The Fever and the Flame

Also by Mary Hooper

Historical fiction

At the Sign of the Sugared Plum
Petals in the Ashes
The Remarkable Life and Times of Eliza Rose

Contemporary fiction

Megan
Megan 2
Megan 3
Holly
Amy
Chelsea and Astra: Two Sides of the Story
Zara

The Fever and the Flame

A SPECIAL OMNIBUS EDITION
OF

At the Sign of the Sugared Plum

AND

Petals in the Ashes

MARY HOOPER

BLOOMSBURY

Special omnibus edition published in Great Britain in 2006 by
Bloomsbury Publishing Plc, 36 Soho Square, London, W1D 3QY

At the Sign of the Sugared Plum first published in 2003
Petals in the Ashes first published in 2004

A CIP catalogue record of this book is available from the British Library

ISBN 0 7475 8670 5
9780747586708

Typeset by Dorchester Typesetting Group Ltd
Printed in Great Britain by Clays Ltd, St Ives plc

1 3 5 7 9 10 8 6 4 2

All papers used by Bloomsbury Publishing are natural, recyclable products
made from wood grown in well-managed forests. The manufacturing processes
conform to the environmental regulations of the country of origin.

www.maryhooper.co.uk
www.bloomsbury.com/childrens

Contents

At The Sign Of The

Sugared Plum

Chapter One

The first week of June, 1665

*'June 7th. The hottest day that ever I felt
in my life . . .'*

To tell the truth, I was rather glad to get away from
Farmer Price and his rickety old cart. He made me
uneasy with his hog's breath and his red, sweaty face
and the way he'd suddenly bellow out laughing at
nothing at all. I was uneasy, too, about something
he'd said when I'd told him I was going to London to
join my sister Sarah in her shop.

'You be going to live in the City, Hannah?' he'd
asked, pushing his battered hat up over his forehead.
'Wouldn't think you'd want to go there.'

'Oh, but I do!' I'd said, for I'd been set on living in
London for as long as I could remember. 'I'm fair
desperate to reach the place.'

'Times like this . . . thought your sister would try
and keep you away.'

'No, she sent for me specially,' I'd said, puzzled.
'Her shop is doing well and she wants my help in
it. I'm to be trained in the art of making sweetmeats,'

I'd added.

'Sweetmeats is it?' He'd given one of his bellows. 'That's comfits for corpses, then!'

He left me in Southwarke on the south bank of the Thames, and I thanked him, slipped down from his cart and – remembering to take my bundle and basket from the back – began to walk down the crowded road towards London Bridge.

As the bridge came into view I stopped to draw breath, putting down my baggage but being careful to keep my things close by, for I'd been warned often enough about the thieving cutpurses and murderous villains who thronged the streets of London. I straightened my skirts and flounced out my petticoat to show off the creamy ruff of lace I'd sewn onto it – Sarah had told me that petticoats were now worn to be seen – then pushed down my hair to try and flatten it. This was difficult for, to my great vexation, it stuck out as curly as the tails of piglets and was flame red. Nothing I wore, be it hat, hood or cap, could contain it. I pulled my new white cap down tightly, however, and tied the ribbons into a tidy bow under my chin. I hoped I looked a pleasant and comely sight walking across into the city, and that no one would look at me and realise that I was a newly arrived country girl.

It was a hot day even though it was only the first of June, and all the hotter for me because I was wearing several layers of clothes. This wasn't because I'd misjudged the weather, more because I knew that whatever I didn't wear, I'd have to carry. I had on then: a cambric shift, two petticoats, a dark linsey-woolsey skirt and a linen blouse. Over these was a short jacket which had been embroidered by my mother, and a dark woollen shawl lay across my shoulders.

I'd been studying the people carefully as we'd neared the bridge, hoping that I might see my friend Abigail, who'd come from our village last year to be a maid in one of the big houses, and also hoping to see some great lady, a person of quality, so I could judge how well I stood against her regarding fashion. There was no sign of Abby, however, and most of the quality were in sedan chairs or carriages, with only the middling and poorer sort on foot. These folk were wearing a great variety of things: men were in tweedy country clothes, rough working worsteds or the severely cut suits and white collars of the Puritans, the women wearing everything from costly velvet down to poor rags that my mother would have scorned to use as polishing cloths for the pewter.

'That's a fine red wig you've got there, lass!' a young male voice said, and I realised that I'd paused beside a brewhouse.

I turned indignantly on the speaker. 'It's not a wig. It's my own hair!' I said to the two men – one young and one old – who were leaning against the wall, mugs of ale in their hands.

'And fine patches across your nose, too,' said the elder.

I opened my mouth to say more and then realised that the youth and man outside the Gown and Claret were making fun of me.

'They're not patches, William, they're called sun kisses!' the first said, and they both roared with laughter.

I picked up my basket, feeling my cheeks go pink. I

hated my hair, but even more than that I hated my freckles, and one of the first things I intended to do in London was to visit an apothecary and see what treatment the great ladies were using for their prevention. I pushed my nose into the air and moved on, only just avoiding a deep rut in the road full of all manner of foul-smelling muck. As I faltered, my foot slipped out of my wooden clog, but I regained my balance, picked up my skirts and carefully negotiated around the rut.

'Well danced, young miss!' called over the older man.

'It's a young red bantum fresh up from the country!' said the youth, and I pretended not to hear. At home I was always being teased about my vivid colouring but I hadn't thought I'd stand out in London, too.

'A spring chicken ripe for the plucking!'

'You mind a piece of old Cromwell up there don't fall on you!' the first went on.

'An eyeball or an ear!'

Before I could stop myself I'd glanced up to the over-arching gateway to London Bridge, where there was a collection of human heads pierced by poles, and let out a small shriek of horror.

I heard further mannish laughter behind me and was annoyed for being so green, for I'd known well enough that the heads of felons were displayed on the bridge – and I'd even been to a public execution – so it should have been nothing to me. The thought of a piece of one of those heads, though, one of those mouldered skulls, falling as I passed underneath – well, I forgave myself that shriek.

I walked on sniffing the air tentatively. London was

crowded and smelt foul. And not just farmhouse-foul, but a churning mixture of rotting meat, kitchen slops, boiled bones, sulphurous smoke and the sweat and discharge from a thousand animal and human bodies. The bridge was teeming with people because – unless you took a ferry – it was the only way you could get across from Southwarke into the City. I knew this because my sister Sarah had told me many times the route I should take to reach her in Crown and King Place, where she traded under the sign of the Sugared Plum.

It had been arranged a year or so back that if Sarah needed my help, and if mother could spare me at home, I'd come to London to work with her, and two months ago I'd been near overcome with excitement when a letter had arrived, a letter with my own name on it brought over by our church minister, saying Sarah's trade was increasing and that she would welcome me there as soon as possible.

'But you'll get lost in London, I know you will!' she'd said on that last visit home. 'You're such a cod's head you lose yourself going across the fields from home to church on a Sunday.'

'That's only because I don't want to get there,' I'd said. Why sit on a hard bench listening to a two-hour sermon when there were so many other, more interesting things to see and do on the way?

Our family home was in a small village called Chertsey which was a good half-day's journey away from the City, and if I could find things to interest me *there*, then you might imagine how I stared around me, marvelling, on London Bridge. There were a great variety of houses faced with brick, timber and all manner of coloured and decorated plasters, and they were of every shape and size, some crammed into minute spaces and others which towered and leaned this way and that. Even more interesting were the shops, and I peered, amazed, into the windows of those that were clustered along the parapet of the bridge. I had never seen such an array of things for sale in all my life: books, china, wooden toys, brooms, ribbons, wigs, buckles, pots, feathered hats and girdles – London had everything!

I began to plan what I'd buy when I was rich. We *would* be rich, I was sure – Sarah wouldn't have sent for me unless the shop was doing well. We weren't poor at home by any means – we had several fine chairs and settles, some pewter plates and space enough so that I only had to share a bed chamber with Anne, my younger sister (my little brothers had a room of their own) – but it was impossible there to follow the fashions. And besides, even if I could buy the silk jackets and flowered tabby waistcoats I craved, who would see me wearing them in the country, apart from booby gamekeepers or woodcutters' sons? In London, though, I might have the chance to make a good match – or at least be taken by a fine young man to a coffee house or one of the pleasure gardens.

Coming off the bridge I steadied myself as a great fat sow, grunting madly, and a litter of piglets swept by me and began rooting for nourishment in the mud and foul refuse outside a shop door. At home, mother always fed our pigs on the best scraps and leavings, but here I could see precious little that they could eat. Mother said that the tenderness of the bacon depended on the pigs being well fed, and Father sometimes remarked that they ate better than he did. The last time he'd said this, though, Mother had served him up a mess of muddy potato peelings on our best pewter, and he hadn't said it since.

I dawdled, sweating gently in the heat, staring at everything, listening to the cries of the street pedlars to 'Come buy!' a hundred different things, and wondering and exclaiming to myself by turn. So many busy, interesting people . . . what were they all doing? Where were they going? Two gallants passed swiftly on horseback in a blur of jewel-coloured velvets and gold lace, their spurs and stirrups glittering in the sunlight, then came several sedan chairs, then a bright yellow carriage drawn by four fine horses with gilded leather bridles. The carriage door had a family crest on it and at the window sat a lady dressed in rich silks, peering at the world over a mask held up to her face.

She was going to a romantic assignation, I was sure. I'd heard many tales of the court and the intrigues which went on, for it was said that the king had many mistresses and the gentlemen and ladies of the court not only approved of his carryings-on, but did the same thing. My mother and I had soaked up such rumours when they reached us through the ballads or the news-sheets sold us by street pedlars, but *now* I was set to hear them first hand.

Reaching the other side of the bridge, I turned right along a broad street and then paused at a water conduit in a small, paved area. The streets stretched out in seven directions here, like the spokes of a wheel, and Sarah had told me to go down the one which had a tavern called the Toad and Drum at the top. I did so, and found the street narrow and mean, with mud instead of cobbles underfoot. The houses were so tall here that rays of sunlight could only occasionally peep through the gaps between them, and their protruding bay windows meant that anyone living at the top could have put out a hand and touched a person in the room of the house opposite.

At the bottom of this street there was a series of alleys and I went down the first, past a dunghill and some piles of rotting refuse, and through into a small, busy market selling all manner of roots and herbs. Laid out here were rough trestle tables loaded with produce, and there were more traders selling from baskets or sacks on the ground. Food shops stood close by, their coloured signs announcing them in vividly-painted pictures and words to be: The House of Plum Pudding, The Gingerbread Man and the Pigeon Pie shop, and, being hungry, I started to wonder what Sarah would have prepared for supper.

I peered into the windows, then lingered by a stall selling strange, brightly-coloured fruit. I'd seen oranges and lemons before – I'd once saved to buy a lemon, Abigail having told me that it was most excellent at fading freckles – but most of the other vivid, oddly-shaped objects were new to me. I stopped, fascinated, amid the jostling people, but the shrill cries of the stallholders urging customers to, 'Come buy before night!' reminded me that I had to get on. If I got lost in the backstreets in the dark I knew for certain that I'd get my throat cut and never be seen again.

A little further on was another small square with a

number of ways leading off it and I stood there, perplexed, for a moment. Sarah had told me that the city was like a cony-warren and it surely was, although I'd had plenty of time since her last visit to go over the route in my mind. After some thought I went along an alleyway, passed more shops and entered the churchyard of St Olave's where I came across six small children standing amid the tombstones playing a game. One was evidently pretending to be the minister, for he had a long dark piece of cloth round his shoulders as a vestment and was proclaiming in a solemn voice. One was a corpse, lying 'dead' on the ground muffled in a winding sheet and the others – the mourners – were wailing and crying. I deduced they were playing at funerals and after staring at them for some moments – fascinated, for I'd never seen children play such a game at home – I stepped past the 'body' and went out of the back gate of the churchyard. Going across a small bridge over a river I took to be the Fleet, I finally found myself in Crown and King Place.

Excited now, I looked up at the swinging shop and house signs, searching for Sarah's. I saw the Black Boy, the Half Moon, the Oak Tree, the Miller's Daughter – and then, in a line of four or five shops, found the one I'd been looking for: a painted representation of a sugared plum. I swung my bundle of clothes over my shoulder and broke into a run, slipping and sliding on the cobbles in my effort to get there quickly, and thinking all the while how happy Sarah would be to see me.

Nearing the shop, seeing it close by, I have to own to a feeling of disappointment. From how she'd spoken of it I'd been imagining it to be large and painted in gay colours, like some of the shops on London Bridge, with a bowed window crammed with sweetmeats. It was not, though. It was like the others in the same row: small, with no glass in the front, and it had a wooden casement of the type that divided into two when the shop was open, the top forming an awning above and the bottom part making an open counter.

Sarah was in the back of the shop, chopping something on a marble slab and looking very cool in a cotton dress with a starched white apron over it. She was tall – as tall as Father, with a shapely figure, thick dark hair that I'd always envied, and no freckles. Not one.

I went in to greet her, sniffing in appreciation, for the shop smelt of spices and sugar water and its wooden floor was thick with strewing herbs, which was pleasant after some of the odious smells outside.

'Sarah!' I said. 'Here I am.'

She looked up at me and I was disconcerted to see that she seemed surprised – even shocked – at the sight of me. Surely she hadn't forgotten that I was coming?

'Hannah!' she said. 'How did you—'

'Just as we planned,' I said blithely. 'I took Farmer Price's cart to Southwarke and then walked from there. But what a muddle and a mess it all is in London. What stinks! What crowds!'

'But what are you *doing* here, Hannah?'

I put down my bundle and my basket. 'I've come to help you, of course – just as you asked. The Reverend Davies brought your letter to me and I was that excited – Father said *he's* never had a letter in his life.

But where is your living space? Where shall I sleep? Can I look round?'

'But I wrote to you again,' she said. 'I wrote two weeks back and said not to come.'

'*Not to come?*' I said in disbelief. 'Surely you didn't—'

'I wrote to you care of Reverend Davies again. Didn't he come to see you?'

I shook my head, upset and bitterly disappointed. I couldn't bear it if I had to go back to Chertsey! What about all my grand plans for living in London, for wearing the latest fashions, for attending playhouses and bear gardens, going to fairs and maybe meeting a handsome gallant?

'But why don't you want me here?' I asked. 'I'll be of such a help to you! Mother has given me some recipes for glazing of fruit and I'm much improved in my reading and writing. I'll be able to help you in all manner of things.' I couldn't understand why she didn't want me there and began to wonder what I had done in the past for which she might not, after all, have been able to forgive me. Accidentally tearing the new lace that she'd been making into a cap, perhaps, or running out of the house early on St Valentine's day in order to greet Chertsey's only comely young farmer before *she* did.

'It's not because I don't want you here, Hannah,' she said. 'It's because . . . well, haven't you heard?' She dropped her voice as she spoke.

'Heard what?'

'About . . . about the plague,' she said, looking round and shuddering slightly, as if the thing she was talking about was standing like a great and horrible brute behind her. 'The plague has broken out again in London.'

I breathed a sigh of relief. 'Oh, is *that* it!' I said. So it wasn't because of me or anything I'd done. 'Is that all? Why, there's always a plague somewhere and as long as it's not here – I mean, not right here—'

'Well, it's not in this parish,' she admitted. 'But there are some cases in St Giles – and a house has been shut up in Drury Lane.'

'Shut up?' I asked. 'What does that mean?'

'One of the people inside it – a woman – has the plague, and they've locked her up with her husband and children so it can't be spread abroad.'

'So there – it's all contained!' I said. 'And it's just one house, Sarah – we don't need to worry about *that*, do we? Doesn't a place like London have all the best doctors and apothecaries? I bet we're safer here than anywhere.'

'I don't know—'

'But I'm here now, Sarah. Don't send me back!' I pleaded, realising now that it must have been the plague that Farmer Price had alluded to in his strange expression. 'Oh, do let me stay!' I burst out. 'I can't bear it if I've got to go home.'

She sighed. 'I'm not sure.'

'I'll do everything you say,' I went on anxiously. 'I won't go anywhere I'm not supposed to. I'll be such a help to you, really I will—'

While I'd been pleading with her Sarah had been slowly looking me over from top to toe. Now, she shook her head. 'You look such a goose, Hannah! What a dog's dinner of clothes you're wearing – and why ever have you tied your cap so tightly about your head? Everyone leaves their ribbons dangling now, and that terrible old skirt – where did you get it?'

'The vicar's daughter,' I said, noting that Sarah's dress was of a pretty light blue with white collar and cuffs, and her cap was untied, its ribbons hanging loose. I frowned. 'Do I look so unfashionable, then?'

'As green as a country sprout!' said Sarah. She gave a sudden smile. 'But come and give me a hug and we'll close the shop early and go out and buy a venison pasty to celebrate your coming.'

'I can stay?' I asked joyfully.

She nodded. 'You can for the moment. But if the plague comes closer—'

'Oh, it won't!' I said. 'Everything is going to be perfectly fine.'

For so it really seemed.

Chapter Two

The second week of June

'Great fears of the Sickenesse here in the city, it being said that two or three houses are already shut up. God preserve us all.'

Sarah leaned over my shoulder to touch the sugar I'd been pounding for the sweetmeats we were preparing that day. She rubbed some grains of it between finger and thumb and shook her head. 'It must be finer than that,' she said. 'Like soft powder. When you've finished you should be able to sift it so that it falls like snow.'

I carried on pounding sugar in the pestle and mortar, keeping my sighs to myself. When, the day before, I'd complained about the amount of time and hard work it took to chip chunks off the sugar loaf and pound them, Sarah had retorted that if I didn't wish to work so hard I could take myself home again and return to my usual jobs of wiping the noses of our little brothers and minding the sheep on the common. So I wasn't going to say another word.

Sarah's shop sold all manner of comfits, candied flowers, and sugared plums, nuts and fruit. The shop had belonged to our Aunt Martha – mother's widowed sister – who'd gone to start a new life in Norwich with a farmer she'd met when he'd walked his five hundred turkeys from Norfolk to the livestock market in London. Mother and I had often talked about this, wondering who was the more footsore after their journey – the poor farmer or the weary turkeys – and if they'd driven him distracted on the way down by trotting off in all directions like wanton puppies.

Sarah was four years older than me. Anne and I were closer in age – there were only two years between us – and at home Sarah had been the grown-up sensible one who'd helped mother. She'd always been closest to Aunt Martha, who at one time had owned a little bakery shop in Chertsey, where Sarah had helped from the time she was ten. Sarah had a knack for making things. Mother said she made the tastiest gingerbread and crispest biscuits this side of heaven. She was good with figure work, too, and used to help Father with his accounts, even when it meant missing a dance on the village green or a visit to the travelling fair. When Anne and I used to tease her about not having a beau, she'd laugh and say getting married wasn't the only thing in the world and, anyway, she wasn't going to marry the first booby farmer who came along.

There were two rooms to the shop: the front one where the sweetmeats were prepared and sold, and the back one which was Sarah's living quarters, and now mine as well. There were two more rooms above us.

Sarah told me that a family had lived there until recently, but now it was just used as storage space by a local rope-maker. Our own living space held a small table and chairs, a chest of drawers for our possessions and an iron bed which Sarah and I shared. I'd asked Sarah to let me sleep nearest to the window, for from here I could sniff the fragrant rosemary bush just outside, which reminded me of the one by the back door of our cottage in Chertsey. I hadn't asked for this because I was homesick, it was just that London smelt so bad and was so smoky, grimy and grey even when the sun was shining, that sometimes I could not help but think of our pretty cottage with its straw-thatched roof and its door wreathed with roses and sweet honeysuckle. Alongside us was the old barn where Father made staves and spokes for his wheelwright's business, and in the garden were a great many neat rows of vegetables – so many that there was always spare to take to market – and our apple orchard which fair burst with fruit each October. Further off still was the village green with its cattle grazing peacefully around the pond, and the manor house, tavern and church. Chertsey was a whole world in miniature, Mother used to say, and she saw no reason why any of us should want to go running off to London.

That day Sarah and I were making candied rose petals, so that morning we'd risen at four o'clock to go to market. I was already quite awake by then, for I'd heard the first cheery call of the watchman – 'God give you good morrow, my masters! Nigh four o'clock and a fair morning!' – and needed little encouragement to rise.

We had gone to the flower market at Cheapside to buy pink and red roses and Sarah had bought six perfect blooms of each, first examining them carefully for signs of age, or bruising, or greenfly. 'Note carefully what I'm looking for, Hannah, for soon I'll be sending you to market on your own,' she'd said.

I'd watched her closely, of course, but my eyes had also been on the giggling maids buying armfuls of flowers: delphiniums, lupins, crimson roses and alabaster lilies to decorate the great houses. I looked for Abigail again, too, but with no luck. I watched the maids to see what they were wearing and how they behaved, envying them their confident manner and the way they traded glances and banter with the apprentice lads. I noticed one or two boys looking my way but I kept my head down, for I wanted to get rid of my freckles before I spoke to anyone. I was wearing my so-called best dress which was of plain brown linen and quite drab and hateful, but I'd undone the ribbons on my cap so that they hung loosely about my face, thinking that at least one part of me must be in fashion. Sarah had promised that as soon as we had time to spare she'd take me to the clothes market in Houndsditch, so I could have a new outfit. It would be less than a year old, she told me, for apparently as soon as any new mode from France reached our shores the great ladies – who would sooner be dead than out of fashion – would rush to order it, and have their servants sell at market any outfits purchased the previous season.

I carried on pounding the sugar, changing arms and trying to use my left hand as well as my right, and at last Sarah said it would do well enough.

'Now watch me,' she said, and she took a sharp knife, severed the head of the reddest, fullest rose, then carefully separated the petals, cutting any pieces of white (which she explained could be bitter) from the bottom of each. She told me to lay the petals side by side, touching them as little as possible, on white paper in a large shallow box. The same fate befell five more roses, until all their petals lay within boxes in long, perfect lines of pink and scarlet. Sarah then sprinkled them alternately with rose water and the finely sifted sugar and gave them to me.

'Put the boxes outside in full sunlight,' she instructed me, 'and turn the petals in two hours.'

Carefully holding the first box, I went into the yard at the back which we shared with three other shops. It was a tiny space, but Sarah said we were lucky in that we shared a privy here with just our near-neighbours instead of all the street. Just outside our back door was a rack of shelves which Sarah used to dry out flowers and sweetmeats at their various stages of preparation. There was room in the ground here, too, for a few herbs – one bush each of rosemary, sage and bay, which Sarah had brought as cuttings from home and had managed to root in the beaten-down soil.

I put the petals on the top shelf of the rack. 'Watch that it doesn't rain on them!' Sarah called through to me, but she was jesting, for it was a hot, dry day. The weather had been fine in London for six weeks, she'd told me, with not a drop of rain falling in all that time to cleanse the streets. Maybe, I thought, that was why it smelled so bad.

I pounded more sugar, and by the time I'd finished it to Sarah's satisfaction my arm and shoulder were aching fit to scream. I was allowed to stop so I could go out into the yard to turn the petals, and Sarah, after inspecting them, told me to sprinkle more rose water and sugar over them. The idea was to candy them to a crisp so that they'd retain their original colour and hue. 'Done properly, with enough care,' she said, 'they'll still look fresh at Christmas.' Then she added, 'Although they won't keep until then because they're so fragrant and delicious that they'll be eaten long before that.'

I sprinkled and sifted carefully. I tasted a small one, but it still seemed to be exactly what it was: a rose petal, reminding me of the ones I'd eaten with Anne as we'd played make-believe with our dolls, sitting outside our cottage with oak tree leaves as plates and acorns as cups.

When I'd finished dowsing the petals I lifted my face to the sun, happy to be outside. Then I remembered that more sun meant more freckles, so hastily pulled my cap lower over my forehead and vowed again that I would go to the apothecary the first chance I got.

Something brushed against my foot and I looked down to see Mew, one of the cats that seemed to come and go between our line of shops. There was a menagerie of cats around – tabby, ginger, grey, tortoiseshell, black and white – and I loved them all.

I picked up Mew and held her to my cheek. She was still quite a kitten and fluffy, with a soft grey coat like Tyb, our big grey cat at home. We'd had him since a kitten, too, and once Anne and I had dressed him up in a baby's gown that mother had discarded and taken him into the village wrapped in a shawl. When our neighbour, Mrs Tomalin, had asked to see him, saying she'd had no idea that our mother was with child again, we'd thrust the cat at her and run away home, cackling like chickens.

'Hannah!' Sarah called, breaking into my thoughts. 'Come in and serve this gentleman some sweetmeats, please.'

I hurried through into the shop, bobbing a curtsey before the man. He was wearing elegant satin breeches, an embroidered jacket and flounced shirt and was carrying a vast plumed hat under his arm. Taking all this in, I made another curtsey – a little deeper and longer – for I knew Sarah wanted to encourage such dandies into the shop. It was her ambition, she'd told me, to rise in fame and perhaps be asked to supply the Court with sweetmeats.

The man paused, his kid-gloved hand to his face, hesitating over crystallised rose petals or violets. 'Which taste would a lady prefer, do you think?' he asked me.

'The violets are very fine, sir,' I answered immediately, for although they both tasted exactly the same to me, the violets were more costly. 'They've been crystallised with pure loaf sugar,' I assured him.

He nodded. 'The violets, then.' He was wearing face patches and had a great flapping wig, but they did not detract from his lack of teeth, or the gums which showed pale pink and shiny as he smiled. 'Young Miss is fresh from the country, I'll be bound,' he said. 'Such fetching hair and skin is not often found in London.'

I didn't say anything but, flicking a glance at Sarah, saw that she wanted me to.

'Thank you, sir,' I said demurely.

'It would take a good many patches to cover those sweet freckles!' the fop went on.

'Indeed, sir,' I forced myself to smile back. 'Will there be anything else?' I weighed his violets and poured them into a twisted cone of paper. 'Sugared almonds? Herb comfits?'

He ignored these questions. 'And such hair as I've only seen before in the playhouse!'

I said nothing to this, just stood there, smiling as if I liked him, and eventually he produced a silk kerchief from his pocket and mopped his brow. 'It is most monstrous hot!' he complained.

'Perhaps some suckets – sugared orange or lemon?' I asked. 'Most refreshing on a hot day.'

He nodded again and the wig wobbled. 'Give me three of each,' he said, 'and some of your herb comfits, too.'

'Certainly, sir,' I said, raising my eyebrows at Sarah as I wrapped them. She took some coins from him and he turned to wink at me as he went out.

'That was the Honourable Francis du Maurier,' Sarah said, as we moved to watch his sauntering progress down the street. 'A real Jack-a-Dandy.'

I sniffed. 'A bumble-bee in a cow turd thinks himself a king.'

'Hannah!' she reproached me.

I giggled. 'Sorry. That's one of Abigail's favourite sayings.'

'Not now she's in service at a big house, I hope.'

As we watched, the 'Honourable' man hailed a sedan chair. As he climbed in, we noticed he had red leather heels to his shoes.

'Look at those!' Sarah said admiringly. 'He's been

here before but never bought as much.'

'See!' I said. 'I'm bringing you luck.'

'Maybe,' she said. 'And maybe we'll need it, for the Bills will be published later today.'

'What Bills?' I asked, puzzled.

'The Bills of Mortality,' she said. 'They list everyone who's died in the parishes of London in the past week so we can see what they've died of. We'll know then if the plague is taking hold.'

She sighed a little and her eyes darkened, so I thought it best to make light of the matter. 'What a long face,' I said to her cheerfully. 'Left to you, we'd all be in mourning weeds before supper!'

She did not respond to this banter, but simply turned away.

Later that day, Sarah gave me leave to go to an apothecary's shop. 'Although why you want to change your looks, I don't know,' she said. 'You saw how your colouring was admired by the Honourable Francis.'

'I don't wish for the sort of colouring he admires!' I said.

The nearest apothecary was Doctor da Silva at the sign of the Silver Globe, in the adjoining parish of St Mary at Hill. 'He's as honest a man as any,' Sarah said. 'I've used him for many cough remedies before now.'

I looked at her enquiringly. 'So they don't work, then?'

'How so?'

'You said *many* cough remedies. But if the first had worked you wouldn't have needed the others.'

'Get off with you, Miss Impudence!' she said, but she laughed as she said it and I felt she was glad that I had come to live with her.

I went out with instructions from her to buy caraway seeds from the apothecary, and some fresh milk from the first milkmaid I saw.

I took a long time getting to the Silver Globe, for there were many distractions along the way. The small shops next to us, six in a row, sold, in order: writing parchment, buttons, gloves, books, quill pens and hosiery, and I found it necessary to look into each one of them. Further along was a run-down tavern called The Tall Ship, a barber-surgeon's shop, some dark and mean alleys and a row of narrow houses with twisted chimneys, then another series of shops. Outside some of the houses women sat gossiping, or sewing, while at their feet children played with dolls or sticks, drew pictures in the dust, or teased their cats or dogs. Chickens pecked between the cobbled stones and occasionally a pig or goat came by to see if there was any food to be had.

The shop at the sign of the Silver Globe was large and wide, with bull's-eye glass windows. Inside, the space was deep and lit by candles, and its shelves were laden with all manner of fascinating objects. One wall held strangely-shaped roots and dried grasses, trugs of herbs, a huge egg – surely belonging to a dragon? – and baskets containing dried matter and layers of wood bark. On another wall differently-hued powders in glass phials were ranged, and there was a shelf full of ancient tomes and yellowing papers, and also a vast cupboard containing bulbous jars of coloured and distilled waters inscribed in a strange language. I took this to be Latin and could not decipher a word of it, for Latin was just for gentlemen to know, and the petty school in our village had merely covered reading and writing in our own language.

I was rather nervous on entering the shop, for I had heard that apothecaries could be sinister and powerful people, and I was half-expecting a man with a beast's head and a black cloak covered in signs of the heavens. But the young man weighing powders behind the counter had not either of these things. Instead, he had a comely, clean-shaven face with very dark eyes, and was neatly dressed in serge breeches with a white linen shirt and black velvet waistcoat.

'Good morning, madam,' he said with a merry smile which showed his even white teeth.

'Are you Doctor da Silva, the apothecary?' I asked rather timidly.

'No, indeed!' he said, laughing, and I felt myself blush. 'And if you knew the doctor you'd not mistake me for him.'

'Is he here?' I asked, feeling as foolish as a mutton chop, for now that my eyes were used to the dim light I could see that this fellow was only a year or two older than myself.

'He is not,' the boy said. 'But if you would care to state your requirements, I'll see if I can serve you.'

I now found myself in a dilemma, being too embarrassed to ask for a remedy against freckles from such a fine, good-looking lad. I therefore just asked him for the caraway seeds. While he weighed them up, he asked if I was new to the area and I said I was. I told him my name, and that I had come here to help Sarah in her shop.

He said his name was Tom, and that he knew our shop. 'And a mighty attraction you'll be to it too,' he added, making me blush again. 'Although it's a pity you've come to London at such a time.'

I hesitated. 'Are . . . are you talking about the plague?'

He nodded solemnly. 'The Bills for last week have just been published and the figures for St Giles Parish have doubled.'

'But there are no deaths in this parish?'

He shook his head. 'No deaths. But the doctor has heard of some cases in Lincolns Inn Fields, and some in Fleet Street, and he's gone to the Hall of Apothecaries now to discuss what's to be done. We will need to prepare some plague preventatives.'

'But perhaps it may not spread! Couldn't it just die out?'

He shrugged. 'The plague is said to go in twenty-year cycles – and it's almost that since the last big outbreak. Besides, there have been signs in the heavens.'

'Do you mean the flaming comet?' I asked, for even in Chertsey people had seen a comet which had flashed across the skies and left a trail of light in its wake.

He nodded. 'And last month there was a cloud formation showing an avenging angel holding aloft a sword. The people say that such a thing foretells a terrible disaster.'

I shivered, just a little. 'And do you think so, too?'

He gave a bow as he handed over my screw-paper full of seeds. 'I can hardly believe such a thing, Hannah, for according to Doctor da Silva, a cloud is just steam and vapour pushed into shapes by the wind.'

'So we are all right, then!' I said. I paid him, and he showed me to the door and opened it for me with a bow, just as if I were a real lady. I had other questions to ask but was so taken with his smiling dark eyes and the way he'd said my name, 'Hannah' – so softly, like a whispered breath – that they went out of my mind. Besides, I really didn't want to know any more about the plague. It sounded a fearful thing, but whatever I found out, I had no intention of going back to Chertsey.

Chapter Three

The third week of June

*'The Sickenesse is got into our parish this week; and is
got indeed everywhere, so that I begin to think of
setting things in order . . . '*

A few days later I contrived a reason to go to the
apothecary's shop again. Sarah was making sugared
almonds and was colouring the sugar syrup in pink,
pale blue and green from the various tints she had. I
suggested that pale gold almonds would look very
well amongst these, and asked if I should go to Doctor
da Silva's to buy saffron.

She looked at me and smiled. 'Saffron, is it? Or do
you wish to make the acquaintance of young master
Tom again?'

'That as well,' I said, for after I'd told Sarah about
our meeting I'd thought of little else but him. At home
there had been no one to think about – think about in
that sort of way – so I'd had to be content with
dreaming about impossible, faraway heroes like the
king, whose image I'd seen on coins and portraits.

Now, though, I had a flesh-and-blood person I could close my eyes and think of before I went to sleep.

I put on a clean apron, changed my cap and rubbed the merest drop of pink colouring into my lips to redden them. However, to my great disappointment, I did not find Tom in the shop, but instead met the doctor himself. He wore black flowing robes, and was old, with a grey beard, knotted hair and bulbous nose. He looked solemn and wise, but kindly as well.

I explained who I was and said that I'd come for saffron. When I said it was for colouring, and not for cooking, he said the cheaper variety would do as well, and took a glass jar from a case. As he turned away from me to weigh out a quantity on some little gold scales, I took the opportunity (for I knew I would blush) to make bold enough to ask if Tom was nearby.

'He is not,' he said. He fumbled around in a pocket of his gown and placed some spectacles on his nose. Then he looked again at the scales and added a few more spidery stamens of saffron to the pile. 'I have sent Tom to High Holborn to see what measures the new French quack doctor is taking against the plague.'

I wanted to ask more but was nervous about what I might hear; also I was very much in awe of him. However, after a moment he turned to me and explained further himself, speaking rather scornfully. 'The Frenchman says he's discovered a method of preventing the visitation. He says he stopped the plague in Lyons and Paris.'

'And is that true?' I asked.

'Bah!' he shook his head. 'If any man could prevent the plague then he would become as rich as a king. And *this* is what the Frenchman seeks!' He spat on the floor. 'Frenchmen! They are good at nothing but being dancing masters.'

'Then nothing can stop the plague?' I asked, suddenly rather alarmed.

He looked at me gravely over his spectacles. 'We all have our preventatives and talismans, and sometimes they work and sometimes they don't. To my way of thinking, though, once that dread disease takes hold, be it on a person or a city, then it has to run its course.'

'Does this Frenchman make pills to take? Is it something you can eat?' I asked, thinking that I'd go there myself, right now, and buy whatever it was, for it surely couldn't hurt to try it.

The doctor shook his head. 'He has a method of smoking . . . of fuming out a house. A fire of sulphur is lit; sulphur and some other ingredients which the Frenchman keeps secret. It stinks the place out and – so he says – cleanses it of plague germs.' He spat again. 'The Lord Mayor of London has ordered that this method be tried. He must be in the man's pay.'

'And was there plague in the house that's being fumed?'

'Indeed there was,' he said gravely. 'Seven dead – the whole family – although the city authorities are not yet admitting that it was plague which carried them off. It will probably go down in the Bills of Mortality as fever, so as not to alarm the people.'

I, for one, was most certainly alarmed. Seven dead in a house!

Handing over the saffron and receiving his payment, the doctor then asked if there was anything else I desired. I thought about my freckles but decided

– in view of our previous conversation – that the matter was too trivial to speak of. I was surprised, then, when the doctor looked at me searchingly and said, 'Your complexion. I suppose you wish it to be pale?'

I nodded. 'Oh, I do!' I said eagerly. 'I've tried things myself – I've washed my face with May-dew, and bathed it with the juice of lemon, but nothing works.'

'What sign of the heavens were you born under?'

I shook my head, bemused. 'I do not know, sir.'

'I ask you because I use the methods of Nicholas Culpeper.'

I shook my head, not understanding. I had heard of this man and knew he was a herbalist, but did not know the methods of which Doctor da Silva was speaking.

'Culpeper decided that the planets in the heavens were responsible for the various diseases which afflict us, and that the planets also govern different parts of our bodies – our blood, skin, heart, and so on.'

I nodded, frowning with concentration.

'So to cure people he uses plants governed by planets which are in opposition to those associated with the parts of the body.'

I did not really understand, but I tried to memorise his words so that when I saw Tom again he would not think me totally ignorant of his chosen calling. The doctor asked my birth date and when I told him I was born on the 23rd day of July he said that it was no wonder I had fiery colouring, because I was a subject of the sun. He pulled out a drawer beneath his counter and showed me a long, papery-dry leaf. 'This is yellow dock,' he said. 'You must steep it in warm water and vinegar and leave it for three days, and then bathe your face with the resulting liquid.'

He wrapped the leaf in a fold of brown paper and, when I asked him what I owed, he said that Sarah was a good customer and I could have the leaf for nothing. After a moment's hesitation I asked if there was anything I could do to make my hair less red and less curly.

'You can comb it with a lead comb,' he said, 'I have heard that darkens the hair considerably.'

'Do you—?' I began, but he shook his head, staring at me over his glasses.

'I do not sell brushes, combs or complexion paints for the ladies. But if you wish your hair less curly, you may find that Lad's Love – a little of that plant in a herbal infusion – may help to straighten it, and you can find this herb at any wayside.'

I thanked him kindly for his advice, and for the leaf, curtseyed, and went to leave. On opening the door of the shop, though, I had to tussle with a great black-and-white hog which tried to push me back in. While I was engaged in pushing it out several chickens ran in, for there was a market at the end of the street that day and a greater variety of animals than usual were sniffing and grunting and trotting around outside. I caught two chickens but another ran towards the doctor, its claws skittering on the marble tiles, but the doctor roared at it so that it turned tail immediately and ran out squawking, its tawny feathers flying. I could not help but laugh.

Once outside in the street, I blinked against the strong sunlight. It was another very hot day and the air felt clammy. Smoke and fumes curled out of the leather tanners in the next street, a soap chandler was boiling stinking bones in a cauldron at the front of his shop and there was a disgusting smell coming from the piles of human refuse which had been scraped into a heap by the night-soil men.

The runaway hog had been claimed and was now being used as a pony by two of the children playing nearby. These two young boys, Dickon and Jacob, lived in an alley near us and often hung about our shop, hoping that (as occasionally happened) a comfit or two would turn out to be misshapen and either Sarah or I would throw it to them. They were about five or six years old and worked as errand boys, taking messages between shops and their customers, sweeping a path through the muck for well-to-do visitors or obtaining a sedan chair for people who wearied of shopping and wished for someone else's legs to carry them to their next appointment. They asked me if I would like a ride home on the hog and though I was tempted – in Chertsey I would have hitched up my petticoats and ridden him as if he were the king's nag – in London I was different, and I laughingly refused and went on.

Now I was out and once again surrounded by London life, by busy folk going about their business, all felt normal. Already the horror of the story the doctor had told me was receding. Seven were dead – but High Holborn was a way off, and possibly the plague would be stopped in its tracks by the efforts of the French doctor. Mother had always taught us never to worry about something before we had to.

When I got back to the shop, Sarah was weighing out a quantity of crystallised violets to a customer. As

I bobbed a curtsey to the young woman, she was speaking of how the violets revived her spirits and freshened her breath, and said that the ladies she worked with enjoyed them, too.

I looked at our customer with interest. She was dressed in a low-cut, primrose-yellow silk dress, ruched up all round the bottom (as was the latest fashion) to expose a yellow and red spotted petticoat. On her head was a little velvet cap embroidered all over with coloured beads, and under this – how I stared! – her hair was as red as mine.

She and I smiled at each other and it seemed to me that, as well as the hair, we matched each other in age as well. The pity was that I couldn't see whether she had freckles because she had some whitening on her face, and several black heart-shaped patches.

Sarah coughed. 'Will there be anything else?' she asked, and I glanced at her, wondering why she sounded so cold and remote.

'Not at all, thank you kindly!' the young lady said, seeming not to notice Sarah's tone. She paid, tucked the paper cone of violets into her yellow silk muff and went off, smiling at me again. She stood at the doorway of the shop for a moment, attracting stares and a murmur of appreciation from a passing gallant, all of which she ignored. Suddenly, she put her fingers in her mouth and gave a piercing whistle. A sedan chair came up, the door was opened for her and she got in and went off. As she climbed in the sedan I noticed that her shoes were spotted yellow and red to match her petticoat.

'Oh, who was *that*?' I asked Sarah breathlessly.

Sarah sniffed. 'That was Nelly Gwyn.'

'But who *is* she?'

'Well, she used to be an orange-seller at the playhouse, but now I believe she calls herself an actress.'

'An actress!' I'd heard, of course, that women and girls were appearing on the stage, but I'd never ever seen an actress before.

'You needn't sound so impressed,' Sarah said, 'for she's as common as kennel dirt. Her mother is famous for being drunk, and no one ever knew her father.'

'Well, whatever she is, she must be a very good actress to be able to afford clothes like that,' I said (and I spoke enviously, for I was still wearing cast-offs from the vicar's daughter).

'Oh, it's not acting that brings in the money,' Sarah said with an edge to her voice. 'It's something else.'

I looked at my sister. 'You mean . . . you mean she's a *whore*?' I said daringly – for although I'd already heard this word used several times in London, such language was forbidden to us in the country.

Sarah gave me the faintest of nods.

'I see,' I said. 'But anyway, she's very pretty. Can we go some time?' I asked suddenly. 'Can we go to a playhouse and see her?'

'Well,' Sarah said, and she frowned. 'I don't know that we should.'

'Oh, please!' I said. 'It's quite all right to go now – even polite company attend playhouses, don't they? Even the king goes!'

'It's not how it would look,' Sarah said, 'for we are known to so few people in London, that would hardly matter. No, I'm thinking of the plague. People are saying that you shouldn't attend any large gatherings, and the nobility are already leaving London for the country.'

'But there's nothing official, is there?' I said, and was glad that I'd not yet told her about the seven dead in High Holborn.

'We'll ask someone's advice,' Sarah said. 'We'll ask one of the clerks at the church whether it would be wise to attend a play at the moment.'

I said I would go to ask at St Dominic's, for I meant to couch my question to the clerk in such a way that his answer – the one I would bring back to Sarah – would allow us to attend. I very much wanted to see a play and, now that I'd met her, I especially wanted to see a play with Nelly Gwyn in it.

However, before I could go to the church – in fact, that very evening – a crier came round the streets. After ringing his bell so loudly that Mew fled into a box under the bed, he called that, by order of the Lord Mayor and because of the feared visitation of plague, all playhouses were to be shut up forthwith, and drinking hours in taverns were to be restricted.

I was bitterly disappointed, for I'd heard so much of what went on in the theatre – the shouting and singing and throwing of tomatoes by the groundlings if they did not approve, and of how the great ladies and gentlemen vied, like peacocks, to outdo each other in gaiety of dress. Now I'd have to wait until the scare was over before I could see it all.

And only Heaven knew when that would be, because the following Thursday, when the Bills of Mortality were published, it was found that there had been one hundred deaths of plague that week in London. And at this figure, the authorities declared that the plague had begun.

That afternoon Sarah sent me out for water. She gave me leave to take as long as I wished and make an outing of it, for we had stayed up late the previous night, working by candlelight to blanch and pound a goodly quantity of almonds to a fine powder, and she'd told me I had worked excellently and she couldn't think how she'd ever managed without me. While we'd worked we'd discussed the plague and told ourselves that it might not be as bad as people feared. For good or ill, however, Sarah could not send me back to Chertsey, because, as our neighbour in the parchment shop had told us, the magistrates were restricting travel out of London for fear that infection would spread to the provinces. This same neighbour, Mr Newbery, a short, stout man with a merry smile who loved nothing better than morbid gossip, had also said there was little hope of escape anyway, for if you had been chosen by the Grim Reaper then he would just come along with his scythe and cut you down.

I went to draw my water from Bell Courtyard. Although there were closer watering places, I favoured this one because it was a fine, paved area with trees and seats, and was much frequented by maids and apprentices from nearby houses. Also, the water there came from the New River and was judged to be pure.

The queue to draw water being quite long, I put down my bucket and enamel jug and waited patiently, looking around me at what the others were wearing (all were more fashionable than I) and wondering when Sarah would have time to take me to the clothes market.

As I waited, amused by a pedlar selling mousetraps with a monkey on his shoulder, there was a sudden burst of laughter from the front of the queue, and a hand waved madly.

'Hannah!' a girl's voice called. I saw to my great delight that it was my friend Abigail Palmer from home.

'There was no mistaking that hair!' she said, coming up and hugging me.

'Indeed not,' I said, for though I'd bought a lead comb and had been stroking it through my hair night and morning, it didn't seem to be making my curls any darker. My freckles, too, were just as bright and, as a result of the continual sunny days, now seemed to crowd across my nose and cheeks jostling for place.

Abigail had put on weight and it suited her. She was pretty, with dark curly hair which had sparks of copper in it, deep brown eyes and a curving mouth. She had on a black fustian dress cut up the front to show a lacy white petticoat, and looked very neat and comely.

'How long have you been in London?' she asked.

I told her, and said where I was living.

'And are you still in your position?' I asked.

She nodded. 'With Mr and Mrs Beauchurch.' She was about to say more when a cry came up from the front of the queue. 'Maid! Will you come to take your place?'

Abigail waved her hand. 'No, everyone can step up,' she said. 'I'll wait in line here with my friend.'

'And a pretty sight you will look,' the youth's voice replied. 'Two fair maids together!' The rest of the queue laughed, for a musical entertainment of the same name had recently been on at one of the playhouses.

Abigail blew a kiss to the youth who'd spoken, and linked her arm with mine. 'Now Hannah, tell me every piece of news from Chertsey, for I swear I have not heard a word of gossip from my mother or sisters since I came here.'

By the end of an hour, Abby – for that was how she was known in London – and I had caught up with everything that had happened to each other. I'd told her of the small goings-on in Chertsey, and about Sarah's shop and Nelly Gwyn coming in to buy sweetmeats, and I'd also told her about Tom, for though there was but a little to tell, Abby had a sweetheart herself and I didn't want to be thought backward.

We touched on the plague and she said that her master and mistress would have left the city already, except that eight weeks ago Mrs Beauchurch had given birth to a daughter and, due to childbed fever, was not yet strong enough to travel any distance.

'Do you think the plague will be really bad?' I asked.

She shrugged. 'It is bad every twenty years, they say. And I have seen some portents myself.'

'Which ones?'

'I saw the angel in the clouds with the flaming sword,' she said, and then she frowned. 'At least, they said that's what it was, though to tell the truth I could not make it out to be a figure at all. I have seen something else, though – the children playing at funerals. It seems that all over London they are play-acting the same thing.'

'I've seen them too!'

'Mr Beauchurch told us that children discern things because they are close to nature. They can foretell the future.'

I shivered. 'Pray it isn't so.'

Abby gave my arm a squeeze. 'Even if the plague does come, you and I are of healthy stock and as sound as 'roaches. We've nothing to fear!'

At home that night, Sarah and I stayed up late shelling and skinning more almonds while I told her all about Abby, and it was midnight before we went to bed, which was the latest I was ever up in my life. Just before we went to sleep we heard the night watchman on his rounds:

'Twelve o'clock
Look well to your lock,
Your fire and your light
And so good-night!'

Chapter Four

The last week of June

'This day much against my will, I did in Drury Lane
see two or three houses marked with a red cross
upon the doors and "Lord have mercy Upon us"
writ there . . .'

The gown being held aloft by the aged stallholder was of pale green taffeta. It had full sleeves and a round neck, the bodice was boned, had narrow tucks all down the front and went into a point in the middle. The skirt was set in pleats and its front edges were drawn open to show a dark green silk lining and matching ruffled under-skirt.

'Oh, this one!' I said, taking it from her and holding it to me. I looked at my sister pleadingly. 'Please, Sarah!'

It was Sunday morning and Sarah and I had already walked the length of Houndsditch market where we had easily sold both the vicar's daughter's skirt and blouse and my own drab brown gown. With the money from these I'd bought a dark blue cambric dress, and Sarah had offered to advance my wages so I could have another.

'You'll find no lice or bugs in my clothes,' the toothless stallholder told us. 'This very elegant gown once belonged to a countess.'

Sarah didn't take any notice of this, though I was quite willing to believe it, for I liked the idea of having a dress that had been owned by someone titled.

'It's rather grand but it does look well on you,' Sarah said. 'The green suits your colouring.'

'It doesn't make my hair look more red, does it?' I asked anxiously, and Sarah assured me that it didn't.

'That gown is only two seasons old,' the old woman went on. 'The countess brings all her clothes for me to sell.'

'What else of hers do you have, then?' I asked.

The woman hesitated, then from an old trunk behind the stall she brought out a clover-pink velvet cloak with black silk lining and matching velvet hat with pink curled feathers.

'Oh!' I gasped, and I put out my hand to stroke the velvet. 'It is *most* beautiful. May I have this as well, Sarah?'

'Of course not!' my sister said. 'It's much too grand for the likes of us. And, anyway, it's far too warm at the moment for such a covering.'

'I could keep it until I needed it,' I said longingly, for it seemed to me that the pink velvet cloak was the finest and most beautiful thing I had ever seen in my life.

Sarah frowned. 'You wouldn't get the wear out of something like that. Besides, pink with your hair—' She shook her head at me and said no more.

I wondered afterwards whether she'd spoken about the colour of my hair just to put me off the cloak, but anyway, I settled on the green taffeta and was mighty pleased with it.

As we left the market a street-seller called to us, bidding us to buy her fresh gooseberry syllabub, and we did so, sharing a dish between us and finding it most refreshing, for it was again very hot. On the way home we also bought some gay coloured-paper parasols against the sun, and some new pattens to wear over our shoes. They made us seem very tall, but Sarah said they needed to, for when it rained the waste would wash along the street outside the shop to a depth of several inches. In view of their height, though, we decided to practise walking in them at home before we went out in them.

Throughout the trip to Houndsditch we had not seen nor heard one mention of the plague, apart from a poster on the door of the Green Dragon Tavern which read:

A most efficacious cordial against the plague may be obtained at the Green Dragon. The only true guard against infection at six pence a pint'.

Because we were in a happy mood, talking of home and our brothers and sisters, Sarah and I both affected not to see this notice.

Back in our room, I tried on the green dress, patted my curls down as much as possible and tied them back with a green ribbon. I then put a few drops of orange water behind my ears and, feeling very fine, my skirts rustling about me, I walked up and down outside the shop to take the air, hoping that someone might come along and see me. I suppose the 'someone' I was thinking about was Tom, but my friend Abby would have done nearly as well.

However, the only persons around whom I knew were young Jacob and Dickon, who engaged me in a game of gleek. This was easier played sitting on the ground, but as I was not willing to kneel on the dirt in my finery, I let Dickon play my turn for me. Pretty soon, a minister of the church came by and chastised us for playing a gambling game on a Sunday, and though the boys protested that we were not playing for tokens or money, he bade us put away the counters and act in a way which was more suited to the Lord's Day.

I went indoors a little later, musing on the fact that I had not been to a church service at all since coming to London. This was not because of a sudden turning away from the teachings, but because (and I must confess I was not displeased at this) there always seemed something else to do: cooking or cleaning, washing or repairing our clothes. And with the shop open all the other days of the week, there was only Sunday to do these things. Sarah told me it wasn't just us who did not keep the Lord's Day, for since King Charles had been restored to the throne in 1660, far fewer people went to church on a regular basis. The ministers blamed the king himself for this, for they said that he and his court were a byword for gaiety and freedom and did not set an example to the people by leading pious and godly lives as the nobility were supposed to do.

Indoors, I found Sarah was starting to make marchpane fruits. It was for this sweetmeat that we'd prepared all the almonds a day or so before and, as I was anxious to learn all the secrets of our trade, I changed out of my new gown and hung it in our room with a sheet over it against the dust.

The marchpane mixture was made by blending the ground almonds with sugar and rose water and dividing it into several portions. Each portion was then coloured by Sarah with either red, green, pink, or orange tinctures, and a little extra was made brown with cinnamon. Once divided, we took a portion each and stirred and pounded until it came together in a stiff dough.

The miniature fruits were to be strawberries, oranges, apples and plums, and Sarah took the utmost trouble with these, using a paring knife and other small instruments – which she said grand ladies used on their nails – to carve their shape. The strawberries were especially pleasing, being the rightful size and plump triangular shape with tiny indentations, as the fruit truly has, and a green leaf and stalk atop of them. I was allowed to make the apples on my own, and I did them green, with a dimple on top from which protruded a cinnamon-brown stalk. When the little fruits were completed Sarah instructed me to take a fine paint brush and give each apple a blush of pink on its side, then roll it in ground sugar.

To make the fairy fruits took us several hours altogether, but it was a most enjoyable task and, once finished, they looked pretty and delicate enough to tempt any passing elfin. We placed them on white paper and gave them another frosting of sugar before putting them in trays to harden slightly overnight and be ready for sale the following day.

The next morning I woke early to the usual cry of a milkmaid calling, 'Fresh milk! Fresh new milk!' and Sarah bade me take the jug to the door and buy some. After we'd drunk well of the foaming liquid – and Mew had her portion, too, with some bread in it left from the day before – we washed and dressed and tidied the shop ready for that day's trade.

At seven-thirty, as I opened up the shop, a town crier announced that certain Orders had been issued on behalf of the Lord Mayor and were being posted at every main water conduit and well. Every citizen was asked to take note of these and do as they commanded.

Sarah, who was arranging our marchpane fruits under muslin cloths to keep off the flies, looked at me in concern. 'That's sure to be news about the plague,' she said. 'Run and get some water and find out what it's about.'

I was pleased to do this, for I was wearing my new blue cambric dress and was mighty keen to give it an outing. Going to Bell Court I found Abby just about to leave there with a full pail and an enamel jug of water. She looked pleased to see me and put her containers down to give me a hearty kiss on the cheek.

'I've come up to read the Orders,' I said. 'What do they say?'

'Oh, 'tis just about the plague,' she said. 'Beggars must stay within their parish, and everyone is to water, sweep and cleanse the street in front of their door every morning and dispose of any slops in a clean manner . . . 'tis not very interesting and just means more work for us maids.'

'But how is your mistress?' I asked.

'Middling well,' Abby said. Her face brightened. 'But she has bid me go to the Exchange tomorrow morning on an errand. Why don't you ask your sister if you can have leave to go, and we can meet up.'

'Where's that?' I asked, puzzled.

'You goose!' she said. 'Have you not heard of the Royal Exchange? 'Tis the most fashionable meeting place in the city! At least, it is apart from the coffee houses – and no decent girl would be seen in one of those without a gentleman.'

I tried to cover my ignorance by assuring her that I had heard of the Royal Exchange, but wanted to know exactly where it was.

''Tis at Cornhill. But I'll meet you here about midday.'

I said I would do my best to be there, and went to read the Orders, which were just a list of rules and instructions for the prevention of further contagion. They included directions for medicines to be prescribed against the sickness – different ones according to whether you were rich or poor – the banning of all needless gatherings of people and a ruling that beggars must not be allowed to go about from parish to parish in case this spread the disease.

Several folk were gathered about the poster and many of them, not being readers, begged me to impart its contents. As more people arrived I was asked to do this several times over, until I almost knew the words off by heart. As I read them once again it came to me that those who surrounded me did not seem overly worried about them. They made good-humoured comments about the contents, laughing and saying it would be more work for death-mongering coffin makers, and naming doctors and apothecaries as quacks and charlatans.

'They would as soon kill you as cure you – for they get paid either way,' one woman said to me cheerfully, and again I could not bring myself to believe that these Orders – this plague – was any great matter. The sun was shining, the day was fair and the people around me were bonny and of good heart. Perhaps the authorities had just been thrown into a panic by a few deaths.

Returning home, however, I was given some cause to change my mind, for I blundered unawares into the very heart of the dread plague-land. Going the long way back – for I was trying to make my journey lead me past Doctor da Silva's shop – I found myself approaching the parish of St Giles. Sarah had told me this was a disreputable area and that many derelicts and paupers had made their homes amongst its slums. It being daylight, however, and the streets being busy, I did not worry about entering. As I ventured further into the mean and shabby streets though, I began to feel considerable unease, for in some passageways shops were closed up and there were few people about, almost as if it was a holy day. I pressed on, for though I had never been this way before, being a country girl I knew by the position of the sun in the sky that I was going in the right direction.

After a few moments I reached Cock and Ball Alley and judged I should turn left into it. But a man lounging by the first house held his hand up to bar my way. He held a sharpened halberd aloft and was a dirty and ugly-looking fellow with a red, sweaty face and several teeth missing at the front.

'I need to get along here,' I said, somewhat nervously.

'No, you don't,' he said, and he pointed to the door of the house behind him.

This was a stout oak door, cast all about with heavy chains and locks, and as I stared at it my heart seemed to contract, for it had a great painted red cross on it and a written notice saying: LORD, HAVE MERCY ON US.

I gasped, my stomach lurching. I knew already, of course, what these signs meant, but the ill-favoured fellow was eager to explain further. 'Four dead of plague in there and the rest shut up for forty days!' he said. He pointed with his halberd. 'And further down Cock and Ball Alley two more houses are enclosed.'

I stared up at the house before me. One small window was open on the second floor, but apart from that it was shuttered and silent.

'But . . . but how do they eat? Who gets their provisions?' I asked.

'I does their errands,' the fellow said, 'and buys their milk and bread.'

'But how do they get on, shut up all that time? How do they take the air?'

'They don't take no air,' he said. 'The only time that door will be opened is to bring out a body.' He scratched his head and I saw something – some small insect – dart along his greasy scalp. 'Four dead so far and two more expected before nightfall.'

As I stood there, horrified, staring at the shuttered windows and trying to imagine how the people fared inside the house, there came from within a sudden wailing, turning to a high-pitched scream which went on and on without any end. There was the sound of running feet and another scream joined the first.

I stared at the man waiting for confirmation, for I was rooted to the spot and felt unable to leave until I knew the worst. He looked at me and shrugged. "Tis another,' was all he said.

A woman walking by us on the other side of the road crossed herself and hurried away. As several others gathered outside a shop and spoke together, looking with frightened eyes towards the house, I began to back away, going home the way I'd arrived, getting out of St Giles with all haste. Before I'd got very far, I heard the bells of the parish church, tolling mournfully to tell of that latest death.

Chapter Five

The first week of July

'Asking how the Plague goes, the Parish Clerk tells me that it increases much, and much in our Parish . . .'

Sarah, being pleased with the way I was working, gave me permission to take an excursion with Abby, and the following day we met at midday as planned.

'Well, the plague cannot be that far advanced,' said Abby as we walked through the vast stone pillars into the Royal Exchange, 'for the king and his courtiers are still in London. They would surely have left if there was any chance of the pestilence coming near to his royal person.'

I shrugged, not knowing the answer to this.

Abby lowered her voice. 'Although I've heard that the royal person is not that fussy about who he *does* get near. The likes of actresses and whores . . .' Here she paused and we looked at each other gleefully. '. . . have had bastard children by him.'

'Have they really?' I said, and I would have asked more except that I was entranced and amazed and distracted on all sides by the scene before me.

The Royal Exchange was a great blackened stone building, open in the centre, with a gallery around each of its two floors. Small, alluring, candlelit shops lined these galleries, each with its own bright metal sign hanging over its doorway proclaiming its wares. Groups of young men gathered in the centre court, looking intently at the women who passed – who, in turn, affected not to see them at all. Occasionally, I heard a long low whistle or a comment of, 'By gad!' or 'Look at that filly!'

I tried to memorise what people were wearing to tell Sarah later, for it seemed to me that each group was more dazzling and brilliantly dressed than the one before. The men were mostly in velvet breeches in rich colours, gartered in gold at the knee, with handsome thigh-length black coats which bore silver-and-gold embroidered cuffs. Some carried swords or three-cornered hats with vast plumes, and some had short periwigs. The very finest wore elaborate curling wigs and their faces were powdered and patched almost as carefully as those of the women.

The women themselves were like birds of paradise in summer gowns made of lace, spangled satin, muslin or watered moiré in all colours of the rainbow: jade green, palest ivory, rich plum, lavender and dusky pink. Most of them had tumbling blonde hair (all false, Abby said in a whisper) and their whitened skin contrasted greatly with their dark eyebrows and sweeping lashes. Their bodices were low – so low, in fact, that it was a wonder that their voluptuous bosoms did not spill out of their gowns – and most carried elaborate, feather-loaded fans. Those who did not affect to hide behind their fans were wearing vizards or masks, held up to their faces on sticks.

It was difficult not to gawp, and in the end Abby had to tug my arm to make me move. 'Do come on, Hannah,' she hissed. 'You're staring about you like a country bridegroom at a whorehouse.'

'Sorry,' I murmured, for my sights had just been engaged by a woman wearing a striking bright fuschia-pink dress with pearl-grey under-skirt and the largest, most ludicrous headdress of flowers and dressed hair I had ever seen. She was an old woman, at least sixty, and her face and upper body were painted waxy-white and covered in black, spangled patches. Her lips were blood red and her eyebrows painted on in large semi-hoops, giving her a permanent expression of surprise.

'Who *is* she?' I asked Abby in a low voice. 'Someone's mistress?'

Abby looked where I was staring and shuddered. 'Years ago, maybe,' she said. 'And now she wears whitening and patches to hide the wrinkles and pox marks. Pray God you and I find good husbands who live long, Hannah, for I would not like to be on the market again at her age.' She tugged my arm. 'Come on, I have to get some silver ribbons for Madam. She's feeling a little better and has a fancy to bedeck herself.' She stepped confidently towards one of the small shops and I scuttled behind her, my eyes darting everywhere.

The little shops sold a thousand varieties of luxurious things: tortoiseshell boxes, silver comfit holders, velvet capes, soft leather gloves, jewelled bags, satin petticoats, watches and clocks, masks, birdcages, linen handkerchiefs and every possible item of haberdashery. The one thing I did not see was a confectioners, and I immediately began to dream of having a shop here, of me and Sarah being at the Royal Exchange, our Sugared Plum sign hanging here amongst the glittering signs of so many others.

Abby made her purchase and, very reluctantly, we set off for home, but not before we'd taken a turn of the inner court once again and seen a most beautiful, very elegant tall woman in flame-coloured silk whom Abby said was Barbara Castlemaine, the king's mistress. I was able to see little more than this lady's head and fine shoulders, however, because a small crowd of gallants were surrounding her, each, it seemed, trying to outdo the others in swaggers and elaborate courtly gestures.

I left Abby at Belle Vue, the house where she was in service. It was a handsome five-storey dwelling set in a cobbled and flowered courtyard, with stables alongside, and Abby promised that the next time the master and mistress were out, she would show me around it. 'We'll be quite safe,' she said, 'for the cook spends her afternoons drinking and playing cards with the grooms and the housekeeper has a lover and is never here. When Mr Beauchurch is out and the mistress is asleep I have free run of the house.' She eyed me quizzically. 'But talking of lovers . . . you have not spoken of your beau. Tom, isn't it?'

I blushed. 'Really, I hardly know him,' I had to confess to her.

'Is that so?'

'Although, if knowing him could be advanced by thinking of him, then I own I know him well enough to marry him!' I said.

She laughed. 'You'll have to contrive another meeting. 'Tis easily done. My sweetheart is 'prenticed to a bookbinder and I find all sorts of excuses and reasons to go in and question him on the book business, although I find it horribly dreary.'

I said I would think of something, and see her soon, then we kissed and parted.

When I got home, I told Sarah in great detail everything I'd seen at the Exchange, and also assured her that I was determined that one day we would have a shop there.

She was in a happy mood and joined in, saying that we might easily do that – for she had done well that day and almost sold out of our fairy fruit. 'Everyone who passed admired it,' she said, 'and several ladies said they would tell their friends about us. There is just one thing—'

'What's that?' I asked absently, my mind still on all the things I'd seen.

'We must close the shop early this afternoon and set to making some more,' she said.

Inwardly, I groaned a little, thinking of the cracking of the almond shells and the laborious peeling and pounding of the nut kernels, but did not say a word.

That evening, while Sarah and I were still grinding nuts, the crier came to say that because of fear of the dread visitation, that very day the king and his courtiers were leaving London for Isleworth. Meanwhile, to try to avert the sickness, his people were ordered to take to the churches and observe some days of fasting and solemn prayer, the first of which was to be the following Wednesday. On this day all shops, markets and taverns were to be closed and everyone was to attend church at least once. Hearing this, I immediately thought of Tom and what a chance it was to see him – for I would make sure to attend the church in his parish as well as ours – and how fine I would look in my new green dress with its matching petticoat.

When, though, three days later, the new Bill of Mortality was published with the news that across London, five hundred persons had died of the plague in that first week of July, I upbraided myself for my vanity and made a silent promise that I would attend church as devoutly and sincerely as a nun, and not give another thought to how I looked that day.

I did not see Tom at church, and indeed it was a most grave and seemingly never-ending sermon in St Mary at Hill, so that I was mighty sorry I had decided to attend it and not go back to the shop with Sarah after the service at St Dominic's. The vicar there wore a rough woollen shirt and had ashes on his forehead, and he roared from the pulpit that if the plague struck in its full terror, then we were all to blame by our corrupt behaviour. He said that if we wanted to avert the full might of it then we must change our sinful ways.

I looked round at my fellow men, wondering what they had to confess and thinking that they must all have souls as black as those of heathens if the vicar was right. Try as I might, however, I could not think of a single really bad thing of my own to confess. There was vanity, of course, but I had quite given up on my freckles and was almost resolved to live with them, and could such a seemingly small thing like wishing to have darker hair and finer gowns really bring down the wrath of God on us?

That afternoon, while we were supposed to be fasting in silent contemplation of our fate (in reality, partaking of bread and cheese and talking of home) there came a tap on the door of the shop.

Going through, I was disconcerted to find Tom standing there and, moreover, Tom in Sunday best starched shirt and red fustian breeches, a felt hat on his head.

He gave me a slight bow, his eyes raking my face and smiling, and bade me good day. I curtsied and bade him the same, but then I was stuck and did not know what was the correct thing to do. At home in Chertsey I would have invited him in to take some small beer, but here in London I did not know if it was appropriate. Sarah, though, seeming to sense I was at a loss, called to me.

'Don't leave Master Tom standing on the doorstep like a boot scraper,' was what she said, and it made him laugh. He tugged off his hat as he came through to our back room, and his eyes fell on Mew. I had tied an old ribbon around her neck and she was rolling across the floor playing with the fraying edge of it. 'Oh, haven't you heard?' he exclaimed.

I looked down at Mew in some concern. I feared that he was going to say that Mew belonged to someone important and was being sought by them, for I'd grown very fond of the kitten and would not have liked to give her up.

'Heard what?' Sarah asked.

'By order of the Lord Mayor all the cats and

dogs . . .' He hesitated. 'All cats and dogs are to be killed.'

Sarah and I both gasped, and I picked up Mew immediately and held her tight.

'Why?' we both asked together.

'They think the sickness may be caused by cats and dogs running abroad and spreading it to different houses. Doctor da Silva does not believe this is possible, but . . .' he shrugged, 'this is what the authorities say. There are carts going round and the drivers are being paid two pence for the body of each dog or cat they club to death and bring in.'

I gave a little scream.

'Is that really true, Tom?' Sarah asked. 'You would not joke with us?'

'Indeed not!' Tom said. 'I can see how fond you are of the little thing.' He put out his hand to stroke Mew's soft fur. 'All is not lost,' he said, 'for if you keep kitty inside they won't see her. The men have no authority to come into the house and club the animals there – although in view of the bounty being paid, some no doubt will try to do so.'

'Then we must keep Mew indoors!' Sarah said.

I nodded. 'From now on she mustn't even go out in the yard.'

Sarah pulled a slight face, turning up her nose, for she took pains to ensure that our shop and living quarters were always clean and sweet-smelling.

'She could go outside on a leash of string,' I said. 'And you or I will watch her to see that she doesn't bite through it and get away.' I held Mew at arm's length and she seemed to look at me reproachfully with her big round eyes. 'It's for your own good!' I said. 'And when all is well with the world, then you can go out properly once more.'

Tom gave a slight cough. 'Miss Hannah. I came to ask if you wished to come picking violets with me,' he said.

I smiled at him, pleased and excited to be asked.

'Where do you intend to go for them?' Sarah wanted to know.

'To Chelsea,' Tom said. 'Doctor da Silva is busy now preparing a great many remedies against the plague and he needs several herbs which only grow wild. I know you use violets a great deal yourself, and there is a patch known only to myself on the banks of the Thames there.'

I glanced at Sarah, who was nodding. 'Violets – yes, we always need many!' she said. 'It has been harder to buy them at the market lately. And if you should see any wild strawberries, Hannah, or borage, I would have some of those too.' She glanced at Tom. 'But of course Master Tom must have first pick.'

Tom smiled. 'There is plenty enough to go round,' he said. 'I know all the secret places.' He patted the canvas bag which he carried over his shoulder. 'This will be full by the time we come home.'

Sarah found me a trug, and asked me in a low voice if I would rather not change out of my green gown and into another more modest one. I stopped her words with a frown and shake of my head, however, and she smiled and let me go.

Chelsea was about five miles away but a pleasant walk once we got through the press of London, and it only took us just over an hour to reach the meadows

Tom had spoken of. We talked all the way. Tom told me about Doctor da Silva, saying that he was a clever man and a good master to his apprentices – which seemed just as well, for Tom still had another four of his seven years to serve. He told me that his mother had died in childbirth several years ago, his father had married again and it was then that Tom had been bound to the doctor.

''Twas to get me away from home, for my stepmother can't abide me,' he said. 'She has no time for the children born to my father before she came.'

I hadn't had such an interesting life, but I told Tom about my family in Chertsey, and how Sarah and I were faring in the shop, and also about meeting Abby again. Then I told him about our visit to the Exchange and all the elegant and fashionable people we'd seen.

'There won't be so many of these elegant people around soon,' Tom said. 'Now that the king and his court have left London, they'll all be going after them.'

This led to us talking about the plague, and I asked what remedies were most effective. Tom said that everyone had different ideas. 'Some say the best thing is to hold a coin of gold in your mouth whenever you go out – and the best of these is an angel from Elizabeth's reign,' he said.

I shook my head, astonished. 'I have never even seen a gold angel,' I said, 'much less have a spare one to put in my mouth!'

'There are many other remedies. You can hold a piece of nutmeg in your mouth. Or a sprig of rosemary. Or a clove,' he said, laughing. 'Or a roasted fig, or some tobacco, or a quantity of snails without their shells.'

I shuddered.

'The doctor has all cures for all prices. For the rich he will provide a cordial made from unicorn's horns and honey, for the poor a decoction of clover and cat's-foot. There is a great deal of money to be made from the plague.'

'So is he a quack, then – your doctor?' I asked wonderingly.

Tom shook his head. 'Of course not. What he prescribes he truly believes in.'

'What then will *you* take against the plague?'

He thought for some time. 'The seeds and leaves of cornflowers taken in wine are said to be most effective for those born under my planet.'

'And should I take the same?'

'You're a sun subject – so the doctor told me,' he said, and I felt a moment's pleasure at the knowledge that he had been talking about me. He thought for a moment, frowning. It caused a small line to appear between his eyes which I had a longing to smooth out with my finger. 'The peony is a flower of the sun,' he said at last, 'though I have not studied enough to know . . .' His face cleared, 'but it is well known that chopped with rue it will promote pleasant dreams and take away fears, and this is all to the good.'

I nodded. 'And where shall I get these things?'

'I shall steep the leaves and begin making you a decoction tomorrow, Hannah.'

There it was again, his voice, saying my name in that soft way. I stopped walking, turned to him, and caught him staring at me. We smiled at each other and I felt a shiver run through me, moving down my spine like a trickle of iced water. He said nothing, but he caught hold of my hand and held it to his face for a moment before letting it go. I felt that we both wanted to say or do something but, ignorant of what this thing should be, we just walked on.

Chelsea was a pretty little village on the Thames, its thatched cottages, farms and uncrowded streets reminding me a little of Chertsey. A field fronted the river, a field thick with lush grass and bright with starry white daisies and golden marigolds. Tom led me through this pasture to the river edge where green rushes grew thickly, and tangled masses of reeds floated out like green hair. We took off our shoes and sat peaceably for some time with our feet in the water, watching the river craft go by and listening to the birdsong. I said there seemed to be more boats about and Tom told me that because of the fear of plague, many people had taken to the river, intending to live on barges and makeshift craft until the danger was over.

Tom had a list of flowers and herbs which the doctor needed. These included angelica, cornflowers, wild garlic, scabious, chervil and sage, all of which he said would be used in plague remedies. Along the edges of the field and in certain places already known to Tom he collected these, snipping off the flower heads and putting them into muslin bags and then into his canvas holdall. Afterwards, he showed me where the patches of wild violets were, and helped me gather a large number to put in my trug. There were many borage flowers, too, which I knew Sarah wanted to candy. Tom took some of these as well, for he said that an infusion made from the flowers expelled melancholy. 'The doctor always says that a merry heart does good like a medicine,' he added.

Setting off for home, we were light-hearted, but as we neared London an invisible pall seemed to gather over us and stifle our laughter. A stillness lay upon the city (Sunday being the day of atonement) as if it was waiting, hushed, for something to befall it. I shivered for I knew now that this thing was plague.

As we reached the shop Tom moved near to me, took a lock of my hair and, looking into my eyes, curled a ringlet around his finger so that I had to move my face closer and closer to his. I was quite breathless, thinking he was about to kiss me, when suddenly there came down the quiet street the loud clattering of clogs on cobbles, and Tom and I sprang apart from each other. Two women appeared – but such women! Frightening old hags, clad in sacking, with deep hoods over their heads, carrying long white staves in front of them.

I instinctively shrank back, fearing their very appearance, and Tom did too, pressing into the shop doorway beside me.

'Who are they?' I asked with a shiver as they passed us. 'Where are they going?'

'They are the searchers of the dead,' Tom said. I looked at him, alarmed, and he added, 'They are employed by the parish. In the event of a death it is their gruesome duty to search the body and ascertain why that person has died. If they find the plague marks on them then the sexton has a grave prepared and sees that their house is shut up for forty days.'

'But there have been no cases of plague round here!'

His expression grew solemn. 'I fear there may have been,' he said. He squeezed my hand. 'But go in and tell your sister what you've seen – she may know something further.' He caught my eyes and smiled. 'Try to be of good heart whatever the news is. I shall call on you with your cordial as soon as it is made.'

Chapter Six

The second week of July

'But Lord, how everybody's looks and discourse in the street is of Death and nothing else.'

When I went inside there was just one taper burning in our back room, and Sarah was sitting quietly on our bed, her hands folded in her lap.

'What is it?' I asked, alarmed, for normally she would have been busy doing something: weighing up sugar, writing the accounts or mending an apron. Now, though, she was just sitting there, her face shocked and pale.

I put down the trug and went towards her. 'I saw two horrible old women on the road. Tom told me they were searchers of the dead. Did you see them? Where have they been?'

Sarah's hands clenched into fists. 'They've been nearby, Hannah. In the first alley off Crown and King Place.'

'And where did they search?'

She looked down. 'In the old house hard by the sign

of the Blue Goose.'

'Dickon and Jacob's house?'

She nodded. 'It was the babe. Their little sister Marie—'

I gasped. 'Not—'

Sarah swallowed hard. 'She was taken poorly only yesterday, but her mother, Mrs Williams, told no one for fear they'd call in the authorities. She said it looked like just a rash. She thought it was a sweating sickness. But then this morning two buboes came up on the child's body.'

'What are they?' I asked fearfully.

'Hard lumps of matter. They come up in the groin, or in the neck or under the arm.' She hesitated. 'They are a sure sign of plague.'

'And then what happened?'

'Mrs Williams called for an apothecary, for they couldn't afford a doctor. And it wasn't Doctor da Silva, it was someone else. But before he could arrive the buboes had become so engorged with matter that the baby could not move its legs or head without screaming.'

I shuddered.

'And although the apothecary tried to lance the buboes it was too late. They said she screamed out one last time – the most terrible sound – and then died.'

I pulled up a stool and sat next to Sarah, not saying anything for some moments, trying to absorb and understand what this meant. I hardly knew Marie, for she was barely two years old and had not been walking long enough to be out and about much with Dickon and Jacob. I'd just seen a sturdy, grubby, child staggering about the place trying to catch hold of one of the cats. Once I'd given her a few candied rose petals and she'd gabbled in baby-talk at me and run off.

After a while I asked Sarah to tell me more of the tale.

'The first I knew that the child had . . . that is, the first I knew what had happened was that the bells of St Dominic's started tolling. And then Mr Newbery banged on the door here and shouted that there had been a terrible event. I went outside and everyone seemed to be at their doors, just standing there, silently. I went from house to house asking what had happened, but they were all crying and could hardly tell me. And then Mrs Williams ran into the street. She was tearing at her clothes and screaming, pulling her hair out like she was going mad with grief. Only then did someone tell me it was Marie who had died, and it was thought to be of the plague.'

I went to our fireplace and put the kettle on to boil so I could make some camomile tea for us both. I felt cold and hollow, hardly believing what had happened. How could that child be among us one moment, running about happily, and dead the next?

'The worst thing,' Sarah went on, 'is that this poor woman . . . this mother quite demented by grief...could mayhap have been comforted by someone's voice soothing her and telling her that she must look now to her other children, but no one would go near her.'

'She has no husband,' I said, remembering what Sarah had told me about Jacob's father being a sailor, and dying at sea earlier in the year.

Sarah shook her head. 'No husband, no comforter at all. I felt I wanted to do something for her, put my arms around her and console her, but I could not bring myself. The fear of the plague was too great. And so she suffers in her grief alone.' Sarah began crying. 'But you have not heard the worst,' she added – and I knew it was selfish of me but I immediately looked round to see where Mew was.

'It's not Mew,' she said, shaking her head through her tears. 'He's in a box under our bed and hasn't been out.'

'What, then? Tell me quickly,' I begged her.

'The eldest child has it. Kate – she has the same symptoms And their house is being shut up.'

'Oh,' I breathed.

We were both silent as we waited for the water to boil. I tried to imagine how it would be in that house, with Mrs Williams just sitting and waiting for the signs of plague to appear, waiting to see if Death would visit any other of her children.

'What if *she* dies?' I asked suddenly. 'What if Mrs Williams dies next and the children have to fend for themselves alone, shut up in the house?'

Sarah shook her head. 'I don't know. Maybe they will all be taken to the pesthouse – although there are not many of those and I hear they are already full.'

'Is their house already closed?'

'I fear so,' Sarah said. 'And now they must stay inside for forty days.'

'The boys will hate that.'

Sarah glanced up at me and I knew what she was thinking: they would probably be visited with plague and die before then.

'Maybe we could give them something,' I said suddenly.

She nodded. 'I was thinking that. Something to cheer the children, perhaps. Some comfits.'

The kettle was rattling on the fire, so I poured boiling water on the camomile flowers and let it steep for a few moments. 'Even if the house is already locked and barred, we could ask their guard to give them the sweetmeats.'

Sarah dabbed at her eyes with her apron and stood up. 'It will make us feel better if we do something – even just some little thing – for the family,' she said. 'What flowers did you harvest today?'

I showed her the trug and its contents, and while we drank our tea I told her something of my hours with Tom, and how thoughtful and pleasant a companion he was. I did not tell her of the times when we'd been rapt in each other's glances, however, for they were private moments, for me to think on later.

I changed into my working dress and Sarah busied herself putting more water on to boil in a pan, then she chipped a goodly piece of sugar from a new loaf and put that in as well. 'Tomorrow we will begin to candy some borage flowers,' she said, 'for they are said to have virtues which may help lighten their hearts. Tonight, though, we'll make some little violet cakes. And we will take them to the house together and try not to be alarmed at anything we might see.' She shook the pan to help dissolve the sugar. 'Whatever fright we take will be nothing compared to what they are going through.'

She set me to nipping the violet flowers from their stalks and washing them, while she boiled the water to melt the sugar. Several times she skimmed it of foam, until it was a thick, clear syrup mixture. Then I was allowed to take the violets – about a quarter of all I'd picked – stir them thoroughly in the mixture, then quickly pour it out into a wetted tray.

The mixture began to harden almost immediately and we let it be while we washed the rest of the violets and borage flowers for the next day. When we turned to it again the flat cake was almost firm, and Sarah carefully cut it into small squares, lifted them from the tray and put them on white paper. They looked very pretty, for I had made sure to choose a variety of colours for the violets, and they ranged from white through pink down to deepest purple. Not, I realised, that it was likely that our poor family would appreciate this careful harmonising of colour.

When the violet cakes were quite cool we folded them into a small package and set off for the house. The windows and door were already barred, and marked with the red cross. Above the cross I could see the same paper sign that I'd seen on the house in St Giles: LORD, HAVE MERCY ON US.

Sarah and I held each other's hands tightly as we approached, for I can't convey how much fear was struck into us to see these words so close to home, and to imagine the terror of that little family on the other side of the door.

The guard, a youngish bearded man, was sitting outside on a stool, his halberd standing diagonally across the doorway of the house.

'Could you give these sweetmeats to the children next time you see them?' Sarah asked, giving the package into his hands.

He nodded. 'That will be in the morning,' he said, 'when I takes in their milk and bread.'

'Are they . . .' I hesitated. I'd been about to ask if they were all right, but of course they were not, and I did not know what else to say.

'They're sleeping now,' he said. 'An apothecary has given them all a draught.'

I was torn between wanting to make our stay there as brief as possible and finding out more, but Sarah was already pulling at my hand to come away.

We walked to our shop, looking back only once at the enclosed and silent house.

'Violet cakes – they seem but poor reparation,' Sarah said. 'What can they do to help?'

I shrugged. 'I don't know.'

But we were glad we had gone.

The following day we took some candied borage flowers up to the house and left them with the guard, but had no way of knowing whether they actually received them or whether the guard ate them himself.

The Bills for that week showed 750 deaths in London and to our great dismay our trade began falling off a little. This was because many of our customers, being mostly of the middling classes, knew how to obtain a Certificate of Health, and were going to their country houses. The king and his court moved further out, too – from Isleworth to Hampton Court – for it had been said that Isleworth was not far enough away from the contamination in London and it was feared the plague might still be able to reach him there.

On Saturday a fruit-seller came to our door calling,

'Cherry-ripe!' and although Sarah said they were too early to be Kentish cherries, and must have come on a ship from the Netherlands, she bought some on my urging, for I was anxious to try out the recipe for sugared cherries which mother had given me. After washing a scoopful of these, I carefully stoned and halved them, then set them over the heat in a preserving pan with a little water. When they were scalding hot I shook them in a sieve, then put them in a cloth to dry, after which I put them back into the pan, layered with a good amount of sugar that I had previously ground down. Putting this pan back on the fire, I scalded the cherries and cooled them three times all together, so that they picked up the sugar and it crystallised on them. After this I dipped them quickly in cold water and placed them in the hot sun to dry out.

Sarah watched me and said this was a new recipe for her, and she had not worked with cherries before, but thought they looked very pretty and tasty.

That evening came the information from Mr Newbery that there had been another death at the top of our street, although as the person there had lived alone there was no need for the house to be shut up. We had received no further news of our Williams family these last three days, so as we closed the shutter of the shop, Sarah and I resolved that we would go and enquire after them.

The guard outside their house was asleep and snoring, so Sarah tapped on the next-door house to enquire how they did.

The woman who answered, Mrs Groat, shook her head. 'I've heard nothing of them these last two days,' she said. 'That first night – and the next day – there was a wailing and a crying and carrying on, but for the last two days there's been nothing.'

'Has food been taken inside?' Sarah asked.

She shrugged. 'The guard has money to buy their everyday provisions, and get milk for the children, but to tell the truth I fear he takes it for ale. I was going to ask the minister at church tomorrow what I should do.' She looked at us and lowered her voice, 'I don't even know if they live.'

Hearing this, Sarah did no more than go straight to the guard outside the Williams' house and try to rouse him, and I fear he *had* been on ale, for it took a great deal of shaking and shouting before he was awake to our questions.

'We want to know how the family within are,' she said and, seeing his rather blank and stupid face, added some falsely polite words of praise for his care of them.

'Has a doctor called on them?' I asked, thinking that if nothing else I could run and get Doctor da Silva and see what he could do.

The man smiled, a drunken, lop-sided smile. 'This family give me no trouble at all. Quiet as the flowers, they are.'

'But we want to know if they're all right!' Sarah said. 'When did you last see them?'

'Can you ask them how they're doing?' I said. 'Can we see if they need anything?'

The man leaned over and picked up his glittering halberd, waving it in front of our faces. 'I has to guard this house. No one can go in!'

'*You* can go in, though, can't you?' I said. 'You can

see how they fare.'

He looked at us suspiciously. 'Are you family?'

I was about to say no, but Sarah broke in and said yes, they were our dear cousins and we were fair desperate to know how they were doing.

'We hoped such a kind and reasonable man as yourself would be looking after them,' I added, for I could see that flattery might be the only thing to move him. 'Would you be able give us news on how they fare?'

Grinning now, the man got out a set of keys and proceeded to open the two padlocks which held together the chains which had been hammered across the doorway. He pushed at the door, which opened to nothing but silence and darkness.

'How do you keep?' the guard hollered into the hallway. 'Is there owt you need?'

Holding each other, Sarah and I looked through into the hall, where not a candle or a taper showed through the darkness. And then the air from the newly-opened house billowed to reach us and we smelled a stench so foetid that we had to step backwards.

'I very much fear all is not well,' she whispered to me, and then braced herself to call, 'Hello! Mrs Williams. Is there anything you need?'

No reply came.

She and I looked at each other nervously, for I felt sick from the smell and would not have been brave enough to enter.

'Will you go in?' Sarah asked the guard.

'Not I!' he said. 'I'm not paid to enter charnel houses.'

'And you mustn't go in either!' I said, holding fast to Sarah's arm.

Behind us, Mrs Groat had come up to peer into the dark abyss of the house.

'I'd best shut 'm up again,' the guard said, but there was suddenly a tremendous crash from inside the house, making us all cry out in fear, and the next moment a small pale figure jumped or fell down the stairs and shot past us, running down the cobbled streets as if the devil himself was after him.

'A ghoul!' Mrs Groat said, and she fell to her knees and began praying.

'No!' I said, looking after the boy in disbelief. 'It was little Dickon!'

'Stark naked and running for his life,' Sarah said.

I watched his progress down the street and would have turned to go after him, but Sarah knew what was in my mind and held me fast. 'You must not,' she said. 'He will have the plague on his skin.'

'But who will look after him?'

'It can't be us! If you catch him it will be a death warrant for us both.'

When we turned back the guard was standing in the doorway, still reluctant to enter. He sniffed and then curled his nostrils in disgust. 'I smell death!' he said.

'You must go and see,' Sarah insisted. 'We cannot just shut the house now. You must go and see who's dead.'

After some persuasion – and Sarah had some small coins on her which we handed to him – he went inside and came back a few moments later to tell us that there were two children dead in a bed upstairs, and the mother was lying dead by the kitchen table.

As the news spread, a small crowd gathered outside the house, most of whom were openly crying. Sarah, brushing back tears herself, asked one of them to go down to the minister so that women could be called in to dress the bodies and make them ready for burial.

We went home, but could not sleep for thinking about the poor, dead children and for wondering what had become of young Dickon. We were not to find this out, however, for we never saw nor heard a word of him again.

Chapter Seven

The third week of July

'But how sad a sight it is to see the streets empty of people, and very few upon the 'Change . . . and two shops in three shut up.'

When we closed shop on the day following the Williams family's deaths, Sarah and I resolved to go along to their house to try and discover when their funeral would be, for she said it was not right that a mother and her innocent children should be buried with no one to cast flowers into their graves.

We had enquired after Dickon that day, but had failed to find any trace of him, and Sarah had said that we must try to think that a kindly family somewhere were looking after him, or at least that he'd been taken to a workhouse or pesthouse for shelter. Neither of us wanted to think that he might still be on the streets of London, frightened, naked and hungry; that he might have ended up living in the sewers with the rats, or on the edge of the stinking Fleet ditch at Westminster where, Sarah said, the river ran thick and stagnant and the poorest, foulest beggars ended up, living on peelings and scraps.

At the Williams' house the wooden boarding had gone from the door and windows, and the fearful red cross had been replaced by a white one to signify modified quarantine, although it would be twenty days and the house would have to be fumigated before anyone could live in it. There was no man guarding it now, but neither were there any housewives chattering outside or children playing nearby. It seemed that people passing knew of the deaths, for they were walking in an arc past the house, as far away as they could get, as if they were trying to avoid breathing any of the air coming from it.

When we asked at the adjoining dwelling, Mrs Groat came to her door with a full pipe of tobacco in her hand which she puffed continually as she spoke. She apologised for doing so. 'But I have heard that it is the only true prevention against the plague,' she said, 'and I am not going to be seen without it all the while people are dropping faster than flies.'

'We came to enquire about the children's funeral,' Sarah said, standing back so as not to be enveloped in smoke.

Mrs Groat shook her head. 'There will be no funeral,' she said, 'for the mayor has issued orders that there must be no gatherings of people.'

'But there must be some small ceremony!' Sarah said, concerned. 'At least a minister must stand by their grave and offer up a prayer to send them on their way.'

'I think not,' the old woman said. She coughed a little herself with the smoke. 'There have been so many funerals already that now they are saying the dead must be dispatched with as little ceremony as possible. All that will mark their passing will be the tolling of a bell.'

'But there haven't been that many deaths in this parish, surely?' I asked.

Mrs Groat shrugged. 'Two in Crutched Friars Alley yesterday. *Said* to be dead of the fever,' she added meaningfully. 'Then our poor Williams family, a house at the sign of the Crooked Bear – there are four dead there, two dead in the Shambles, and one dead in a house just newly shut up in Stinking Lane. They say that at St Dominic's there's been funerals every day for two weeks.'

'I had no idea,' Sarah said in a shocked voice, while I tried to take in these numbers. As if to confirm what she was saying, I could hear, from several points across the city, the dull tolling of church bells.

The woman lowered her voice. 'It's said that St Dominic's and the smaller churchyards will soon be filled to overflowing, so they won't be able to take more bodies. And what will happen then? My husband says they'll just be left in the houses to rot!'

Sarah and I gasped.

'They're already collecting the bodies in a cart instead of on a pallet,' she went on. 'They came last night for the children and took them all of a heap together.'

Sarah and I looked at each other. 'Then it's far, far worse than we thought,' she said to me in a voice a little above a whisper.

Mrs Groat nodded. 'Aye,' she said. 'I fear we've all been deceiving ourselves. My husband and I would go out of town if we could – but where would we go? Who is going to take in someone from this city when God knows what airs and humours we're carrying on us? Besides, we could not afford the certificates.'

Sarah asked which brand of tobacco Mrs Groat was using and she told us, though I could not imagine me or Sarah smoking a stinking pipe, or even how you managed to smoke and breathe at the same time without choking to death.

We wished the woman well (though privately wondered if the poor thing had already contracted the plague by being so close to the contagion) and began to walk back to the shop. We had work to do, for we had almost used up our supply of rose water and must make a quantity soon, for it was needed in almost every recipe we used for our sweetmeats.

We passed a sedan chair carrying someone being taken to a pesthouse, with a man in front holding a white stave and clanging a bell to warn people to keep out of the way. As we stood back to watch it pass Sarah linked her arm with mine and drew me close. 'I feel so guilty about bringing you here and making you go through all this, Hannah,' she said. 'If only you'd received my second letter before you left Chertsey.'

'But if I wasn't here you'd be all on your own!' I protested. 'It wouldn't be right if you had no one to befriend you. Besides,' I hesitated a moment, then said, 'if you fell ill, who would look after you?'

What I didn't say – for I was ashamed of even having such a feeling – was that I *wanted* to be here, that I found it dangerous and exciting to be in London at this hour. Some of this was to do with having met Tom, and some to do with the heightened sense of tension and anxiety that now seemed to surround us. At home in Chertsey, life had been peaceful. The milk turning sour or getting blackfly on our beans had been the only disturbances to our calm existence. Here, though, *now*, there was a bitter, heart-stopping danger in each day. We were walking on the very edge of a chasm of fire.

We had been to market that morning but had not gone very early, as we usually did in order to get the freshest blooms, for Sarah had said that to make rose water it hardly mattered what condition the flowers were in. We had gone, then, to find bargains rather than perfection. The blooms we'd bought had been placed in enamel jugs of water outside our back door and when I went to get them in (first checking on Mew, who was safely under the bed) Sarah suggested that before we started making rose water, we should take some of our blooms down to St Dominic's churchyard.

'No matter if the family are not having a proper funeral,' she said. 'We can at least say a prayer over the graves of those children.'

We took one red rose for Mrs Williams, and three pink roses: one for Kate, one for Jacob and one for Marie, and walked along to the churchyard with them. It was a warm night and not yet dark – the watchman called eight of the clock as we walked – but there was hardly anyone about.

'They are staying indoors,' Sarah said. 'And have you seen how people now try to avoid each other in the street?'

I nodded, for I'd already noticed that during this last week or two, people would step in the kennel ditch muck in the middle of the roadway rather than come face to face, breath to breath, with someone who might be infected with the sickness.

We talked of our family in Chertsey as we walked, and both fervently hoped and prayed that the plague would not reach them there.

'And even if I got a Certificate of Health, how could I go back home now?' I asked Sarah. 'I could be carrying the plague on my clothes.' I looked down at myself. 'I could be carrying it from London into our home and give it to our brothers and sisters.'

Sarah shook her head slowly. 'No, I can see we are both here for the duration, so we must follow all the rules. We must keep the space in front of our shop swept clean, and take care not to eat anything unwholesome. We must examine our bodies carefully each night to make sure no spots or lumps appear. We will chew a sprig of rosemary when we go abroad, and we will take a cordial and make ourselves an ABRACADABRA talisman, for I hear they are most effective.'

I nodded. 'One other thing – when I went to the grocer's I found I had to put my payment coins into a jar of vinegar.'

Sarah nodded. 'Then we shall have our customers do that, too,' she said. 'With care, you and I can survive.'

I smiled back at her and squeezed her hand. I was full of optimism and could not believe I could die, for I had everything to live for.

The bell was tolling mournfully as we approached our parish church, and over the small lychgate which led into the graveyard a tall wax candle burned.

Hearing noises and looking over the wall, we discovered four men digging a large hole. To one side there was a piece of tarpaulin on which – my heart contracted – seven corpses were lain. These were not enclosed in wooden coffins, but wound in rough shrouds with a clumsy knot tied at each end.

I clutched Sarah's hand, and nodded towards them, my teeth beginning to chatter with fright. I had seen dead corpses before, but only one at a time, and then each body had been settled, washed and neat, arms crossed at the breast, in a pine coffin. These corpses, though, were just piled carelessly on one side like stale loaves.

'Oh, we should not have come!' Sarah said in a low and shaky voice. 'We should have stayed away from this horror.'

'Do you think that is . . . is *them*?' I asked, nodding towards the corpses.

'Maybe,' she whispered. 'Them and some others.'

'Or maybe our family were buried yesterday,' I said, looking across the churchyard. 'Look at all the new mounds!'

There were many piles of freshly-dug earth, but no way of telling if each held more than one body. Some sort of white powder had been strewn across the whole churchyard, and it covered the ground like snow.

'It's lime,' Sarah said in answer to my question. 'Lime to stop the infection and to encourage the bodies to . . . to . . .' she shuddered and could not finish.

The men were still digging steadily, throwing the earth to one side and singing a bawdy song as they worked. They did not acknowledge us in any way.

'Shall we . . . shall we ask if the bodies they are burying are those of the Williams family?' I asked.

Sarah shook her head. 'They will have no way of knowing who they bury. And as there seems to be no clergy to ask, I think we may as well go home. We can do no good here, and it fair turns my stomach to see such things.'

'Let us throw in our flowers before we go, then,' I said.

Sarah nodded. 'And say our own prayer.'

So we leaned over the wall and threw in our roses, and the grave-diggers, on seeing us, fell silent. I said a prayer for the Williams family, and then we went home.

When the Bills were published, we found out that one thousand people had died from plague during that week.

'One thousand!' everyone whispered in shocked voices, although it had quickly become common knowledge that this figure was much lower than it should have been. Mr Newbery told us that the bereaved would bribe the searchers of the dead to have a death recorded as spotted fever or the purples, rather than have plague noted against the name and cause the rest of the family to be shut up for forty days. Most of the searchers, he told us, were brutal and common types who would sell their own mothers for a flagon of gin.

That day was a black one for us, too, for Mew disappeared. I had hardly been in our back room at all as I had spent the morning in the shop making orange-flower water: boiling water on our fire, steeping the orange blossom in it, then straining and re-straining the resulting pale primrose liquid through muslin. At dinner time Sarah bought a pigeon pie from a pie-man, and when we went into the back, calling for Mew to come and have a scrap with us, she wasn't there on the end of her tethering string. Discovering this, Sarah and I stared at each other in horror.

'Was she there this morning?' she asked me.

I nodded. 'I gave her some bread and milk. Her string was tied tightly – I checked it!' I assured her.

We looked under the bed and, finding that Mew had wriggled her head through the neck loop, both began to cry.

'One of the catchers has taken her – I know they have!' I said. I was already imagining her sad fate, for I had seen a creaking old farm cart the day before stacked to the brim with the carcasses of dogs and cats in a carelessly jumbled pile of fur and hair.

We looked around the room carefully, in case she was hiding herself (although there were precious few secret places). Then Sarah looked out the front door while I went to the back. I searched our yard and privy, and called, 'Mew!' across the roofs several times, all the while banging one of our old bowls with a spoon to try and attract her. Our yard stayed empty, though, and I thought sadly that if we'd have done the same thing just two weeks ago, a stable-load of cats and kits would have come to our door to be fed.

Sitting down, we ate some of our pigeon pie, although found we had little appetite for it.

Sarah sighed. 'We must imagine to ourselves that,

like Dickon, Mew has gone to a happier home,' she said. 'Maybe she's jumped on a cart and gone out of town, or maybe she's got herself into a cosy household where meat is on the menu every day.'

I nodded, my heart heavy. What I was thinking and was scared to say was, what would happen if, after a day or so, Mew came back? We wouldn't know where she'd been. She might have been scratching for mice in a newly-dug churchyard beside a body rotten with plague, or have lodged a while in a house struck down with it. Maybe her thick grey fur would be harbouring the very sickness that we dreaded so much.

But Mew did not come back, and it seemed certain that she'd slipped her string to go after a mouse or two and been found by one of the fat-gutted ruffians who were employed on the shameful job of clubbing animals to death. Sarah and I cried ourselves to sleep that night, but after that we did not speak of her again, for it seemed to be tempting fate to mourn the loss of a kitten when all around us people were losing parents, children, brothers and sisters.

More and more people were departing for the country. One morning I had an errand to run for Sarah which took me along the Tyburn Road, and I saw several coach-and-fours laden with cases and servants, trundling along with their thick brocade curtains closed tight to protect the occupants from the stares of the common people. I knew that the travellers must all be either of the aristocracy, or at least affluent merchants or rich landowners, for apart from the fact of their having a coach and horses of their own, and a place to go in the country, I had not heard of an ordinary person being able to obtain a health certificate.

I saw, too, a pretty yellow-varnished carriage sway past me pulled by two chestnut horses, their manes and tails tied with green ribbon, and the coachman wearing smart green livery. I glanced inside, for this time the curtains were not closed, and was sure I saw Nelly Gwyn sitting there in a peacock-blue gown, for the girl looked up just at that moment and though her ribboned bonnet partly obscured her face, I could see a flash of unruly red hair.

Sarah laughed when I told her this and said I had just seen what I wanted to see, but I am sure it *was* Nelly, for her carriage was heading towards Salisbury, and we had heard that the king and his court were on their way there to be further off still from London. I like to think she was obeying an invitation from His Majesty to come and dance some lively jigs for the gentlemen of the court to console them for being away from the entertainments in the capital.

That day, walking back from my errand which was to obtain an amount of rose oil from a grocer, I could not help my ears being assailed by the constant tolling of the church bells announcing more deaths, or seeing the red crosses on doors as I passed. Most of these doors were in the poorer parts of the city – although not all, for I saw a substantial house in Blackfriars which had been enclosed, and one big dwelling in Fleet Street also. In this house someone had dislodged a plank over the first-floor window and from this space two small, tear-stained children peered out, scared and bewildered. I could not help but wonder what was happening within. Had their mother and father succumbed to the disease? Who was looking after them? There was no way of telling and no one seemed to care.

Two more things I noticed. One was the activity in the churchyards, for each contained at least two grave-diggers going about their gruesome business, and some had been dug over so constantly for new burials that they resembled ploughed fields. The other thing which assaulted the eye was the number of posters offering preventatives against the sickness. On almost every tree and shutter they hung, advertising amulets, powders, cordials, charms, pills and enchantments. There were some herbal preventatives that Tom had already told me of, and others made from all manner of strange things: powders made from dried toads, an amount of mercury contained in a walnut shell, or a talisman made from a verse from the Bible written in a certain mystical way. All promised to shield against contagion and prevent malignant humours from affecting the body.

Which of these would be effective, though?

With so much at stake, which to choose?

Seeing all these promises and writings together made me think of Tom, for I had not heard a word from him since our day out. I vowed, therefore, that I would go to Doctor da Silva's as soon as I could to ask Tom about the cordial he had said he would prepare for me. This was a good enough reason and could be my excuse, but the truth was that in spite of all that was going on around us, he filled my thoughts and I longed to see him again.

Chapter Eight

The fourth week of July

'And they tell me that in Westminster there is never
a Physician and but one Apothecary, all others
being dead.'

Out of the darkness of Doctor da Silva's shop a
monstrous figure came towards me, causing me to
scream aloud. The creature was broad and imposing,
its head was that of a great bird of prey, with a tiny
shining eye and a great hooked beak, and its breathing
as it lumbered towards me was hoarse and rasping.

'Keep away!' I screamed. I backed away, trembling,
feeling behind me for the door through which I'd just
entered. I tried to recall some holy words to banish
such an evil and unearthly creature, but in my panic
could not think of any.

There was the sound of running feet across the shop
and Tom's voice called, 'It's all right, Hannah!' he
said. 'It's just Doctor da Silva.'

I burst into tears of fright and relief and Tom put
his arms around me. 'It's the doctor in the outfit he

uses to visit the stricken.'

I drew in a shuddering breath, peering through my fingers at the figure. Now that I could see more clearly in the dim light I discerned that it was, indeed, only a man in a strange headdress and covering gown of heavy waxed material, and not a creature from hell at all. 'Is it truly him?' I asked, for I felt comforted in Tom's arms and did not want to stir myself from them.

'Doctor, will you take off your head?' Tom asked, and the frightening creature lifted his arms and pulled off the leathery headdress of his outfit, beak and all, revealing himself indeed as the doctor.

'Yes, it is I,' he said, trying to flatten his tangled grey hair. 'I am dressed to go and treat plague victims.'

My fright disappearing, I thought I had better let my arms fall from Tom's shoulders, for I did not wish to appear too forward. 'And is this what you have to wear?' I asked breathlessly.

The doctor nodded. 'All the apothecaries and the doctors – that is, those who are still in London and have not gone away to the country with their wealthy patrons – have them now.'

'The thick gown prevents any infection touching the doctor's skin, and the beak contains strong herbs,' Tom said. 'Every breath he takes will come through these herbs and be cleansed.'

'And the herbs are . . .?' Doctor da Silva asked of Tom.

'Alehoof, ivy, sage, chervil and scabious, sire,' he answered, and the doctor nodded. He looked at me. 'And how are you and your sister, and how do you find yourself in your shop? Do you have good health?'

'We are doing quite well, I thank you,' I said.

'Though we have . . .' My voice choked in my throat and I had to pause a moment. 'We have lost some of our neighbours to the sickness.'

The doctor shook his head reflectively. 'It is said that Thursday's Bills will contain some 2,000 deaths.'

I gasped. 'But that is double that of last week!'

'And it will increase, I fear, unless they stop shutting up the houses and entombing the living with the dead,' he said.

'Doctor da Silva thinks it would be better to take the sick person off to a pesthouse and isolate him there,' Tom explained.

'Although the city is not supplied with nearly enough of those,' the doctor said grimly. 'In the meantime when one person sickens and they are shut in with their family and servants, then they *all* fall sick. There is nothing more certain. One might just as well bury them alive.'

'But can people catch the plague and live?' I asked, for this was something Sarah and I had been pondering.

'It is possible – with the right treatment at the right time. The buboes have to burst, however.' The doctor turned to Tom as he said this, looking at him enquiringly.

'A root of the Madonna lily mixed with hog's grease makes a poultice to ripen plague sores,' Tom said, on his cue.

The doctor inclined his head. 'They must burst and discharge their poison, for if they do not then the matter goes inward and infects every organ of the body.' He paused. 'What preventatives are you taking?' he asked me.

I felt my cheeks flushing. 'I came today because Tom said he would prepare me a cordial,' I said. 'I wondered if he had finished it yet.'

'The flowers had to be steeped and the liquid boiled and strained by turn. It took over a week to make,' Tom said apologetically. 'And then we have been so busy with our new patients and with making up preventatives I have not found time to bring it to you.'

'So you have been taking nothing all this while?' the doctor asked me.

'Well, Sarah and I always chew sprigs of rosemary before we go out,' I said. 'And we each have a rabbit's foot. And a cabalistic sign.' I pulled from my bodice the piece of paper on which a travelling pedlar had written ABRACADABRA in a certain way, as a magical triangle.

The doctor looked at the paper. 'I cannot think that this will help. But, Tom, what is Hannah's cordial?'

'A compound of peony flowers and cornflower leaves steeped in wine,' Tom replied. 'A general preventative, for I thought both her and Miss Sarah would take it.'

'Then fetch the bottle now, and I will delay my visits to our troubled neighbours until you have taken both her and it back safely. But be quick.'

When Tom returned with the bottle I noticed that the cordial was thick and brown and did not look very appetising, but under the doctor's eye I was given instructions for taking it. Tom and I then walked together back to the shop, seeing on the way two fellows closing up a house at Friars Alley and fastening locks and chains across the door. I told Tom of the Williams family, and of the way Dickon had burst out of the house and gone off. Tom said he had heard before of people running mad when the sickness was on them.

'I know tales of folk who have thrown themselves out of windows or run to the river and jumped in to drown themselves,' Tom said, shaking his head, 'for there is such pain while the buboes are swelling that some fair go mad with it.'

'But the doctor said that it is possible to catch the pestilence *and* survive.'

'Aye,' he said. 'If the swellings burst and heal, there is a chance. And if the tokens have not appeared.'

'What are tokens?' I asked fearfully. 'Is that another name for the buboes?'

He shook his head. 'They are little marks under the skin.'

'Like freckles?'

He smiled at me, tapping my nose with his finger. 'Not like freckles!' he said. 'Like pink blotches. They come up on the chest or arms. And if *they* appear then there is no hope at all, even if the buboes have burst.'

Our hands touched and, saying nothing, we linked our little fingers so that no one else could see. 'But how are you faring within yourself, Hannah?' he asked me. 'Tell me truly.'

I sighed and told him about Mew, and he said that the doctor had two pet dogs which had also been taken by the catchers. 'It is sad,' he said, 'but if this helps the spread of the disease, then this is what must happen.'

On our way back I noticed several shops had been shut up, including a grocer where we sometimes got our sugar, and I wondered aloud what would happen if more and more of them closed, and where we would buy our provisions.

'It will be difficult,' Tom said, 'for already there are many less pie-sellers and hawkers around. We have heard a rumour that Leadenhall Market might close because the country farmers are no longer willing to come into the city with their goods.'

'So what will happen if we can't get food?'

Tom shrugged. 'I suppose the city authorities will feed us somehow – at least with our daily bread,' he said. 'Although the doctor says that very little provision has been made. There are no public funds for relief of the poor, and no grain stored against such an event.' There was a moment's silence, then he looked at me sympathetically. 'But were you very frightened when you saw the doctor in his outfit?'

'I was!' I made myself shiver in what I hoped was an appealing way. 'I thought he was a fiend from hell!'

Tom laughed. 'Yes, he can be. But he's a good master.'

We reached the shop and Sarah, looking out and seeing that Tom was with me, bade him come in, saying that it was nearly midday and he might like to take some dinner with us.

'Thank you – but the doctor has asked me to go straight back,' Tom said to her. 'And I have many potions and preventatives to make up.'

'Another time, then,' Sarah said. She turned and busied herself over the fire, tactfully averting her eyes from us as we parted. My mouth felt dry, for I could see a certain look in Tom's eyes and was very nervous as to whether he would try to kiss me and if I should allow it.

He told me to take all necessary precautions against the sickness and said that he would see me as soon as he was able, then leaned forward and quickly brushed across my cheek with his lips. I was cross with myself afterwards, for I offered my cheek to him so quickly that he actually ended up kissing one of the ribbons on my cap.

But then again, perhaps I should not have allowed him such freedom anyway. I resolved that I would ask Abby, and went in thinking that for the last four whole minutes I had managed to forget about the plague altogether.

Three days later – for there was much to do and, as Sarah was rather low in spirits, I did not wish to leave her – I went up with our water jugs to Bell Court, hoping to see Abby. There was water to be obtained closer, but I knew she favoured this place and I was anxious to know how she was faring.

She was not in the queue for water, however, which was half as long as it usually was, for a great many of the quality had gone out of town now, either taking their servants or leaving them to fend for themselves. I could remember where she lived, so leaving my jugs unfilled for the moment, I made my way there. As I passed the various churches: St Bride's, All Hallows, St Sepulchre's, each was tolling its bell to tell of someone's passing.

I would not have dared to knock at the front door of the house, but there was a young boy in the yard grooming one of the horses, and I asked him if Abby was at home. He ran off and a few moments later came back with Abby behind him.

To my great relief – for there had been a horrid dread in my mind – she looked perfectly fine and healthy. We hugged and I said I'd been anxious about her, having not seen her at the conduit.

She pointed to a well in the yard. 'Mr Beauchurch says we must use this water now and not gather in Bell Court. He says that being in crowds is dangerous.' She pulled a face. 'And so I have to miss my afternoon gossips!'

She took my arm and we walked across the yard into the coolness of the dairy, which was a big, airy room tiled in blue and white. Milk churns stood along the floor, and there was a butter and cheese maker, and several big round wheels of cheese. 'But Hannah, what d'you think!' she said excitedly. 'I am to travel to Dorchester with my mistress and the babe!'

'Where is Dorchester?' I asked, for I had never heard of it.

'It's in Dorsetshire, southwest of London. We are to go to a great estate belonging to my mistress's sister, who is a titled lady, and there we will be safe from the sickness.'

'Oh,' I said, feeling a little forlorn. 'When will you go?'

'As soon as the mistress is well enough to travel.'

'And just you with her?'

She nodded. 'Mrs Beauchurch says that out of all the servants, I am best with the babe.' She smiled. 'For sure having six little sisters has helped me there.'

'But what about your master – doesn't he want to travel out of London as well?'

'He has to stay at his mercers' company to run the business,' she said. 'Besides, only two travel

103

certificates can be obtained, and they are fearfully difficult to get because they have to be signed by the Lord Mayor himself. No other signatures are being accepted!' She danced a few steps around the floor. 'Just think, it will take four days to travel there and we have to stay at inns along the road, where I shall meet all sorts of young gallants!'

I laughed at her, for she was twirling around and lifting her petticoats as if she was ribbon-dancing around the maypole at home. 'But what about your sweetheart?'

She pulled a face. 'He's nothing but a niggardly hog-grubber,' she said. 'I've seen him walking out with one of the girls from the coffee shop.'

I was quiet for a moment. 'I shall miss you,' I said. 'But when do you think your mistress will be well enough to travel?'

'Next week, maybe. Though she was monstrous sick in the night and I had to go into her three times.'

'But is the babe well?'

'Aye. Healthy and hungry.'

Just then, a very well-rounded woman in a maroon gown, and a young girl in a black servant's dress, came through the dairy, both carrying shopping baskets. The fat woman frowned slightly at Abby, who just gave a beaming smile in return.

'All the house are very jealous that I'm going to Dorchester!' Abby whispered, and then laughed aloud. 'Lord, but did you see the size of Cook? That gown sits on her as tight as the skin on a plum.' She slipped towards the back doorway of the dairy. 'Come on – almost everyone's out now, and the mistress is asleep. Come in and I'll show you all the furnishings!'

The house was very large, the largest and grandest I'd ever been in. Beyond the dairy was a still room, with bunches of herbs drying and blossoms being prepared for pot-pourri and flower water, and beyond that a laundry, with ropes on which aired white linen smocks and damask bed-sheets. There was a kitchen and dining room on the next floor, but we did not go into these because Abby said the housekeeper was around. We tiptoed up to the next floor and Abby opened the door to the drawing room, showing walls hung with black and silver striped silk, delicate carved furniture and small settles bearing purple velvet cushions shot with silver. There were many portraits, too, although Abby said she didn't know who they were, and thick patterned rugs covered the floor.

The next room was even more sumptuous, with diamond-paned windows which overlooked the flowered courtyard below and a vast carved wood fireplace which reached the ceiling. This room had silver-gilt chairs and nests of drawers patterned in flowers, with Chinese vases and silver candlesticks atop, and was all very fine, so that I could not but gasp at the beauty of it all. 'I never thought furnishings of a house could be so elegant,' I said to Abby, for indeed all the houses I'd been into – big and small – had been in the country and of rustic style.

'Oh, 'tis all for show!' she said. 'They never come into these rooms. But you should see the bedrooms! The mistress's room has Venetian mirrors all over, and she sleeps in a four-poster with gold hangings that are said to have come from Persia.'

Once she'd told me this, I longed to go upstairs and

see these things, but Abby said she didn't dare take me. She did say, though, that if I went up the servants' stairs to her room, then she would go to the nursery and bring the babe to see me.

To tell the truth I was not that bothered about the babe, having seen more than enough of my little brothers and sisters as infants, but Abby said it was a pretty one and seemed so eager to show it off that we went to her room and I waited while she fetched it.

It *was* a pretty babe, about three months old and still swaddled, with thick dark hair. She was awake and smiled up at us, so Abby loosened the cambric sheet around her and let her wave her arms.

'This is Grace,' Abby said. 'And she must think I'm her mother, for it's been me who's been looking after her since she was born.'

'How is she fed if your mistress is so ill?' I asked. 'Does she have a wet nurse?'

Abby shook her head. 'They won't allow a wet nurse for fear of contagion, so a maid with the milch-ass calls here twice a day.' She stroked the baby's cheek. 'I trickle the milk down my hand and this little squab sucks my fingers.'

I was silent for a moment, and then I asked in a low voice, 'It's not plague that your mistress has, is it?'

Abby laughed. ''Tis not! Plague would have carried her off by now. It's just childbed fever. Though, to tell the truth,' she added, 'when I wash her, I always look her over for the tokens, for I know that plague is no respecter of persons. It can visit a lady as quick as an ale-house wife.'

'And do you take a preventative yourself?'

She nodded. 'The mistress's doctor made us up

some treacle with conserves of roses before he went into the country. And we all chew a piece of angelica root when we go out.'

Talking of the preventatives made me think of Tom, and, rather embarrassed, I brought his name into the conversation and asked Abby whether I should allow him the liberty of kissing me or not. 'I mean proper kissing – on the lips,' I explained.

She laughed. 'Of course!' she said. 'For what's a sweetheart for if you don't get one or two kisses from him!'

'Mother used to say—'

Abby waved her hand dismissively. 'It's different in London,' she said. 'And different now, when no one can count on living two days at a time. If you're visited by the plague—'

I gave a little gasp of fright.

'You don't want to go to your grave unkissed, do you?'

I smiled and blushed. 'Indeed I don't!'

'Well, then,' she said.

Laughing, I said I would think on it, and bid her goodbye.

Chapter Nine

The first week of August

'And I frighted to see so many graves lie so high upon the churchyard where so many have been buried of the Plague.'

'Praying is all very well,' said the stout woman in church, 'but I cannot fast! And I do not see why I have to. I don't believe the king will be fasting. I'm sure he and his court will be sitting down to their grouse and oysters and lobsters and geese just the same as they always do!'

Sarah and I smiled at the woman, who was as wide as she was high, and moved slightly further down the pew and away from her. She was hot and red-faced and we did not wish her breath to fall on us, for the latest rumour was that you should keep cool and keep your distance from others as much as possible in order to avoid contaminated air. It appeared that the authorities did not know this rumour, however, for we were still required to attend church regularly, and without fail on the first Wednesday in each month.

The Bills had shown that near two and a half thousand had died of plague in the past week, and on the way into St Dominic's that morning I had not been able to avoid seeing how the ground in the graveyard had risen; how corpses had been laid upon corpses so that the ground on each side of the pathway had swelled to a height of several feet. It made me shudder to see it, for I could not help but imagine them all lying there in the cold earth in their winding sheets – for few were given the sanctity of a coffin – old piled upon young, men upon women, laid without care or ceremony.

Once seated in church, we discovered that our own minister had moved to the safety of the country, and another now stood in his place. He gave a violent and frightening sermon which lasted nearly two hours, telling us that the plague was a judgement on the behaviour of the people, and of the terrible death and hellfire which awaited us unless we truly repented of our blasphemies and sins. He affrighted me so terribly that I had to take Sarah's hand, but she whispered to me that he could not mean the likes of us, for a just God could not account any sins *we* had committed as being evil enough to take us to Hell.

Going home, we saw a sad sight: a young woman carrying a small box in her arms, weeping aloud and calling, 'Oh my child . . . oh my precious!' as she trudged towards St Olave's churchyard. Sarah whispered that she probably wanted to take the baby to the graveyard herself and make sure it had a decent burial. 'For she will surely be shut in as soon as the authorities find out the child has died,' she added.

Another strange sight we saw was that of a poor

madman, raving deliriously, clad with only a cloth about his loins. He was beating his naked breast and screaming out to the Heavens to deliver him from his life on earth, for his whole family had been taken with the plague and he no longer wished to live. Sarah threw a coin to him and we hurried past without speaking.

When we got home, we found that a letter we had tried to send to our family telling them that all was well with us, had been returned undelivered. A man from the carriers told us that, despite this letter being steamed over a pot of boiling vinegar to kill any contagion, the authorities in Chertsey had refused to accept it. He said that many towns were no longer taking letters from London unless they concerned official business, or were a matter of life or death.

'Do you suppose they will know in Chertsey that the plague is upon us?' I asked Sarah.

'They are sure to,' she nodded. 'And Mother will be worried, no doubt. But they will think no news is good news.'

We changed out of our church-going clothes and, both being very hungry – for we had not yet broken our fast – we ate some of our sweetmeats. Sarah said it could not count as proper eating just to sample the stock, and besides, we had been left with rather a lot of crystallised violet and rose petals of late, because our trade had fallen off so much.

'To be plain, I am worried,' Sarah said. 'Our takings are down to less than a half of what they usually are.'

I was rather distracted, for I'd finished my violets and was looking at myself in a little mirror that I'd bought from a pedlar. It seemed to me that, despite all my efforts, my hair was wilder and curled more than ever.

'Hannah!' Sarah said. 'Did you hear me? With more and more of the quality going out of town, I fear we will soon not be making enough money to buy our daily food.'

'There won't be food to buy anyway, will there?' I said, putting the mirror away. 'Half the shops are already shut, and if it gets any worse Mr Newbery says we'll all starve!'

Sarah shook her head. 'We will not,' she said, 'for I have heard today of where we may buy provisions.'

'Where did you hear that?'

'While we were waiting to go into church this morning and you were staring at the graves and thinking of God knows what horrors, I was speaking to a man who lives near Lincolns Inn. We talked of the difficulty of getting food and he said that there are some country wives who are not willing to come into the city for fear of contagion, but who bring their wares to town and set them up for sale by the city gates. They bring rabbits and chickens and all manner of pies, and they are there every day of the week.'

'And we will always be able to get bread – so we will not starve after all!' I said.

Sarah shook her head. 'No, indeed. But about our trade. How can we sell more sweetmeats?'

We both fell to thinking.

'I could go out with a tray,' I said, and at Sarah's frown, added, 'Indeed I would not mind a bit.'

Sarah shook her head. 'I don't think it would be wise for you to walk the streets any more than you have to.' She thought some more. 'If we could make something which the poorer people needed, then we wouldn't worry about the quality going out of town.'

And then I thought of the answer. 'We must make sweetmeats which prevent the plague!' I cried.

Sarah clapped her hands. 'The very thing! Why didn't we think of it before?'

'We must look through our recipes and see what seeds and herbs are of most use,' I said, then hesitated. 'But how do we know anything will truly work against the sickness? How can we say what will work more than any other thing? Won't we be just like the quack doctors who set up stalls overnight and sell pellets of stale bread and call them plague pills?'

Sarah shook her head. 'There are a hundred different preventions now, and who is to say what works and what doesn't? Even the real doctors and apothecaries – even Doctor da Silva – don't know for certain what is of use.'

I nodded slowly. 'We may make the very things which make a difference.'

'We will make sugared comfits from the little spikes of rosemary! Everyone says rosemary is most efficacious.'

'And it will cost almost nothing, as we have a bush of it just outside our back door,' I said.

We sat and thought for a while, and looked through some of our aunt's papers, and in the end I went to see Tom at the apothecary's, for I assured Sarah that he would know as well as anyone what would be the best plants to use.

To my regret, Tom was not there, having apparently gone to the docks to fetch some very rare mineral compound. Doctor da Silva, who was boiling herbs in a pot, assured me, however, that rosemary comfits would be beneficial.

'And even if not beneficial, at least not harmful,' he added.

'And what else could we make into sweetmeats?'

'What of angelica? This is a most powerful herb of the sun in Leo and it would be right to gather it now.'

I nodded eagerly. 'We can candy the stems of angelica into sugar sticks.'

'And chervil has a root similar to that of angelica,' the doctor went on thoughtfully, 'and is said to be as effective, and there is also dragon-wort, which expels the venom of plague – although you may not know where to find it at this time of the year. The root of the scabious boiled in wine is a very powerful antidote, although I do not know how you would convert this into a sweetmeat.'

'But rosemary, angelica and chervil,' I said thoughtfully, 'we can use all these.' I spoke slowly, looking around the shelves of the shop, at the dusty bottles and phials, and hoping that Tom would arrive back before I left.

'And the flowers of garlic may also be candied,' the doctor said. 'Garlic is an efficacious remedy for all diseases.'

Some more customers arrived to see the doctor then, and feeling obliged to go home, I bobbed the doctor a curtsey and thanked him for his trouble.

''Tis nothing. We must all help each other in our distress,' the doctor said, and as I went to the door, added, 'Oh, by the way, some young ladies swear that an ointment made from cowslips rids them of their freckles.'

I was tempted to ask further, but as I did not wish to be thought of as an empty-headed baggage, I just said, 'When we are over our troubles, perhaps,' and asked him to please commend me to Tom.

Two days later, Sarah and I rose at the call of five o'clock, for we were going out to see if we could find angelica growing on the marshes. I had washed and left my washing water ready for Sarah – for it was not at all dirty – when she suddenly cried out my name in a most despairing voice.

I looked round, alarmed, and she was sitting on our bed in her shift, her face flushed and a hand pressed against her jaw. I immediately began to shake with fright, for I knew what must have happened: *She had found some swelling* . . .

I crouched down beside her. 'What is it?' I asked her urgently. 'Is it a lump?'

'I believe so,' she said shakily, feeling along her face. 'Just here.' She took my fingers and pressed them against her face, although – God forgive me – for an instant I wanted to recoil and snatch them back. 'Can you feel it too?'

I felt along the line of her jaw. 'I . . . I think so,' I said.

'There is pain, too, all down the side of my neck. And it has been so all night.'

'And on the other side?'

'Nothing.'

'Do you have any other symptoms?' I asked, my voice trembling. 'Fever? Do you feel sick? Have the giddiness? Do you have a headache?'

She shook her head to all of these except the last.

'Let's go quickly to Doctor da Silva, then,' I said, and she nodded speechlessly, her face as white as her shift.

While we dressed my mind was whirling ahead of me. If it indeed *was* plague, then without more ado we would be shut up in the house with a brutal minder at our door. I would have the same symptoms in one or two days, then Sarah would die, and I would follow. Mother and Father would find out in a letter from someone – a minister at the church, perhaps – and would come to London, but would be unable to find our grave.

And I would die unkissed, before I had hardly lived.

To our great relief the shop was open and the doctor was in, although it was his consultancy morning and there was a queue of people outside waiting to see him. They were going in one by one and talking to him privately, so we waited our turn, keeping our thoughts to ourselves and staying a good distance from everyone else. Indeed, some of them looked most alarming: one woman was greasy with sweat and moaning softly under her breath, and a man was naked to the waist, with great open wounds under his arm and on his chest. They were most gruesome to look upon, and I averted my eyes. Sarah whispered to me to keep away, for they were plague sores which had burst, and the man must be attending the doctor for healing herbs to be packed into the wounds.

It was Tom who opened the door to us, and when he saw it was me and Sarah waiting to see the doctor a look of such horror crossed his face that it almost brought tears to my eyes, for I knew then how he felt about me, and that it was the same as the way I felt about him.

This was some small comfort to me for my mind was a perfect blank of dread. I began to pray, something I had not done properly, really meaning it, for many a month. I began to make God any number of entreaties and promises if only he would make Sarah well again.

I had already told Sarah of Doctor da Silva's strange outfit, so she was not too shocked when our turn came. We were led behind a screen and she saw him sitting there with his bird's head, his breath rasping through the beak of herbs.

'I have a . . . a lump,' Sarah stammered. 'Here.' She took off her cap and lifted her head, turning her face slightly so that he could see it more clearly. 'It's very painful,' she said.

The doctor lifted a candle high and looked at the swelling, which to my eyes seemed to have grown since we left home. He pressed it with his fingers, and Sarah winced, then he directed her to open her mouth and probed inside with a small wooden stick.

'Is it plague?' I asked fearfully, begging God to spare her. 'What can you tell?'

The doctor pulled off his beak headgear and put on his glasses, then he looked in Sarah's mouth again. He smiled – a smile most delightful for us to see. 'It is a tooth in your lower jaw,' he said. 'It has an abscess underneath which is full of poison, and this is what is swelling your gum.'

Tears began to swim in Sarah's eyes and, seeing them, my eyes filled too. 'Are you sure?' she asked.

'I am indeed!' said the doctor, 'and happy to be so.'

He reached behind him for a small bottle. 'I will rub some oil of cloves on it, and Tom will give you a root of saxifrage to chew if the pain gets too much. But you must go and get it pulled.'

'Can you not do that?' I asked.

He shook his head. 'But there is a man who pulls teeth at the sign of the Red Bull, by the coffee shop in Covent Garden. He wields a fair instrument.' He gave Sarah an awkward pat on the shoulder. 'I am glad to have given you good news.'

'We . . . we must pay you,' she stammered.

He shook his head. 'No need. Instead, Tom and I will have some of your fine new sweetmeats against plague.'

Tom had heard everything and was smiling fit to burst when we came around the screen. He gave us a piece of dried root of saxifrage and explained again exactly where the man who drew teeth was to be found, then opened the door so that we could be released and the next poor customer could enter.

The feeling I had on walking home was one of such joy and relief that I felt I wanted to dance and sing aloud, and without thinking I began to hum a tune I'd heard the balladeers singing, linking arms with Sarah and swaying with her. My poor sister, though, was still in some pain and said to me quietly, 'The plague is still around, Hannah. We are not through it yet. We must still be vigilant.'

I stopped humming and swaying when she said this, for indeed I had heard – could always hear – the bells of many different churches tolling for more deaths.

Sarah, being very frightened of the tooth-puller,

waited to see if the medicaments that the doctor had prescribed had any effect. They worked but a little, though, so at noon we went down to Covent Garden and found the tooth-puller at his booth by the sign of the Red Bull, and indeed we did not have to hunt for him, for the fellow – a man as big and as sweaty as an ox – was waving a frightening instrument in his hand and calling at the very pitch of his voice that he cut out ulcers, drew wormy teeth and lanced boils in the mouth.

Sarah hung back when she saw him. 'He looks a dirty and ignorant fellow,' she whispered.

'But the doctor recommended him,' I reminded her. I held her hand and led her towards him. 'And it will be over in a minute and then you can forget all about it.'

The man sat her on a little stool, bent her head back and pushed his fingers into her mouth so she had no choice but to open it widely. He looked at her gum, then he unclipped some pincers from his belt and thrust them in her mouth so that her face twisted into a strange shape. He fitted the pincers on to the tooth and pulled. There was a gurgled scream from Sarah and she squeezed my hand so tightly I swear she almost broke my fingers. Then, suddenly, he was holding the tooth aloft and proclaiming himself the fastest tooth-drawer in the city.

Sarah was pale and trembling all over, so I paid the fellow and we went home, only stopping on the way to buy an infusion of blackberry flowers and leaves to help heal her mouth. Sarah then went to bed and slept most of the rest of the day, while I opened the shop (but sold little) and amused myself by finding a stub of pencil and making a list of what sweetmeats we were going to make and the ingredients we would need to buy for our new undertaking. I was reasonably content as I did this, for I knew Sarah would be well, I had Tom to think on, and – apart from losing dearest Mew – all was well with us.

That night, though, I heard it for the first time.

The plague cart.

There came the noise of wheels trundling on cobblestones and I went to the shutters to look out, for lately there had scarce been any traffic by our door.

What I saw was a big farm cart, like the one I'd ridden on to London with Farmer Price. At the front sat two men, gruesome-looking ruffians, unhatted, wearing long black coats, and holding flaming torches aloft in the darkness. Instead of their load being hay, the harvest they carried was bodies: about twenty of them, wrapped in winding sheets or tied into knotted shrouds, two or three of them stark naked, their limbs gleaming pale under the light from the torches.

'Bring out your dead!' they cried, ringing a bell. 'Bring out your dead!'

As I looked on, horrified, a door opened in one of the houses opposite and an old man called to the drivers. One of them then went to the door of the house with what looked like a shepherd's crook in his hand and, taking a step inside, he thrust in the hooked part and dragged out the body of an old woman wearing a nightshirt. This tumbled down the doorstep and on to the ground, prompting a cry of despair from the old man.

The back of the cart was let down and the men

manipulated the body with their crooks, throwing it all anyhow on to the cart, so that the poor corpse's long grey hair tumbled to her shoulders and her nightshirt came up, exposing her white and wizened limbs to the world.

Without another word to the one who stood alone on the doorstep, the men stowed their hooks, got up on their seats and drove off. I watched their progress down the street, listening to the cry of, 'Bring out your dead!' until the words and the sound of the cart wheels were too far off to be heard.

When I crept back to bed I longed to wake Sarah, wanting to share with someone the awful sight I'd seen. I did not, however, feeling that she'd been upset enough that day. Instead, I laid in the darkness, going over what I'd seen and seeming to feel within me a thousand dormant symptoms of plague stirring into life. Would we survive?

Why should we when so many others were dying?

How cheap life seemed. How random.

Bring out your dead . . . The words echoed around my head until dawn.

Chapter Ten

The second week of August

'The people die so, that now it seems they are fain to carry the dead to be buried by daylight, the nights not sufficing to do it.'

We had managed to get all the ingredients we needed for our new venture, and were now selling sugared chips of angelica and chervil, herb comfits containing leaves of rosemary and caraway seeds, and candied garlic and rosemary flowers. We had also prepared lozenges from rue which we had chopped with caraway seeds and mixed with sugar and rose water. Although we had not been told that this herb, rue, was a plague preventative, its old name was herb of grace, and Sarah felt that anything with that name was sure to be beneficial. Besides, a green man had called at our door selling flowers and herbs, and he had given us a large bunch of rue very cheaply.

I had prepared a notice to go outside the shop which advertised our new produce. In order to help our customers who could not read I had merely written the word PLAGUE and drawn a cross through it, for now all, even the most ignorant, knew that dread word by sight. For those who could read I gave more information.

Excellent electuaries against the Plague may be bought at the sign of the Sugared Plum.

When you go abroad, chew the sugared root of Angelica or the herb, Rosemary.

Also take our lozenges made with the ancient Herb of Grace.

I had copied some of these words from bills I had seen posted on tavern walls and windows, and I was very pleased with the result.

Even though the streets seemed thin of people, within three days we had sold out of everything we had made and had to prepare more. One of our customers – a proper gentleman, with velvet and gold-laced jacket and long curled wig – told us that he had never found the taking of medicine more delightful than when it was coated with sugar candy.

'And never has it been served by two more delightful gals,' he added, chucking me under the chin and giving me an extra twopence when he handed me his payment. I could see by the look in his eye that, given any encouragement, he would have come round the counter and put his arm about my waist, so I merely dropped my eyes and thanked him demurely.

Scowling at his departing back, I asked Sarah who he was.

'Someone at the Admiralty,' she said. 'I forget his name. Someone very high up, I believe.'

Soon after his visit, Mr Newbery came in to buy some lozenges from us.

'For I've heard that these are very tasty and strong,' he said, and I assured him that indeed they were, and that they had been praised highly by members of the Admiralty.

Sarah came through from the back and asked if he knew what the Bills were for that week.

'I do, and I wish I didn't,' Mr Newbery said, 'for they are three thousand!' As Sarah and I gasped, he added, 'Three thousand – with another thousand of what they call "other causes".'

Sarah shook her head worriedly. 'The plague is now in every parish of London, I have heard.'

'That's true. And I have heard that there are five plague pits dug to accommodate its victims.'

'We have heard of them – have you seen one?' I asked Mr Newbery. 'I did wonder how . . . how big they are.'

'Hannah!' Sarah rebuked me.

'For I cannot imagine . . .' my voice trailed away. We had heard reports of these pits which had had to be dug because the churchyards could not take any more corpses. Rumours said that they were vast holes that held forty . . . sixty . . . eighty bodies or more.

'I have heard that the biggest can hold two hundred!' Mr Newbery said. 'They are dug as deep as a man can stand in the ground, and can be as wide as the church of St Paul's. They are needed, too, for I have heard that in some parishes the death cart is coming by day now as well as by night, for the hours of darkness are not enough to take all the corpses.'

Sarah went through to our back room, shooting me a glance which meant we had heard enough of such matters.

'But have you heard about the piper?' Mr Newbery asked, and I shook my head.

Mr Newbery popped a comfit into his mouth. 'Well, they do say that a piper – just a common music man – fell down in the street insensible with drink. In the night the plague cart came round and thinking he had been struck dead, hooked him up and threw him on to a cart already piled with bodies. He was buried under more, but the jolting of the cart woke him just as they reached the pit, and he sat upright and began playing his pipes to draw attention to his plight.'

Mr Newbery paused to suck noisily on the comfit. 'The drivers of the cart couldn't see him in the dark, just heard uncanny music coming from the load of bodies, and they bolted in terrible fright, saying that they had taken up the Devil himself on to their cart!' He laughed. 'Now, what think you of that?'

I smiled, although in truth I did not know whether to laugh or cry.

'Truly, the spectre of death stares each of us in the face!' Mr Newbery said cheerfully as he went out.

That night I had a terrible nightmare. I was alive, but lying in a plague pit under a press of bodies which weighed down on me so that I could neither move nor hardly breathe. Something – some foul-smelling piece of dead flesh – was hard against my mouth and my hair was held knotted in a dead man's grip so I could not change the angle of my head to enable me to gather my strength and scream. I had no way of knowing how far down the pile of corpses I was and knew I would suffocate unless I could claw my way through them and reach the top of the heap.

My nightmare was ended when I kicked out and hit Sarah in my efforts to climb, and she woke me properly by shaking my shoulder and calling my name. She went back to sleep quickly but I lay awake for an age, wishing I could feel the comfort of Mew's little body on my feet and wondering when the Bills would show a downturn and we could go back to living an ordinary life.

The next morning Abby came round to purchase some sweetmeats, saying that her mistress had a fancy for something light and delicate to tempt her appetite. We had no crystallised violets or rose petals now, but instead gave her some candied angelica and also some citron chips made from an orange, which Sarah said was held to be good for an invalid, and which we had made the same way as the angelica chips by boiling three times in sugared water.

Abby had a pomander of herbs and flowers which she sniffed constantly as she spoke to us, and she had also tucked some blue flowers behind her ear. She said they were cornflowers and she was wearing them as a plague prevention, but indeed they looked so fetching – the blue against her dark curls – that I resolved that I too would obtain and wear some.

We gossiped at the door while Sarah was weighing up the citron chips, finding it strange that we could now look up and down the street with hardly anything to spoil our view, for as well as being quiet of people and their conveyances, there were no cats, dogs, pigs or goats around either. Indeed, there had been so little traffic that grass and weeds had started to sprout between the cobblestones.

'Your mistress is still not well enough to travel?' I asked Abby.

She shook her head. 'She's improving, but she dreads the length of the journey and the battering and jolting our bodies must take on the way.' She looked up and down the street. 'Are you all in good health here? Praise be, I don't see many shut-up houses in view.'

'There are two newly shut just around the corner,' I said. 'And a woman who was a customer of ours has this morning been taken to a pesthouse.'

Abby shook her head. 'I went past the Exchange just now and when I looked in there was scarce anyone there. And no one of quality at all.'

Before I could comment on this she said, 'And what do you think – our cook was on a ferry going across to Southwarke when the boatman was suddenly struck blind and dumb!'

'And then what happened?' I asked, alarmed.

'Well, the boat started drifting downstream and one of the men passengers had to push the boatman to one side, take the oars and carry on rowing across.'

'Did they reach the other side? What of the ferryman?' I asked.

'By the time they got to the other side, he was dead! And he had the tokens on him in a ring around his neck, though everyone swore they were not there when they got on board, or they surely would not have gone with him.'

'Abby's sweetmeats are wrapped and ready!' Sarah called from inside the shop, but I pretended not to hear her. She was always telling me not to listen to gossip, that it made one morbid, but I took little heed.

'But is your cook all right?' I asked Abby.

Abby nodded. 'Fat and healthy as ever was a sow. But did you hear of the wraith in the woods?'

I shook my head and asked Abby to tell me straightaway, for despite being in dread of what I might hear, I could not bear *not* to know. 'A real wraith – you mean, a ghost creature?' I asked.

'It happened outside the city,' Abby said in a low, storytelling voice. 'At Brentwood, I believe. A maid in a big house had been taken ill of the plague and was removed to a shed in the garden to be away from the family. A nurse who was appointed to look after her went to get some medicines, and while she was gone the maid escaped from a window. When the nurse returned she got no answer to her knocks and, believing her patient to be dead, told the master of the house so.'

She paused for breath and I urged her to go on quickly, fearing that Sarah would come up any minute and I would not hear the end of the tale.

'Well, the master was much disturbed, for none of the villagers would touch a plague victim to bury them, so he went into Brentwood to obtain assistance in getting rid of the corpse. On his way back through the woods, though, he encountered the maid and believing it to be her wraith, ran back home, shouting and raving mad. Finally, it was discovered that the maid had got out of the shed window, then she was found in the woods and put into a cart to be carried off to a pesthouse.'

I gasped. 'And did the master of the house recover from his madness?'

Abby looked surprised. 'I do not know!' she said.

Chapter Eleven

The third week of August

*'And my Lord Mayor commands people to be within
at nine at night that the sick may have liberty to go
abroad for air.'*

For the next few days we were very busy, for news of
our plague prevention sweetmeats was spreading and
they were selling well, which caused us to be up all
hours making more. I did not see Tom but I thought
of him often – especially when I took the cordial he
had made – and wondered how long it would be
before I set eyes on him. I thought too about our first
kiss, and could hardly wait for it.

On Friday evening I was putting up the shutters
outside the shop when a lad came running down the
road looking about him in a distracted way, studying
the signs as if he was looking for one in particular.

As he came closer I saw to my surprise that it was
the boy groom at the house where Abby was in
service. Suddenly spotting our sign, he made a lunge
towards me.

'The sign of the Sugared Plum! You're Hannah?' he asked, panting.

I nodded, rather intrigued, wondering what he could want.

'I have a message from Abby.' He doubled up then, breathless from running, and tried to regain breath enough to speak.

'Is it your mistress? Does she want more sweetmeats?' I asked, thinking to help.

'No – it's our house!' the boy croaked. 'Our house has been enclosed.'

I gasped and stepped backwards. 'It has been visited with plague?'

He nodded.

'And is it Abby who is sick?' I asked fearfully, and while I was anxious for my friend I was also terrified for myself, trying to think how close we had stood while she'd been telling me about the wraith, and whether or not she might have passed on any contagion to me.

He shook his head. 'It's Cook,' he said. 'Cook was taken very sick last night and a doctor came and said it's plague and we all have to be shut up.'

'But *you're* not shut up.'

'I ran off – and one of the maids got out as well. But Abby shouted down to ask me to come and tell you what had happened.'

Shakily, I asked who was left in the house, and he told me his master, mistress, the housekeeper, cook, two maids, and the babe.

'But is Abby well?' I asked anxiously.

He nodded. 'As well as anyone can be knowing they're going to be locked up for forty days,' he said.

'And your master and mistress?'

'Everyone is well except the cook, who is of a fearsome waxwork complexion and everyone says is like to die at any minute.'

I moved myself just a little further off. 'But where will you go now?'

'I will try and get back to my family in Suffolk,' the boy said.

'You don't have a Certificate of Health.'

He shook his head. 'I'll go across country and no one will see me. I'll sleep in barns and under hedges and get a message to my ma somehow so that she will send a cart out for me.'

I looked at him with concern. 'I wish you well, then.'

He grinned at me, not seeming to realise the seriousness of his situation. 'Abby said you would give me something for my trouble in coming here.'

I nodded, went inside and got him a few pennies, and also gave him a hunk of bread and some cherries.

While he ate the cherries he told me that there was now a guard outside the house, but if I went round to the back yard and called up, then Abby would come and speak to me out of the first-floor window. He bade me go there as quickly as possible, and then he stuffed the piece of bread inside his shirt and ran off, leaving me to go inside and tell Sarah this news.

I thought at first that Sarah would raise some objections to my going to see Abby, but she did not, for she had known her and her family as long as I had and was equally anxious to know that she was all right. I was not frightened, for I felt there would be no risk in speaking to Abby from the distance of a window. Just as soon as we had eaten supper, I set off.

The streets were quiet as I hurried along, not looking at anyone nor acknowledging those who might be looking at me. When I got to City Road someone hailed me and shouted that I should go home, but I thought it was just a madman and did not take any notice. A little further on, however, I chanced upon a crier in a square who was ringing his bell and calling nine of the clock as being an hour of curfew. At this time, he called, all able-bodied people were to stay inside their houses and allow those who had been visited by plague to walk the streets and take the air unimpeded.

I panicked then, for of course I had not known about this curfew and immediately visualised a vast crowd of diseased people sweeping through the streets and infecting me with their weeping sores and foetid breath. I turned to go home and, thinking to take a short cut, went down a long, narrow alley. When I emerged I did not know where I was and, the sun having gone down, could not work out in which direction to walk.

I turned to the right but when I reached the Fleet River I knew immediately that I was not going in the proper direction, and turned back. In my haste, however, I missed the alley through which I had come. Breaking into a run, I at length found myself close to the city walls and near the church of St Just. I did not wish to approach the only person who passed, who had his eyes and hands raised to heaven and was praying aloud for God to have mercy on us all, so thought it best to go towards the church and hope to see someone of authority there to ask for directions.

Alas, I could see no minister but, instead, beyond the church my eyes seized upon the most dreadful sight: one of the plague pits that Mr Newbery had spoken of, a cavernous black hole in the ground, lit by the flares and torches of those standing nearby. There were some men inside the pit itself, walking about (perhaps on bodies, I thought), and some more men beside a plague cart which had just pulled up.

This cart was pulled by drayhorses and contained a stack of dead bodies, perhaps thirty or forty of them. I could not help but watch as it tipped up and the pile of bodies tumbled into the pit, a jumbled heap of limbs, hair and rags.

'Here's another load of faggots!' I heard a man call, and there was a roar of laughter.

'Pile 'em in and pile 'em up!' another shouted.

As I watched, the men already in the pit moved across and poked and hooked the corpses so they laid at an even level, and others shook out lime from great sacks and strewed it over them. I did not hear one murmured prayer or exclamation of sorrow, and indeed all was conducted with a callous and cruel indifference to the poor corpses which were now spread out before them all.

As another plague cart arrived I turned away, sickened to my very heart, and by sheer good fortune managed to find the right path home. The horror of that evening was not yet over, though, because on the way back I encountered the dead body of a young man propped in a doorway. He held a Bible in his hands and his eyes were wide open and staring. The sight of him gave me the most dreadful fright.

I arrived home before the plague victims walked

out, however, and after thoroughly washing myself (for I felt clammy and dirty from all I had seen) Sarah and I waited for these poor creatures to appear, watching with a morbid curiosity from behind our shutters. The streets were completely deserted now and it was as silent as a morgue outside, apart from the far-off tolling of a bell, when some tapping and shuffling noises were heard along the cobblestones.

We were expecting to see fearsome monsters, but when the sufferers came into view they were not monsters at all, just a straggling line of pitiful creatures: old and young, stooped and upright, ugly and fair, some recovering from the sickness and walking with an almost confident stride, some bent almost double and held up with sticks, and one or two pushed in a cart by others. The one thing they had in common was that they were all plague sufferers – and wore stained and tattered bandages as their mark of distinction.

'And these are just the ones who are well enough to come out,' Sarah breathed as we watched the pathetic procession pass our shop.

Perhaps forty passed in ones and twos, some carrying flares before them, and then a party from a pesthouse came along together: ten or twelve led by a surly-looking nurse, all carrying white staves in front of them. I imagined them returning to the pesthouse and telling the inmates who had not been well enough to walk of the things they'd seen, of a strange London, shut up and unearthly quiet, seemingly populated by none but plague victims.

I went to sleep that night worried because I had not been able to speak to Abby, and Sarah said I should go first thing the following morning.

In the morning Mr Newbery was standing outside his shop telling early passers-by that four and a half thousand had died of plague that week, and making much of a tale he'd heard of one of the plague walkers of the previous night who'd dropped down dead just outside St Saviour's.

'He was a frowsy-headed old man, rich with lice,' he said, 'and when he dropped to the ground, those coming after threw him over the wall into the churchyard. They just picked him up and chucked him over like a bundle of sticks!'

I made noises of surprise and disgust.

'Well, it saved the cart coming!' Mr Newbery said. He scratched his fat belly. 'But where are you heading so early on this hot morning?' he asked, and I told him the truth: that I was going to see my friend Abby, who'd recently been enclosed.

He stepped back from me and crossed himself, looking at me in alarm. 'Those enclosed are fuel for the carts,' he said. 'She'll not make old bones!'

I was about to make a witty return, for I'd found that this was the only way to deal with Mr Newbery, but to my horror I found my eyes filling with tears. I turned away, saying nothing.

I found London very different that day, perhaps because something had happened which touched me personally. The sun still shone but it seemed to have drained the colour from the City, for the house signs no longer glittered and the people (what few there were abroad, and none in the bright colours that denoted them to be of quality) were slow and dull of spirit, going about their business with their eyes cast down and none of their usual laughter or banter. The houses were desolate, too. Amid those that had crosses on their doors were many which had been deserted by their owners. They stood empty and lifeless, having been cleared of anything of value and boarded up. I missed the animals, too: the pink grunting pigs, the fighting dogs and the cats which had silently slipped in and out of the shadows. Their robust farmyard smell had disappeared and been replaced by an unwholesome and putrid stink which those such as Doctor da Silva called a *miasma*: a sickening, invisible fog emanating from the graveyards which were now choked with rotting bodies.

When I arrived at the front of Abby's house I saw a most fearsome sight, for the plague cart was at the front door and the carters were taking away a large bundle. Of course, my first fear was that it was Abby, for notwithstanding that the groom had told me last night that she was perfectly healthy, I had heard many tales of persons being well one moment and dead the next.

I held back for a while in the shadow of the opposite building, my heart pounding, but then, having judged by the size of the corpse that it could not be Abby, went around the back of the house to call up to her.

She was already at the first-floor window, standing looking out with the babe in her arms, and she looked so thankful to see me that I almost fell to crying. She still had a flower tucked behind her ear, but that flower was fading now, and her face was pale, her dress creased and stained.

'I have been here since daylight,' she said and, when I began to apologize for not getting there earlier, added that it was not because she was especially waiting for me, but because she wished little Grace to draw in what fresh air she could from outside and not let her breathe in the foul atmosphere of the house.

'I saw the cart outside,' I said. 'Who was it that died?'

'Cook,' she answered.

'So quickly?' I gasped.

She nodded. 'I did not like the old baggage . . .' Here she stopped and struggled to compose herself. '. . . but I would not have wished that death on her.'

'How did she . . . did she have the buboes?'

Abby nodded. 'In her groin. She screamed for four hours last night.'

'Was there nothing could be done?'

'Nothing. She cried out that she could not bear the pain and was going to fling herself out of the window, and the nurse had to tie her to her bed.'

I shuddered. 'And then what—?'

'Then she fell into a deep sleep and woke before dawn to start screaming again. She found the strength from somewhere to break the ropes that bound her, then ran through the house and threw herself down the back staircase.' Abby drew in a little breath, making a sound between a sob and a laugh. 'She knew her place even then, see, for she made sure it was the servants' stairs.'

She dipped her head and wiped her eyes on the swaddling sheet. 'And now her neck is broke and she is no more.'

'And you. Are . . . are you well?' I faltered.

She struggled to compose herself. 'I am. I'll be all right. For aren't we good country stock and as strong as 'roaches?' She smiled faintly.

'And what of the others in the house?'

'The master complains that he cannot sleep for pains in his arms, so they are going to send the doctor round,' Abby said. 'And one of the maids says she has a sick headache. But every little sniff and ache is the plague to us!'

'Is there anything you want?'

She shook her head. 'The milch-ass comes twice a day, an apothecary calls with fresh tinctures and the wretch at the door buys our food for us. We have everything we need.' She looked at me bleakly. 'We just have to wait.'

'Forty days?'

'Forty days from the last death,' Abby said wearily. 'If another of us dies in a week's time, or two weeks' time, then that forty days will start again.'

I swallowed and my throat was dry with horror, for I knew I could not bear being shut up in that house for those weeks amongst the dead and dying. 'I have brought you some sweetmeats,' I said quickly. 'Candied angelica and some rosemary comfits.'

Comfits for corpses. The thought came to me unbidden and I quickly brushed it aside.

Abby looked a little cheered. 'I will send down a basket,' she said, and holding the babe deftly in the crook of her arm, she put out a little wicker basket on a string and lowered it to the ground. Carefully – I did not let my fingers come into contact with the basket – I put the cones of sweetmeats in and stood back to allow her to pull it up.

'Will you come again, Hannah?' she asked.

I nodded. 'I will try to come every day. And if you need anything, you must tell me and I will try to get it for you.'

We blew kisses, said goodbye, and I turned away.

Abby called me back. 'Hannah!' she added, with a touch of her old spirit. 'You be sure to kiss your sweetheart!'

Chapter Twelve

The fourth week of August

'Every day sadder and sadder news of its increase . . .
it is feared that the true number of the dead this week
is nearer ten thousand.'

For the next few days the church bells seemed to toll incessantly for one death after another, until an Order came from the Lord Mayor that they should be stopped, for everyone was much cast-down by hearing them. The weariness of spirit I'd noticed around me when visiting Abby had spread and it seemed that some people no longer cared what happened. This led them to go one of two ways: either they sank into a deep gloom, or they began frequenting the ale houses (for these had begun to open again) and drank themselves past false joviality and into a stupor.

Although our herbal sweetmeats were still selling quite well, no one had much faith in preventatives any more – not when the dead were to be found clutching the very talismans that they'd hoped would save them. There were no directives from the authorities and it seemed that they had washed their hands of us, for the only new instruction we heard was that it was forbidden to build plague hospitals near to the dwellings of persons of substance and quality.

I had a mind to visit Abby again, but the next morning, after sleeping badly (for I still had the fear of the plague pit on me), I could hardly rouse myself up, and my legs trembled as I put them to the floor.

Sarah bade me stay in bed. 'For if you feel weak you may be more likely to take infection,' she said.

The next morning I was the same and I slept most of that day, weary, tearful and, for the first time, wishing myself safe back in Chertsey with my brothers and sisters. It crossed my mind – and of course it crossed Sarah's – that these were the first stirrings of plague about my body, but praise be, the third morning, I felt better and was anxious to go out and see how Abby fared.

Before I could do this, however, Mr Newbery came in to tell us a fresh and morbid tale, which was of a friend of his, one Josiah Brown, who, he said, was as well and as merry a chap as ever you could meet. 'He took all the precautions against the plague, and when he was out he carried a cloth of vinegar over his face, and never failed to change into fresh garments after going abroad. I saw him last week and he stood as healthy as you or I!' he said. 'Well, on Monday, my friend Josiah met someone in the street – an astrologer – who took one look and told him that he saw the mark of death on him.'

Sarah and I exchanged glances, knowing what was coming next.

'Why, Josiah laughed in his face,' Mr Newbery went

on, 'and said he had never felt so well in all his life. But when he got home he changed his clothes and saw to his horror that he had the tokens on his breast. And he knew that the tokens were gangrene spots and that the plague had gone inwards and mortified his flesh.' He paused for breath. 'And then my friend Josiah just sat down and died.'

Sarah tutted, shook her head, but I was silent, thinking of Abby.

'Eat, drink and be merry for tomorrow we die!' Mr Newbery went on. 'You may as well die happy as any other way.' He winked at me. 'Or catch the French pox, eh? That's worth a try!'

I didn't know what he was talking about but when he left, Sarah blushingly told me that it was thought that if a man lay with a prostitute and caught a disease, then that would stop him catching the plague. 'But 'tis all just a rumour,' she said, 'for no one knows anything of what is true and what is not any more.' She frowned. 'But I cannot believe that God would allow a man to be saved by sleeping with a . . . a whore, for this wouldn't be right.'

On the way to Abby's house, to my horror, I saw another corpse on the street (a woman, seemingly big with child) and heard the agonised sobs of people from an enclosed room, and so began to fear of what I might find when I reached Belle Vue House. But Abby was at the window once more, though looking pale and weary. There was no flower behind her ear now, and her hair was hanging in lank tails on each side of her face.

I asked how she was and she shook her head listlessly. 'I am well enough and I have no lumps,' she said, 'but I fear I shall go mad with being enclosed here.'

'But how is your mistress – and the babe?' I added anxiously, for I could see she was not nursing it as usual.

She shook her head. 'The babe is well and sleeps. But Mistress Beauchurch does nothing but cry and 'tis difficult to tell whether she is sick or well. My master has now a lump in his groin and groans aloud – I fear he is failing – and Becky, the other maid, lies in bed with such a sweat on her that we cannot keep her dry no matter how often we change the sheets.'

I gasped. 'Is it plague, then?'

Abby did not reply for a moment and I had to ask again.

'We fear so,' she then answered in a low voice. 'For she was often enough with Cook.'

'And do you have to nurse her?'

She shrugged. 'We have a nurse-minder sent in by the parish every morning, but she is a haggard old crone who knows next to nothing, and Becky is terrified of her.' Abby's hands gripped the sides of the window frame. 'Hannah, if I die you must promise you'll get a message to my mother in Chertsey.'

'Of course!' I said before I could stop myself, and quickly added, 'But you won't die! We're strong as 'roaches, remember?'

But her eyes had glazed over and she was thinking I knew not what terrible thoughts. I tried to think of things to speak about to lighten her heart, but it was hard, for all that was on my mind – indeed, all that was on the mind of anyone in London – was the plague, the pits, the corpses on the streets and horrid tales of those who had been afflicted. I left her, promising that I would go back as soon as I could, and I vowed to myself that I would do this even if I had the lethargy on me again, for it seemed little enough in comparison to what she was going through.

At home I had the most pleasant surprise, for Tom was there taking a glass of small beer with Sarah. She had sent a message to Doctor da Silva while I'd been out, to ask for something which would help me sleep soundly and prevent nightmares, and Tom had brought up a phial containing oil of lavender.

He told me to put one drop on my tongue on retiring, and one on my pillow.

'No more,' he said, 'for it is extremely potent.'

'And will it help her sleep?' Sarah asked him anxiously.

He nodded. 'It helps in all manner of night terrors and passions of the heart.' He smiled at me mischievously as he said these last four words, and raised his eyebrows. I could not help myself smiling back at him.

He could not stay, for at Doctor da Silva's they were busy day and night with making preventatives, for although it seemed that people no longer believed in them, they still wanted to take them.

'The doctor says they must have hope in something, for if that goes then all is lost,' Tom said, draining his glass.

He and I went to the door of the shop together and I told him the latest news about Abby and asked if he could offer any advice. He could not, however, apart from saying that I should tell Abby not to sleep in the same room as Becky, that she should keep to her own chamber as much as possible.

I hesitated before asking my next question. 'Do you think it is . . . is dangerous for me to speak to Abby from some distance away?'

He shook his head slowly. 'I do not think so,' he said. 'But no one knows for sure.' He took my hand and spoke earnestly to me, 'Hannah, you *will* take care, will you not?'

I nodded shyly.

'I think about you often, and if I could do what the necromancers say they can do, and cast a cloak of protection over you, then I would.'

Our gazes locked and I could not reply for the fullness of my heart and the tightness in my throat.

'And when all this is over . . .' he said softly.

Our hands touched, I lifted my face to his and let my eyelids drift down, ready . . . then I heard a jovial laugh beside us and Mr Newbery's voice saying, 'Ah, that's right – gather ye rosebuds while ye may!'

Unwillingly, I opened my eyes.

'That's what the poet tells us,' Mr Newbery went on, 'and in this dark time it would be as well to remember it!'

I glared at him, thinking that if ever there was an inappropriate time for Mr Newbery to appear with one of his stories, then this was it. But he did not seem to notice, just looked from me to Tom, casting his merry and unwelcome smile on each of us in turn. 'If I'm not mistaken, you're the 'prentice lad from the apothecary's!' he said. 'Now, tell me what faith you have in holding a gold angel in your mouth to keep off the sickness, for I have heard 'tis the very thing.'

Tom cast a sorry look at me, twining his hand in mine, and I squeezed his fingers for goodbye and dropped a small curtsey, for I knew Mr Newbery could speak for a great deal of time when he had a mind to.

'If you'll excuse me . . .' I murmured, and Tom smiled at me – a bright, tender smile – before I went inside again.

I used the lavender oil that night, and, thinking of Tom before I went to sleep, did sleep sounder and felt better. To my great shame, however, I let two whole days elapse before visiting Abby again. I had no excuse to offer for this, except my own selfishness, for while I stayed with Sarah and kept within the confines of the shop I felt I was out of harm's way. I did not feel safe in the city any more, for Death stalked its streets and no one was immune. I no longer thought London an exciting place to be.

Abby was not waiting at the window when I went round, nor did she come when I called up to her. I waited and called again, several times, and at length, fearing the very worst and chastising myself for staying away, I went round to the front of the house and spoke to the man guarding the door. At least there *was* a man still guarding them, I thought, so there must be someone alive inside.

I told him that I had come to speak to my friend the maid but had not been able to rouse her, and fearfully asked him if there had been other deaths in the house. He told me there had, but he could not say who they were.

'For the usual fellow is taken sick and I only came

here last night,' he said.

I began trembling, and felt ashamed and low, for what if Abby had died since my last visit . . . had dragged herself to the window to look for me, but I had not come?

'How many have died altogether in the house?' I asked.

He shrugged. 'Three, I believe. Or four.'

I went round to the back again and threw some gravel up to the window, and called and called. At last, at very long last, someone appeared. It was Abby, yet not the Abby I knew, for this person had a wild eye and a pain-filled face, and her forehead glittered with beads of sweat.

I could see at once that she had been deeply and fatally afflicted, but I tried to swallow down the fright I felt at her appearance. 'At last,' I said, 'I have been a-calling this hour or more.'

Abby smiled down at me. A strange smile she had, and an odd gleam in her eye.

'I have been visited, Hannah!' she said, and to my extreme surprise her voice had the tone of one telling another that a favourite friend had called. 'Visited at last. It courted me but I resisted it for days . . .'

'I . . . I see,' I said.

'Death called me to come into his arms! And what is a maid to do?' She gave a sudden cry of pain and clutched her head with both hands. 'Oh, but it is a hard and spiteful master!' she cried.

I choked back tears. 'Are you in great pain, Abby? Where is the nurse to look after you?'

'The nurse hasn't arrived today, Hannah. No nurse.' She shook her head gravely. 'She must be dead too.

They are all dead. And I have two fearful lumps come up in my groin so that I cannot walk as far as the privy but must lie in my own soil.'

I was sickened at this, but tried not to show it. Poor, poor Abby, who so loved her pretty gowns and her silk ribbons and who had come out with me on many a May morning in order to bathe her face in the dew and be beautiful.

'Is *everyone* dead, Abby? Your master and mistress too?'

She nodded. 'Within an hour of each other. In the beautiful chamber with the mirrors from Venice and the hangings from Persia.'

'But – *all* dead? What about the babe?'

'The babe!' A sudden light lit her face. 'Little Grace survives. But she cries – oh, how she cries! She is a poor orphan babe though, so she is right to cry.' Abby was leaning against the window frame and suddenly slipped sideways so that she disappeared from view. I called to her again.

'Abby!' I said urgently. 'What can I do for you? Is there something I can get you? Anything at all?'

I didn't think I would get a proper response, for I could see that the horror of what she must have seen in that house had already driven her half mad, but suddenly her two hands appeared, gripping the sill, and she pulled herself to her feet.

She looked at me with glittering eyes. 'Yes, Hannah,' she said. 'I almost forgot. You must take the babe.'

Astonished, I thought I must have misheard her, so did not reply.

'I promised Mrs Beauchurch, my mistress, that you

would get the babe away if I could not. It is all planned. There is a letter for you . . .' Abby flinched with pain and pressed her hand to her head, then raked it through her hair, knotting a handful of it around her fist as if she would pull it out.

Filled with pity, I waited for the spasm to pass from her before I prompted her to continue. 'A letter?'

She nodded and felt among the folds of her dress for her pocket, then dropped the letter out of the window.

It fell on to the cobblestones and lay there for a moment (for to tell the truth I feared to handle it) until Abby cried that I must take it up. I was forced to do so then, and holding it outstretched before me, I ran home with it.

At the corner I looked back, but Abby had again disappeared.

Chapter Thirteen

The first week of September

'A saddler who had buried all his children dead of the Plague, did desire only to save the life of his remaining little child, and so prevailed to have it received stark naked into the arms of a friend.'

I sobbed all the way back to the shop and people avoided me as I ran, for they probably thought I was afflicted and half-mad.

Sarah was standing in the doorway with a grave expression upon her face, but my sudden tearful appearance distracted her from whatever had caused this. I gave her the letter and explained in a few words about Abby. Without speaking she shut the shop and we went through to our little room in the back.

She turned the letter over in her hands. 'We should steam it over vinegar,' she said.

'But I have already handled it in bringing it here!'

She shrugged, and I knew she was trying not to alarm me. 'Then we won't bother.'

We sat down together on the bed and she peeled up

the seal and opened the folded piece of paper. It was a page torn from a book, the handwriting being on one side.

'It is written in an educated hand,' Sarah said, 'although you can see that whoever it is from—'

'It is from Abby's employer, Mrs Beauchurch,' I said.

'Her hand wavers and she is in some distress.' Sarah then read out the letter, which was addressed to me.

'Dear Hannah,

I beg and beseech you in the name of the Almighty that you take my child, Grace, upon receipt of this letter, and carry her with all speed to my sister the Lady Jane at Highclear House, in Dorchester. My child is lusty and hearty now, but if left in this house of death she will surely perish. There are Certificates of Health for you and your sister, but you must travel under the names of Abigail and myself. A carriage has been procured and will be at the sign of the Eagle and Child in Gracechurch Street each day awaiting your arrival. The driver is my sister's man and has a Certificate to travel.

On reaching Dorchester, Lady Jane will ensure that you and your sister are well cared for. You will be permitted to stay until the Visitation has left London, when you will be given safe passage back.

May the prayers of a mother melt your heart and you find it within yourselves to grant my dying wish and save my child.

By my hand this 30th day of August 1665.
Maria Beauchurch.'

'Abby is terribly sick and so strange that I could scarce believe it was her,' I said to Sarah. I lifted a corner of my skirt and wiped my eyes on it. 'What will we do?'

She put down the letter and turned to look at me. 'We will go, of course,' she said calmly, 'for our own sakes as well as that of the babe. We will not get another chance of leaving London and it grows more dangerous here by the minute.'

I was still shaking from the shock of seeing my poor friend, and from hearing what was asked of us. 'Must we really go?' I asked.

She nodded. 'For when you appeared then, I had just been told a terrible thing by Mr Newbery.'

I looked at her. 'But there are so many terrible things.'

'The Bills. They show six thousand dead in London in the last week.'

'Six thousand!'

'And nearly two more thousand dead of "other causes" – and they fear it will get higher, for there are so many dying all around that there are no longer enough men to board up and guard the houses. Mr Newbery says the afflicted will now begin to walk the streets and infect others, and the whole population may fall.'

I put my face in my hands, uttering a cry of distress. How had I ever thought that living here in this city . . . this charnel house . . . was preferable to living in the serenity I had enjoyed in the country?

Sarah was already moving about our room, pulling things out of our nest of drawers and stuffing them into a cloth bag. 'We will wear our good gowns,' she said. 'For if we are to act the rich mistress and her nursemaid, then we must look the part.'

She stepped out of her workaday dress and apron and threw them on the bed, then took down her best grey taffeta gown and jacket, and put on her little lace hood. ''Tis not the height of fashion,' she said, 'but I daresay that the men at the city gates won't know any better.'

She came to me and clasped my hands in hers. 'This is our way out, Hannah. This will save us!' I did not reply or move and she shook my shoulders gently. 'Set to, Hannah. You can wear your blue and put my little travelling cape over the top.'

I rose and turned so Sarah could unbutton my gown at the back, my mind a mess of thoughts: Tom, Abby, our journey, the babe . . .

'We will shut up the shop and not tell anyone where we're going, for who knows but there might be some law against impersonating a person of quality and using their Certificate of Health,' Sarah said. I nodded obediently. I would let Sarah take charge, for I did not wish to have to decide things myself.

Two bags were packed with some clean shifts and a change of clothes each, and somehow I found myself dressed and ready, a cape around my shoulders and a clean white cap on my head. Sarah decided to leave what there was left of our plague sweetmeats outside the shop for the poor to eat (which they would, of course, immediately) for she said it would just encourage rats if we left them inside.

'And who knows – our sweetmeats might do someone some good,' she said.

There was a knot of fear in my stomach as we

closed our shop behind us. Suppose it was discovered that we were travelling under false documents? Would we then be consigned to the pest hospital (which I had heard was little more than a burial ground)? And – worse still – suppose little Grace carried the plague germs on her? If everyone else in that house had succumbed, why should she be spared?

Sarah secured the door and then, having thought of something else, went back inside and came out carrying a folded linen sheet.

'We mustn't take anything from Abby's house,' she said, pushing the sheet into the bag. 'For they say you should remove nothing from a house which has plague in it.'

'But we are taking Grace—'

'We will have to trust that she is healthy. But she must have no clothing or swaddling cloths on her. Nothing in which plague germs could hide.'

She closed the door again just as Mr Newbery came out from his shop. 'I'm shutting up,' he said. 'What is the point of making parchment and fine writing papers when no one's buying them?' He looked at us curiously. 'But are you shutting up too? I would have thought your business was doing well.'

'We are . . . are . . .' Sarah stumbled.

'Going to church!' I finished for her.

'Well, that's very good and commendable,' Mr Newbery said. 'Though you may not get in through the gates, what with all those corpses lying about!'

'We will somehow manage to get in and pray,' I said piously.

'And spend the rest of the day in silent contemplation of our fate,' Sarah added.

'Well, say a prayer for me,' Mr Newbery said. 'I'll be in a pew in the Three Pigeons.' He gave us a wave and walked off in the opposite direction.

Sarah and I did not speak for some moments, for I was deep in thoughts of what might lie ahead. Deep in thoughts of Tom, too, and as we approached Doctor da Silva's I asked if I might go and say goodbye to him.

'I'd rather you did not,' Sarah said. 'For the less people know about our flight from London, the better.'

'But Tom can be trusted,' I pleaded. 'And think how worried he'll be if he comes down to see me and finds the shop empty. He'll think we've both been taken by the sickness.'

She sighed, but in the end gave me leave to see him. 'Hurry, though,' she said as I pushed open the door of the apothecary's. 'With Abby so very ill, every moment is precious.'

Tom *was* in the shop, and I quickly explained to him and the doctor what was happening, and they were most anxious and concerned for us. The doctor gave me a sleeping draught for the babe, a strong purging elixir for Abby, and also two onions which I was to tell her to roast and place on the buboes to try and bring them to a head. He packed these things into a small valise and told Tom to escort us to Belle Vue House to ensure that we had safe passage.

Any other time I would have been merry whilst walking with Tom through the City, but this was very different. The three of us barely spoke as we hurried along, and when we did it was just to murmur in low tones of the dire things we saw around us. There were more corpses placed outside houses for collection – I saw at least three – and other sad sights: a woman sobbing, 'Dead, all dead!' from a top-floor window and a man dressed only with a rag around his private parts, crying aloud and tearing at his flesh with his fingernails so that his arms and chest ran with blood. We also saw a death cart trundling along, so over-full with corpses that some were slumped across the bench seat with the driver.

Tom hurried us past all these sights until we arrived in the vicinity of Belle Vue House, and here the streets became quieter, most of the residents having gone into the country some time before.

Going round to the back of the house my heart was heavy, for I was fearful of what condition Abby would be in. If she was well I feared the effect giving the babe away would have on her, for she loved Grace, and caring for her gave her something to live for. If she was worse – well, I did not dare think on that.

As before, there was no answer to my call. We all tried, calling softly at first and then more loudly, and in the end Tom gave a most piercing whistle, like a blackbird, but even this did not bring her to the window.

'I fear she may have fallen into a deep sleep,' I said. For I had heard that this is what happened just before plague sufferers died.

'I fear she—' Tom began, but then glanced at me and did not finish.

We looked around us. A large green and gold vine encircled the house, going right up to the fourth floor, but Sarah decided that it was not strong enough to climb, or Tom might have shinned up it.

We called some more but then had to stop, because the watchman on duty at the front of the house came round wanting to know what we were at. Tom, luckily, having been warned of the man's arrival by the sound of his boots on the cobblestones, ducked into one of the empty stables and so was not seen by him.

'Our sister is the maid in this house and we are concerned for her welfare,' I informed the guard – but very politely, for I knew we must not arouse his suspicions or enmity.

'When did you last take in food to anyone in there?' Sarah asked anxiously.

'The milch-ass called this morning as usual and a flagon of milk was sent up,' he said. He looked suspiciously at our bundles of clothes on the ground. 'Anything which goes into this house must go through me. And nothing must come out!'

We assured him that of course it would not, and he went back to the front of the house again.

Tom reappeared. 'I have an idea,' he said. 'As this looks to be a slow business, why don't you go to the Eagle and Child and secure the carriage, while I wait here for you. I will call Abby meantimes, and when you return, if I have not roused her, I will insist on being let in the house. I will say I am an apothecary and that I have been sent by the parish.'

'We cannot ask you to do—' Sarah began, but Tom hushed her.

'Go and get the carriage,' he said. 'You must act with all haste.'

Sarah knew the Eagle and Child, which was a large and notable inn in Gracechurch Street with stables at the back. While Sarah waited in the courtyard, I went in to ask for the inn-keeper's wife and, when she appeared, informed her that I was the maid at Belle Vue House and that my mistress was Mrs Beauchurch.

'Do you have something for us?' I asked.

She was obviously expecting me and, nodding her head, she went to a locked cupboard and took a roll of parchment from it. She then fetched a deep canvas bag. Unrolling the parchment I found it contained a sum of money and the two Health Certificates of which Abby had spoken, one in her name and one in that of Mrs Beauchurch. They stated that, being free of the pestilence we should be granted safe passage out of London. They were signed by the Lord Mayor himself, Sir John Lawrence.

In the canvas bag there was a soft white woollen shawl for Grace, a flask of wine, a travelling rug and cushions for Sarah and myself, also some kid gloves, a lantern and some other little items for our comfort during the journey.

I went outside to the courtyard and rejoined Sarah, and in a few moments two horses were brought out of the stables, and a groom had wheeled out a small blue-varnished carriage, a coat of arms on its door, from the coach house. While we waited there a boy ran helter-skelter through the yard, and returned a few moments later with a stout and bald man of perhaps fifty years. This fellow bowed and introduced himself to us as Mr Carter, coachman to the Lady Jane.

Sarah, holding her head high, told him that she was Mrs Beauchurch.

'Indeed,' he said, giving a slight wink. 'And you are hardly changed since your last visit to Dorchester.'

Sarah inclined her head, and managed very well not

to look askance at this.

'I have been expecting you, and I am to be your coachman and your guard for the journey,' Mr Carter went on. 'Your passage has been considered and your stops planned ahead of us. I only hope you will not find the journey too arduous.'

Sarah, in her role as gracious lady, smiled her thanks. 'We are looking forward to it,' she said, and then hesitated. 'When we are all prepared here, I have to go back to my house to collect my child,' she added. 'It is just a short distance away.'

'I am at your service,' Mr Carter murmured.

As the horses were bridled and prepared I was still in an agony of fear about Abby, but could not help but marvel at the smooth way everything had been made ready for us. Sarah said to me quietly that it was all to do with money, and that anything, any service, could be procured if someone was willing to pay enough for it.

Feeling very nervous, but also very grand – for neither of us had ever been driven in a carriage before – Sarah directed Mr Carter to Belle Vue House. On drawing close by, we asked him to stop just out of view of the courtyard, for we were both anxious about being noticed by the watchman. If this happened, Sarah said, if it became known that we were stealing a child away from an enclosed house, then he would certainly lock us all into the house and inform the magistrates.

Alighting and going to the courtyard, we found that Tom had not been able to rouse Abby, and that he now proposed to go inside the house. 'For what could be more natural than an apothecary should attend his patient,' he said, holding up his valise. 'Doctor da Silva does it all the time.'

'I don't think you should go,' I said worriedly, but although part of me wanted to beg him not to risk such danger, I had no idea how we would secure little Grace otherwise.

Tom took my hand. 'It's nothing. I see plague sufferers every day of the week. Just wish me well and wait here for me.'

'Be careful,' was all I could say in return, and though I knew that these words sounded pitifully inadequate, my mind was so full of fear and dread that I could not think of any others.

While Sarah and I waited, Tom went around to the front of the house. I do not know what he said to the guard, but a few moments later his face appeared at the first-floor window we had been calling up to for so long.

'Is it all right?' I asked breathlessly. 'Have you found Abby?'

He did not reply and I asked again, already knowing in my heart what he was about to say.

'I have,' he said gravely.

Sarah took my hand and held it.

'She is here on the stairs,' he went on, 'but, Hannah, I do not think she suffered much, for there is a look of hope on her face.'

'Her hope was that you would come back,' Sarah said, looking at me with great pity. 'She must have been looking out for you.'

So Abby was dead.

Dead. The word struck me cold and brutal, and the image which came into my head of my lovely friend being no more than a heap of rotting flesh made me want to scream and sob and pull at my clothes like the mad people in the streets did. I dared not indulge myself, though, for we had much to do if I was to carry out Abby's last wishes. I did not even allow myself to weep, but knew I must put my feelings to one side until later.

'What . . . what of the babe?' I asked Tom, and I was bitterly scared now, for if she too was dead, then all this had been for nothing.

Tom disappeared, and came back a moment later with a bundle in his arms. 'I have her here,' he said, holding up Grace. 'She was sleeping, but now she smiles at me.'

At this I felt a rush of tears to my eyes. 'Is she well?' I asked anxiously.

'She seems well enough,' Tom said, looking her over. 'I am no expert but her eyes are bright, she seems well-fed, and she is pink-cheeked.'

'Will you bring her out to us now?' Sarah asked in a low voice.

'And risk being seen by the guard?' Tom said. 'I think not. We must—'

'Is there a basket nearby?' I asked suddenly. 'There was one with a rope attached which the household used to get its provisions.'

'There is,' Tom said, bending down for it. 'And I think it will be just big enough.'

'Will you take off her things, Tom,' Sarah said. 'We have brought a clean sheet to wrap her in.'

Tom disappeared for a moment or two to do this, and while he was out of view my mind was a perfect whirlpool of fear. He then reappeared with Grace naked within the basket. Lifting this into the air, he tested the rope that held it, and then Sarah and I stood with arms outstretched as he carefully lowered the precious bundle to the ground.

I took little Grace out – and indeed she did look healthy, with plump pink limbs and a fine head of hair – and as we wrapped her in the clean sheet she looked so pretty and innocent that Sarah and I both fell to weeping at her sad destiny in being orphaned so young.

Tom, watching from above, asked us what the matter was. 'Have you seen some mark on her body?' he said anxiously.

I shook my head. 'We are just weeping for . . .' I began, but found I could not explain why.

'For the sadness of the occasion,' Sarah finished with a sigh.

Tom said he was mighty relieved that the babe was well and had no marks on her, and told us that he had a mind to remove Abby's corpse from the stairs, and not leave it in such disarray. He disappeared to do this, but a moment later, to our great horror, we heard a shout inside the house, and the face of the watchman appeared at the same window.

'What mischief are you doing?' he yelled to us. And then he saw the basket and the rope, and Grace in my arms, and began roaring at us to stop, saying he would call the magistrates and have us locked up as kidnappers and common thieves.

We were in a terrible confusion then, for we did not know what to do for the best. I felt that we could not just run off leaving Tom in the plague-torn house, for it would be known that he'd had a part in our stealing of Grace.

Sarah picked up our bundles and pulled my arm, though. 'We must go! If we want to get away, we must go now!'

And I knew she was right. Holding the babe tightly, cradling her head, I began to run with Sarah towards our coach. Mr Carter was still sitting atop in the driver's seat, and reaching it, Sarah opened the door and clambered in, then turned to take Grace from me.

Panting and shaking with fright, I handed the babe to her. I then climbed in myself as quickly as I was able, calling to Mr Carter to drive off with all speed.

As we started off and the carriage turned into the main street, my attention was caught by a blur of movement as Tom came running from the house, sprinted across the roadway and arrived on the corner just as our horses galloped past him.

We had time for just one thing: to blow a kiss to each other.

I leaned forward in my seat, trying to see Tom until the last possible moment, and in this way saw the watchman run out of the house and stare after our coach. Tom ran off, and it looked as if the watchman was hesitating, wondering whether to go after him. He chose us to chase, however, and began to run down the centre of the road ringing a bell and shouting.

This did not alarm us unduly, for within no time at all the horses had gathered speed and we had left him behind. We were going at a goodly pace now, swaying and bumping on the uneven cobbles, and found we had to sit well back, bracing our legs, to enable us to keep our positions. We sat on opposite seats, gazing at each other in a mixture of excitement and fear.

'Close the curtains,' Sarah said. 'A lady and her maid would not allow the common people to gaze in on them.'

I did so, then begged Sarah to let me hold Grace. Smiling, we had a small dispute about who should nurse her, but Sarah at last agreed that it would be more usual for the babe to be held by the maid rather than the lady, and passed her to me. Grace was quiet, the movement of the carriage having almost sent her off to sleep again.

We galloped and jolted through the streets, twisting and turning down narrow passageways, and found out later that Mr Carter had taken us a complex way around in case the watchman found means to follow us. Peeping through a crack in the curtain, I saw few passers-by, and none who looked at us with any interest, for people were very much keeping within their houses now and only going out to buy what food was necessary to keep them alive. After some minutes of fast, jolting driving, we heard Mr Carter shout at the horses and rein them in. They fell into a walk.

Sarah pulled the curtain to one side. 'Mr Carter,' she said, 'can you not maintain the speed?'

'I can, Ma'am,' he said, 'but we are approaching the gate on London Bridge and I do not think it meet that we should arrive there all of a hugger-mugger.'

'No. Indeed!' Sarah said hastily, and she sank back once more on to her seat. We shared an anxious glance and composed ourselves as best we could.

After a moment we heard a 'Whoa!' from Mr Carter and the carriage came to a standstill.

'Be calm, Hannah,' Sarah said quietly. 'Remember that everything depends on us being who our

Certificates say we are.'

I nodded but could not reply, for my throat felt tight and constricted. I put out a finger and stroked little Grace's cheek, praying that things would go well.

Mr Carter was hailed by a rough-sounding voice and someone asked his business. In reply, we heard him explain that he was taking a lady of high breeding to stay with her sister in the country. 'As she has a new-born infant, I wish to make good time and proceed with speed,' he finished.

The curtain was then pulled aside and a dishevelled, bearded fellow looked in on us. He carried a blunderbuss in his hand and did not look as if he'd hesitate to use it.

'Your name?' he asked bluntly.

'I am Mistress Beauchurch,' Sarah replied haughtily. 'My infant daughter is Grace Beauchurch and my maid here is Abigail Palmer.'

'Your certificates to travel?' the fellow asked, and Sarah drew our passes from the canvas bag and handed them over.

'Is there not one for the child?'

Sarah shook her head. 'She is but newly-born. We were told she wouldn't require one.'

His brawny hand plucked at the covering which held Grace and as he looked at her, frowning, I was thankful that Grace was small for her weeks, and that the fellow apparently did not know what size a new-born child should have been.

Losing interest in Grace, he held our certificates up to the light. 'There have been forgeries.'

'Those are no forgeries,' Sarah said with spirit. 'Sir John signed these himself in my presence.'

The fellow spat on them, then rubbed at the ink signature with a grimy finger until it smudged. He thrust them back at Sarah, looking her up and down searchingly.

'And you are Mistress Beauchurch, are you?'

'I am,' Sarah's voice rang out like a true aristocrat and I looked at her admiringly.

'First lady I've seen with rough hands,' the man said. 'Looks more like you've been in charge of the washhouse.'

Sarah looked at him witheringly. 'My good man,' she said, 'the plague is rife and most of my servants are fled. A lady must learn to fend for herself – and besides, I do not trust anyone except myself to wash and tend to my precious child's needs.'

The man gave a bitter laugh. 'Oh, 'tis right, the plague is a great leveller. Even a great lady has to stoop to the washtub nowadays.' He still did not move out of the roadway, but stood there looking at us through narrowed eyes. I felt a cold trickle of sweat begin its journey down my back and was mighty scared.

He brought his face to the carriage window. 'Would you risk anything to get out of London?' he asked.

'I don't . . . I don't know what you mean,' Sarah said.

'What is it worth to you, lady?'

Sarah quivered. 'How dare you!' she said. 'I should have you birched for such impudence.'

'Call the other guard, then, if you've a mind to,' the fellow said easily. 'He'd be interested to see someone like you – someone who is only play-acting a fine lady. There are strict laws against what you're doing.'

Sarah was transfixed and I could not contain a gasp of horror. Did he actually know something, or was he just trying his luck?

'Although, if you were to grease my palm a little—'

'Wh . . . what?' Sarah faltered.

'He wants money!' Mr Carter barked from above. 'Give him what you have and let's be on our way.'

Sarah started, then rummaged in the canvas holdall for the little bag of gold coins we'd been given. Taking out three of these, she thrust them at the fellow.

He looked at the coins, then at us. He seemed astounded, but still he did not move. Panicking now, not really knowing whether what had been given was enough, I snatched the bag from Sarah and pushed another two gold angels into his palm.

'Drive on!' I called to Mr Carter, and as he whipped up the horses the fellow staggered back, staring at the coins he held as if they were stars fallen from the skies.

'We gave him far too much!' Sarah said as we galloped across London Bridge.

'Never mind!' I said. 'We're on our way.'

Leaning forward slightly, I pulled back the curtains a little so I could see out. We had crossed the bridge now – that same London Bridge I had approached with such anticipation and excitement only a few months before. The traitors' heads were still there on their spikes over the gateway, but I also saw the desolate sight of a newly-hung corpse, a man who – no doubt having contracted the sickness and despairing – had made away with himself.

How green I'd been when I'd arrived. I knew now that it was not only cut-throats and villains that one should be wary of in London, but something far more deadly, something unseen and altogether more terrible.

I looked down at the face of little Grace and breathed out a sigh. She must live on, for her survival was all I could do for Abby.

Abby. My friend. I would think about her later, and would earnestly try to think of the sunny, joyful girl who'd been my sweet companion, and not the pitiful wraith I'd last seen at the window.

I leaned against Sarah for comfort and her head inclined towards mine. We were well on the road now, and I felt we would reach Dorchester and survive, for we had not come this far to be overtaken by man or plague. London would survive, too, and I would return to it, and to Tom, and I knew I would not die unkissed.

Petals in the Ashes

Chapter One

The Journey

'A saddler who had buried all his children dead of the Plague, did desire only to save the life of his remaining little chil', *and so prevailed to have it received stark naked into the arms of a friend.'*

'Rouse yourself, Hannah,' Sarah said, shaking my shoulder a little. 'Tie your hair back . . . and can you not splash your face with water from the flask? We don't want to arrive at Milady's house looking like frowsy kitchen wenches.'

With a big effort I opened my eyes and looked at my sister, who was sitting on the opposite side of the carriage from me and holding the babe, Grace, asleep in her arms. I yawned hugely.

'And put your hand to your mouth when you yawn,' Sarah said, 'or Lady Jane will think we've no manners at all.'

But I just yawned again and closed my eyes, for the effort of trying to keep them open was too much. After nearly three days on the road and two nights at wayside inns, with Grace hungry most of the time and squealing like a piglet, neither the constant jolting, the clatter of hard wheels on rough road nor the continuous thud of horses' hooves could stop me from sleeping.

Dimly, as if from far off, I heard Sarah address Mr Carter, our driver. 'Is it much further now to Dorchester?' she called, but I could not hear his reply over the drumming and the rattling and the clanging.

London seemed further away than just three days' travel. Already everything was so different. When I peered out of the curtains of our carriage there were no corpses slumped in the streets, no crosses on doors, no screams of those enclosed within foetid houses and no death carts conveying raddled bodies to the plague pits. There were just fields and farm animals and the occasional village, and the endless dusty road which threatened to jolt us to bits before we ever arrived at our destination. Our lives in London, threatened by the monstrous plague which had stalked and caused the deaths of our friends and neighbours, seemed a great way off, as if it had all happened in another existence.

My dear friend in London, Abby, had been nursemaid in one of the houses of the nobility. When this house had fallen to plague and been shut up for forty days, one by one those within had succumbed to the sickness and died. Towards the end, only Abby – and Grace, the babe in her charge – had remained alive in there. When Abby, too, had contracted plague, the babe had been entrusted to our care. My sister Sarah and I had stolen her away from the house and, using the Health Certificates meant for Abby and her mistress, Mrs Beauchurch, were taking Grace to her aunt, her mother's sister, Lady Jane Cartmel in Dorchester.

I must have fallen asleep, because the next thing I knew Sarah was shaking my arm. 'Were you having a bad dream?' she asked. 'You were murmuring to yourself and twisting in your seat.'

I raised my head from where it had lolled forward and shivered. I *had* been dreaming and it had not been pleasant, for Abby had been standing before me as I'd last seen her, her body ravaged by plague sores, holding out little Grace for me to take. I had not seemed able to hold the babe, though, for as I had reached for her she had become small and slight, like a changeling child, and had slipped through my fingers and floated away on the air, and Abby and I had watched her glide past us and wept together.

'I dreamed of Abby,' I said to Sarah, my eyes filling with tears. 'And of Grace. I was trying to hold her, but she just floated away.'

Sarah looked at me with some pity. 'We've got Grace safely now,' she said, and gave a wry smile. 'No one who has heard her yells could doubt that.' She leaned across the carriage and stroked my arm. 'And Abby is at peace, with no pain and no plague. Perhaps she's even watching over us to make sure we're taking care of Grace.'

I nodded and sniffed back my tears. 'I'm worried that she may not be getting enough milk,' I said. Although we had obtained flasks of ass's milk, we knew, of course, that this was no substitute for a mother's milk. 'Mayhap there'll be a wet nurse at the big house so she can feed properly.'

'Of course there will,' Sarah said, nodding. 'Lady

Jane will have prepared for our coming. There'll be a proper nurse and a lady's maid and a nursery, and for all we know some little cousins for Grace to play with. The poor lamb needs clothes as well – all she has is that little cloth she's wrapped in.'

When we'd had Grace lowered from the window of her plague-torn house we'd made sure she'd been naked, so she didn't take any plague germs with her. We'd wrapped her in a soft linen sheet we'd brought with us, but we'd been tearing off strips of it for her napkins all along the journey, so that now it was one quarter the size.

'If the journey takes much longer we'll be tearing up our shifts for her,' I said.

Sarah moved on her seat towards me. 'Will you take her for a moment, Hannah, while I adjust my dress? Mr Carter said that we're nearly there and I want to look tidy.'

'Are we really there at last?'

Sarah looked out of the window. 'Almost. He said we'll know we're at our destination when we turn into a park which is planted with all manner of fine and rare trees.'

'And these must be them!' I said, for I could see that around us, on either side of the wide drive and as far as the eye could see, were many shapely and beautiful trees with leaves of gold, lime, emerald, amber and deepest plum.

I took Grace carefully, being sure that the small round head was cupped securely in my hand. She was a pretty babe, with delicate pale skin and thick dark hair, and her eyes were as blue as forget-me-nots. I'd never seen Mrs Beauchurch, her mother, but Abby had said that the babe took after her rather than Mr Beauchurch, whom she'd once described as a red-faced booby with a nose like a tomato. But both of Grace's parents were with God now, I reminded myself, and it was not meet that I should speak ill of the dead. Indeed, if Grace, once grown, should ever ask me what her father was like, I would lie and say that he was the very model of princely good looks with all elegant attributes known to man.

Our destination being close, I began to think about how we would be greeted by Lady Jane. 'Milady will certainly be very pleased to have her infant niece here safely,' I said to Sarah as she rose and, holding on to the carriage straps, tried to smooth the creases out of her gown. 'Do you think she will reward us?'

'Tush!' Sarah said reprovingly. 'We are not doing this for gain. There's enough reward in saving Grace's life and gaining safe passage out of London for ourselves.'

'Yes, but she may reward us as well . . .'

Sarah permitted herself a small smile. 'Yes, she may.'

'I wonder if she will keep us there as companions in the big house with her. Or do you think we will be made to live as servants?'

Sarah shrugged. 'I cannot guess. We don't know her circumstances or whether she has a big family and children of her own – or even what age she is.'

'But I'm sure she will be so grateful to us that she will treat us like family and give us lovely rooms with four-poster beds in her elegant house!'

'When we get there I shall sleep for a week, whatever our rooms are like,' Sarah said, rubbing the back of her neck. 'I swear I am black and blue with being bounced in this box.'

'Abby told me that the house is newly built,' I said, 'and that it has a room just for bathing in, with cold water and hot water coming from a tap in the wall.'

Sarah's eyes grew wide. 'Indeed! I have never heard of such a thing.'

After thinking on this wonder for a moment, my thoughts turned once more to London. And from there, of course, to Tom, my sweetheart. 'But how long do you think we'll have to stay in Dorchester?'

Sarah shrugged. 'Until we get word that London is free from the plague. When we hear that the king and his court have returned, then we'll know it's safe.'

'And then perhaps Milady will give us a grand carriage to travel back in, and we can visit Chertsey on the way and see our family!' I said. But we wouldn't stop there too long, I told myself, for I would be dancing on coals by then to get back to Tom.

'We must pray that Chertsey, and our family, remain safe from plague,' Sarah said, very serious. 'For they do say that what is suffered in London one year spreads out from there the next.'

I fell silent at this, for I could not bear to think of the plague spreading and my family contracting it . . . of my mother, father, brothers or sister being visited. Surely it was enough that around us in London so many had died that their corpses rotted in the streets for want of people to bury them? Hadn't everyone suffered enough?

'Highclear House!' Mr Carter called suddenly, and Sarah and I scrambled to the window to look out and see our new home.

When we saw it we both gasped, for it was very large and immensely grand, with tall white marble columns to each side of the entrance, and steps going upwards to the doors. It had a great gravelled drive which swept across the front of the house with a fountain in its centre, and the water from the fountain rose into the air in a sparkling flume, catching the sunlight and making a rainbow.

I gazed at it in wonder, thinking that I had never seen a house more noble than this in my life before, nor a sight prettier than the rainbow in the fountain.

'I did not realise it would be so grand!' Sarah said, when we had stared and marvelled and found our voices again.

'And we have only the clothes we stand up in!' I wailed, trying to pull back my unruly hair and straighten my cap with my one free hand. 'I didn't even wear my best gown. I should have worn my green taffeta!'

The carriage came to a standstill and, as if knowing she was at her new home, Grace awoke and immediately began struggling to sit up. Anxious to be out of the carriage, I leaned forward to open the door. Sarah, however, motioned to me to sit back.

'Let Mr Carter do it,' she said. 'It's what he's used to.'

And so we waited while Mr Carter climbed down from his high seat and tied up the reins of the horses, then came to open the carriage door for us and lower the steps. Sarah got out first and I handed Grace to her, then I climbed out myself and gazed about me. The house in all its beauty stood before us, backed by more trees and a great park and, far off, what looked like a lake. Lady Jane's husband, I thought, must be monstrous rich.

'What shall we do now?' I whispered to Sarah, taking Grace back from her. 'Go and knock at the door?'

'I don't know,' Sarah answered, looking troubled.

We thanked Mr Carter for his great care in bringing us here, and he bade us farewell and began to lead the horses and carriage across the drive and towards the back of the house. A moment later the great doors opened and a woman dressed in black ran down the steps of the house.

'Mrs Beauchurch!' she called, with something like joy in her voice, and then she reached us and stopped. 'Oh, you are not . . .'

'No. No, indeed,' Sarah said, while I stood awkwardly, not knowing if I should curtsey to this woman, or indeed if she should curtsey to me. Was this a maid – or was it Lady Jane? Indeed, I thought it was not Lady Jane, for this woman was dressed quite modestly in a black moiré of half-mourning, with just one row of pearls around the high, ruffled neckline.

'Is she not with you?' The woman peered into the windows of the carriage as it moved away.

'No, we . . .' Sarah looked at me helplessly, but I did not know what to say, and so pretended to be very much occupied in keeping little Grace quiet. We had not thought of this: that those in Dorchester might not know that their relatives in London had died, and that strangers were bringing Grace to them.

'Mrs Beauchurch is . . . is not with us,' Sarah said hesitantly. She indicated Grace. 'But this is her child.

We have brought her from London.'

Hearing the word 'London', the woman took two steps backwards, and I noticed that she made a little hiccupping noise.

'But we are quite well and healthy!' I added quickly.

'May we speak with Lady Jane?' Sarah asked and, without another word, the woman turned and ran back into the house, leaving us standing outside as if we were peddlers selling ribbons.

For some minutes we just stood there, waiting. Grace began crying fitfully but I walked with her to the fountain to soothe her. She watched the water droplets falling and was amused by them, holding out her hands as if to catch them and making baby noises.

'Hannah!' Sarah called to me suddenly and, when I turned, another woman was coming out of the house with the woman in black.

This, we knew straightaway, must be Lady Jane. Although not tall, she was imposing, with fair hair caught on top of her head and styled into a hundred tiny curls. She was wearing a fashion that I'd seen worn by the quality in London: a cerise flowered silk dress cut low in front, with much gold lacing above the waist, slashed open to show a froth of petticoats. She carried a posy of flowers which she was to sniff throughout the time she spoke to us.

Instinctively, Sarah and I both curtseyed as she reached us.

'Who are you?' she asked sharply.

This was not the welcome we had hoped for, and we hardly knew how to begin our reply.

'Where is my sister? Where is Mrs Beauchurch?' she asked, speaking accusingly, as if she thought we might have stolen her from the carriage and made use of it ourselves.

'Were you not expecting us?' asked Sarah.

'I was expecting my sister,' came the reply. 'I sent Carter with my carriage and he's been waiting some two weeks for her fever to subside so he could bring her out of London.'

'She is . . . ' Sarah began, but I interrupted.

'The letter!' I urged her. 'Give Lady Jane the letter.'

Sarah looked at me, and then she delved into the canvas bag she was carrying. 'This letter,' she said, holding it out, 'is from your sister. You will recognise her hand.'

Lady Jane and the other woman stepped back together. 'I will not touch it!' said Lady Jane. 'Read it to me please, if you are able.'

'I am able,' Sarah said, adding gently, 'and I am very sorry for what you are about to hear.' She then read out the letter, which had been given to me by Abby.

'Dear Hannah,
I beg and beseech you in the name of the Almighty that you take my child, Grace, upon receipt of this letter, and carry her with all speed to my sister the Lady Jane at Highclear House, in Dorchester. My child is lusty and hearty now, but if left in this house of death she will surely perish. There are Certificates of Health for you and your sister, but you must travel under the names of Abigail and myself. A carriage has been procured and will be at the sign of the Eagle and Child in Gracechurch Street each day awaiting your arrival. The driver is

my sister's man and has a Certificate to travel.

On reaching Dorchester, Lady Jane will ensure that you and your sister are well cared for. You will be permitted to stay until the visitation has left London, when you will be given safe passage back.

May the prayers of a mother melt your heart and you find it within yourselves to grant my dying wish and save my child.

By my hand this 30th day of August 1665.
Maria Beauchurch.'

As Sarah reached the end of the letter, Lady Jane's face grew pale and her mouth tightened with distress. She shook her head to and fro several times, but did not speak.

'I am Hannah, and this is my sister, Sarah,' I said into the long silence which followed. 'Abby was Mrs Beauchurch's maid and was also my dear friend. She . . . she died of the plague.'

'As did your sister, shortly after writing this letter,' Sarah said gently. 'And her husband being already dead, we secured the safety of Grace and brought her to you, as she wished.'

Lady Jane's face did not change, but she took several more sniffs of her nosegay.

'Grace would have been alone in the house in London,' I said. 'She would have died.'

'I did not know of this,' Lady Jane said at last. 'I sent a messenger to the house to bring me news, but he did not return.'

'London is devastated by the sickness,' Sarah said. 'People are dropping like leaves from trees.'

'Eight thousand died last week alone,' I said. 'Your

messenger may have caught the sickness too.'

'But little Grace is well and lusty,' Sarah went on, 'although we are woefully inadequate at feeding her and hope to discover that you have a wet nurse here.'

'Wet nurse!' Lady Jane said scornfully. 'How would you expect me to find a wet nurse for a child, however well-born, that is come from a house where plague has taken its mother and father?'

'But Grace is healthy,' Sarah protested. 'As healthy as we are. See!'

She lifted Grace towards Lady Jane, who made agitated movements with her arms and moved away from us. 'No! Get back!'

'We have Certificates signed by the Lord Mayor himself,' I said, and then realised how stupid a statement that was.

'They are not in your names!' said Lady Jane immediately. 'They verify the health of my sister and her maid – and how little they are worth may be judged by the fact that both are now dead!'

'But for pity . . .' I held up Grace for her to see. 'Here is your niece and she is a beautiful child.' My voice shook, for not only did it seem that the lavish welcome I'd been expecting was not going to be forthcoming, but it also looked as though we were going to be turned away. 'Surely you'll let us stay?' I cried.

Lady Jane was silent for some moments, causing me much anxiety, but at last she spoke.

'I will not turn you away entirely. Indeed, it pains me to keep my own flesh and blood from my side, but I have my household here to consider. You must be quarantined until I am sure that you have not brought the sickness with you.'

'But we are well . . .'

'Please consider . . .' Sarah began, but her voice trailed away for, like me, she felt that to protest was useless. Lady Jane would have heard what the conditions in London were like and would know how the plague proliferated – and had I not told her myself of the numbers who'd died in the previous week?

'How could I live with myself if I were responsible for bringing the plague to Dorchester?' Lady Jane asked. 'No, to vouchsafe my family here, the three of you must go into a pestilence house for a period of isolation.'

Sarah gasped. 'Oh, not that!' she cried, and she moved closer and put her arm around me.

I felt tears of fright spring to my eyes. To go through all we had done, only to be sent to one of those beggarly, foul-smelling places where the Angel of Death kept constant watch beside each bed! It would have been better if we'd not journeyed here at all, but had taken our chances in London.

'And what of Mr Carter?' the woman in black asked Lady Jane. She had not spoken in all this time, just made more of the strange hiccupping noises. 'He has been living amongst the sickness in London too. Must he go to the pesthouse?'

'Carter was afflicted in the last outbreak twenty years ago,' Lady Jane said. 'He recovered and will not catch it again.'

'But . . . but where is there such a house?' Sarah asked. 'Where must we go?'

'There is a pestilence house for travellers located on the road into Dorchester,' Lady Jane said. 'You must stay there for forty days – until we are sure that you are not contagious.'

'But we sought to secure the life of Grace by bringing her here – how will she fare in such a place?' I asked. 'We have no milk for her, nor clothes or coverings. All she has is the sheet she lies in.'

'I will have the milch-ass call there, and you may have whatever comforts I can provide,' Lady Jane said. 'After forty days you may return to Highclear House.'

'We might be dead by then!' I said bitterly.

'And how will we get there?' Sarah asked, tears now running down her cheeks. 'Must we walk?'

'No. I shall arrange for Carter to convey you,' Lady Jane said. She turned and spoke some words to the other woman, who hurried off towards the stables. 'But now will you show me the babe once more?' she asked.

I felt like refusing, but did not dare. I held Grace out towards her, loosening the sheet so that Lady Jane could see her healthy complexion and strong limbs.

'She is very like my dear sister,' was all she said, and then she turned and began to walk back towards the house.

'Not a word of thanks,' Sarah said as we watched her go inside.

'And sent to the pesthouse for our reward! Shall we just run away?' I said desperately. 'We could hide in the woods somewhere or make our way into a town. Anything rather than go to a pesthouse!'

Sarah shook her head wearily. 'How could we run away? We have no food nor means of shelter. Where would we go?'

'We have some money . . .'

'But not enough to last. And what of Grace – we couldn't live like animals in the woods with a child of such a tender age. Besides,' she added, 'I am so weary that I could not run anywhere.'

'So you mean for us to go to the pesthouse and live among the beggars?'

'I fear we have no choice,' she said. 'We must make the best of it.'

Chapter Two

The Pesthouse

'This month is the first decrease we have yet had in the Sickness since it began, and great hopes that the next month it will be greater.'

Upon the door of the pesthouse being opened, the first thing which arrested our senses was the stench which derived from it, as thick and foul as the miasma which had hung over London. It told of filth and rotting food and excrement and uncleansed bodies and was enough to turn the strongest stomach. Sarah and I both gagged and would have backed out again, but the parish officer, in whose charge we had been put, was close behind us.

As our eyes grew accustomed to the dim light inside, we looked about us, quaking with fear. Sarah had Grace in one arm and she and I linked hands and held on to each other like lifelines.

After the smell, the next most apparent things were the gloom – for it seemed as dark as a burying vault – and then the decay. No covering or cloth hanging relieved the rough walls or cobweb-encrusted beams, and the windows were high and narrow, with no glass in them. The floors were of trodden earth and littered with all manner of disgraceful objects: old, stained plaisters and blood-soaked bandages, full chamber pots, tattered cloths and rags, and what looked to me like the detritus and waste left behind by a dozen different plagues. Amidst this filth stood perhaps eight beds, some five supplied with a patient, either sitting or lying down, and covered with a grimy sheet or rough blanket.

'It is . . . foul,' Sarah said faintly, and she loosened her hand from my grip and pressed a white holland kerchief to her mouth to breathe through. She turned to the parish officer, Mr Beade, a rank and ratty-faced man with a good many pox scars. 'My sister and I are gentle born,' she said in a low voice. 'Is there not another place we may lie?'

I indicated Grace. 'This child is Lady Jane's niece,' I said. 'It is surely not right that she should be in such a place.'

'But Lady Jane herself has sent you,' he said, looking astonished that anyone should question the desirability of living there, 'and she will pay me for accommodating you and letting you wait out your quarantine. Come,' he went on, 'the time will go quickly, and with God's grace you will be out of here as healthy as you came in.'

Sarah and I exchanged despairing glances.

'And such pretty wenches – and you with your flaming locks!' he said, sliding his eyes to me. 'Two such frisky creatures will gladden the hearts of some of our poor patients!'

I gave him a hard stare at this, for I had no

intention of being a form of entertainment for the other inmates. 'May my sister and I at least stay close to each other?' I asked.

Sarah nodded. 'And, as we have a young child, may we have a corner or recess where we can attend to her needs and not disturb those who suffer here?'

Mr Beade – who was as ill-smelling as his pesthouse – looked doubtful.

'We are not seeking special treatment,' I said. 'We are thinking of the comfort of your patients as much as ourselves. The babe wakes frequently for milk and cries as often as any other infant.'

After much deliberation, and after dragging a poor person who looked half-dead from their mattress and moving them elsewhere, Mr Beade found a bed in the corner for Sarah, with my bed at an angle from this, thus enclosing Grace within the small square made by our two bedsteads. For her (no doubt wanting to secure the good opinion of Lady Jane), he procured an empty drawer from the adjoining almshouse where he lived, saying we could fill it with whatever material we wished and it would make a fine cradle.

Sarah looked around at the patients. 'Do any here have the plague?' she asked him in a low voice.

He shook his head. 'No, indeed!' he said. 'No one has the plague here. There is no plague in Dorchester.'

She pointed around us. 'Then what . . .?'

'Two have the spotted fever,' he said, 'one the bloody flux and one suffers the sweating sickness. One other is come back from London to Dorchester, which is their home town, and must sit out forty days, as you do.' Saying that, he went off about his duties, which seemed mostly to consist of chivying people to bestir themselves and not lie around succumbing to whatever ailed them.

'It is certain that at least one of them will have plague, whatever he says,' Sarah warned me as he left us. 'We must keep apart from those abed as much as we can.'

'Of course,' I said. I surveyed the grim scene before me and then sat down on the bed which had been allotted to me, for I suddenly felt very weary and tearful and wanted nothing more than to lie and weep a while.

Sarah immediately hauled me to my feet. 'The person who was lying on this bed before you looked like to die at any time!' she scolded me. 'We must gather some fresh straw to stuff our mattresses before we lie on them.'

I sighed, for I felt so careworn that right then I did not give a jot what infections I caught. I felt, too, that niceties such as fresh straw were useless, for I knew already that the plague respected neither person nor precaution, and would touch or leave whomever it pleased at its whim. However, on Sarah's insistence, we took our mattresses outside and emptied their contents on to a pile of refuse just by the door, which stank very badly and was buzzing with all manner of flies. The soiled covers we could do nothing about, but we shook them in the air and then filled them with dried grasses and heather (for the pesthouse was built on a common and there was much of this type of material around) before taking them back inside.

By the time we'd finished these tasks, Grace was crying fit to raise the Devil and this led us to a new dilemma, for the flask of milk we'd obtained from the inn where we'd stayed the previous night was now empty. On applying to Mr Beade, however, and emphasising to him how important it was that Lady Jane's niece should thrive, he sent his wife to a house on the other side of the common and, quite soon (while Sarah and I took it in turns to try and pacify Grace by walking round and round outside the pesthouse with her), a young girl came up leading an ass, which she proceeded to milk into an enamel jug.

Thus provided, we fed Grace using the same method that Abby had employed – trickling the milk down our fingers and letting it drop into her mouth – and left the rest of the milk, covered, in a shady place for later. We then took Grace inside and changed her undercloth, using another strip of the sheet, and made her as comfortable as possible on a nest made of hay in the drawer. As we were monstrous hungry ourselves by this time (for we'd not eaten since breaking our fast at the inn that morning) I went to find Mr Beade to ask how we got on for food, and what time it would be supplied.

The man fell to laughing in an uncivil way. ''Tis not a tavern!' he said. 'Do you think then to order yourself a dish of roasted pigeons or some grouse soup?'

'But how do we eat?' I asked him.

'My patients have food sent in by kindly neighbours living hereabouts,' he said. 'I'm sure Lady Jane will have something sent over in good time. In the meantime you may help yourselves to the leavings of what's already been provided.'

I went to tell Sarah this, and she pointed to a sturdy deal table at one end of the room. 'I think there are some scraps there,' she said. 'See what's left for us.'

I went to look and, shuddering, reported to Sarah that there was a small piece of green cheese, two hunks of hard bread and some dried-up cooked potatoes.

Sarah looked at me ruefully.

'But we cannot eat any of that!' I said, looking over to the table in disgust. 'We will starve.'

'No, indeed we will not,' Sarah said. 'We have two gold coins left, and if no food arrives from Lady Jane, we will ask Mr Beade to purchase food for us.'

'But what about today . . .'

'Today we will have to eat the potatoes and the bread,' Sarah said. 'It is not what we're used to but it will not harm us.'

I shuddered again.

'We must keep our strength up and our hopes,' she went on. She sat down on the bed and took my hands in hers. 'For didn't your sweetheart tell us that a merry heart does good like a medicine?'

I could not but smile at this, for it warmed me to hear Tom referred to as my sweetheart again and to remember what his master, the apothecary Doctor da Silva, had told him at the height of the plague.

We did not have to force down the stale bread, however, for as I turned to go back to the table and select the least objectionable items, a woman's voice called, 'Young ladies! I have a nicer loaf and would be glad to share it with you.'

This call, I was relieved to see, did not come from one of the half-dead who were lying prone, but from a woman who had just entered the pesthouse. She came over holding a loaf wrapped in a cloth, and I glanced over at Sarah, for I didn't know if I should accept it or not. The woman pressed it into my hands before I could decline, however. 'My family are nearby and keep me well supplied with food while I am here,' she said in a soft country voice. 'I can easily spare you this.'

I think Sarah might have wanted to keep both the woman and her bread at some distance, but it did not seem kindly to do this (and besides, I was very hungry), so, thanking her heartily, I bade her sit down beside us.

Our benefactor was a woman of perhaps thirty, with a round, honest face and a bird's nest of hair on which a battered white cap was perched. She was rather grubby and her apron was stained, but this was not surprising, for I did not anywhere see a wash bowl or any water where she could have cleaned herself.

'I'm Martha Padget,' she said, 'and I came from London some three weeks ago.'

I told her our names and said that we had just arrived from London that day. 'And the babe here is named Grace,' I said.

'She is your child?' Martha asked Sarah with some curiosity.

'No, indeed not!' Sarah said hastily. 'She is an orphan and the niece of Lady Jane Cartmel, who lives nearby.'

'Lady Jane!' Martha said, her eyes round.

'You know of her?'

'Of course,' Martha said. 'She is a great lady and known to everyone in Dorchester.'

'She may be a great lady,' I said bitterly, 'but she made us come to *this* foul and stinking place!'

'Hush!' Sarah said to me, and then added to Martha, 'We thought to be staying with Lady Jane – and indeed we might in the future, but first we have to live out forty days here.'

'As I do,' Martha said. She sighed. 'But tell me, does the plague rage in London as fiercely?'

'Ever worse,' Sarah nodded. 'The death cart is never absent from the streets.'

Martha shook her head. 'I fear London may become completely abandoned. All in my house perished: master, mistress, children and servants too. I was the cook – and thanks be to God that I was spared! I obtained a Certificate of Health and travelled back to Dorchester, for this is my home town and where my sister lives.'

'And how do you fare here in the pesthouse?' I asked.

She gave a shudder. 'I speak to no one, eat nothing that my sister does not provide and keep apart from those who have any fever. I have nineteen days to go before I can be released.' Grace murmured in her sleep and Martha got up to look at her, smiling kindly on her repose as people do with a babe. 'But what of you?' she asked.

I hesitated and Sarah gave me a warning look, but of course I would not say that we had travelled on false Certificates. 'When Grace's mother died, my friend Abby had care of the babe,' I said, 'but then she . . . she too was taken ill of the sickness, and she bade us take Grace away. We obtained Health Certificates, had a carriage to convey us, and arrived at Highclear House just this morning.'

'Were you in service in London?' Martha asked.

Sarah shook her head. 'We have a sweetmeat shop at the sign of the Sugared Plum in Crown and King Place.'

'We sell frosted rose petals and sugared fruits.' I looked around. 'It is different indeed from this frowsy place!' All the time I'd been speaking I had, unthinkingly, been breaking the soft bread between my fingers and putting small chunks in my mouth. Normally I would not have dreamed of eating bread without a preserve on it, or at least dipping it in sugar water, but being starving I found I did not miss these garnishings at all. Indeed, I think I might have eaten the whole of it, but I suddenly remembered Sarah and, with an apology, hastily passed her the rest.

Sarah, after thanking Martha for her kindness in supplying us with the bread, asked in a low voice if anyone in the pesthouse had died in the time she had been living here.

'Two,' Martha said. 'A week apart. And it was the plague that took them, for sure. I know the signs as well as anyone who has been in London. An old crone came in, however, one who had been employed as a searcher of the dead, and gave out that the first had died of French pox and the second of the bloody flux.'

'Why was this?' Sarah asked.

'Because Mr Beade would not have it any other way,' Martha said, after looking over her shoulder to make sure that he was not nearby. 'He is employed to keep the plague out of Dorchester, and that is what he does. He keeps out the plague by not allowing any mention of it.'

'So – forgive me – but why have you not caught it?' Sarah asked.

Martha shrugged. 'Why not indeed? I spend most of my days out of doors – but if I knew why some catch plague and some do not I would bottle it and make myself a fortune!'

'We try to chew a sprig of rosemary every day – and we each have a talisman in our pockets and took a cordial when we were in London,' I said, 'but which of these helped us we don't know.'

While we were speaking we became aware that Mr Beade was outside, speaking to someone and employing a good deal of bluster and affability. A bit after this he called to me and Sarah, saying that a small crate had arrived for us from Lady Jane, with a message that the rest of the pesthouse was to benefit from anything that we didn't require.

In some excitement, Sarah and I took in the crate and, lifting the lid, discovered some linen sheets, patched but very clean and soft, a quilt, some gloves, three dresses (which were rather out of fashion but, judging by the quality of the lace, her Ladyship's own) and several cotton smocks and petticoats, as well as face cloths, a towel and a small bar of soap. Grace was supplied with some two dozen napkins, a quantity of smocked and tucked gowns, two loosely-knitted shawls and some pretty bonnets with ribbons. As well as these things, there was a basket containing two fresh loaves of bread, some wine, a whole round cheese and some fruit: one orange and a great many apples and plums.

The note with the crate said:

Mistress Hannah and Mistress Sarah. Lady Jane has bade me send you these items which she hopes will

go some way towards making your stay at the pesthouse a less irksome one. I will ensure you receive adequate amounts of food, and please apply to me at any time if I may supply further items for your needs, and be assured that I am your diligent and faithful servant,
R. Black,
Housekeeper to Lady Jane Cartmel

Even the fact that we had heard Mr Beade exclaiming over the crate a while before and were certain that he had already helped himself to a few items, did not detract from our pleasure. We immediately set to changing into the clean undersmocks and dresses (for we had travelled four days in the same things) and asked Mr Beade for a washing bowl, that we might wash both ourselves and our undergarments. Before we did these things, we pinned up one of the sheets across the end of Sarah's bed so none could see us undressing. We must preserve our modesty, Sarah said, adding, 'Although the rest of the inmates look half dead, you cannot be too sure.'

Although the ordeal to be endured in the pesthouse still seemed very wearisome, we felt a deal better after the supply of these items and the knowledge that we would receive regular food. We knew our friendship with Martha would help, too, for she was a good source of information both on pesthouse conduct and on Mr Beade.

Over the next few days, with our new friend's help, we began to clean up the ill-smelling place. Already there was a nurse of a kind who called daily to see how the bedridden fared, but now we asked that a maid be sent in to keep the floor swept clean, and also to wash the mattress covers and change their contents regularly so that the air would smell sweeter. We had the pile of refuse moved from outside the front door to a good way off, strewed herbs on the floor and indeed employed most of the methods that had been decreed in London to prevent the plague from spreading. We asked that, unless a person was on the verge of death, everyone should go outside and use the privy for their business, for it was not at all decent that chamberpots be used and left under the beds for days on end, especially as the weather continued very warm.

The weather, indeed, was a blessing to us, for if it had rained we would have been forced to stay inside the pesthouse amid the foul vapours and humours. As it was, though, we spent a good deal of our time in the walled garden which surrounded it, separating it from the hamlet beyond. We asked for paper and pencils to be sent and amused ourselves by gathering herbs and any flowers we could find and pressing and naming them, and also taught Martha the basics of the alphabet and how to form her name, for she had never been to school.

We kept Grace outside as much as possible, and she thrived on country air and grew plump on fresh ass's milk, especially when a bone feeding-cup with spout arrived in one of the regular deliveries from Highclear House. This enabled her to drink more milk and at her own pace, for she quickly learned to gulp from it and bang it on the floor when she wanted it refilled. Sarah had more patience with Grace than I and spent longer in her company for, although I loved her dearly, to tell the truth I had seen rather too much of my three little brothers mewling and puking to have any great affection for infants. One of the inmates of the pesthouse carved a little wooden poppet for her, and Sarah and I made dresses and bonnets for it from scraps of sheeting (although Grace, who was teething, ignored these coverings and just gnawed at the dolly's head).

Some two weeks or so after we'd arrived in the pesthouse, Martha was seen by a doctor from Dorchester, pronounced fit, and allowed to go on her way. We knew we would miss her very much, but we promised that we would see each other again – and indeed she said she could not wait to visit us in Highclear House.

One person died over the next week (it was given out that he'd died of spotted fever) and two more people were admitted for quarantine: an old man and his son. They too had come from London and brought the welcome news that at last there had been a downturn in the numbers dying from plague. From a tragic high of ten thousand deaths in one week, the numbers had gradually fallen. The first week in October showed three thousand, with further falls expected.

'We must write to our family,' Sarah said, on learning this news. 'Now the numbers of dead are decreasing, they may allow a letter through.'

I nodded. 'Besides, we are not writing from London, but from Dorchester, and that will make a difference.'

We deliberated a good while on what to say about

the death of Abby, for Abby's mother, a widow, lived just a short distance from our house in Chertsey and would not yet have heard of it. We did not know if we should put our own mother in the difficult position of passing on the news.

In the end we decided we would not mention it, for neither our mother nor father could read well, and it would have been too difficult to explain the circumstances of Abby's death and to say how we had taken over the care of little Grace and brought her to Lady Jane. Accordingly, we just wrote the following:

> *Dearest Mother and Father,*
> *We trust that you remain in good health as we do, thanks be to God. You will have no doubt heard of the unhappy conditions in London at present and we write to tell you that due to certain circumstances we are at present staying in Dorchester. On our journey back to London we shall be sure to visit you, and in the meantime send love to John, George, Adam and Anne, and remain your loving daughters, Sarah and Hannah*

Folding the parchment and sealing it with wax supplied by Mr Beade, we sent it care of the Reverend Davies at our parish church in Chertsey, trusting that he would pay the necessary small sum to take delivery of it and pass it to whichever member of our family came to church the following Sunday.

'Imagine the excitement when it is received!' Sarah said fondly.

I nodded. 'Anne will carry it back home to Mother . . .'

Sarah laughed. 'And John and George and little Adam will fight to see it first . . . and they will try to read the words . . . and Mother will show them their own names at the end.'

'And then the boys will practise their writing by making a fair copy underneath!'

We were silent for a good while after this, and I felt very low and as if I could weep. Though it was only five months since I'd seen my family, a great deal had happened to me in that time, and I wished most desperately to be back safely in our little thatched cottage in Chertsey with them all.

When our forty days had elapsed, Mr Beade applied for the local doctor to call and examine us. He did so and pronounced the three of us fit and healthy. He must have then supplied the same information to Highclear House, for that afternoon the coach which had conveyed us from London to Dorchester called at the pesthouse and Mr Carter, bowing, requested that we collect up our belongings, as Lady Jane wished to receive us.

Immediately, very excited, we dressed Grace in her best dress and bonnet, attended to our hair and gowns and made ourselves ready for the short journey. Mr Beade, whose person who had not been part of the pesthouse improvements and who still stunk worse than a polecat, ran beside the carriage for some distance, seemingly sorry to see us go.

'Don't forget, ladies, to tell Lady Jane how I have nurtured and taken especial good care of you!' was his last cry to us.

Chapter Three

Highclear House

'Called at my booksellers for a book writ about twenty years ago in prophecy of this year coming on, 1666, explaining it to be the Mark of the Beast.'

The contrast between Highclear House and the pesthouse could not have been more marked. We had first seen Highclear in the sunlight so that the marble columns gleamed and the windows glittered silver, and though when we returned it was raining, with storm clouds above as thick as pease pudding, the sight of it was still enough to make you catch your breath. It was imposing and stately, with something of the grandness of the Royal Exchange about it, and looked far too splendid to be a house built merely for people to live in.

Mr Carter drove us around to the back, past a chapel, brewhouse, laundry, stables, and coach houses. There seemed enough of these buildings to form a small village, and this impression was strengthened by the large number of people we saw going about their duties: clerks, maids, grooms, valets

– even two reverend gentlemen.

The carriage stopped in a paved courtyard and, alighting, we entered the house through a heavy oak door and went down steps into the kitchen. This was a room as big as an alehouse, its walls lined with pot cupboards and shelves. Along one wall was a vast black-leaded cooking range, and above this were two complete rows of shining copper pots, pans and moulds. There were several deep pewter sinks and two fireplaces, each holding a roasting animal turning on a spit, and the bright flames of the fires reflected off the lines of copper pans, making the whole room cheerful. Indeed it looked so warm and welcoming that for some moments we just stood there staring about us, for it was such a contrast to the dark and dirty aspect of the pesthouse where, in spite of all our efforts, rats scuttled across the floor at night and lice and fleas bit us into wakefulness, that I felt I could scarce look at it enough.

Grace, secure in my arms, was silent and wide-eyed too, and the several women in white aprons who were busying themselves about the room smiled at her – and us – in a friendly manner. We were both astonished and delighted to see that one of these women was our friend Martha from the pesthouse: Martha in a long white apron, her unruly hair pushed up and almost hidden under a new starched cap.

'I've been waiting for you!' she said, coming up and kissing us in turn. 'Mrs Black told Cook that you would be arriving here one day this week.'

'But what are you doing here?' I asked, very surprised.

'Well, my sister has a new husband and I could not

abide him,' she said. 'I heard that her Ladyship wanted a cook-maid and so I applied, knowing that you would be coming here soon.'

She stroked Grace's cheek and the babe, recognising her, began to babble at her in nonsense baby-talk. Meanwhile, I still stared around the room in awe, for here was a grand home, a stately home, such as I'd never entered before. Through a doorway I could see into a still room, where thick bunches of dried flowers and herbs were hanging, and another doorway led into a buttery, with vats of cream and butter standing by to set. I wondered about the rest of the house and concluded that if I was in such great awe at the kitchen, I might possibly be struck dumb by all the rest of it.

'What are we to do here – do you know?' I asked Martha, for Sarah and I had often talked about how we might be received by Lady Jane and what she would do with us.

'What will be our status?' Sarah added.

Martha shook her head. 'I have no idea,' she said, 'for though we maids keep our ears pricked for gossip, we rarely hear anything of merit. The undercook is above me, and the cook is above her, and the housekeeper is above us all. I have never even seen Lady Jane! I do know that Lord Cartmel is something to do with Parliament, but he's away in Oxford where they're sitting.'

'Why sitting in Oxford?' Sarah asked.

'Because of the plague still being in London,' Martha replied, dropping her voice on the dread word.

'But we did hear that the numbers of dead were

falling,' I said.

Martha nodded. 'They say there's an improvement now the cooler weather is come. Thanks be to God,' she added.

Grace made a grab for Martha's cap and pulled it sideways and I moved her on to my other hip and so away from temptation. 'Is this a good house to work in?' I asked.

'It is,' Martha assured us, 'for although Mrs Black is strict, she's fair. And it's most beneficial to the staff that the poor lady suffers permanently from—'

But she did not continue, for just then there was a strange little noise from the doorway and a moment later the woman in black we had first spoken to some forty days before appeared. This was, in fact, Mrs Black (which name I thought most appropriate for someone wearing such sombre clothing), housekeeper to Lady Jane. As such, she supervised all the female staff: cooks, maids, governesses, needlewomen and launderesses.

Another moment and we were to find out what Martha had been about to tell us of Mrs Black, for as she came towards us she hiccupped twice, tiny movements which jerked her head back and caused a little inward breath. I felt a laugh rising inside me but managed to keep it down, for Mrs Black was holding out her arms for Grace.

'At last! You are welcome to Highclear House,' she said, adding, 'and indeed the little one is more than welcome.'

Sarah and I both bobbed curtsies – I as well as I could, for Grace was plump and heavy now. Mrs Black took her from me and I think Grace might have cried at being handled by a stranger, indeed she opened her mouth to start, but Mrs Black gave two more hiccups and Grace forgot to bawl, looking at Mrs Black with such an astonished expression that again I felt I wanted to laugh.

'You are to come upstairs now and speak to Lady Jane,' Mrs Black said, 'and be sure to say how very grateful you are for her kindness in receiving you here.'

Sarah and I exchanged brief glances and, as Mrs Black led the way through the kitchen, I said to her in a whisper that it should be the other way round: *she* should be grateful to *us* for rescuing Grace. Sarah shook her head at me to be quiet.

Mrs Black, hiccupping gently, led us down a long corridor, and through doors, and up and down short flights of stairs, and then said we were entering the part of the house where Lady Jane and her family lived.

Going through a door into this part of the house, the difference was apparent immediately. One moment we were in a narrow, dark stairwell without a rug under our feet, the next we had entered another world where the air was heady with the scent of pot pourri, and where we trod on thick, soft carpets and looked up to walls hung so generously with portraits, mirrors and tapestries that the wallpaper behind could scarce be seen.

'You will never be in this front part of the house again, except by invitation,' Mrs Black said, 'for the house has been designed so that the staff and the family lead completely separate lives. The servants here have their own staircases and corridors and are not seen by the family.'

Sarah and I both looked surprised at this, for we had never heard of such an arrangement before.

'It is so that the gentry walking up the main stairs in the morning do not see last night's chamber pots coming down to meet them,' Mrs Black said.

'And is there really a room for bathing,' I asked, 'in which the hot water comes out of a tap in the wall?'

'There is,' she said, 'but it means two maids working four hours each to fill the tank with hot water, so it has been used once only, and that after my Lady's last confinement.'

We paused outside a door gilded all over with carvings and Mrs Black shifted Grace into a more comfortable position and rubbed a smudge from her plump cheek, then looked at me and Sarah critically. 'Can you not calm your hair a little more?' she asked me. ''Tis all over the place like a storm.'

I adjusted my cap. 'It is tied at the back,' I said, turning slightly to show her. 'I fear it has a mind of its own, though.'

'And such a colour,' Mrs Black murmured. 'Do you not find it over-bright?'

I did, of course, and had tried many times to subdue its redness, but since finding out that Nelly Gwyn had hair of the exact same colour and type, I had begun to bear it a little better. Hearing someone criticise it now just caused me to run my fingers through my curls so that they stuck out further.

'Hannah's hair is much admired,' Sarah put in, hiding a smile. 'All the gallants comment on it.'

'There are no gallants here,' said Mrs Black dryly. She gave us a final look-over and brushed a leaf from

Sarah's skirt, then tapped at the door gently and ushered us into the room.

I just managed to stop myself gasping at the sight before me, and indeed I could not describe it in any detail, but knew that there were vast purple velvet drapes and many mirrors hung with crystal droplets and studded with candles (for the day was already dark), and that the whole effect was one of glitter and light and richness. Three golden bird cages hung from the ceiling, each with several brightly-coloured birds within.

In the middle of all this glory sat Lady Jane at cards with three other ladies around a small table. All four had high, glossy wigs and were dressed in the finest silks and satins: Lady Jane was in stiff gold brocade over gold moiré, one of her companions was in brilliant green silk lined with silver and the remaining two ladies were in pink: one deep plum, the other clover. The overall look was as rich and elegant as a painting.

The ladies put down their cards and stared at us, causing Sarah and I to sink unbidden into curtsies as deep as if we were faced with the King of England.

Lady Jane rose from the table and, ignoring us, made straight for Grace and took her from Mrs Black. She snatched her too abruptly, though, for she immediately began to cry.

'Hush, you minx!' Lady Jane said, then made an ineffectual try at pacifying Grace by lifting her into the air and swinging her about.

'She dislikes that!' I blurted out, and would have taken her back again but was somehow stopped by the glances of my sister and Mrs Black.

'Then pray take her, Mrs Black!' Lady Jane said, seeming to lose interest. 'I know you have her nursery all prepared.'

Dropping Grace into Mrs Black's arms, Milady sat down once again at the card table and it seemed that we were dismissed (and had as much value as fleas on a counterpane, I said to Sarah later). But Mrs Black delayed, nodding at us meaningfully.

'Oh! Thank you for your great courtesy in receiving us here in your house,' Sarah said.

Her Ladyship nodded and, as she glanced at me, I asked, 'What are we to do now?'

Mrs Black gave a hiccup and another hard look and I added, 'Your Ladyship. If you please.'

'You will both stay here, of course, until the plague leaves London,' said Lady Jane, picking up her cards and studying them intently. 'And then Carter will take you back there in the carriage.'

'But how will we know when it's all right to return?'

'We have news every week,' Lady Jane said, waving her hand dismissively. 'There are newspapers and letters now coming out of London – we'll know when it's safe.' She turned away from us back to her hand of cards and, as Mrs Black and Sarah were both in the doorway and making big eyes at me, I withdrew.

'Lady Jane must not be troubled by such as yourselves,' Mrs Black chided and hiccupped, once we were outside. 'She has more important matters to think on.'

'So we saw,' I murmured, but Mrs Black did not hear me above Grace's cries.

With Grace still bawling, Mrs Black led us through more corridors to the nursery wing, which she told us was where Lady Jane's children and their staff lived and were schooled. She explained that Grace was to have a room of her own and a nursery maid to tend her, and accordingly we entered a small, whitewashed room and found a young girl of perhaps fourteen blowing on some coals in the grate to try to get them to catch. This was obviously to be Grace's nursery, for as well as a narrow bed there was a stout wooden cradle and a table and chair, and also a wooden rocking horse which looked as if it had been well used by Lady Jane's children, being battered and having most of its mane missing.

The girl jumped to her feet as we appeared and gave a curtsey to each one of us in turn. Not used to being curtseyed to and unsure of what my reaction should be, I returned this compliment, although Sarah frowned at me.

'Anna here will have charge of Grace from now on,' Mrs Black said to us. 'She's a careful girl. Her mother died in childbirth so she's brought up her three little sisters on her own.'

Anna smiled shyly at us and then held out her arms for Grace, who'd gone silent as we'd entered the room but who'd now started crying again. Anna did not seem perturbed at this, though, but settled Grace into the crook of her arm and, with her other hand, popped something into her mouth. Grace immediately began to suck greedily.

''Tis a raisin tied in muslin,' Anna said. 'It always works.'

'Oh! We have left her poppet behind in the pesthouse!' I said, suddenly remembering Grace's dolly.

Mrs Black made a face of displeasure. 'She won't

need any dirty things from that place,' she said. 'She'll have all manner of fine toys and games from now on and will play nicely with her cousins. When she's mastered Dobbin there . . .' she nodded towards the make-believe horse, '. . . she'll learn to ride a real one.'

Although Grace's lips still moved in rhythm as she sucked at the muslin comforter, her eyelids had closed by the time we said our goodbyes. She looked so bonny and pretty as I bent to kiss her that I felt a great ache of sadness, for I had tended her like a mother for six weeks, and she was my last link to Abby. Feeling the tears well up I let out a small sob, which caused Sarah to begin to weep too, so that Mrs Black led us from the nursery in quite a gentle manner, telling us that we could visit Grace whenever we liked.

We were then shown to our room, which was quite plain, with an iron bedstead and several sets of shelves, and told by Mrs Black that as long as we kept to the back part of the house we could come and go from here as we liked. The only time our presence was essential was in the chapel every Lord's Day.

When Mrs Black had left, Sarah and I felt such a sense of relief that our ordeal at the pesthouse was over that we sat down together on our bed and wept, nor hardly stopped for the rest of that afternoon. We were weeping for all the horror we'd left behind in London, and for our friends who were dead, and for the relief in delivering Grace safely. On my part I was also weeping because of Tom, for I had a dreadful fear that I might never see him again.

Our time in Highclear House passed slowly, for we had no regular duties and it seemed that Lady Jane had forgotten about us. As we waited to hear that the plague had left London, weeks turned to months and the weather grew cold and frosty. We had a fireplace in our room and a weekly allowance of coal, and so spent a deal of time there either trying to improve our reading (there was a large library, though with monstrous dull books), embroidering our clothes or learning still-room recipes. Martha was skilled at these and showed us how to make pot pourri, scented washing waters and pomander balls. She also showed me how to make a herbal infusion with rosemary and lad's love to condition my hair and stop it being quite so unruly (although it did not subdue its redness). We occupied ourselves too by playing with Grace, and with the cats and dogs around the house, for in London we had not seen either of these for several months as they'd been put to death in case they spread plague.

We heard that the plague had moved from London to Sherborne, in Dorsetshire, where it was presently rife, and also to Southampton and the Isle of Wight. Mercifully, it continued to abate in London. We heard from *The Newes* (which arrived at Highclear every week and appeared downstairs a few days later), that in December there was a frost in London so hard that the Thames froze over and a Fair was held on it, and that this exceeding brutal weather had caused the numbers dying of plague to fall even more. *The Newes* informed us, however, that the king, the court and most others who'd fled still hesitated to return to the capital, not yet convinced that it was safe.

The regular servants in the house tolerated me and Sarah, although some, I felt, rather resented the fact that we had no real work to do. Their burden of duties was unceasing, and watching them – especially the housemaids – busying themselves from morn until it pleased their betters to let them retire at night, made me vow that I would never go into service.

We helped them occasionally, making sweetmeats and comfits for several of Lady Jane's musical evenings and again when there was a ball to mark his Lordship's return from Oxford. He arrived in a flurry of pomp just before Christmas, bringing a number of personal staff: a valet, butler, groom, footman, gentleman of the wardrobe and bootboy, which swelled the numbers below stairs even more.

The bootboy, I am ashamed to say (for he was a scurrilous little wretch), became somewhat attached to me and would follow me around the gardens when I was looking for feverfew – for this herb had many useful properties – or for herbs which might be turned into comfits, talking all the time and distracting me from whatever task I was set upon. As he listened at doors and was a great gossiper, however, we found out quite a lot of information from him. He told us that there was no plague at all in Oxford, and that the gentry did not spare much time to think of those who suffered in London.

'The only talk in Oxford is of Lady Castlemaine's imminent lying-in,' young Bill told me one morning when I was in the kitchen garden looking for winter-flowering herbs. 'There are those who say that it is not the king's child she bears.'

'Lady Castlemaine is at Oxford with the court?' I asked in surprise, for though we all knew who the king's mistresses were and spent many hours discussing their various merits and who was the most beautiful, I had not realised he took any away with him.

He nodded. 'The king has made Lady Castlemaine a Lady of the Bedchamber to the queen, so now she accompanies them everywhere.'

'The queen is there too?'

'She is – though nobody gives a tuppeny jot for her. It is Lady Castlemaine who has the power.'

'And is she very lovely?'

'I have only seen her at a distance,' Bill said, 'but they say she has fine eyes and a mane of hair that is all her own, and when she is in a room nobody looks at anyone but her.' He came close to me. 'But I daresay you could hold your own against her, Sweeting.' He put a grimy hand on my arm and his nails were so dark with boot-blacking and dirt that I gave a little scream and moved away.

'Tell me more about what it was like at Oxford,' I said hastily, pulling my plaid shawl around me against the wind. 'Do they really not care about those left in London?'

'They say they do,' he said, 'but I say they do not, for they continually hold balls and masques and entertainments. They say it is to keep their minds from the horror of the plague.'

'And do they talk of when they will move back?' I began, but we had heard a hiccup which meant that Mrs Black was close by, and Bill suddenly darted back towards the house, for Mrs Black had a sharp tongue and would not hesitate to report him to his master for slacking. I bent over the ground again, finding some rosemary growing between the cracks of paving and picking it.

'Ah,' Mrs Black said, gliding up to me, 'I was looking for either you or your sister, and Martha said you might be out here.'

'I'm looking for herbs,' I said.

'It was that of which I came to speak to you. Of . . . herbs and simples.'

'I have not much knowledge,' I said hastily, for I knew it did not do to be a woman and confess to understanding of these things, for a neighbour of ours in Chertsey had been bitten by a mad dog and had consulted a local wise woman who'd given him the herb plantain. When he'd later died, she'd been accused of witchcraft.

She hiccupped twice. 'You may have noticed this . . . my affliction.'

I nodded solemnly.

'I would have it treated, but I fear going to a doctor in case he tells me that I have something else. Something worse. Is there anything I can take? Any cordial you can make me for it?'

'I'm not sure,' I said. Sarah and I had written down various recipes and some cures which had been given to us by Doctor da Silva the apothecary, but I wasn't certain if we had anything which would cure hiccups.

'Perhaps you could ask your sister and then let me know,' she said.

I spoke to Sarah later that morning and we came to the conclusion that Mrs Black suffered so because she liked highly-spiced foods, so we looked through our writings and found several herbs which were said to be good for the digestion. All of these, unfortunately, only flowered in summer, but luckily we had preserved a few stalks of hawkweed, a useful herb with several medicinal properties, so we ground up the dry flowers and steeped them into a cordial. After sipping this mixture after meals for only two days, much to our surprise Mrs Black's hiccups ceased. She was so grateful to us that a whole extra pail of coal appeared in our room, and she also gave us five pairs of fine white kid gloves that Lady Jane had discarded.

However, having now lost notice of the housekeeper's imminent arrival anywhere, the other servants were not so grateful.

The Highclear Ball was held on the eve of the New Year: 1666, which was forecast and predicted to be a year of great import because of the triple occurrence of sixes. We discovered this from *Lily's Almanack*, which Cook had purchased, even though she could not understand much of the writing. When it was quiet or Mrs Black was occupied elsewhere, Cook would ask me to read from it so that we could learn what was to happen in the coming year, and also to tell her and the other servants their fortunes according to their astrological signs.

Late on the night of the ball we did this in the kitchen, sitting at the long table while the ball was going on over our heads, for, a great meal having been eaten in the dining hall earlier (and Mrs Black having retired to her own room), the staff were free to make merry. Indeed, some bottles of sack had been given for this purpose, and we had also been supplied with the carcasses of several roast capons, geese and pigeons which had been barely touched by the gentry above, so stuffed were they with the multitude of lavish dishes which had gone before.

I didn't fully understand what I was reading from the *Almanack*, and I didn't believe that many of the servants did either, but the most important prediction was that a momentous change would occur during this year, 1666. 'For in the Book of Revelation it says that 666 is the number of the beast,' I read out.

'Well, whatever does that mean?' Martha asked, and we all shook our heads.

'The beast is capable of bringing fire from heaven and causing the houses of the mighty to fall,' I continued, while everyone made wide eyes at each other, pretending to be affrighted.

The serious manner in which I presented this news to the servants was, however, somewhat spoilt when Bill came up with some mistletoe and, pulling me backwards off the table, tried to kiss me. I, screaming, ran helter-skelter across the kitchen with him in pursuit, locked myself in the dairy and only came out when he promised not to handle me so.

Later we all drank to the coming-in of the year, and Sarah and I hugged each other and said that we were grateful and relieved that the old year was over.

'Whatever happens in this one, it cannot be as cruel as the last,' she said.

I shook my head. 'Indeed it cannot!'

Chapter Four

Chertsey

*'But now the Plague is abated almost to nothing, and
I intending to go to London as fast as I can, my family
having been there these two or three weeks.'*

'Aren't we near yet?' I asked Sarah. 'We *must* be
nearly there now.'

She looked out of the carriage window and into the
sky to judge the position of the sun. 'Mr Carter said
we would arrive near sundown,' she said. 'And we're
a way off that yet.'

I sighed, long and loud. Never had a journey
seemed so wearying. Even travelling from London to
Dorchester seemed nothing to this, for we'd had Grace
with us then and much to do in keeping her fed and
pacified.

'We'll soon be there, Hannah.' Sarah smiled into the
distance. 'And just think how excited the little ones
will be to see us.'

'And Father will grunt a bit and nod and look
pleased!'

'And then Mother, after she's got over her shock,

will cry with happiness that we're home.'

I nodded with satisfaction. All that. All that and more: Mother would have one of the boys catch a chicken and cook it for supper, with a flummery to follow that had been made with cream from our own cows. After we'd eaten we'd all sit down, light the candles and tell our news: Mother and Anne would want to know about the shop, what sweetmeats were most popular and the fashions worn by the quality who came to buy from us, while the boys probably would want to know how many bodies we'd encountered when the plague was at its height, and if we'd seen anyone with the buboes on them. Later, I would be sleeping once again in the bed-chamber where I'd been born, with the damp patch on the wall which was shaped like an oak tree, and Tyb, our big old cat, would sleep on my bed and wake me in the night by leaping around the room trying to catch moths. I was so longing to be there.

Our stay at Highclear House had continued until the numbers dying from plague on the London Bills of Mortality had come right down and it was considered perfectly safe for us to travel. We'd heard at the end of February that the king and his court had returned to Whitehall, but it had taken us some time to arrange our journey, as Lady Jane had by then gone out of England to stay with relations in France. Mrs Black, however (who could not do too much for us since we had cured her of the hiccups), had written to her mistress asking that Carter might take us in the carriage as far as Chertsey. Permission had been granted, and Sarah and I were to stay with our family for a week or two before we made the last stage of the journey to London by whatever means was convenient. We had bid farewell to the Highclear household, but had only been really sorry to leave Grace and our good friend Martha.

I stretched my legs in the cramped carriage, then lifted my skirt to rub at my knees. 'Every part of me has been jolted to bits,' I complained. 'I swear I am black and blue under my shift.'

Having rubbed at my aches, I pulled my skirt down again and patted the pleats carefully into place, for the material was costly and the colour vivid blue and I loved the gown dearly. By and large, Sarah and I had managed to obtain several new outfits during the time we'd been at the house. Lady Jane was generous with her cast-offs and, in addition, a bolt of deep plum linsey-woolsey had arrived from abroad, the colour of which Lady Jane had not liked, so she had passed it to Mrs Black. With her help, and that of the needlewoman at the house, Sarah and I had made skirts and matching jackets of it, which we later embroidered and which looked very fine.

We came to a crossroads and I peered out of the carriage window. There was a set of stocks here, and also a double gallows where the bodies of two highwaymen hung, swaying gently in the wind. This caused to make me think of Gentleman Jack, the highwayman who'd plied his trade around our home town and on the roads into London – a dashing figure always dressed in the finest silks and satins who oft stole a kiss from the ladies when he took their diamond rings. I asked Sarah if she thought he were still on the roads.

'I think not,' she answered. 'I am sure that our neighbour Mr Newbery said to me that he saw Gentleman Jack hung at Tyburn and his head stuck on a pole over London Bridge.'

I was just taking in this news when there was a shout from outside and a yell and swearing from Mr Carter, and one of our horses neighed and reared up, causing the carriage to skew across the road. I screamed, for it seemed obvious to me what had happened. 'It's highwaymen! We're going to be robbed!' I cried to Sarah.

I had no jewellery, but I immediately pushed my small bag under the seat so it was out of view. Our gowns and capes were in a chest on top of the carriage and they would be stolen straightaway, but at least they would not see my bag containing my own special things: brushes, pink kid gloves, a little silver box and two pretty fans.

Sarah, too, pushed her bag out of view, and tucked her only jewellery (a gold neck-chain that our grandmother had given her) into her neckline so that it was hidden.

There was another shout, but we were too frightened to lean out of the window for, apart from Gentleman Jack, most of the highwaymen were violent, lewd fellows who would shoot first and rob second, and think nothing of stripping a lady's dress from her and leave her standing in her shift. Indeed, we had heard of one who had a mind to take a lady's petticoats too and leave her stark naked on the road.

Our carriage came to a halt all of an angle, and Sarah and I clung to each other. We heard Mr Carter shout to someone, employing a good deal of swearing and blaspheming.

'Take heart, my man!' an answering hail came. 'I am not a highwayman. I have merely been assaulted by one.'

'Get out of the way!' Mr Carter swore again and whipped up the horses but (as it turned out) one of our back wheels had gone into a ditch and we did not move an inch.

'I assure you I am speaking the truth!' the man's voice came again. 'I have been abroad and was travelling from Southampton back to my home when I was set upon. My two horses were taken – and my luggage. All I have is what I stand up in.'

'A likely tale!' Mr Carter retorted.

'Indeed not, Sir. I am Giles Copperly and my family lives in Parkshot.'

Sarah's arm gripped mine. 'The *Copperlys* . . .' she said.

I gasped and nodded. Parkshot was a hamlet only a spit away from Chertsey, and we knew of the Copperly family, for they were rich spice merchants and had endowed a stained-glass window at our church.

Sarah put her head out of the carriage window. 'Mr Carter,' she said, 'my sister and I know the Copperly family.'

'Do you indeed?' Mr Carter said stoutly.

'I am sure he . . .' she paused. 'Mr Copperly, what is the name of your father?'

'It is Thomas, Madam,' the answer came.

'That's right.' Sarah opened the carriage door and Giles Copperly strode over. He was about twenty-five and swarthy, with dark eyes and good teeth.

'Your servant, ladies,' he said, bowing very deeply, and I felt that, had he had one, he would have flourished a plumed hat as he made his addresses.

There was a *hurrumph* from Mr Carter. 'If you're sure, Ma'am,' he said.

Sarah nodded her assent to Mr Carter. 'I am Sarah, and this is my sister Hannah,' she said to Giles Copperly. He gave a nod towards me and I smiled and inclined my head slightly, as I had seen the quality do. 'We live at Chertsey and are going home to our family,' Sarah went on. 'We're sorry for your predicament and will be pleased to convey you to Parkshot.'

'Thank the Lord!' said Giles Copperly, and he seized Sarah's hand and kissed it. She looked at him, smiling, and, to my great surprise (for gallants coming into the shop often flirted and it was nothing to us), blushed scarlet.

Mr Carter called for Giles's aid in setting the carriage straight, and (while Sarah, I noticed, was patting her hair and pinching her lips together to make them pink) he helped get it from the ditch and back on to the road. He then joined us for the rest of the journey. While I had hoped for some lively talk – for it turned out that he had just returned from the South Sea Islands – he and Sarah kept most of the conversation between the two of them, and spoke of little but spices and sugars all the way to Parkshot. We left him there, and indeed I was glad to see him go, for I thought him a bore, and we were then driven the short distance home.

We drove through the high street of Chertsey, and – it being rare to see such a beautiful and costly coach-

and-four going through the town – people stopped and stared at us and we, seeing folk we knew, laughed and waved to them. As we drove I was mighty relieved to see that nowhere in the town were there signs of plague: no houses enclosed, no doors with the dread sign on them, and the churchyard stood as tranquil as before, the ground not raised and swollen with bodies as had been the case in London.

Leaning from the coach window, I directed Mr Carter down our lane. Our cottage, cosy and newly thatched with golden straw, stood just beyond the apple orchard, and my brothers were perched on the gate which led into this, playing Jack-come-up and pushing each other from the top bar, as they always did. Suddenly, though, they saw the smart carriage coming towards them and became still as statues, their mouths perfect circles of astonishment.

We just had time to admire our beautiful orchard, alight with white blossom, and the barn where Father worked, which was covered all over with glossy ivy and starry forsythia, before the carriage halted and Mr Carter got down to open the door and lower the carriage steps for us.

Sarah and I exchanged glances and she put her finger against her lips. We lifted our skirts and climbed out in a genteel manner, being sure to keep our faces low so that the boys could not see who we were – but I had reckoned without my hair, and there was no hiding *that*. Before I had even taken a step on to the ground Adam shouted, 'It's Hannah and Sarah!' and all three boys flung themselves on us with squeals and shrieks of laughter. At the noise they made, Anne ran from the cottage, closely followed by Mother, all set to admonish the boys for acting familiarly with two such grand ladies. These two halted on the path and then we had the bigger surprise, for we could see that our mother was expecting a child, and indeed was so very large that it seemed she might produce it at any moment.

She hugged us as close as she was able, and wept, and we wept too, and were glad to be safely home. 'All my children together,' she said, 'gathered in like the harvest.'

Near a week later Sarah and I were ourselves sitting on the orchard gate amid the fast-falling blossom. We had just returned from Abby's cottage, where we'd had to tell her mother how she had died of plague. Although we'd emphasised how brave she'd been, and that it was due to her that the life of little Grace had been saved, it was obvious that Abby's mother would rather have had her own daughter safe and did not care two jots for some other person's child. She had cried, too, because she would have no tranquil churchyard to visit or lay flowers in, Abby's body having gone into a plague pit along with so many others.

'I wish we had taken some memento from Abby,' I said as Sarah and I sat on the gate, talking of what had been said. 'A lock of her hair or some trinket – or at least a word or two from Abby to her mother.'

'There was no time for things like that,' Sarah said. 'We were too anxious to snatch Grace and get away. But mayhap we should have made up some last words to be of comfort to her mother.'

I sighed and nodded, for it had been a difficult and

awkward visit and we'd been only too anxious to leave the poor woman and come home. After some moments I tried to put this sad matter out of my head, however, and looked at Sarah to try to judge her mood, for she'd been acting rather oddly the last day or so. 'When do you think we'll return to London?' I asked.

'You seem in a great hurry.'

I shrugged. 'Well, I thought we agreed we wanted to get our business going again, the shop open and the customers back and . . .'

'And see Tom!' she finished.

'That as well,' I said, my heart giving a little leap.

There was a long pause. 'Hannah, you may not be altogether happy with this, but I think we ought to stay until our mother's lying-in,' Sarah finally said.

'That long!' I protested, for in spite of Mother's girth, there was more than a month to go before our new brother or sister would be born.

'Mother is not so strong as she was for birthing or for the demands of a new baby. We know how hard *that* is from looking after Grace,' Sarah said.

'But Anne will help! And the maid from the village comes in every day.'

'The maid has enough to do with the boys – and Anne is just a lazy flibbertigibbet!'

I laughed, but it was true, for Anne's head was stuffed with games and fashions and fol-de-rols. Further, as she had not bothered overmuch with school, she could barely read or scribe her name.

'She'll be no help at all to our mother!' Sarah said. 'And as we are the eldest daughters, I feel we should stay.'

I sighed. 'But for how long?'

'Eight weeks or so – maybe twelve. We'll see.'

I gave a cry of protest, counting on my fingers. 'Twelve weeks will be July! We'll have lost all our customers by then – they'll have gone elsewhere for their sweetmeats.'

'Tush!' Sarah said. 'There are only a few sweetmeat shops in the west of the City – and we are most certainly the best. They'll come back to us.'

'But . . .' I sighed again, for I could barely explain how much I wanted to go back to London, for I hardly understood it myself. I'd hated the stinking city when we'd left, could hardly bear to think on its name, but now that the plague had disappeared from the streets the people would be back, the theatres and shops would be open and we would find everything as cheery as it had been before. Besides (and this was what I most feared), if I was too long in returning, Tom might find another sweetheart, for there had been no words spoken or pledges given, nor even a kiss.

'Hannah, I think we must stay here a while,' Sarah said gently.

Cross and disgruntled, I jumped down from the gate to go inside, leaving Sarah sitting gazing into the distance. I loved my home and my family, but while I'd been away I'd grown apart from them. Although close in age, I now fancied myself much more mature than Anne, and as for John, George and Adam – well, they drove me quite demented, following me around and putting on my voice until I could scream. Moreover, although Mother was as sweet as she'd always been, Father was often crotchety and preoccupied with his business, seeming none too pleased that he would soon have a new babe in the house. All in all, now the excitement of our return was over and we had told and re-told all our adventures, Chertsey was in every way as tedious as I'd always known it to be.

I went into the cottage and sat at the window seat, staring down the lane. Another twelve weeks! How would I bear it? I could write to Tom, perhaps, care of his master Doctor da Silva to whom he was apprenticed, and tell him that I had not forgotten him and would be returning soon. I had done this once before from Dorchester, but had not had a reply, and indeed I was not sure it had ever reached him, for our letter to Mother and Father had not done so.

As I thought on, my attention was caught by a movement further down the lane. There was a horseman riding towards our cottage, and I knew immediately that it was Giles Copperly, for he'd visited us the day before, and the day before that, each time to thank us for conveying him home. Three visits in a week!

As I watched, he stopped where Sarah was sitting on the gate and jumped from his horse. Sarah took his outstretched hand but, instead of helping her from the gate, he put her hand to his lips and kissed it. They then gazed at each other so long, with the blossom falling all around them, that I was embarrassed and felt obliged to turn away.

It was then that I realised. Of course! *That* was why she did not wish to return to London . . .

The boys were in bed and the candles lit when, that evening, Sarah told Mother she would be staying in

Chertsey to help her through her lying-in.

Mother was so content with this news that it made me feel guilty that I did not really wish to stay. Yet I could not resist a sly dig at Sarah, saying that I had noticed Giles Copperly had called a third time – surely he hadn't wanted to thank us *again* for our trouble?

'No,' she said, blushing. 'No, he merely called to ask if I wished to see the extent of spices they have in their warehouse at Parkshot. I will be visiting there next week.'

Mother, Anne and I looked at her. 'Indeed?' Mother said.

Sarah rose and pretended to tend the fire. 'Yes. They have vanilla, nutmeg, aniseed and a type of cinnamon I've never heard of. Mr Copperly feels we may wish to use some for our sweetmeats.'

'Giles Copperly!' said Mother. That was all, but the way in which she spoke said much.

'He is very handsome. Is he your beau?' Anne asked eagerly, but Sarah did not reply.

'So you two girls will be staying here and eating like horses for another two-month, will you?' Father put in.

I looked at Sarah. 'We will be back in London by the middle of July for definite, won't we?' I asked.

'Of course,' Sarah said. 'Our new babe will be settled in and Mother will be recovered by that time.'

'And mayhap you will have seen enough cinnamon by then,' I teased, and had the satisfaction of seeing her blush again. We sat gazing into the fire and the only sound was the crackle of wood and a *phut-phut* as Father pulled on his pipe of tobacco.

'Hannah,' Anne suddenly piped up. 'If you are so

anxious to get back to London, why don't you go ahead by yourself?'

I looked at her, my heart giving a great leap. Never had Anne said anything so clever.

'You couldn't do that,' Mother said immediately.

'Of course you couldn't,' Sarah said. 'And you couldn't manage to make sweetmeats, run the shop and serve folk all on your own.'

'Well, then!' Anne said. 'What if I went with her? We could do these things between us.' She looked around at everyone beseechingly. 'If I was in London I would work very hard! You would be surprised at how hard I would work.'

I gave a little gasp at this suggestion, but as it did not get shouted down straightaway, began to get fearful excited.

'What do you think, Father?' Mother asked after a moment.

'I think it's a sound idea,' he replied. 'Anne could learn a trade and we would have two less mouths to feed.'

'But do you think Anne could do such a job?' Mother asked Sarah.

'Of course she could,' I put in quickly. 'She could do all the tasks that I used to do: shopping and fetching water from the conduit and grinding down the sugarloaf. She can serve in the shop while I do the skilled work,' I added, for I had already learned much of the trade from Sarah.

'And what would Anne do when you returned to London, Sarah?' Mother asked.

'Well,' Sarah said slowly. 'If things work out with Anne in London I will bide my time here and stay

229

with you a while longer, Mother. Until the babe is weaned, perhaps.'

'And then Anne could come back to Chertsey or we would find her another job in London,' I said, and I spoke joyfully, for in my mind's eye I could already see the reunion of me and Tom – of us meeting and kissing and walking through flowers together, like in the ballad sheets.

'But are you perfectly sure that it's safe?' Mother asked.

'Of course, Mother!' I flew to kiss her. 'London is as safe as houses!'

Chapter Five

London

*'May Day and thence to Westminster, on the way
meeting many milkmaids with their garlands upon
their pails, dancing with a fiddler before them.'*

'What is that great hulking place?'
'Oh! Who does that forward baggage think she is!'
'Hannah! Look at their gowns!'
'What a beautiful barge!'
'Do look at that!'
As we made our steady progress up the River
Thames, Anne was testing my patience sorely, leaning
first to the left of the open wherry, then to the right,
pointing, exclaiming, gasping and calling for me to
look at first one thing then another. It was May Day
and it seemed that most of London was on the river.

Mother had asked that we stay in Chertsey until
May Day, and on the previous evening she, Sarah,
Anne and I had gone into the orchard as we always
had on this day, and spread linen cloths under the
trees. At dawn we had risen, run into the orchard
(although Mother had not run) and pressed the damp

cloths over our faces and arms, for everyone knew that washing your face in the dawn dew gathered on the first of May was a great beautifier.

Thus refreshed, we had gone home for bread and milk, and then the whole family had walked to the village green where a maypole had been erected and where there was a small May Fair with stalls selling pewter and china and fruit and toys, and sideshows with jugglers, tooth-pullers and dancing milkmaids. Anne and the boys were highly entertained at these, but it was not much to me after the amusements of London – although I did not say as much.

It was a happy farewell to Chertsey, though, for after spending all morning at the fair, Anne and I had walked down to the wharf with our family and caught the boat to London, which was to bring us all the way in four hours. Mother and Sarah had wept as we boarded the craft, but Anne and I had not, for neither of us could contain our excitement at the adventure before us.

We had passed Hampton Court (where the king, it was said, kept two spare mistresses in case he should stay overnight) and also the great palace at Richmond where Good Queen Bess had died. With each mile we covered, the number of craft on the Thames increased until, near the City, a myriad of little boats covered the water from side to side: sculls, skiffs, wherries, decorated rowing boats and the magnificently ornate barges that belonged to the various Guilds of the City.

About two hours into our journey, Anne (who carried two lidded baskets made by our father) said she had a confession to make. I, being in the best of moods, said that I would forgive her, for the day was fair and nothing could be *that* wrong.

She then pulled out the smaller of the baskets, which I had noticed her fiddling with for some time, opening and closing its lid. 'I have brought a friend,' she said, looking at me imploringly, 'for I could not bear to part with her.' Saying this, she lifted the lid and presented me with a white kitten, which she put upon my lap, saying, 'Isn't she pretty? Just look at her pink ears! I could not bear to leave her behind.'

The kitten immediately crawled up to my shoulder and, as she seemed about to make a leap into the river, I took her up and placed her back in the basket, sighing a little. I felt it was fitting that I should sigh, being the older sister and the one in charge, but to tell the truth I loved cats as much as she did and did not mind a bit. Besides, I knew London still had a shortage of animals and that she – and her kittens in time – would be welcome there.

'You're not very cross, are you?' Anne said. 'One of the farm cats had five kittens and I couldn't leave them all behind. I almost brought two—'

'It'll be you who'll look after her,' I warned. 'You must find scraps for her to eat and clean up any messes.'

'Oh, I will!' she said fervently.

'And you must keep her in that basket and not let her out until we reach the shop.'

Some of the bigger craft had musicians, or a fiddler or singer, and these provided entertainment for the passengers who, dressed richly and to be seen, lounged on the decks drinking wine and partaking of food. As we passed Chelsea we came across a skiff containing four rather drunk gallants, and they, seeing us, urged their boatman to follow us upstream. For two miles or so they did so, calling us 'Charmers' and 'Sweet Angels' and sending extravagant compliments across the water, promising not only undying love, but all manner of jewellery and fine things if only we'd join them. We did not deign to even look their way, of course, but there was much giggling between me and Anne and we were rather sorry when, their boatman seeming as drunk as they were, they lost us amid the crush somewhere before the king's palace.

Here, at Whitehall, we had the biggest thrill of all, because the royal barge sailed by us with the king himself on board. His Majesty was seated on an ornately carved chair at the prow, and looked the very image of the man we had seen depicted on news-sheets and inn signs: handsome, strong and lusty. He had olive skin, long black hair which fell curling to his shoulders, and a narrow dark moustache, and was magnificently clothed in satins and lace with a fur-trimmed velvet cape hung about his shoulders. He smiled and waved to those around him, exuding a charm and a presence which drew all eyes. Several spaniels must have been playing about his feet, for we could hear them yapping, and when a barge piled with animal skins passed by, two of them jumped up to a ledge at the stern and hung there, sniffing the air, like tiny figureheads.

His Majesty's barge had lavish ornamentation and was most excellently carved and gilded, with all manner of bright pennants fluttering from its awning. Queen Catherine was quietly seated under a tapestry canopy in the shade (for it was said that she was expecting a child), and looked a neat body, and refined, and on seeing her our eyes raked the area to the back of the barge, hoping we might glimpse Barbara Castlemaine or another of the Ladies of the Bedchamber, but we did not. On board there was a quartet of musicians and all around us on the water people were shouting, 'Long live the King!' and 'God bless His Majesty!' We joined in, shouting, 'A Health to King Charles!' louder than anyone else, for we were fair excited out of our wits to see him there.

Indeed we could not have travelled by river on a better occasion, for there was so much to see that, when Anne was not giddily exclaiming at the sights around us, she was struck speechless at them. I, too, was both awestruck and astounded, but sought to appear more knowing, mindful that I was eighteen months older and had lived in London before.

Passing the great warehouses, tanneries and chandlers along the quayside of the City, our wherry landed at Swan Steps just before London Bridge (at which sight Anne almost collapsed with wonder and astonishment). Here we alighted, which was no easy matter for the landing jetty was slippery-thick with mud and detritus. We had no clogs or pattens to lift us out of the mud, but were wearing leather mules with our best gowns and carrying bundles and bedrolls as well as baskets and the kitten. The waterdog who'd rowed us there came to our aid, however, taking our baggage first and then sweeping us up and throwing us over his shoulder to carry us in turn to the top of the steps. Thus safely landed, I paid our fare and gave a generous tip and, with kitty in the basket meowing piteously, we set off for Crown and King Place and the shop. I was tingling all over now, happy to be back, thrilled at the thought that I'd soon be seeing Tom again.

Anne stopped at the top of Fish Lane. 'Can we go on to the bridge?' she asked breathlessly, looking back at it. 'Just to look . . .'

I shook my head. 'We cannot!' I said. 'Not with all the things we have to carry. See how crowded it is up there! We would be pushed this way and that and robbed of everything we have.'

Anne looked sorely disappointed, so I added that although we ought to get to our shop quickly for the sake of the poor enclosed kitten, we'd return as soon as we could. Our load was such that I was tempted to take a sedan chair, but did not because I had never hailed one before and was not sure of the correct procedure. Besides, it being May Day, some skipjack chair-carrier would be sure to overcharge me, and I had promised Sarah that I would look after the sum of money she'd given me, trade sensibly and not get fleeced.

It was taking an age to get through the crowds for, in spite of the incessant mewling of the kitten, Anne was stopping on every corner to gawp and gaze at the streets, the shops and the passers-by. I thought how different London looked from the way I'd last seen it. Looking now at the hoards of people, the crowded shops, the noisy taverns and the countless street-sellers shouting their wares, it was difficult to picture the City as it had been: bleak and silent, its streets rank with death. It felt to me now as if that other, plague-infested city had been but a dream.

'I never thought there were so many people in the

world,' Anne said wonderingly, as we paused at Cheapside and looked down the wide cobbled street thronging with horses and carriages and people dressed in their best. 'And such things to buy!' she added, darting to a window where all manner of luxurious silk and satin collars and scarves were displayed. 'I swear I will not rest until I have visited every shop in London.'

'Then I fear you will never sleep!' I retorted.

We walked deeper into the City, away from the crowds and through the lanes and alleys. Here I could see traces of the year before, for there were shops still closed and shuttered and houses – once shut-up – which still bore marks of the red cross which had been painted on them, or had their doors still barred. In some of these, whole families had died and no one had come forward to take over the accommodation.

Anne paused before one of the churchyards, looking through the railings curiously. 'Why is the ground raised on each side of the walkway?' she asked. 'It is fully six feet above the path.'

Something caught at my heart and I stood quietly for a moment, for it was this churchyard, St Dominic's, which early on in the plague time had taken the corpses of the four young children who had been neighbours of ours, and their mother as well. 'Because so many died of plague they had no space to bury them all properly,' I explained to Anne. 'They just had to pile bodies upon bodies until they could put in no more. And when the graveyards were full right up they took to throwing corpses into plague pits.'

Anne gasped. 'Bodies upon bodies . . .' she breathed.

'They say one hundred thousand died in all.'

'One hundred thousand!' Anne said wonderingly. 'I do not know and cannot think what that number is.'

'And it is better that you don't,' I said.

We moved on. We were very near our shop now and I began to be nervous, for I had no idea what I'd find. Had all our neighbours perished? Had our shop been looted of what little we had left? Had some drunken hawker, seeing it was empty, set up home in it? Where would I turn for help if things were not as they should be?

'There's our sign!' I said to Anne, pointing above the row of shops to where the metal sign swung and creaked. 'See the sugared plum!'

We reached the shop and stood outside, staring up. The floor above had been rented by a rope-maker who had stored his twines there; but I didn't know whether he had survived the plague or not.

'Is this it, then?' Anne asked, disappointment in her voice, and I remembered that when I'd arrived a year back, I'd been disappointed at the sight of it too. 'It's quite small,' she said.

I nodded. 'I know. It's not like the shops on the bridge – or in Cornhill or Cheapside. Were you expecting more?'

'I thought it would be bigger,' she said. 'Varnished in bright colours. With a glass window.'

'Well, maybe if we work hard and make our fortune we'll be able to have one of those soon. A little shop in the Royal Exchange, perhaps!' I put my bundles on the ground, found the key (which Sarah had placed on a long ribbon around my neck for safekeeping) and opened the shop door. It was dank and gloomy in there, though, and we needed the shutters opened before we could see anything. These, however, were fixed with pegs and a turning device, and a damp winter had swelled them so that they no longer turned. After a struggle I went to the shop of our neighbour, Mr Newbery, who, trading under the sign of the Paper and Quill, sold parchments and fine writing paper.

I pushed open the door of his shop somewhat nervously, for I had last seen Mr Newbery at the very height of the plague when people had been dropping like flies around us. The day Sarah and I had left London he'd informed us he was going to shut up shop and take up drinking at the Two Pigeons instead.

He was back in his shop now, however: a short stocky man bent over the counter reading *The Intelligencer*, his oversized wig pushed to the back of his head. He looked mighty surprised when he saw it was me.

'Young Hannah!' he said. 'How are you? Not dead of the sickness, then?'

'No, indeed not!' I said, smiling to myself as I remembered Mr Newbery's relish for conversation of a morbid nature. 'I am here to open up our shop.'

'Your sister Sarah is with you?'

'No, she—'

'She's dead?'

I laughed. 'No. She is well. I have my younger sister with me – Sarah is staying at home to help our mother with her lying-in.'

'Ah, lying-in,' he said. 'A tricky business. Midwives kill more than they save.'

'Well, it is our mother's seventh and she will more

than likely deliver it herself,' I said. 'But I am here to beg your help, Mr Newbery. Our shutters are jammed and we need a man's strength.'

'You're going to start trading again?'

'We are.'

He shook his head, sighing. 'Your rooms are like to be in a terrible state – fair eaten away by rats, I should think. Or dripping damp from the rain we've had over the past months. And to be in London now – don't you know that there have been bad omens about this year? There is a hellfire preacher at St Paul's who says that God's dreadful punishment will be meted out to sinful London soon.'

'But you're still trading,' I pointed out.

'Well, that's as maybe,' he said gruffly, pulling his wig forward on his head and straightening the curls.

He took a small hammer and a stool from beneath his counter, then followed me outside. I presented my sister to him and, after scaring her by telling her about a pamphlet detailing a seer's vision of the City set all in flame from one end to the other, he got up on the stool and tapped on the turning peg with a small hammer to release the shutter. This shutter, when lowered, allowed light into the shop and also formed a counter from which to sell our sweetmeats.

'As I thought – all of a muddle and a mess,' Mr Newbery said with satisfaction, peering into the room and shaking his head.

He went back into his own shop and Anne and I then surveyed the room before us, which was not much spoiled – although the walls were mould-ridden and would need washing, and the herbs we'd strewn on the floor were black and gave off a musty, unpleasant smell. The fireplace was laid neat and tidy, however, with the fire irons all in place and the saucepans set above, and there was the small burner to heat the sugar water nearby. To one side of the room was the marble working surface on which stood various sizes of wooden drums. These were empty and dusty now but, after a visit to the market, would soon contain sugar, spices and the various fruits and herbs with which we worked.

'It is a good business, and we must work hard and make a success of what we do, for Sarah's sake,' I said to Anne.

'Of course we will!' My sister took Kitty (for thus we had named her) from her basket and began to walk around the shop with her, and then into the living quarters beyond, telling her that this would be her new home and she wasn't to stray but must stay with us and be a good, playful kitty.

'Anne, are you listening?' I asked.

She nodded. 'You said we must work hard.' She put Kitty down and turned to me, looking puzzled. 'But what was that that your neighbour was saying – about the City in flame?'

'It was nothing,' I said. 'Mr Newbery likes to scare.'

And if God's dreadful punishment was being meted out to the City, I thought to myself, then surely it had happened last year. The plague. Nothing could be worse than that.

It is well known that a London housewife may buy everything she needs from her own doorstep, and we proved this by setting our shop to rights without needing to go abroad for any of our purchases. Within two days the walls – both in the shop and our room beyond – were newly limewashed, the floor was scrubbed with soda and strewn with fresh herbs, and a new water carrier and some enamel jugs had been purchased. There were fresh wax candles in all the holders and two shimmering sugar loaves standing ready to be used. Thus all was prepared, and it just remained for us to go to Covent Garden market to buy the blooms and the fruits we needed to start making the sweetmeats.

Before I'd left Chertsey, Sarah and I had talked about what should be made first, and had decided upon frosted rose petals, orange and lemon suckets and herb comfits. These were simple sweetmeats which Anne could help with and which we knew sold well. Once we had a few regular sweetmeats in stock, we would then begin to make the more time-consuming things: the marchpane fruits, the crystallised violets and the sugared plums.

All was prepared, then, and I was mighty pleased with myself. There was one thing I had not done, though, and it was on my mind constantly. I had not yet been to Doctor da Silva's to speak to Tom.

We were too busy, I told myself, there was much to put to rights, and I could not leave Anne, for she needed to be instructed all along the way. These were my excuses – but what truly delayed me was the thought that Tom might have forgotten about me in the eight months that I'd been gone – for it was said that 'prentices bedded where they could, and why should he wait for a girl who might not ever return to him? Moreover, a girl he had not even kissed. All the while I did not go to see him, then, I could pretend that all was well between us.

Late on the afternoon of our third day there, however, all being done in the shop, the part of me that wanted to see Tom won over the part that was afeared, and on an impulse I took off my work clothes and put on my best green taffeta gown, which I had worn all that time ago when Tom and I had walked to Chelsea to pick violets, and which I'd left in our back room. I caught up my hair in a top-knot, as was now the fashion in London, and put some sprigs of deep blue rosemary flowers into my curls. Rosemary for remembrance, I thought, and prayed that I had not slipped far from his mind.

Before I left I circled the shop, swirling my skirts around to show the darker green lining and ruffled underskirt. 'Do I look very fine?' I asked Anne. 'Do you think my Tom will be fair overcome at the sight of me?'

She laughed and nodded. 'But you must pull your bodice down a little to show more of what a man likes to see!'

I pretended to look shocked. 'You have been learning such things from the minxes in our village, I suppose.' Anne blushed and I added, 'I am quite confident of Tom's good opinion without doing that, thank you kindly.' (Although truth may have it that I did go into our room and lace my bodice a little tighter, which had more or less the same effect.)

Going up the lane towards Doctor da Silva's shop I felt both excited and nervous. I would not take for granted that we were sweethearts, I decided, but would act as if I were someone recently returned from the country calling on an old friend.

As I rounded the corner I saw, glinting, the sign of the Silver Globe hanging outside the apothecary's shop, and my heart caught in my throat. How often over the past months had I dreamed of coming back here and seeing Tom, of him looking up and seeing me standing there, then coming to me and taking my hand . . .

But . . . but when I reached the shop the windows were shuttered, the door was barred with two planks of wood across it and – oh, foul thing! – a faded red cross was upon the door.

Plague!

My heart began beating loudly – so loudly that I could hear it in spite of the noise all around. I stood quite still for some moments, trying to control this, and then I began to walk around the shop examining the shuttered windows in case there was a crack I could see through. There was not, however, and I came once more to the door and stood before it, pressing my hands against the wood as if it could impart some secret to me. I closed my eyes and saw again the shop as it had been last September: windows full of plague preventatives and a trail of people outside, some with plague tokens on them, some with discharging buboes, all waiting to see Doctor da Silva and be treated, for many physicians had already left the City and the poorer folk had nowhere else to go. It should be no surprise to me that he and Tom had succumbed to the disease. Why had I thought that they had some special immunity?

Behind me I heard a street-hawker's cry of 'Hot faggots! Five for sixpence!', but I did not turn.

'You want an apothecary, dearie?'

I opened my eyes and an old woman was looking up at me, bent low under the burden of a tray of faggots which she carried tied around her neck.

I shook my head. 'I don't want an apothecary – well, I do, but only this one.'

'Doctor da Silva? He stayed to help us, didn't he? Poor man. He went the way of most of 'em that stayed. He and his lad both.'

'They . . . they both contracted plague?'

'Aye,' she nodded, swaying on the stick. 'They was taken ill just when we was athinking it was all over. Near Christmas, it was.'

'Do . . . do you remember what happened?'

She shrugged. 'What happened? Only the usual thing: one day they was here, the next they was poorly, the next they was dead.'

'They are . . . truly dead, then?' I asked.

'Aye. Both of 'em. Dead and in the pit. I kept indoors most of that time meself. Didn't go out for three months and near starved.' She suddenly gave me a suspicious look. 'But why do you need a 'pothecary? Do you have a fever?'

I shook my head.

'They say plague may return if we don't take care.'

I didn't speak.

'I keep three spiders in my pocket whenever I go aselling faggots. What do you do?'

But I couldn't reply to this for my throat was thick with tears and I felt near choked with them. After a moment she moved on, looking at me strangely. 'Five for sixpence! Five faggots for sixpence!' she called as she moved down the lane.

I stayed leaning against the shop front for some

time, tears falling down my cheeks and marking the green taffeta gown. And then I pulled the rosemary sprigs out of my hair and let them fall, for there was no one here to remember me.

Chapter Six

Nelly Gwyn

'Saw pretty Nelly standing at her lodgings door in Drury Lane in her smock-sleeves and bodice – she seemed a mighty pretty creature.'

Anne did not find me good company in those days after I had first learned of Tom's death for, being full of sorrow, I made a hard task-mistress. Not sleeping well, I rose before dawn, worked all day and continued toiling by the light of a candle at night, and expected her to do the same.

I found it hard to believe that I had lost Tom for ever. With my friend Abby I had seen her grow weaker and more pitiful, day by day as the plague took a tighter grip on her. That she would die had seemed inevitable. Tom, though . . . the last I'd seen of him he had been strong and healthy and brave, blowing kisses to me as our carriage had driven away from London. How could he be dead?

I lay awake at night with Anne sleeping peacefully beside me, and couldn't help wondering in which way he had been struck down. I had seen or heard of plague taking many forms: brief and so violent that the sufferers were dead before they knew they had contracted it; painful but drawn out over a long, weary period so that they almost believed they might survive; or so prolonged and maddening in its intensity that the victims dashed their brains out against a wall in order to find peace.

Which had Tom endured?

I knew again, too, the sorrow of not having a grave to visit. After our grandmother in Chertsey had died we would go to the churchyard several times a year to take flowers or – on her birthday – to decorate the grave with cut-out pictures and black ribbons. I would have felt greatly comforted if I could have visited Tom's grave, for I would have taken paper love-hearts as well as flowers, and sat and told him what was in my heart. There was nowhere to go, though, no grassy mound to sit beside, and although I made enquiries at the parish church, they told me that on contracting plague he and Doctor da Silva had been taken to a pesthouse in another parish. On asking there, I was told they had died and their bodies tipped into a plague pit. It was not even known which pit it was, except that it had been outside the City walls.

After two weeks of continual moping my dark mood was arrested, however, by Anne's announcement that she wanted to go back to Chertsey.

We had just shut the shop and I had put her to grinding down sugar for the next day's sweetmeats, hardly noticing that she was tired and unhappy.

'Hannah,' she suddenly announced. 'You're not the same sister that I remember. You're miserable and hag-ridden and I declare I want to go home.'

I could scarce believe my ears. 'Why, what are you saying?'

'I know you've lost your sweetheart, and I've held my tongue thinking you would get over your bad humour, but it looks to be getting worse and you're more miserable by the minute,' she said defiantly. 'I'd thought we'd have a rare old time here in London and enjoy each other's company and be going to fairs and plays and suchlike, but all I do is grind sugar day and night – and moreover, be held up to ridicule for not doing it well enough!'

I stared at her in surprise, for this speech was so unlike Anne that I could only think that she had been rehearsing it for days.

'So if you'll pay me my wages to date I'll take Kitty and make my own way home,' she continued, 'for I'd rather stay in Chertsey with the heifers than be in London with a shrew!'

'Oh!' I gasped.

'So there. I've said it and am glad on it.'

I looked at my little sister standing there so defiantly and, although I was very much hurt, recognised more than a little of the truth in what she'd said.

'A shrew, you say . . .'

'I didn't mean that last bit.'

'Yes, you did!'

'Well. Only sometimes.'

There was a long pause. 'Am I really so bad?' I asked.

She nodded. 'I can never speak to you. You're always miserable. You stand and watch everything I do and then say it's wrong.' Her bottom lip trembled. 'I don't like it here now!'

I felt so ashamed at these last words that I went over and put my arms around Anne. 'I'm sorry,' I said. 'I've thought of no one but myself and I've been horrible and beastly.'

'Indeed you have.'

'But please don't go home,' I said, hugging her tightly, 'for I couldn't manage without you.'

'Well,' she said. 'You must promise to be nicer to me, and if you are, perhaps I'll stay . . .'

So we became friends again and I resolved to myself that I would put Tom out of my mind as much as I could, for I knew that everyone had lost someone in the plague: parent, employer, friend, husband, child . . . and if we all went around in low mood and foul temper, then the world would become an awful place indeed.

I began to see another side of Anne, a London side, for here she became a quick and neat worker and not at all lazy. As the weeks went by and the markets became fully open across the City, I allowed her to go off on her own in the mornings to buy the fruit and flowers we needed. She was good at this, for she drove a hard bargain with the stall-holders and, unlike me, was bold enough to return a bloom she later found to be damaged or an orange with a worm at its centre. I did not allow her to handle money, however, for on the two occasions when she had gone out with a pocket of coins under her petticoats, once she had been rooked of all she had by a fortune teller in a booth, and once she had purchased a whistling wooden bird to amuse Kitty, which had broken within the hour. After this I sent her out with trading tokens, or she went to one of our regular suppliers where we had an account.

We spoke often of our family, and whether Sarah and Giles loved each other, and also if our mother had been confined safely and whether we had a new brother or sister. I felt that things had gone all right for our mother, for Sarah would have found means to let us know if this were not the case.

It had been feared that with the coming of warmer weather the plague would return, but although there were always a few plague deaths on the Bills of Mortality, thanks be the numbers did not increase. People continued to pour into London – either returning to their old jobs or coming to fill up the places left by those who had died – until the City seemed just as crowded and heated and hectic as it had done the previous year.

In the first days after our return we did not have many customers, but we didn't mind this because we didn't have a deal of sweetmeats prepared. By the month of June, however, many of our old customers had realised we were open again and custom began to improve. I was pleased to be in such a trade as ours, for although it is true that sweetmeats are only passing trivial things, our customers held that they made them feel better and cheered their day. One grand lady said to us that if she wanted some sweet delicacy and could afford it, then she would have it, for life was too short to do without.

One day, we made an excursion to see the shops on

London Bridge. It took us fully one hour to fight our way across to Southwarke, for there were forty shops open on the bridge, and as many stalls, and a press of people on foot, horseback, carriage and sedan fighting with each other for space. Here we purchased two pairs of scented gloves each, and a set of nutcrackers at a new cook shop, for one of our most popular sweetmeats was miniature fruits made from marchpane, which meant two or three nights sitting cracking a deal of almonds with a hammer, and the nutcrackers would greatly speed this work.

Leaving the bridge to go around the myriad of little shops near the Tower, we heard a terrible roaring coming from the king's menagerie, making me jump mightily and Anne shriek with fright. We were told by a garlic-seller that it was feeding time for the king's lions and tigers and, hearing this, I promised Anne that we would visit the menagerie soon and see these lions, for they were said to be most enormous and fiercesome, yet related to our own Kitty (which I could scarce believe).

Another day, obtaining some lengths of parchment from Mr Newbery (who asked me if I wanted it to write my Will and said it was wise to do so), I wrote a list of all the sweetmeats that we made, to be advertisements for our goods. This read:

Frosted rose petals
Crystallised violets
Sugared plums
Herb comfits
Sugared angelica
Glacé cherries

Sugared orange peel
Lemon and orange suckets
Violet cakes

As well as these we made the marchpane fruits, of course, but as they took a monstrous long time to make, we could not always hold them in stock. I took great pains with the spellings of these items, even though many of our customers would not have known any better and, after getting some coloured inks from Mr Newbery, drew a likeness of the sweetmeat next to its name for those who could not read. I made two copies and nailed one to the wooden shutter to be on show when we were open, and put the other inside on the wall.

We also began to make pomanders as Martha had instructed us, for at a warehouse in Wharf Lane I'd seen a barrel of cloves going very cheaply and had made bold to buy the lot. Oranges were costly, but we did not need the best quality, nor the freshest, so we would buy five or six of a lesser quality at a time, stud them all over with cloves and decorate them with ribbons and lace. Anne was especially good at doing this and would search around the rag markets for scraps of braid or gay trimmings to use. We hung these pomanders in the shop and they did not stay long, for pretty items like this were much in demand with the quality.

I wanted Sarah to see what a success we were making of things, and looked forward to her return so that we could hear how our mother had fared, yet loved what I was doing so much that I did not want to relinquish my place as shopkeeper. I knew, too, that

Anne would not now wish to return home to Chertsey, so began to wonder if the three of us could work together when Sarah arrived. The shop and the living quarters were small, but Anne could have a truckle bed to pull out from under the bigger one, and perhaps a storeroom could be built at the back of the shop, beside the privy.

Anne and I soon became best friends again, for being very near in age we had always played together as children, and it didn't take long for us to regain our old closeness. Things were going mighty well for us and I would have been happy had it not been for the loss of Tom. Though I did not speak on it now, his memory was always at the back of my mind. I wondered if I would find another sweetheart, and when, and what he would be like. Whenever I daydreamed and thought on this mysterious person, though, he always turned out to have Tom's face. Maybe, I thought, there would be no other suitor for me, and I would remain unkissed and die a spinster.

One morning, to my great surprise, a handsome gilded carriage stopped outside the shop drawn by two white horses with their manes and tails plaited with red and gold ribbons. A velvet-coated footman then jumped down, opened the door with a flourish and lowered the steps.

As I hurried to the doorway to greet this important customer, there was some giggling within the carriage (for it seemed that there was a man in there too), and then a young woman with hair as red as mine stepped out.

I brushed down my apron and just had time to call

Anne to come through from the back room. 'Quickly!' I shouted in great excitement, for I had never forgotten her coming to the shop before. ''Tis Nelly Gwyn. The actress!'

Anne came running in and we both curtseyed to Nelly for, as Mr Newbery said later, although she was but a whore she was a mighty pretty one. She was dressed very beautifully: her gown was of the finest silver tissue and over it she wore a most fashionable little cape of black velvet backed with silver fur.

'I'm pleased to see your shop open again at last!' she said. 'I have oft fancied some of your sweetmeats.'

'Thank you, Ma'am,' I murmured. 'We have but recently returned from the country.'

'And all's well and you have survived the visitation?' She looked through to the back of the shop. 'Where is your sister?'

'She is staying with our family at present, Ma'am,' I said. 'But I have my younger sister here instead.'

Nelly laughed and showed little pearly teeth, perfectly spaced. 'So! A goodly supply of sisters.' She looked around. 'Your shop here is a little oasis. London roars outside as wild as a lion, but in here all is sweetness and calm.'

'Thank you, indeed,' I said, bobbing another curtsey and thinking I would write to Sarah on the instant and tell her this.

'And now will you let me have some of your crystallised violets, for I swear nothing revives me after a performance as they do.'

I was instantly filled with remorse, for we had not been able to find fresh violets at the flower markets in the last week and so did not have any crystallised ones to sell. I apologised for this, and, promising that we would have some by the middle of the following week, persuaded her that lemon suckets might be the very thing to refresh her instead.

I counted ten of these into a large cone of paper. 'Are you on stage at present, Ma'am?' I asked, for I could see from Anne's face that she was struck dumb with admiration and would want to know more about our visitor.

She nodded. 'I am engaged to play Lady Wealthy in *The English Monsieur*. Me – a lady! The very thought has put the aristocracy into a fearsome stir!'

Anne and I both laughed.

Kitty wandered in from our back room and Nelly bent down to pick her up and kiss her, saying, 'I have a fur muff of exactly this colour!' Kitty gave a yowl of protest at being handled, for she was not a cuddlesome cat, and Nelly put her down again. 'Oh – are those oranges?' she exclaimed, pointing at two decorated pomanders which hung in the shop. We said they were, and were for hanging in closets, and Nelly said that until recently she had been selling them in their natural state during the interval at the theatre (which I knew, of course, but affected not to) and would take them both because they were so pretty.

'But have you been to the theatre – either of you?' she asked when she had paid us.

'Never,' I said.

'I have always wanted to!' Anne blurted out.

'Then you shall go.' Twirling a red curl around her finger, Nelly said, 'When I return for my violets I shall bring you tickets for next week's performance.'

We, quite overcome, gave our thanks and curtseyed

again – indeed we were bobbing up and down like ships at sea as she went out. By this time, a small crowd had gathered outside our shop, for Nelly was very popular with the people on account of her having risen from such humble beginnings to this position of prominence. Moreover, it was the talk of the coffee houses (so Mr Newbery informed us) that the king, tiring of Barbara Castlemaine, might take Nelly for his mistress, for he had been seen at the theatre on many occasions when she was performing.

True to her word, Nelly did return for the violets and gave us tickets for the theatre, and Anne and I were both monstrous excited at the thought of going, in spite of Mr Newbery telling us that he would not attend a theatre for a king's ransom. 'They are nasty, crowded places and breeding grounds for all sorts of diseases,' he said.

'Then are not taverns those things, too?' I asked nicely, for Mr Newbery was exceedingly fond of alehouses and was often brought home hung about the shoulders of the night watchman. He did not reply to this.

On the day of the play we shut the shop at midday and were at the theatre for two o'clock, for although the performance did not start before three, we wanted to be sure to see everything there was to be seen. We were dressed in our best – I wearing the plum linsey-woolsey suit which I had made and embroidered, and Anne wearing my blue linen gown of the previous year; we both had new starched lace caps and scented gloves.

The King's Theatre was in Rider's Yard in Drury

Lane, which was a goodly way for us across the City and outside the walls. From the road it looked just like an ordinary building in some disrepair, but inside it had a glass roof and was circular in form, filled by boxes separated from each other and divided into rows going upwards. Our seats were in the middle of the theatre and there was a gallery below us and one above, this latter being where the 'prentices sat. At the bottom was a sloping pit area containing benches where well-dressed young men were sitting, and next to the stage lounged the pretty orange and lemon sellers shouting their wares to the quality and, I noticed, casting their eyes upon the young men nearby as they did so.

Anne and I sat down and began staring avidly at the people there, looking this way and that and exclaiming and gasping by turn. Early though we were, the place was already crowded and noisy with laughter and conversation. People were walking about, changing seats, hailing friends, eating pastries and indulging in horseplay, so that it seemed to me more tavern than theatre.

On stage, acts came and went to amuse the audience before the play began: a dancing bear, a juggler, a man playing a pipe and dancing a jig. No one seemed to take much notice of them. At one point, the 'prentice boys on high started a chant of, 'Nel-ly, Nel-ly! Nel-ly!', which the other men took up, causing us to put our hands over our ears until their yelling ceased.

Anne drew my attention to the pit, pointing out that there were a dozen women sitting with the young gallants. Such women, though! In butterfly colours, they flirted and giggled and moved from one man to another, either wearing glittering masks held to their faces on sticks, or so many patches and sequins that you could scarce see their complexions beneath. Their gowns were of rich materials in delectable colours, but seemed to have been made when they were a deal smaller, for their bosoms looked about to fall out of their bodices.

'They're the whores,' I said, leaning over to whisper in Anne's ear. 'They're looking for business.'

Anne gasped and we both watched, fascinated, for none of the women had the least shame about them, nor looked downcast, but instead lorded it over the men with as many airs and graces as if they were duchesses rather than doxies.

''T'would never do for Chertsey!' Anne said, and we could scarce stop laughing.

It was at this time, just before the play started, that there came on to the stage a man all dressed in black wheeling a large box which he set up on its end. Shouting to be heard above the hubbub, he announced in a strange accent that he was a magician and necromancer by the name of Count de'Ath, and he had brought with him his mysterious cabinet.

A little hush came across the audience, for everyone loved to hear of magic and enchantment (and indeed Anne and I intended to pay a visit to Madame le Strange, the fortune teller on London Bridge, for it was said that she had predicted the plague and foretold the exact number who would die).

Count de'Ath stood full square before the audience, twirled his moustache and said that if any member of the audience wished to disappear, either from his wife or his creditors, then he had only to enter this cabinet and he would never be seen again.

'Where will he go, Maestro?' someone asked from above, and the Count said that the cabinet would instantly convey this man to a land across the sea, where he would live as a person of wealth and property.

''Is troubles vill disappear and he vill for ever dwell in a place of warmth and luxury.'

'I dwells there after five pints at the alehouse!' some wit shouted.

Count de'Ath did not appear to hear this. Indeed, he seemed oblivious to all that was going on in the theatre: the people constantly arriving, the yapping from the lap dogs of the ladies, a brawl taking place in the gallery, a new cry of 'Nel-ly!' beginning from a box.

'How much will it cost to go there?' someone wanted to know.

The Count raised his arms. 'No money vill exchange hands,' he said. There was a pause. 'It vill merely cost 'is soul.'

There was quiet at this, and several people in the audience crossed themselves. Even the harlots stopped their chatter for a moment.

'Are zere any takers?' asked Count de'Ath, but of course there were not, because reading the almanacs and visiting a fortune teller was one thing, but selling your soul to the Devil was quite another.

The Count asked again, telling of how a person's life could be changed, how a man could become a king and live on a rich island of his own for the whole of his life. Suddenly, then, from one of the benches in the pit, a young man stepped forward and ran up the steps on to the stage. He was tall and slim, dressed like a dandy in satins and lace. 'I'll go!' he said, sweeping his feathered hat from his head with a flourish.

Those in the audience who were watching the act started in surprise and then strained forward in their seats in order to see better, while others gasped at his bravery. I gasped loudest of all – indeed I gave a little cry – for as the young man turned, I saw that it was Tom.

Chapter Seven

The Magician

*'My wife and I to the theatre where sat the King,
Madam Castlemaine, the Duke and Duchess, and my
wife to her great content had her full sight of them
all.'*

Or was it? Just as the young man turned and walked
across the stage to enter the black cabinet, a couple
pushed past us to their seats and we had to rise. As we
sat down another couple came by, laughing, and made
to engage us in conversation.

'Damned fine play, this!' said the man. 'Saw it
yesterday, too.'

'Have you seen it before?' the woman asked me.

I didn't reply and, stifling a cry, almost pushed them
out of the way so I could see around the woman's
ribboned cap. They passed by, looking at me curiously
and muttering about my rudeness, but it was too late
by then, for the young man was inside the cabinet, his
face shrouded by darkness.

'What is it?' Anne asked in a whisper as the couple
went on. 'Was she a whore too? Is that why you didn't

speak to her?'

I shook my head but was not able to explain, for I was rapt, breathless, watching the stage.

Count de'Ath bowed. From the musicians standing by the stage there came a fanfare. 'If any person vants to examine my cabinet, he vill discover no openings or false doors, and no secret passages vere a man might hide!'

'So where is that man going to go?' someone shouted.

'He vill disappear . . . be changed into air and shadow . . . become a ghost creature who vill travel o'er vast continents until he arrives at the land I have pledged. Only then vill he regain his right shape and substance and become a man again!'

There was quite a stir in the audience at this.

Count de'Ath swirled his cloak around to half hide his face. 'I am trained in the black arts and 'ave studied at the hands of demons! Only through me can zis enchantment be achieved.' He paused. 'And just for the price of a soul!' he added.

There was another gasp at this and two gallants arrived on stage to examine the cabinet. Pronouncing it to be in no way out of the ordinary, there was another fanfare and a black curtain was pulled across the front of the box, obscuring the young man within completely from view. The Count made various strange movements over the box, there was the tinkling of bells and a puff of smoke, then the curtain was pulled open.

It was empty. The man inside – whoever he was – had disappeared.

Some people in the audience cried out in

astonishment. The same two gallants then examined the cabinet again and, looking puzzled, pronounced that the young man had gone and they knew not where.

Count de'Ath regarded the audience with some disdain, then gave a short bow before tipping his cabinet on to its side and wheeling it out again without another word. Some people clapped, the 'prentices cat-called, but for the most part those that had watched the performance sat in awed silence.

Anne, too, was spellbound, staring open-mouthed at the stage. 'A real magician. An enchanter.'

'It seems like it,' I said, stunned.

'I've never seen real magic before . . .'

Slowly my heart stopped pounding and regained its normal beat. It couldn't have been Tom – of course it couldn't. The youth on stage had been taller, thinner, the shape of his head had been different.

And Tom was dead, I told myself sternly. No magic on earth could bring him back again. And yet . . . and yet . . .

More entertainment arrived on stage – a man playing the bagpipes – and ten minutes later the play began, although this did not seem to make a jot of difference to the audience. They continued to walk and talk amongst themselves, calling out to compliment or jeer at the actors and actresses. The plot made no sense to me, for I was still stunned by the performance of Count de'Ath, but this did not spoil my enjoyment at being there. When Nelly came on the audience went wild, and indeed she played solely to them, calling, waving and once even neglecting her part on stage to address someone in the pit. At one time she was disguised as a boy (wearing short breeches and showing her legs, which were very slim and shapely) and when she appeared thus the whole audience rose to her, applauding wildly.

At half-time the orange girls came round selling their wares. One sold sweetmeats, too, and we purchased two lemon suckets and were pleased to find that these were inferior to ours and looked rather limp and stale. On tasting, we discovered that they were not so succulent, either, and we decided that they could not have undergone the six days alternately steeping and boiling in sugar water as ours did, but had been made by a quicker and inferior process.

People came round at this time selling ballad sheets and pamphlets, and holding up bills showing what the following week's performances were going to be, and there was also more entertainment on stage, although not Count de'Ath again.

A few moments after the play restarted there came some noises and barking from the royal box above us, and a stir of anticipation ran around the theatre. The barking, it was whispered, was from a pack of spaniels and meant that the king had arrived.

Anne and I were fearful excited at this.

'Again the king!' Anne said, for we often spoke about how we'd seen him in the royal barge, and how neither our mother nor father nor our brothers had ever glimpsed him nor were likely to. 'Today is the best day of my life!' she went on, clasping my hand. 'I will not sleep a wink tonight for the thrill of it all.'

And now no one was watching the stage, for all eyes were fixed on the royal box, and even Nelly had to take second place to His Majesty. News quickly ran round the theatre of what the king was wearing, what humour he was in, and what mistress accompanied him, and Anne and I practically fell out of our seats trying to crane our heads outwards and backwards to obtain information on these subjects for ourselves. Unfortunately, though, the royal box was stuffed with ladies and courtiers who were fawning about His Majesty and keeping him from our view, and we caught no more than brief glimpses of piled, curled hair, gaily-coloured dresses and waving plumed fans. We could not even see which royal mistress he had favoured that day, although were told by someone in front of us that it was not Barbara Castlemaine, but a girl called Mall Davis who was but sixteen.

When the play was over and the king had left, Anne was anxious to go round to the stage door to mingle with the gallants and fops gathered there for a sight of Nelly. I agreed to do this, but only because I had a mind to say a word to Count de'Ath.

The crowd outside the stage door had just set up a cry for Nelly when the Count came out and began to push his way through them. He was dressed in the swirling cloak he had worn on stage, and a black velvet hood lined with crimson.

'Count de'Ath!' I hailed him and, when he turned, called quickly, 'Can you tell me where that young man in your cabinet has gone?'

He looked at me through narrowed eyes. 'Did you not pay heed to what I said? 'E has gone to a new life, Mamzelle. A better life.'

'And can I go there too?' I blurted out, and Anne started and gasped.

'If you enter my cabinet. Come to Bartholomew

Fair!' he said, and then he disappeared beyond the crowd and out of view.

'Why did you say that?' Anne asked, astonished. 'What are you thinking of?'

'I didn't mean it,' I said. 'It was something to say. I was jesting.'

Of course I had been jesting. And besides, it had not been Tom who had been on that stage and had been transported by magic to another place. Whatever conjuring Count de'Ath could do, he could not conjure with someone who was dead.

This did not stop me from daydreaming, however, and on falling asleep that night I could not but think how terrible it would be if Tom had somehow survived the plague only to have been magicked away from me into Count de'Ath's cabinet, and lost his soul . . .

'Wherever did you get those?' I looked at Anne and burst out laughing. I'd sent her to the conduit for water and she'd been gone an age. When she'd come back, her face was stuck all over with black and sequined patches: a heart on her forehead, clubs and spades on her cheeks, a ladybird on her chin.

'Do they look fine?' Anne said, taking up a looking-glass and admiring herself. 'Do I look a lady?'

'You look a harlot!' I said.

'But everyone wears them now!'

'Not shop-girls,' I said, shaking my head. 'How much did you pay for them?'

'I traded a pomander with a woman who runs a stall in Cornhill.' She picked up Kitty, who looked at her in some surprise and then began to pat at her face, no doubt thinking that the face patches were black beetles.

'I have one for you, too,' Anne said to me. 'It is of a miniature coach and horses and you may wear it across your forehead. The woman said that she sold a Countess one just the same.'

'I would sooner have my freckles!' I said.

But Anne thought her patches mighty fine and wore them for the rest of the day – and the next, too, until I thought I'd have to peel them off when she was asleep to be rid of them. She wore them until Mr Newbery came in to impart some tidbit of scandal and, seeing Anne's face, stepped back, looking aghast.

'Have you the pox, Madam?' he asked.

'No, indeed I have not,' Anne said indignantly.

'But the women who wear patches are mostly raddled old bawds who wear them to hide their sores and scars,' he said, and for once I was glad of his dismal perspective, for even before he had finished speaking, Anne had begun peeling them off.

Mr Newbery gave us the gossip, which was that the king's new mistress, Mall Davis, was an actress, and that Nelly Gwyn was so jealous of her that she'd had a song written which poked fun at her rival's legs, which by all accounts were fat and not nearly so elegant as her own. We laughed and said we were on Nelly's side, and then just as Mr Newbery was leaving I suddenly remembered. 'What is Bartholomew Fair?' I asked him. 'And when is it?'

'Bart's Fair?' he asked, scratching his bald head under his wig. 'Why, 'tis a monstrous big fair held on the grounds in Smithfield, by St Bartholomew's hospital. 'Tis there for two weeks at every end of August.'

Anne had gone through to our back room now. She was having trouble removing some of the patches, for they had set hard on her skin, and every now and then she gave a little shriek as she pulled at them.

'And are there conjurers at this fair, and magic men?' I asked him more quietly, for I did not wish Anne to hear.

'There is everything there!' said Mr Newbery. 'Plays and players, dancing shows, educated apes, puppets and horses dancing jigs! The whole world is there.'

I felt excited already. 'Then Anne and I must go!'

Mr Newbery frowned. 'You'll get your throats cut and lose your pockets as sure as a sow drags its belly on the ground!' he said. 'The place is fair bursting with higglers, hawkers and robbers.'

I could not but laugh. 'It's a wonder we've survived in London so long,' I said, 'and thank you for warning me, but I think we'll take our chances. You have painted too exciting a picture for us to miss it.'

Chapter Eight

Bartholomew Fair

'Carried my wife by coach to Bartholomew Fair and showed her the monkies dancing on the ropes. There was also a horse with hoofs curled like Ram's horns, a goose with four feet and a cock with three. Then to see some clockworks and several scripture stories, but above all there was shown the sea, with Neptune, Venus, mermaids and the sea rolling.'

As soon as we came to Smithfield market, which led on to the fair, I began to be afeared that I would lose Anne, for seeing the field set with such a gay scene stretching in all directions she began uttering little shrieks of excitement and running here, there and everywhere, so that I wished I had her on a restraining tether like a child. As Mr Newbery had said, it was a monstrous big fair and would likely take several days to get around it all.

By Smithfield, forty roast pigs turned on their spits as the butchers cried up their products. There was a rich smell in the air, the sizzle of crackling and the singe of smoke. 'Tender pork! Here's your delicate pig and pork!' they called. 'A good sausage, and well made!'

'Hot sheep's feet!'

'Rare beefsteaks!'

'Trotters all hot!'

I stopped to sniff the tantalising odours, suddenly feeling hungry.

'What d'you lack, sweet ladies? What d'you lack?'

Two peddlers stopped before us, their trays laden with an assortment of braids and tassels, ribbons and silk flowers.

'Oh, what lovely colours!' Anne said, straightaway delving into a tangled skein of ribbons.

'Fine ribbons, pin cases, lovely flowers – what d'you lack?'

'We lack nothing at the moment,' I said to them, pulling Anne's hand away. 'For we have just arrived and must see everything else before we buy.' But we had made the mistake of pausing and looking, and now found ourselves surrounded by a dozen or more hawkers.

'Fine pears!' one called.

'Sweet gingerbread!'

'Ballads, fine new ballads!'

'Fresh fish . . . fresh new fish!'

'Fine singing birds!'

'Ink – seven pence a pint! Very fine, bright ink!'

'Strawberries ripe! Cherries! Asparagus!'

'A powder for a flea!'

A crowd of them were round us, and indeed it seemed that every London peddler and street seller was today at Bartholomew Fair trying to do business.

I grasped Anne's hand. 'Come and we will run for it!' I said to her and, dodging through the sellers, we ran across the grass towards the bigger booths and the striped tents and awnings, all bright with fluttering flags and streamers.

Pausing by a puppet show, I spoke to Anne seriously. 'You must show no interest in buying anything,' I said, 'or you will find we have spent our money before we have even started. You must stay beside me all the time, and not go wandering off. And you must keep your hand on your pocket all the time, for everyone has told us of the cut-purses here and Mr Newbery seems to think that we'll be lucky enough to get home with our heads on.'

'But it's all so thrilling!' she said breathlessly. 'And I've never before seen such sights in all my life. Nor so many of them!'

I could not but smile. 'Neither have I. But we must be cautious,' I added.

Arm in arm we began to stroll through the tents and booths, admiring, exclaiming and gasping by turn and not knowing what our eyes would fall on next. There were rare sights to see, and the dress and appearance of the visitors (who were of the quality as well as tag, rag and bobtail) were almost a show of their own. The ladies were dressed in their best, but it was a mixed best: some wearing full wigs, face masks and vast plumed hats, some up from the country in out-of-fashion moiré dresses with straw bonnets, some in neat riding habits and some attired as if they were attending a ball at the palace.

We paused outside a tent showing a drawing of a tiny person standing by a daffodil, and refreshed ourselves with a glass of juniper water. 'Shall we go to see this sideshow?' Anne asked. 'What does it say?'

I read from the printed notice: '*Inside sits a girl of sixteen years of age, not above eighteen inches long. She reads well, sings, whistles and all very pleasant to hear. You may see this wonderful creature for the sum of two pence.*'

'Oh, do let's go in!' Anne said.

I shook my head. 'It must be some trick,' I said, trying to peer around the curtain to see what was within. 'It cannot be a true person.'

'A girl as real as life!' the showman cried, seeing our interest. 'Only come in and see for yourself. And ladies only may see this creature in her shift.'

But Anne was now looking at the canvas booth next door, which was painted to look like a horse's stable and had, in fact, a real horse peering out of the flap on the door.

'What will happen here?' she asked me.

'*The Mare that counts money,*' I read out. '*Come and see this beast who is as clever as a man. She counts, gives wise advice on investments and imparts knowledge.*'

'That cannot be!' Anne said.

'No, it cannot,' I said, laughing.

'Come see the horse that counts!' the showman called. 'Wisdom truly from the horse's mouth!'

We walked on and Anne moved closer to me, for three chained lunatics came along, gibbering and dancing with a bear who wore irons on its legs. A man with them carried a notice which announced that they were released for the day from Bethlehem Hospital, which was a madhouse, and were available to come to the houses of the quality to amuse their guests for a small fee.

As we walked on my eyes were everywhere, darting through spaces and over people's heads, trying to see the one show that I was really looking for: was Count de'Ath going to be at the fair today?

A man passed with six or seven monkeys sitting all over him, and another wore the head of a great beast and carried a board which announced that all should repent of their sins, for this was the Year of the Beast and judgement was at hand.

Anne pointed towards a large tent with a board outside. 'B . . . best sh . . . show,' she began reading out haltingly, for I had been helping her with her letters and her reading and writing were slowly improving.

'. . . in the fair,' I continued. 'A *wonderful curiosity. A man with one head and two bodies, both masculine, who is lately brought over from the country of the Moguls, and with him his brother who has hair down to his knees.*'

'I don't think I should care to see those,' Anne said. 'I would rather see the little creature as tall as a flower.'

'Or what about this,' I said, reading out from the next-door booth: '*A tableau recently come from Russia of curiously preserved people who are enchanted and lay between life and death. You may touch and examine these people as much as you wish for no extra charge.*'

Anne gasped. 'I should like to see those!'

There were more of the same at the other sideshows: dancing apes, a dog that played the tabor, a man twice the size of a Lincolnshire heifer, a hare that did a morris dance, a woman with a prodigious beard. I could not see the Count and his magic cabinet, however.

After much deliberation we decided to go into the booth with the Russian tableau for, as Anne said, we would get several people for the price of one. Paying our money, we went behind a curtain and came across a strange scene, which so startled me that I turned to go out again, thinking that we had somehow gone the wrong way and strayed into some lady's drawing room by mistake.

In the tent was a long upholstered sofa, and on this sat three people: two women and a man. Each was exquisitely dressed in velvet and satins, and each engaged in drinking tea, either holding a cup to their lips or conveying it delicately towards its saucer.

This in itself was not strange. What was most surprising, though, was that none of the people was moving, but rather seemed frozen in that moment, each teacup neither touching their lips nor ever reaching its destined saucer. More strange still – for people could, mayhap, play at statues, but *animals* couldn't – there was a golden-haired lapdog sitting on one of the lady's laps, its pink tongue hanging forth and its head coyly on one side.

'Oh!' Anne breathed and, after standing in silence staring at them staring at us, we circled the trio, examining them minutely.

'They do not breathe,' Anne said timidly. 'Are they alive?'

'They do not even blink!' I said, passing my hand in front of the man's eyes.

Daringly, I put out a hand to touch the hand of the woman. It was smooth and cool, almost like skin but not quite.

'It *looks* like skin,' I said, peering at her cheek as closely as I dared, for I was in a mind to think that these people were enchanted and would be released from their spell in a moment and chastise us for examining them so rudely.

We tiptoed around them, looking at their hair, their clothes and their shoes. Every aspect of them was considered and refined. One of the ladies was wearing mules and I could see the tips of her toes, pink-painted, while the other carried a little silver-mesh bag in which could be seen her red lip-crayon and patch box.

'Is one of them the sleeping beauty who was put under a wicked spell?' Anne asked in awe.

I shook my head. 'I don't know,' I said wonderingly, 'but they are mighty strange.'

The entrance curtain was just then pulled aside again and two well-dressed ladies came into the show, starting with fright just as we had done at the sight of the trio there.

Then one began to laugh. 'Do not fear – they are made of wax!' she said to her companion. 'I have seen similar at Southwarke Fair.'

'But so real!' said her friend in awe.

'I believe the maker is a skilled artist who does likenesses on tombs.'

The other said, shuddering, 'I don't like them. They're too lifelike for me.'

'Too death-like!' corrected the first as they went out.

Anne and I now looked again, rather disappointed, at the wax statues. 'Then they're not enchanted sleeping beauties,' she said.

I shook my head. 'I suspect that little in this fair is what it seems to be.'

Feeling hungry, we went to Pie Corner and had hot pasties and a dish of peas, followed by gilt gingerbread and buttered ale, all of which were excellent. We saw a Dog Toby dance the hornpipe, then Jacob Hall – who was rumoured to be the lover of several high-born ladies – performing on a tight-rope high in the air and making everyone scream with fright at his antics. We heard bands and bagpipes, kettledrums and fiddlers, and saw many more sights, including the educated ape of whom Mr Newbery had spoken.

Anne then found a gypsy who, on her hand being crossed with a piece of silver, promised to tell you who you would marry and how many children you would have, and said she would return your money if it didn't come true.

'Oh do let me go!' Anne implored me. 'She says she sees spirits walk and fairies dance – and I do so want to know who I'll marry.'

'But it costs a piece of silver!' I said. 'And how will you get your money back from her if none of it comes true?'

Anne looked shocked. 'She is a high-born gypsy queen!' she said. 'She has second sight. Of course it'll come true.'

I might have relented and gone to the gypsy as well (for of course I, too, was anxious to know if I would marry) but then, at last, I saw on the edge of the field a board announcing *Count de'Ath and his Magick Cabinet.*

I steered Anne away from the gypsy. 'We will go later perhaps,' I said. 'But for now we must go and find the man I came to see.'

The Count was standing on some steps by his tent, which was of a large oval shape and looked as if it could contain a hundred people. Tall, dark and strange-looking, he was pointing with a stick at the words on the board before him. I read them out to Anne. *'An enchantment so strong that men can be turned to air! See someone enter my cabinet and be transported over land and sea, never to return!'*

'You're not going into that cabinet!' Anne said in sudden fright, putting her arm round my waist. 'I shan't let you go!'

'Of course I'm not going in it,' I said. 'I just want to see the magic performed again, and perhaps speak to the Count.'

The board announced a show starting on the stroke of every hour, and we paid our three pence and entered, ready to wait the twenty minutes or so. Evidently Count de'Ath had quite a following, for there was already a small crowd inside sitting on benches and waiting for three o'clock.

We sat towards the back and began talking of all the sights we had seen that day, and indeed were glad of the rest in the cool darkness of the tent, which was lined in some black cloth and had only some tapers to light it.

More people entered, and then it was three o'clock and Count de'Ath himself came through from outside and walked on to the small wooden stage at the front, where his cabinet stood ready. As before, he went through the same talk – asking if there was anyone who wanted to escape from his wife or creditors and saying they could enter his cabinet and be transported away.

As before, no one in the audience moved.

He asked again for someone to enter the box. 'And ze price vill merely be your soul,' he added.

There were a few gasps, then an eerie silence, as if everyone were holding their breath.

I scanned the front rows. No one. No one who looked like Tom.

But then someone got to his feet. 'I will go!' a man called. 'I will leave this land of horror and plague, and if I lose my soul then so be it!'

The man who'd spoken was a monk, in rough brown habit tied with rope and a deep hood over his head which half-concealed his face. A stir ran around the audience at seeing his garb. 'A holy monk to lose his soul!' Anne said, shocked, for indeed it did seem terrible that a man of God should have truck with the Devil's work.

Count de'Ath spent some moments telling the monk exactly when it would be necessary to extract payment for the journey he would be making, and how there was no going back on this strange bargain, and through it all I sat enraptured, listening to everything, watching avidly and hardly breathing, so intense was my scrutiny of everything that was happening on the stage. The man would go to Hell, sure as anything. How desperate he must be!

Two men from the audience examined the cabinet carefully, tapping it back and front, and then the monk silently turned and entered it. It was then that my heart stood still, for under the hood I saw that it was Tom, and no other.

How could this be?

Amazed and unbelieving, I wanted to call out, yet could not, for I felt as frozen and petrified as the wax people we had seen. The curtain was pulled across, concealing the monk from view. Count de'Ath muttered something in a strange language and then a moment passed, the curtain was opened again and the monk was gone.

Several women in the audience screamed and there was a groan from a man in front of us.

'Oh, where has he gone?' Anne whispered.

Count de'Ath bowed stiffly, then the audience was dismissed and began to shuffle out, looking mystified and amazed.

'Real enchantment!' Anne said wonderingly. 'Now that was proper magic, wasn't it?'

'I . . . I do not know.'

She stood up and tugged at my hand. 'Where shall we go now?'

I didn't move, for I was confused, and couldn't come to terms with all that was in my head. First Tom was dead, then I saw him go into a magic cabinet at the theatre and vanish, then he appeared as a monk – and then disappeared again.

Was he really dead?

Had he become a monk?

Had he sold his soul?

'Come on!' Anne said. 'We must see more things before it gets dark.'

I shook my head. 'I have something I must do. I

think . . . I think I know the person who went into the cabinet.'

'What?' Anne looked at me strangely. 'How do you know a monk?'

'He may not be a monk.' I shook my head as if to clear it. 'Wait for me, Anne. I have to go to see Count de'Ath.'

I ran outside, but the Count was not yet back on his stand at the front of the tent trying to entice people for the next performance, so I went around to the back. Here there was a square canvas tent about as tall as a man, with a flap-door tied up with rope. Someone was within, that was certain, for the canvas was moving about as if someone were divesting themselves of their clothing.

'Count de'Ath?' I enquired uncertainly, and then, 'Tom?'

The movement ceased.

'Tom?' I asked again, 'is it you?' And at once a surge of joy and certainty ran through me so that I felt filled with light and happiness. 'It's Hannah.'

The canvas door was pushed aside and Tom was there looking at me in disbelief: he was thin, pale and shorn of his hair, but not dead at all. Not a monk. Nor changed into air and transported over seas.

'Tom!' I said, a sob half-choking me. 'It's really you. I thought you were dead!'

'I thought *you* were!'

And then losing all modesty, I put my arms around his thin frame and held him as if I would never let him go.

From beside us, there was a drawn-out gasp. 'What's happening and who is this?' Anne's voice asked. Neither of us answered and a moment later her tone changed and became pert and lively. 'Oh, Hannah! Is this your sweetheart?'

Still holding on to him tightly, I managed to nod. 'Yes, Anne. Yes, this is Tom.'

Chapter Nine

2nd September

'My maid called us up about three in the morning to tell us of a great fire they saw in the City. So I rose and went to the window . . . but thought it far enough off and so went to bed again and to sleep.'

The following day I was in an agony of suspense as I waited for Tom to arrive – mostly because I could hardly believe that he was really coming. When I'd woken that morning it had seemed to me that I'd imagined the whole thing and had only dreamt that I'd found him at the fair, for to meet someone you thought was dead seemed a strange and incredible thing – and to discover that person in the cabinet of a magician even more fantastical. It was only Anne's questioning of me as soon as my eyes were open that told me that it had really happened.

'But what do you *think* he was doing there?' she asked, leaning up on one elbow in our bed to stare at me.

I shook my head, still as baffled as she.

'Is he really a monk? Did he not go into that

cabinet? How could he just disappear from it and be outside all the time?'

'I don't know, I don't know, I don't know!' I said.

'Will he really come round today?'

'He promised he would . . .'

Rising, I found we were out of water, so I threw a shawl over my nightshift and went down to the well at the end of the lane to draw some. As I walked back, I swung the buckets I carried and felt like bursting out singing. Tom was alive. I'd found him. He hadn't died of plague at all!

The afternoon before, when I'd stopped crying, he'd peeled my arms away gently and told me to go to the front of the stand before Count de'Ath came and found us speaking.

'I will explain all to you tomorrow,' he'd said. 'Are you living at the shop again?'

I'd nodded. 'But do you truly promise to come to me?'

'I truly promise! It's Sunday and the fair will be closed. The Count owes me some free time.'

'But how have you—'

'It's been a deal of do,' he'd said, 'but I will tell all tomorrow. Go now, or I'll lose my job!'

Now, as I carried the water into our shop, Mr Newbery was just coming out of his. He was not wearing his wig and his face was fuddled with sleep, his eyes rheumy.

I bade him good morning, but he scowled at me and held his head, and I guessed he had spent overlong at the alehouse the previous night. I was very anxious to tell someone my news, however. 'Anne and I enjoyed Bartholomew Fair, Mr Newbery!' I said. 'And the most surprising and excellent thing – you remember my friend Tom who worked with Doctor da Silva the apothecary along the lane?'

'The 'pothecary died of plague,' he said gruffly. 'And so did his lad.'

'But he *didn't*, though,' I said. 'For I found him at the fair. Tom, my sweetheart!'

He grunted. 'Is he much changed and crippled by having the sickness?'

'Hardly changed at all!'

'Then the disease went inside,' he said, nodding sagely. 'More than likely he will be mad.'

I could do naught but laugh. 'He's not mad at all! He's as sensible as you and I and he's coming round today!'

But Mr Newbery just gave another grunt and shuffled off down the road.

By the time the bell-man rang two o'clock, though, I was getting concerned. Anne and I had spent the morning busily preparing frosted petals and making several violet cakes with some flowers we'd bought at the fair, but by noon our rooms were straight and I was ready – more than ready, for indeed I'd changed my dress several times. Though I loved my green taffeta gown best of all, I remembered that Tom had seen this when we'd walked out the previous year, so felt compelled to change into my tabby suit. I then thought my blue linen gown might be more suitable (for it was another hot day) but once it was on me I found that it had several spots on it – from Anne wearing it – so changed back once again into my green taffeta.

All this was regarded very closely by Anne, who watched me with interest and then offered me patches and hair pomade, both of which I turned down. I put some orange flower water behind my ears and a little rose oil on my lips, however, and did not think this too immodest.

'Are you sure he'll come?' she asked, as I settled for the green, hung up my other gowns and swore I would not change again. 'For I still don't understand how he *can*, for he was supposed to be changed into air and sent over lands and seas . . .'

'I don't know either,' I said, walking once again to the shutters and peering out. 'But I believe he'll come.'

By the time the crier called three I was fair distracted out of my mind, but a little after this we heard a tap on the door. Anne sprang to it and flung it open before I could pose myself, for I had thought to be seated demurely with Kitty on my lap, but instead was seen crouched down engaged in picking something off my shoe.

Tom stood in the doorway and removed his hat and bowed, and I rose hastily and curtseyed, which actions seemed formal and strange to me, seeing as I had spent some moments the previous afternoon sobbing in his arms. But then he came over and kissed my cheek and took my hand in his, and we sat together on the wooden bench in the shop, with Anne on the chair a little distance off, surveying us with interest.

'I'm sorry to be later than I wanted to be,' he said. 'I had to run an errand on the way and got tangled in a crowd near the river, for there's much astir there.'

'Why's that?' Anne asked.

'I heard that there's a fire near to the wharves.'

'There are always fires there,' I said. 'There was one at the tallow-chandlers last week which gutted the place right out.'

'Is it a big fire?' Anne asked.

'I couldn't see it. But someone roused the Lord Mayor in the night to tell of it and ask for the fire-squirts to be brought, and he looked on it and said it was nothing and that a woman might piss it out.'

Anne and I laughed, but Tom suddenly looked embarrassed. 'You must pardon me for using such a term,' he said, 'but I have not had female company for many a month and I have almost forgot my manners.'

'Then you *are* a monk?' Anne asked.

'No, I am not.'

'Oh! And you didn't go into the cabinet and get turned into air?'

Smiling, he shook his head. 'No. But you mustn't tell a soul that it's not true.'

'*None* of it is true?' Anne and I both asked at once.

'None of it.'

'Not magic?' Anne said, disappointed.

'I will tell you all, and tell you truly,' he said. 'But first let me ask where is your sister Sarah, and what happened to you after you left London?'

I took a deep breath. 'It's a long story,' I said, and attempted to tell him in as few words as possible (for I was more than anxious to hear *his* tale) about our stay in Dorchester at the pesthouse, and then at Highclear, and our journey home when Sarah had met Giles Copperly, and then about me and Anne coming to London. 'And when I reached London I was told that both you and Doctor da Silva had contracted plague and were dead!' I finished.

Tom was silent a while. 'Doctor da Silva died, God rest his soul,' he said then. 'I was thought to be dead, too – and even taken for a ride on a death cart.'

'You were put on the death cart?' I gasped, while Anne sat open-mouthed.

He nodded. 'The Doctor had already died and I was unconscious when they took up our bodies with some others to convey us to the pit,' he said. 'Luckily for me, though, the buboes under my arm had burst and the poison was slowly draining from me, so that when the cart reached the pit I had recovered my wits enough to sit up and ask for a pigeon pastie.'

I tried to laugh with him yet could not, for his dying was not a matter in which I could find humour.

'I lay abed for some weeks until I was strong enough to stir myself, and then I had to find a job. I heard at a hiring fair that Count de'Ath wanted a thin, strong lad, so applied for the position.' He stretched out his arms. 'Do you find me changed?'

I nodded. 'You are much thinner, yes, and taller – and you have no hair to speak of.'

'That is because I lost my hair to the plague and it is only just now growing again. But I have reason to thank the sickness for my present job, for only a very thin person could fit into the secret space at the back of the cabinet, and on that my job depends.'

'So you just go into the back of the cabinet?' Anne said, looking affronted. 'There is no magic to it at all?'

He shook his head. 'I'm afraid not.'

She sighed heavily. 'It is too bad to think there's no magic in the world.'

'There *is* magic.' Tom's eyes caught mine and locked

with them. 'For those who are lucky. But it is not a matter of cabinets and disappearing monks.'

Tom and I went for a walk. I longed to go to Chelsea again, where we had spent a day last year picking wild flowers, but the sun was already low in the sky and the walk would have taken several hours. Instead we went out of the City by Ludgate and took a route past the prison and over Fleet River (which was stinking very bad after the hot summer we had had) and from there to the Strand to admire the new-built houses of the nobility. We came near to the king's palace at Whitehall and I told Tom about coming back to London on May Day, and seeing His Majesty on the royal barge.

'May Day.' Tom frowned slightly, trying to remember. 'I was in Bath then, appearing at the pleasure gardens.'

'With Count de'Ath?' I asked.

He nodded. 'I've been with him for six months now.'

'Is he a good man?'

Tom raised his eyebrows. 'A cat will be a cat still,' he said.

I looked at him for his meaning.

'He is as good as any quack can be, but he is not a real Count, and not even French.' He smiled. 'When he is not Count de'Ath he is Doctor Marvell. Have you heard of Doctor Marvell's excellent medicine?'

'No!' I said, laughing.

'Doctor Marvell's medicine can cure everything from rupture to measles and from toothache to the bladder stone,' Tom said solemnly. 'Three bottles will fit a man for life and cure any illness he is likely to encounter during all of that time.'

'Can it cure plague?' I asked.

'Everything!' he said firmly, with the glint of a smile in his eye.

'And what is in this wonderful linctus?'

'Nettle water.'

'What's that?'

'A few leaves of nettle steeped in water. And perhaps a leaf of curled parsley for luck.'

I began to laugh. 'That will not cure anyone!'

'But 't'will not kill anyone, either. And if you think it is doing you good then mayhap it will. It'll do the quack doctors good, certainly,' he went on, 'for there were a hundred different cures for plague and men were made rich by them.'

'But why did you not take up a new apprenticeship with another apothecary?' I asked after a moment.

'Because there was no one to pay my premium,' he said. 'When I recovered from plague I journeyed home, but could not find my father and stepmother. I was told they had moved away.' His voice broke slightly and I squeezed his hand and looked at him with tenderness, for I could see that he had felt himself alone in the world. 'But I get on well with Count de'Ath,' he said with more cheer, 'and it is a merry job, for when I am not making bottles of nettle water then I am an actor.'

'So it's always you who appears and goes into the cabinet?'

He nodded. 'Sometimes I'm a monk, sometimes I'm a farmer, on occasion I'm a woman! I have six changes of face and keep a record of what person I am where, for I must never appear in the same guise twice in the same place.'

'I saw you at the theatre dressed as a dandy,' I said. 'At least, it seemed to be someone who looked much like you. That was partly why we came to Bartholomew Fair – so I could see the show again.'

He smiled. 'I'm very glad that you did.'

I hesitated a moment. 'What I cannot understand,' I said slowly, 'is that seeing how you were alive all the time, you did not come round to the shop to see me.'

'I did!' he said. 'I came when we were in London earlier this year – in February or March.'

'Oh! We were still in Dorset then . . .'

'I came round in a rush, dressed as a monk, and spoke to your neighbour – the frowsy-headed fellow at the sign of the Parchment and Quill.'

'Mr Newbery.'

'And he told me you were dead for sure, and he might take over your shop if no one claimed it.'

'The hog-grubber!' I gasped. And then I looked at Tom from under my eyelashes. 'But did you just come round to ask for me once only?' I asked, for this did not seem to me to be enough.

He smiled, his head on one side. 'And did you enquire after *me* once only?' he countered.

'Indeed not!' I said indignantly. 'I saw that Doctor da Silva's shop was shuttered, and spoke to an old lady who said that you'd gone to the pesthouse and died, and then I enquired at the pesthouse and saw it recorded that the death cart had taken you!' I paused. 'But how many times did you ask for me?'

'I was at Death's door for six weeks – so you will excuse me not asking *then*,' he said, laughing a little, 'and then I was travelling across England, to Bath and Warminster and Canterbury to all the fairs and theatres that Count de'Ath could reach. I came to enquire about you both times we were in London, however – the first when I spoke to your neighbour and once again, late one afternoon after we'd appeared at the King's Theatre. I banged at your door but although it was a trading day the shop was still shut and boarded, so I feared that you must really be dead.'

'It was shut and boarded because I was at the theatre seeing you!' I said. 'Nelly Gwyn had been in the shop and given us tickets for that very day.'

We mock-glared at each other, then this gave way to laughter and thence – in myself at least – to something close to tears, for we had so nearly lost each other, and it had been only the most peculiar set of circumstances which had caused us to find each other again.

I wiped my eyes with my fingers and Tom pulled a linen kerchief out of his pocket for me, and with it came a length of bright green silk ribbon.

'For me?' I gasped. 'How pretty!'

'No, it is for my new disguise . . .' Tom began, and then he stopped and lifted my chin, for my face had fallen in disappointment. 'No, indeed it is not! I was only teasing, for I bought it yesterday at the fair. And there is a silver locket too, which is to go on the ribbon and be tied around your neck.'

'Oh!' I said, and could not say more or even thank him because I was quite speechless with pleasure and happiness.

'And I'm glad you're wearing this green gown, for I bought it specially to match it,' he added.

We had walked a good way out of the City by this time, and were in a pretty lane alongside the Thames where Michaelmas daisies grew amass in blue, purple and white clumps. There was a fallen oak tree covered in all manner of ferns and ivies, and we sat upon this and Tom carefully threaded the locket on to the ribbon and tied it around my neck. When it was tied fast his hands moved from around my neck to my face, one finger tracing along the line of my cheek, another trembling on my lips. I lifted my face to his, seeing the sun shimmering the sky crimson and dappling the river with light, and then, as I closed my eyes, his mouth came down softly upon mine.

My first kiss was everything I'd dreamed it would be, and there were two more kisses after it before Tom took a deep breath and said that we ought to be getting back.

'That's what I was thinking,' I said quickly, although I hadn't at all, but did not want him to think of me as a girl ready to throw up her petticoats at any man's asking.

'We'll be together again soon,' he said.

I felt the locket at my neck and ran my fingers over its cool smooth shape, impatient to get home and look at it properly, for I had not had time to see it before he'd put it on me. 'Will we?' I asked. 'For you'll be travelling around all the time with Count de'Ath.'

'Well, we are at Bartholomew Fair all this week, and then go over the river to Southwarke, and from there to Richmond – and I can come and see you from all those places.'

'But what then?' I asked, for I felt I couldn't let him go.

'Then . . .' He shrugged. 'I don't know. With the winter coming mayhap the Count will shore up somewhere for a season. And London is where the money is to be made, so we may stay here.'

I sighed. 'But what if it—'

He interrupted me by kissing me again, lightly, on my nose. 'Wait and see. If I go away then I'll give you a kiss for each freckle and this will last us until we meet again.'

And with this I had to be content.

Walking downriver a little, we came to a landing stage where several boatmen were plying their trades ferrying people across to the other bank, and Tom negotiated a fare of sixpence with a young water-dog for us to be taken as far as Swan Steps at London Bridge. It started off a pleasant trip, for although the sun had almost disappeared, it was still warm with a light breeze, and a soft mist was rising from each bank of the river. There were craft aplenty: families out with their servants, couples deep in each other's eyes, and groups of young men carousing.

It was only when we were coming to the last deep bend of the Thames before the City that we became aware that all was not as it should be. The craft we were seeing were not bent on pleasure; some were being rowed hard, with a purpose, across to the other bank or upstream and away. And then as we came around the river's bend we heard strange sounds: the clashing noise of church bells reverse-pealing, and an awkward crackling sound tempered by the occasional sharp bang of what sounded like fireworks.

Our water-dog hailed another to ask what was amiss, saying that he had only just now begun his evening's work.

'Fire!' the other yelled back. 'Some of the wharves are alight and you'll not be able to land at Swan Steps.'

Our water-dog swore, and said he would land us wherever he could and the rest of the trip could go hang, and so began to row us towards the bank.

As we cleared the bend we could see the fire for ourselves, as it was sending up pillars of smoke in a line all along the river from Black Swan Alley, where I sometimes went for sugar, past Cold Harbour as far as London Bridge. In all, the flames looked to stretch for a quarter of a mile or more.

'This must be the fire that I told you of this morning!' Tom said as we both stared in horror at the bank. 'I had no idea it was this bad.'

''Tis more fire than I have ever seen at once!' I gasped.

The boatman began to swear under his breath for, although he was rowing as fast and as hard as he could, backwards and forwards, he could not find a landing stage which was not crowded with people intent on putting out to river and getting away.

'Your fare will be double!' he shouted to Tom, and Tom could not but agree to pay him.

Up and down the river we rowed without finding a place to alight, and once the boatman threatened to put us out on the Southwarke side of the river, and upped his fare to one shilling and sixpence not to do so. Tom again agreed to pay, for the north side of the bridge was now burning hard, its glistening timbers falling, splashing and sizzling into the water, and we knew we would not get across it if we were landed on the Southwarke side.

Once we were close by to the river banks we could see people running along Fish Hill and Thames Street, some of them pushing their furniture on carts, or carrying chairs atop of their heads. Two or three churches were alight, too, their steeples standing black like witches' hats with the flames rushing up them, and even old Dyers Hall was afire with orange and gold flames reaching towards the sky. As I looked in wonderment and fear at this mighty building, the roof fell in with a terrible crash and a great cloud of dust and golden sparks lifted into the sky. A gust of wind wafted these across to a row of houses in Black Raven Alley, and I saw some thatched roofs catch and then a man running along the street with his clothes alight.

I clasped Tom's arm tightly, for I was much afraid, and it looked for a while as if we would not be able to land at all. In a few moments, however, the boatman put us out a little downriver at Broken Wharf Steps, his boat being immediately taken by two men who were intent on getting away and did not care where. I heard the boatman demand from them the sum of five shillings, and I did not doubt that he would get it, for the men seemed in a passion of fear.

As we reached the top of the steps I looked back to the river. Dense smoke was now hanging over the water like a fog, and sparks and fragments of burning wood and cloth were falling into it, hissing and spluttering. The rising moon showed a family standing by the waterside throwing all their possessions into a wherry: table, chairs, clothes, bedding – all went in. The moon then gleamed crimson and a moment later vanished under billowing clouds of smoke, and the family disappeared into the dark so that I did not see what happened to them.

Tom and I stood speechless, hardly knowing where to go or what to do.

In the streets running alongside the river, all was chaos and noise and stink – for the glue-makers were by this wharf and there was an acrid smell of burning bones and animal fat here. Fires roared to the right of us, windows shattered, barrels exploded and stones of buildings fragmented and fell. The street was thronged with people bent double under the weight of the goods they bore on their backs, or pushing hand carts with furniture atop. I saw a sick man lying on a pallet, moaning as he was carried along, and a whole family of ten or so children sitting on a farm cart, crying with fear.

An old woman was standing outside the door of her house looking around her in wonder, and Tom stopped to speak to her.

'What's happening here now?' he asked. 'Is anyone fighting the fire?'

'Oh, 'tis all in fair order,' she nodded, 'for the king is now come to fight it with his brother the Duke. They have ordered the pulling down of all houses in its path.' She cocked her head to one side. 'If you listen you can hear the crashes.'

'But where did the fire start?'

'Over east a way – Pudding Lane. In a baker's shop, so I've heard.'

'But you must leave here!' I said to her. 'The wind's blowing the fire in this direction.'

'I'll go just as soon as I've seen the king and spoken to him,' said the old woman.

'But he may not have time to speak to everyone! You must shift for yourself and go now!'

'There's plenty of time,' she said comfortably. 'Yon fire is more than two streets away.'

It seemed useless to argue with her, and Tom pulled at my hand. 'Come, Hannah,' he said. 'We must get back and see what danger there is for your shop. And for Anne.'

We were nigh exhausted by the time we reached the shop, for the streets near the river had been teeming with people, carts and horses trying to get away, and we'd sometimes had to employ our hands and elbows to fight our way through. Strangely, though, as we left the river behind, the smoke and roaring and smell all receded, as did the reverse-pealing bells, so that by the time we reached Crown and King Place and I saw our dear shop sign, all was calm and quiet, with no indication anywhere that there was a fire raging elsewhere in the City.

I hammered on the door. 'Are you all right?' I asked Anne, as she opened the door. 'Is all well here?'

'Of course,' she said, and I saw her eyes fall on the silver locket and widen. 'Why?'

'The fire!'

'What fire?' she asked.

Tom laughed. 'See. All's well. It will likely be put out tonight and tomorrow they will start rebuilding. 'Tis always the way.'

He took my hand and kissed it. I'd rather he had kissed me on the lips but as Anne was watching us, had to be content. 'But when will I see you?' I asked.

'I'll come tomorrow. In the evening when the fair

closes,' he said, and he blew me another kiss and ran off.

I watched him go. 'He stays on the fair site at Smithfield,' I said to Anne, a trifle anxiously. ''Tis a way outside the City walls, so he should be safe.'

'Why shouldn't he be?'

'Don't you listen? Because of the fire raging!'

'But you heard what he said . . .' Her eyes fell upon the locket again and sparked with interest. 'Now let me look at that silver heart, and tell me straight what he said as he gave it to you and if he declared love, for I cannot wait a moment longer to know.'

Chapter Ten

The Fire Takes Hold

'Met my Lord Mayor in Canning Street, and he cried like a fainting woman, "Lord what can I do? I am spent! People will not obey me. I have been pulling down houses but the fire overtakes us faster than we can work."'

No crier came to wake us the next morning, but I was awake at first light anyway, wondering if the fire was still burning and if it was, where it was heading. We were at the western corner of the City and a goodly way from the last point I had seen flames, but anything could have happened by now. Tom, however, had seemed sure that it would have been put out overnight, and I prayed that this would be so.

Tom. I felt for the locket around my neck, held it tightly between my fingers and wished on it that he would come to no harm. This thought of him led me to musing on his kisses, and I was about to begin going over them precisely, moment by moment, when there was a knock – nay, a hammering – on the shop door. Leaving Anne still dozing, I slid out of bed, pulled a shawl around myself and went to open it.

Mr Newbery stood there, fully dressed in his Sunday clothes of ribbon-edged breeches, doublet and cloak, with plumed hat over his periwig.

'Fire!' he pronounced gravely. 'A very desperate fire.'

I nodded. 'I saw it last night by the river.'

'And spreading north and like to engulf us all!'

'It will surely not spread as far as us,' I said. 'For isn't the king himself working to fight it now?'

'The king!' Mr Newbery said scornfully. 'This fire is a condemnation of that very man. It has been long said that this year has the number of the Beast and will contain a judgement against him and his depraved court!'

I didn't say anything to this but put on my listening face, for I knew a discourse was coming.

'The court did not change their ways so the Lord brought down a plague and a pestilence. And now he brings a fire to cleanse their souls.' He paused and added in a more general tone, 'What's more, the king has now acknowledged another royal bastard. That makes six of 'em that we know about!'

I stepped out on to the cobbles to look into the sky, which was white and milky with smoke and contained a pale and ineffective sun. There was a strong stench of burning in the air and, as I stood there, a flurry of paper, charred at the edges, dropped out of the sky around us.

'So it burns still!' I said.

'That is just what I've been saying,' he retorted. 'And I must rouse all our neighbours that haven't yet heard of it.'

Two lads passed us in a great hurry, and Mr Newbery hailed them and asked where they went.

'To Whitehall,' one of them called. 'The people are making a deputation for His Majesty to use greater measures to save them from the fire.'

'What can *he* do?' Mr Newbery asked scornfully. 'He is only one man.'

'He is the anointed king!' they said, as if this were enough in itself to preserve us all.

'And 'tis his fault we're stricken in the first place,' Mr Newbery muttered as they went on.

Anne had now stirred herself and came to stand beside me in the doorway. 'Oh! How big is the fire now?' she asked, looking up at the sky. 'Do we still open the shop this morning?'

I shrugged, looking at Mr Newbery for advice. 'I don't know.'

'People still have to eat,' he said. 'But I doubt if they will be eating sweetmeats. I myself intend to go to the market to buy some good cheese and some pies, in case the food markets are all closed tomorrow. And then I will pack the rest of my clothes and my possessions lest I have to flee.'

'Then we must do the same,' I said to Anne.

Mr Newbery licked his finger and held it high for a moment. 'The wind is changing,' he announced. 'It now blows towards the west of the City.'

'Where is the west?' Anne asked.

'Where we are, my good child!'

'But it's a way off yet, isn't it?' I said. 'It may yet be halted – or the wind may change again.'

'Or it may not,' Mr Newbery said.

I looked at him helplessly. 'Is there nothing more

that people can do to help themselves?' I asked.

He shrugged. 'If we had fire squirts we could dowse our houses – but there are none to be had.'

'What else?'

'The booksellers and stationers around St Paul's have taken their stocks and put them into the crypt,' he went on, 'and people are burying their treasured possessions in their gardens so that if the fire comes it will pass over them – indeed I passed a man burying his Parmesan cheese in his garden only yesterday. I myself am taking some of my best things to St Dominic's, so that they may lay safe within its walls.'

'But I saw churches on fire . . .' I said, speaking slowly, for it had just occurred to me that if this fire was a judgement from God, why was He also burning His own churches?

Mr Newbery shrugged. 'Goods will be safer there, stacked tight, than in our flimsy shops,' he said, and then went on his way to warn and befright our other neighbours. And indeed perhaps this was a good thing.

Anne and I got dressed quickly, hardly bothering to wash ourselves, for such was the smoke and smut in the air that to do so seemed a waste of time. I put on my old grey linen dress, which I cared for least, and carefully folded the others in case I should need to flee with them. I then made Anne do the same. After this we took a box and put in it the few things we valued: our kitchen equipment, chafing dishes, pans and bowls. We also took our canvas travelling bags, putting in them those hair combs, fans, favourite gloves, perfumes and odds and ends that are precious to those of the female sex.

Going out for provisions (for I could already see that there were very few bakers or milkmaids around), I decided we should head for Green Place, which was north of the City and just within the walls, rather than go towards the river where the fire seemed to be worst.

Although only one hour or so had passed since my conversation at the door with Mr Newbery, already the air outside was thicker. People seemed unsure of what they should do or where they should go, and several of our neighbours were standing around in little groups talking, glancing often down towards the City, where sometimes could be heard the dead-pealing of bells or a thudding gunpowder-bang where a house had been blown up to try and create a fire break.

We'd not taken more than a few steps when I suddenly remembered Kitty, who'd been curled asleep in a drawer.

'Shall we take her out with us in the basket?' Anne asked eagerly.

I shook my head. 'But we must go and close our back door and keep her inside,' I said. 'We can't risk her straying.'

Anne went back in to make her safe and at that moment a gang of men came running along the lane, some ten or twelve of them, carrying staves and sticks.

'The Frenchman!' I heard one shout. 'Where is he?'

I made to slip back inside our door, for I could see they meant business, but one of them saw me.

'The Frenchman – where does he live?' a heavy-set man shouted at me.

'I don't know of any Frenchman living down here,'

I said, shrinking back.

'There are no foreigners about!' Mr Gilbert, one of our neighbours, called over.

'Yes there is! Maurice is his name,' said the heavy-set man.

I shook my head again and tried to go inside again, but he took my arm. 'If you see him, tell him he'll hang for this.'

'We'll hang him ourselves!' another cried. 'And draw and quarter him as well.'

'What has he done?' Mr Gilbert asked.

'Fired our city. Put an incendiary through a window and set London alight!'

There was an angry murmur from our neighbours at this. 'There's a lodging house at the corner. Over the milliner's shop,' one said. 'He may be there.'

As the men ran off Mr Gilbert called to me that it wasn't safe to be a foreigner in London now, for gangs were seeking out any French and Dutch and accusing them of starting the fire. 'They even seized on an Italian washerwoman and threw her into the river!' he added.

Anne and I made our purchases without difficulty, for Green Place was where the country housewives came to sell their garden produce and their baking, and there were many more there that day who had not been willing to venture further into the City.

We stayed some time gossiping, for some folk there had already been made homeless by the fire and had tales to tell, and there were also those whose houses and shops were now in direct line with the fire and so were on their way out of the City. As in the plague, I saw that it was the poor who suffered most, for they had no carriages or carts to convey their goods or themselves away, nor place to go, and so these newly homeless were making their way to Moore Fields or London Fields to lie until the fire was brought under control.

We gathered around one woman who was telling of how she had seen the king himself amid the flames. 'He was stripped to his linen undershirt!' she said, 'passing buckets of water from the river to try and dowse the fire at Apothecaries Hall. His brother the Duke was alongside him, and both looking the very essence of masculinity and strength.'

'How did you know it was the king?' one asked. 'Was he wearing his crown?'

'Or was there an actress alongside o' him to rub salve into his burns?'

There was laughter before the woman replied with dignity that she knew it was he because a fine black horse had been standing alongside, held by a groom, and the horse's saddle and blanket had borne the royal standard.

Another housewife told of the looting which was going on in the Halls of the Guilds. 'At Dyers Hall, as soon as the fire had cooled, looters came crunching across the ashes and took away all the melted gold and silver they could handle.'

'I heard this too!' another joined in. 'And some twelve full suits of armour have been seen going downriver on a barge.'

'I saw a man killed over the hire of a cart!' one volunteered. 'Two men were bidding the owner five shillings . . . ten shillings . . . then the sum was one pound, and it went up and up until they had reached ten pounds!'

There were murmurs of wonder at this.

'The owner gave the cart over to one of the men and took the money,' the tale-teller went on, 'whereupon the other took out a knife, stabbed him and ran off with the cart!'

'But there is plenty of money to be earned for honest labour!' a man on a stall sought to tell everyone. 'They've set up fireposts down in the City. Each is provisioned with beer and bread, and the king will give a shilling a day to each diligent man who helps fight the fire.'

'That's only because he's fair frighted out of his wits that it'll reach his palace,' one answered dourly.

'It'll not reach that far,' said the stall-holder, 'for they're now pulling down rows of houses in the fire's path with grappling irons.'

'But the flames have a mind of their own and leap over the gaps that are left!' a woman said. 'I've seen it with my own eyes leave two rows of houses untouched and start ablazing in a complete new spot.'

'I heard of a family who lost their direction in the darkness,' another offered. 'A heap of coal on the quay caught fire, sending thick rolling smoke everywhere, and yon folk ended up with their cart in a blind alley and were set upon by a marauding gang. All their furniture and possessions were taken from them!'

Anne and I listened to these tales with bated breath, scarce knowing if we should believe them or if the reports were exaggerated. Anne thought they could not all be true but I, having seen London in the grips of plague and encountered many and worse horrors, was inclined to believe them all.

Having completed our purchases, we both felt full of a strange restlessness and did not want to go back to the shop, for we did not feel we could follow our normal routine and begin frosting sweetmeats on a day such as this. Instead we decided to walk to the north of the City and see if we could climb the City walls and glimpse the fire from there, and thus find out whether it progressed or no, and if so, whether it approached us.

Smoke now hung directly over us like a cloud, and there was the distant rumble of thunder in the air. As we walked, every moment it seemed to grow hotter, and as the sun rose higher, it lost its pale face and became a strange and horrid red disk.

Anne glanced up at it. 'I don't like that sun,' she said with a shiver. 'It doesn't seem natural. Today seems like the day of judgement: the end of the world that the clergy sometimes speak on in church.'

I tried to reassure her but could not do so with any conviction, for the same thought had already occurred to me. I tried to remember what I'd read in the almanac in Highclear House about 1666 being the Year of the Beast, when a cleansing fire would be brought down. I also thought about what I'd said to Mother about London being as safe as houses . . .

When we reached the walls, we found that at any point along them, especially near a gate, the roadways were crowded with carts, carriages, sedan chairs, horses and people on foot, all carrying furniture and fighting and jostling with each other to get out, and thus we could not make much progress. The situation was not helped by a large number of people fighting to get *in*: those looking for their families, going to rescue things from their homes, and also porters, labourers, carters – anyone with a conveyance on wheels for, as we had been told, there was a deal of money to be made from the moving of furniture and possessions. At Cripplegate we found confusion and accidents and fighting crowds, and these at Moorgate and Bishopsgate too, and finally (after we had seen one family's horse fall and break its legs on a pile of abandoned furniture, also a poor cat running for its life with all its fur afire) decided to go to All Hallows church and climb the tower there.

Although on occasion clouded by gusts of smoke, we now had a view which was quite terrible in its aspect, for it could be seen that the whole northern shore of the Thames was aflame from beyond the bridge on our left as far as the sturdy bulk of Baynards Castle on our right. Seeing this dreadful sight, my eyes straightaway filled with tears, for it was most shocking and awful to see those wharves, lanes and alleys and those houses and rooms ablaze, or reduced to sticks and ashes, and to think what devastation and terror must be in the hearts of those who lived and worked there.

Anne and I held each other tightly, both quite speechless with shock. Now that I had witnessed this scene for myself, words could not convey how awful I found it, for it did truly seem as Anne had said: that the end of the world was nigh.

Once I had dragged my glance back from the shoreline of the Thames I realised that our view was unobscured only because there were now very few large buildings between us and the river. Churches were burnt away or still in flames, many Halls of the Guilds were razed, as were the noble buildings in Cornhill and even – I uttered a cry – the magnificent Royal Exchange had surrendered, for I knew well where it had been and it was there no more! Straightaway, the thought of the visit I'd paid there with Abby came to me: the vast marble edifice of stately columns and noble statues, the gaily dressed gallants and so-fine ladies gossiping in the courtyards, the immaculate little shops containing delicate and rare items – all gone!

But even that knowledge was diminished by Anne suddenly screaming and burying her face in my shoulder, pointing with a shaking arm towards the heart of the fire, where now could be seen a wall of flame, some fifty feet high, moving as swiftly as the wind and travelling east to west along a row of houses. As I watched, horror-struck, each building in its path caught and erupted one after the other, small volcanoes sending blizzards of sparks everywhere. Stone buildings were slower to catch, others – according to what was stored within – burned fast and mad. This running fire was only halted when it reached the grey mass that was Bridewell prison on the banks of the Fleet and, beating against this, could go no further.

Thus thwarted, the fire, like a terrible living beast, turned and began to move slowly northward in a maelstrom of heat and noise. Reaching what must have been a storehouse containing spices and peppers, there was a sudden soft explosion and then a shimmer of blue, purple and green in the air which was terrible in its beauty and strangeness and made me and Anne both cry out in wonder. A moment later, an amazing spicy scent filled the air which for a moment dominated the stench of sulphur and gunpowder.

All in all, we stood there some two hours, until the front line of the fire was a mile across and the banks of the Thames were clothed in fire almost as far as we could see. We stood overlong for, although the sight before us was terrible indeed, it was also compelling in its very terribleness. It had something of the air of a public execution about it: spectacle and drama mixed equally with horror and fear.

We might have stayed longer, but I was anxious to see how things stood back at the shop. When the wind changed direction slightly and began to blow thick, sulphurous smoke in our direction, making us cough, we decided to descend. As we did so, two pigeons with their wings still burning thudded down beside us.

'They stayed too long on their perches and caught alight,' a man remarked, and he picked them up by their singed feet and declared he would take them home for his dinner.

Chapter Eleven

The Raging Beast

*'At four o'clock in the morning, my Lady Batten sent
me a cart to carry away all my money and plate and
best things . . . which I did, riding myself in my
nightgown in the cart; and Lord, to see how the
streets and the highways are crowded with people,
running and riding and getting of carts to fetch
away things . . .'*

Anne, beside me on the wooden pew, moved and
whimpered softly in her sleep. It was hot in the small
church and crowded besides, and I had not been able
to sleep at all for wondering what was going to
happen to us.

Last night the wind had been blowing strongly in
our direction, and there had been great discussion
with our neighbours in Crown and King Place as to
whether the fire, still some distance off, would reach
us. Mr Newbery said it would, and declared he was
off to Moore Fields to lie under a bush and be safe,
but others said they were sure the fire would be
stopped long before it came to us, and besides, there

was a vast firebreak being constructed along Lombard Street and it would not get further than this.

Most of the neighbours wavered, swayed first by one argument, then by the other, then one old woman declared that the flames could burn her up if they cared to, for she had not moved for plague and would not move for fire either. In the end, though, only a few stayed on in their homes, while most went to take shelter in St Dominic's church, feeling that there was safety in numbers and we would be able to alert each other quickly in case of danger. Here we had ranged ourselves and our precious possessions (Kitty being amongst these) along the hard benches and tried to make ourselves comfortable. We shared our food companionably, sung some of the old songs to try to cheer us, and several men had firewatched through the night.

I had not heard from Tom the previous evening, but took some comfort from a neighbour telling me that because of the fire, Bartholomew Fair had not opened since Saturday and that most of the fairground folk had already moved off to a fresh site. I felt in my heart that the love we shared (for though unspoken, I felt it was that) meant that we would meet again – for surely we had not lost and then found each other for no good reason?

As I shifted in the pew and rubbed at my stiff neck, there came a scritching and a scratching from Kitty's basket at my feet. It was very dark, however, there being no candles lit, and I did not dare loosen the tied lid, for if I did so she would run off and hide herself in some chink in the church and we would never see her again.

I think I dropped off to sleep shortly before dawn, but when I awoke to the sound of someone calling eight o'clock, it was still dark because of the heavy smoke which surrounded us. For a moment I could not remember where I was, and then I jumped up with a start to find Anne awake and feeding Kitty a cup of milk. Fresh bread had also been delivered, for the king had decreed that every working baker was to bake for the masses who were without a hearth or home.

As we ate, news began coming in from passers-by about fighting and looting in the shops, and about where the flames had reached, and what had caught fire and what had been saved. The previous day Anne and I had seen the fire reach Bridewell Prison, and though its walls were still proving too sturdy to collapse, they were blazing from end to end. Here – alas – the fire had jumped over the high City walls and was now racing west down Fleet Street, devouring the fine merchants' houses that Tom and I had seen on the previous Sunday.

The wind still encouraged the fire towards the north and west of the City; it had not moved east more than two streets away from Pudding Lane where it had started (whether from a baker's failing to put out his oven properly or from a foreigner's incendiary we did not know). The only good news we had received was that London Bridge had so far been saved, for the fire had not burned more than four struts along before it reached a gap in the houses and been halted. There was fire all along the banks and wharves here, though, and strong danger of the Tower of London catching.

'The king's beasts in the menagerie roar to wake the Devil!' a young man with a sooted face and singed hair told us breathlessly. 'For no one dares go near them – and there is no place to move them!'

'Can't they be given some linctus or herbs to send them to sleep?' someone asked.

The young man shook his head. 'The fire rages all around and it is monstrous hot in their quarters – no one can bear the heat enough to get close to them. The beasts pace to and fro and oft-times throw themselves against the bars of their cages in their distress.'

'But suppose the fire breaks down their cages and they escape?' a woman asked him in some nervousness. 'There would be great apes and tigers running in the streets!'

The young man shook his head. 'They would be burned to death before that,' he said. 'And even now they may be dead from the smoke.'

'Then I wish the poor beasts a quick and painless end,' the woman said, 'for all dumb animals must be near out of their minds with terror.'

Hearing this, Anne and I picked up Kitty and put her straight back in her basket. We had lost our cat Mew to the plague, and I did not wish to lose Kitty to the fire.

As our neighbours gradually went from the church – either to go home or to make for safe ground – we fell to talking about what to do next. We had not cleared everything from the shop, and wondered if we should try to obtain a cart to collect our bed and our few pieces of furniture and bring them into the church for safety. On looking outside, however, it became obvious that we would never obtain any sort of conveyance, for everything with wheels had already been pressed into duty and was crowding the lanes around us in great muddle and confusion.

'Do you think that Mother knows about the fire?' Anne asked.

'She's sure to,' I said. 'They say that the smoke from London can be seen rising fifty miles away.'

'They'll be worried . . .'

I nodded, but we had no possible hope of getting word to them that we were safe, for we knew that the post office had been consumed by fire in the night.

I was alerted by some disturbance outside. 'Listen!' I took Anne's hand. 'What can you hear?'

She shrugged.

'The fire!' I said. 'I'll swear that's what it is.'

She put her head on one side and closed her eyes. 'Yes!' she said. 'It's roaring away like Father's furnace – and there are noises like walls crashing.'

I swallowed hard. 'And timber cracking and people screaming.' I began to pick up our things. 'It's coming on apace and we must go,' I said, trying to sound calm, even though my heart was beating mightily. 'There may be a last-minute dash to get out of the City and we must get to the gates.'

'What about the other things left in the shop?' Anne asked. 'What of our bed?'

'Never mind!'

A sudden shouting came from outside and a man, sweating heavily, his face burned and blistered, ran into the church.

'Cheapside has fallen to the fire!' he shouted to those few of us still there. ''Tis fallen!'

There was a general wail of despair at this and Anne looked at me questioningly. ''Tis the road which comes into the city from Newgate,' I said to her. 'The great highway where the kings make their progress and where all the rich goldsmiths' and silversmiths' shops are.'

'But did they not try to save it?' someone asked the man.

'Damn you for a fat gutted dog!' he exploded. 'We've been working all night making a break, but the south side caught fire and all the houses collapsed together sending firebrands across the gap so that the north caught as well!' His voice broke into something like a sob. 'The painted signs collapsed, the windows shattered, the stones cracked and then the great timbered roofs fell and lit up the sky. London's greatest street has been razed to the ground and will never be again!'

We waited no longer after this, but took up our boxes, baskets and bundles and left the church in some haste. Outside hung a thick blanket of smoke and, the lanes being full of abandoned furniture and bundles, it was difficult to walk without falling over something. Every moment we would be jostled by those bearing furniture on their backs or pushed out of the way to allow a cart through. As we dodged through showers of falling sparks, we found it difficult to breathe, for each full breath in made us cough or choke.

At first we just followed where the crowds were going, but then I stopped to think which might be the best gate to head for. We knew the fire had jumped the walls near Ludgate, and was now heading down Cornhill towards Newgate, so it seemed best to me to head towards Moorgate and thence to the safety of

Moore Fields. Accordingly, we turned at the corner in this direction, but had only gone a short distance when we realised (as all those others had before us) that the things we carried hampered us greatly. We would not abandon the basket containing Kitty, of course, and I was most reluctant to leave my green taffeta gown and my canvas bag, but we decided that the two boxes of kitchen things could be left, for they were easy enough to replace and had no great value. Seeing at this moment a woman running along the street screaming, her long hair alight from a falling brand, I made sure to tie my curls back and got Anne to cover them tight with a cloth for, although I did not like red hair, I would rather have it than be bald.

By leaving these kitchen stuffs inside another church we found it a little easier to get along. Still, though, there was the constant roar of the fire at our heels, a blizzard of sparks and firebrands falling over us, and shouted reports that 'There is no water left in the City!', 'Guildhall is a sea of flame!' and 'The water in the Fleet ditch is boiling!', each new cry serving to send us into more of a panic.

Nearing Moorgate and seeing the press of people converging on it from the surrounding streets, I began to despair of getting through.

'A carriage is in the gateway and stuck fast against a cart coming in!' a woman told us. 'We've been here near an hour without moving.'

I sighed mightily at this, for I felt responsible for Anne. 'I fear we've come to the wrong gate,' I said to her. 'I wish I had decided on Cripplegate.'

'There's a crowd fighting at Cripplegate,' said the woman. 'I heard two people have been stabbed over a tin of gold coins.'

'At Bishopsgate there are more people trying to get in and rescue goods than—' another began, but we never heard more, for of a sudden there was a huge roar and something must have given way at the gate, for the crowd in front of us surged forward and Anne's hand was wrenched from mine.

'Keep hold of Kitty's basket!' I shouted to her. 'Never mind about anything else. Make for Moore Fields, stay close to the walls and I'll find you!'

I believed that Anne got through for, as the great swell of people split, some surging one way, some the other, I glanced back and saw her being carried out of the gate by sheer force of numbers. I prayed that she would be safe, but did not know whether or not God still listened.

Now came my darkest time, for I was picked off my feet by the incoming mob and, after having all the breath squeezed out of me so I could neither scream nor hardly breathe, was shoved and manhandled, then knocked to the floor and somewhat trampled on. Several other people were used so, yet I did not feel that anyone meant this, rather that panic overtook the mass of people and the less robust among the crowd suffered the consequences.

Once the dense crowd had receded somewhat, I lay where I had been washed up, testing my limbs one by one and feeling where I had been hurt, and eventually I came to understand that I had no broken bones and was merely bruised and grazed. My green taffeta gown had disappeared, however, and also my canvas bag. A shawl that had been around my shoulders was also missing, and one shoe, but – my hand sprang to my neck and I gave a gasp of relief – my silver locket was still around my neck and my pocket containing our money was still under my petticoats.

As I struggled to lift my weary body from the cobbles, a young woman came along, her hair knotted and her face covered in smuts, and, sitting down beside me, began to cry.

'I've lost everything!' she said. 'My little house . . . my husband . . . all gone in fire so fierce it was as if the jaws of Hell had opened!'

I could not reply to her, for a stupor had come over me and I felt as tired as a dog.

'We thought we were safe, and then the fire dropped on us like a flaming sword from heaven! My husband stayed to fight it and I saw him consumed in the flames.'

'I . . . I'm sorry,' I said, struggling to get myself upright.

'His clothes, his hair, his face – all alight!' Her face came nearer to mine and she smiled sweetly. 'God chose him for an angel and then lit the cleansing fire around him!'

And now I struggled even harder to get on my feet, for I knew the woman to be mad and did not wish to get involved with her. My one thought was to get out of the City and find Anne. Getting to my feet unsteadily I left the woman crying at the side of the roadway and went on, luckily finding my shoe some distance away.

Discovering myself some little distance from Moorgate, I thought it best to try and make my way to a gate to the east of the City, which – as far as I knew – the fire had not yet reached. If I could go out of the City by Bishopsgate, then I could make my way into Moore Fields from there.

It was not that easy, however, for due to the heavy pall of smoke which hung over everything, I could hardly see in front of me and, not being able to recognise the lanes (for I was not often in this area) or see the sun, I could not work out the right direction to take. Some streets that I sought to go down had been closed off by the bands of men who had come together to earn the king's shilling, or they were impassable because of dumped goods or rubble. I turned my ankle and cut it on some sharp stones, was once made sick with coughing, and then was grazed badly by a runaway horse and cart which passed too close to me and then overturned. As well as this my eyes stung constantly and I often had to stop to shake out my skirts when a shower of sparks threatened to catch me alight.

Looking for landmarks, I found that many of these had disappeared and, thinking to find the tavern at the start of the great Lothbury highway which would lead me to Bishopsgate, found instead just a great heap of rubble where buildings had been pulled down with grappling irons. I asked directions, and if this was indeed Lothbury, but people were too frantic with their own matters to pay attention to me, and twice I was directed wrongly and came up against a wall of flame.

Feeling dizzy and by now desperate for water, I stopped a woman with a flask to beg a mouthful from it. She would not allow me any, however, and called me a careless hussy to come out without, saying she needed every drop for herself.

The day grew darker still and the wind began to rage like a beast, the smoke overhead growing thicker and more dense by every minute. Having no idea of where I was or what time it was, I began to be mighty scared, but stepping near to some ruined shops and crunching across lukewarm ashes, suddenly found myself near to St Paul's and felt a sense of relief. While much around this great church had already been laid to waste, and while other buildings still had flames licking up their stonework, St Paul's was built on a hill and looked to be invincible, standing aloft like a mighty castle.

Stumbling through its open doors I found that scores of people had also thought to find shelter there, and many had brought their animals and goods along, too, for I saw a pig, some dogs and a monkey along the wooden pews. Sinking on to a bench, weak with relief, I was given a cup of rough wine and a hard biscuit by a woman, both of which I would have scorned in normal times but now was very glad to accept. I slid into a quiet corner, closed my eyes and tried to quell my beating heart, for I had been traipsing the streets a very long while and felt as exhausted as a hunted deer.

In spite of the clamour within and without, I fell asleep for some minutes, and only awoke when the same woman shook me hard and told me that I must stir myself and flee.

'Surely not!' I said, my eyelids dropping once more. 'We are safe here.'

'If you do not stir you will be burned to death where you lie!' the woman chastised me. 'A flaming brand has fallen on this roof and even His house cannot protect you now.'

This, of course, roused me up and I ventured with a group of others towards a set of doors. Looking out I could see that a flaming circle surrounded us, for even those buildings which had seemed to be gutted now burned with a new lust. So many were the buildings which had been destroyed between my standpoint and the river that when the wind blew and the smoke and flames shifted a little I could see all the way through to the banks of Southwarke, which was very shocking and strange indeed.

Many of those who had been sheltering with me had already fled, taking their chance and looking for a break in the flames to run to safety, and I knew that I had to do the same if I wanted to survive.

Frightened, shivering in spite of the vindictive heat, I looked about me. The dark shroud of smoke above had grown more dense and oily as the fires raged all around, and was now churning like hot black oil. Suddenly, out of its depths, forked lightning began to stab all around, its following thunder almost lost in the terrible roar of the flames and howling wind. Instead of rain, however, the showers that fell were of golden sparks.

Whatever it was that had fallen on the roof of St Paul's must have suddenly flared, for a screaming came from a group of people some distance off and, with one accord, they turned to look back at the vast edifice which sheltered me, pointing at the roof and shouting in awe.

I knew I must run for my life, but the flames scorched all around and I was mighty scared, for such was the glare from these that I could not see what I was running to, and moreover was feared that a lightning fork might come down and strike me dead. I took three steps forward and two back, then started off in a different direction, only to run back again and again, too much affrighted to make a decision.

Four further steps forward . . . then again back, and I screamed aloud in frustration and despair, not knowing what to do for the best. Tears coursed down my cheeks, for I felt now that I was doomed to perish in this church and never to see Tom or my family again.

It was then, at my lowest moment, that I heard the voice that was to save me.

'Mistress!' someone shouted. 'Hannah!'

Dashing my tears aside, I saw by the light of the encroaching flames the silhouette of a lad standing with a small, laden handcart before him. 'Who is that?' I called.

''Tis I, Hannah. Bill!'

But this meant nothing to me and I still could not see him, for the flames were as bright as sun in my eyes.

'Bill! Don't you remember me? Lord Cartmel's bootboy!' the figure shouted. 'Jump on my cart, Mistress!'

My befuddled brain could still not understand who it was who addressed me, and I wavered and swayed and would have fallen on to the smouldering grass, but the lad dropped the handles of the cart and ran to me. Catching me under the arms, he dragged me towards the cart, then kicked a deal of books from it and dropped me on to it without further ceremony.

With me clinging on as best I could, he then began trundling me over the stones and rubble away from St Paul's, faster and faster, until I cried aloud for him to stop to enable me to catch my breath. Even this did not halt him, however, and he did not pause until we had reached a safe place away from the flames.

Here he breathlessly pointed towards St Paul's, shaking his head the while, and sitting up on the cart I could see flames rising at the edge of the great roof, and from this point catching all over and darting in every direction, different colours according to the material they burned: red, orange, yellow, white and gold, each stretching up to the dense fire-storm cloud above. Within just a few moments large parts of the roof, stone and burning timber, fell inwards and the whole cathedral became a roaring cauldron of fire.

Speechlessly we watched as this maelstrom of fury began to melt the lead roof of the cathedral, which then began to flow in silvery streams, sparkling and flashing, making everything it touched erupt in darting pinnacles of flame. Suddenly, like pistol shots, the great windows began to shatter and flames burst through. At this point the heat and brightness of the great fire became so intense that, although we were a good distance off, we had to move or our skin would have blistered.

Both exhausted, we stopped at last in a thoroughfare where the heat from the fire could not touch us, and I knew that my saviour was indeed Bill, Lord Cartmel's bootboy. Realising this, I somehow mustered the strength to fling my arms around him and sob out my thanks for saving me, for I knew that I would not have had the courage to run through that ring of flames and save myself.

'But what are you *doing* here?' I asked when I had left off my speeches of gratitude.

'Making a pretty penny!' he said. 'I'm a beast of burden with a cart for hire and I've been charging the gentry two pounds a load to take their furniture and treasures away to safety out of the City.' His smutty face grinned at me. 'I've made myself a fair fortune in the last two days!'

'But where is your master?'

'Oh, he high-tailed it to Dorchester at the first sign of danger, leaving me and two footmen to clear his house.' He rubbed his hands. 'I tell you, Mistress, I'm a made man! I've earned enough money in this last two days to marry and live in luxury for the rest of my life!'

He winked at me and I knew where his thoughts were heading and sought to distract him. 'Bill,' I pleaded, 'could I ask you for one more thing – to help me find my sister? I told her I'd meet her by the wall in Moore Fields but don't know how to get there.'

'Oh, that's easy!' he boasted. 'The route out of the City is drawn in my head, for I've now done it fifty times or more. But we'll not go through Moorgate but by way of Aldgate in the east.'

And so we set off across the City at a steadier pace – with me riding on the cart like a pig going to market, for he would not let me walk – and only stopped once more: when there was, of a sudden, a tremendous noise from the west and a moment later the whole of the City was lit up with a glow as bright as the noonday sun.

''Tis the crypt below St Paul's,' Bill said grimly. 'The booksellers have packed it full of their precious papers and books and now the fire has reached down there and 'tis all exploded into flame.'

After surveying the roaring and flickering city scene before us – the great heaps of rubble, the piles of ash, the charred stone and, nearby, some vast oak church beams glowing red like coals – we commenced our journey to Moore Fields, for I think Bill was anxious to install me in a place of safety so that he could carry on making his fortune.

Chapter Twelve

Moore Fields

'Going to the fire, I find, by the blowing up of houses and the great help given by the workmen out of the King's yards, there is a good stop given to it . . .'

When I opened my eyes in Moore Fields the following morning, it was to find Anne sitting close at my side looking down at me anxiously.

'You've been asleep for hours!' she said. 'You were curled up like a cat and I didn't like to wake you.'

I looked up at her blankly, as for some moments I could not recall where I was or how I came to be there.

'And if you *are* a cat, then you're a very dirty one!' Anne went on. 'Your gown is filthy, your hair is singed and matted. You look like a sweep and stink worse than a glue-maker!'

I sat bolt-upright and looked around, suddenly remembering where I was – in that hummocky, shrubby place where the laundresses of the City took their sheets and hung them on the bushes to dry. There were no sheets there now, however, for their place had been taken by hundreds – nay, thousands – of people sitting, lying or standing, together with their furniture, bundles, baskets, books and animals, and all so cramped that there was scarcely a space between them.

'However did you find me?' I asked Anne in astonishment.

She smiled. "T'was easy!' she said. 'I fell in with the McGibbons family last night, and at first light this morning I told their six children what you were wearing – although I did not know your gown would have changed *quite* so much – and said that I would give a paper cone of sweetmeats to the one who found you.'

I looked around for the McGibbons, who owned a small pie shop a few doors away from us in Crown and King Place, but for the moment could not see them amid the crush.

'The children took off at first light and by searching diligently along the walls, found you within a half hour!' Anne shook her head ruefully. 'I don't know when I'll be able to pay them the sweetmeats, though . . .'

I gasped. 'Has the fire then reached our shop?'

She nodded solemnly. 'Mistress McGibbon told me that it reached Crown and King Place late last afternoon. There was a trained band of men there and they pulled down the houses behind ours with grappling irons to try and save our row, but the flames leaped across the gap and . . .' She stopped, seeing my eyes brim with tears, and after a moment went on, 'No lives lost, though, Hannah. And look!' She lifted a corner of her skirt and there was Kitty, fast asleep on the grass with a ribbon around her neck, the end of which was tied around Anne's wrist.

I smiled, but it was only a very small smile. We had lost everything – everything except Kitty and the clothes we stood up in – and even *those* were ruined and torn. My hand once again flew to my neck and my smile lightened a little, for I still wore my precious locket – moreover, I knew my pocket was still tied under my skirts, for I could feel the little swell of money resting on my hip.

'But our little shop, though!' I said, picturing its pretty sign, its wooden shutters and limewashed interior. 'Our shop all gone to ashes . . . What will Sarah say? She left me in charge of it.'

'Hannah!' Anne exclaimed. 'She won't say a thing. She'll just be happy that both of us are safe. And how could you have preserved *our* little shop when the greatest buildings in the city have caught fire?'

I sighed and nodded. 'I saw St Paul's alight,' I said. 'What a sight it was, Anne – a great box of fire lighting up the sky and turning it into day. 'T'was hot enough nearby to cook a thousand turkeys.'

'They say that all the big buildings have gone, and thousands of smaller houses besides. The prisons, too – and poor mad people left to burn in their chains!'

I turned away with a shudder. 'Don't!'

'But tell me how you came to be here,' Anne said, 'for I stayed close to the wall as you told me, and watched and watched people coming through the gate until it was grew dark – although it didn't really grow dark because of all the flames – but I never saw you come in.'

'I'll tell you soon, but I have not the heart to talk yet,' I said. 'And I'm fair famished! Is there anything to eat anywhere?'

'There's some ship's biscuit,' Anne said, 'though it's nasty and salty and hard. But there are folk coming in from the country today with fruit and beer and milk to sell, and the king has promised that no one will go hungry.'

'Really? How could he promise that?' I asked, looking across the field where, as far as the eye could see, people were crowded into makeshift camps. 'There must be people holed up in every single safe place outside the City. How will he feed them all?'

Anne shrugged. 'I don't know. *He's* the king, not me.'

We sat there for a very long time, for I felt weary and befuddled – and besides, there was nowhere to go. Occasionally news would come to us of what was now burning, what had been burned down or of where the fire had been stopped. Smoke blew across the walls, eddied around and hung over us, and smuts and burning brands swirled and dropped all around. On the other side of the walls we could hear the fire roaring and the wind blowing, and booming and cracking from different directions where they were blowing up houses with gunpowder, followed by the tumbling crash of falling stone.

By the afternoon of that day, however, which was Wednesday, the news came to us that the wind was blowing itself out. Later still, we heard that the fires in most directions had been extinguished, while those that still burned were thought to be under control.

This information ran around the whole of Moore Fields until it reached every far corner, but there was very little delight or joy shown, for we were all dreadful tired, hungry and disorientated and, as most had already lost their homes and possessions, it meant little. We took in the news and were pleased about it, but could display no emotion. The only time any feeling was shown was when some citizen or other, hearing a rumour, would try and rouse others, calling, 'To arms! To arms!' and giving out that a Frenchman had started the fire, or a Dutchman, or any foreigner at all. During the day we heard many such tales, and also that a man seen throwing fire balls into a shop had been torn limb from limb by the crowd, and that a woman who had predicted the fire had been killed for a witch, but I did not know whether these things were true.

'What will we do?' Anne asked me frequently during the day. 'What will become of us?'

Each time she asked I shook my head, for I just did not know. I felt, too, that I was not qualified, nor hardly old enough, to have to deal with such questions, and wished desperately that Sarah were with us so that I would not have to be the one to make any decisions.

Anne looked dishevelled but was not too far off from her normal self; though she kept looking at me and smiling with some amusement at *my* appearance. Seeing this, I asked leave to borrow a looking-glass from a family we were alongside, and had the shock of seeing what I had become.

'I'm a scabby, sooty, dirty beggar!' I said, holding the glass this way and that and looking at my reflection in shock.

'Indeed you are,' Anne said. 'I don't think even your

sweetheart would recognise you.'

'Have you anything – a cloth or a kerchief I could wipe myself with?' I asked.

She shook her head. 'Nor a comb to de-tangle your hair, or soap to clean you or any flower water to hide the smell of soot on you.' As I uttered a sigh of protest, she added, 'But everyone looks the same, Hannah. You won't be noticed.'

The mention of Tom had spurred me into action and at length, not finding any other cloth, I tore a strip from my undersmock and, walking around the perimeter of the field, wetted this material in a stream. On instruction from Anne on where the worst dirt was, I then began to clean myself as best I could. The singed eyebrows I could do nothing about, nor the bruise on my cheek, nor my hair which, to my despair, had tangled into a vast red cloud, but I managed to get all the smuts from my face and felt the better for it – even if I did not actually look much better.

By and by, people were seen coming round with trays of food from the naval storehouse, and everyone fell to cheering, but these trays proved only to contain more of the hard ship's biscuit which no one liked. Anne and I took some, however, and after eating a little ourselves, pounded up the rest for Kitty and she was glad enough to have it. Others in the Fields fed their dogs with it, and the McGibbons family – who had thought to bring along three chickens from their backyard – fed the biscuit to them and hoped thus to ensure a couple of fresh eggs each day for their children.

We heard later that day that the king had ordered the magistrates and lieutenants of the surrounding counties to ensure that all the food that could be spared, especially bread, should be sent immediately to London, and that temporary markets were to be set up for this just beyond the burned areas at Smithfield, Bishopsgate and Tower Hill. As well as this, any City bakers who had not been gutted by fire were ordered to bake bread around the clock, and extra grain was to be made available for this purpose. These loaves were later brought into Moore Fields, and we managed to obtain some small beer and also milk, and in this way kept ourselves going. I thought often of the sweetmeats and comfits that we had left behind in the shop, and wished that I had thought to put some of them in my pocket. Other shopkeepers, though, had left behind far more costly things: bales of silken fabrics bought ready for the Michaelmas fairs, rare books, boxes of scented gloves from Persia, gold coins (which we heard had melted and fused together in the heat) or silver plates destined for the same fate – so we counted ourselves lucky to have left behind only frosted rose petals and sugared plums.

By that evening we were assured that, although fires still burned in some cellars and warehouses, these would not now spread further. We were urged to stay on the Fields, however, until it was quite safe to move. This suited me very well, for I felt mighty fatigued still and could not have dealt with moving. I just wanted to sit where I was on the grass and feel safe, and not think about what was going to happen next.

As night came, it was the strangest thing to go to sleep (or try to sleep) amongst such a vast company and in such strange circumstances. As far as the eye could see, people were now packed head to tail across the grass, sitting or lying down, squeezed into corners with whatever stuff they had managed to bring with them: a bundle of clothes, say, or a chair or wash stand, a cloth containing food, the household pig or some small treasure. A few had also managed to bring a candle or taper along, so that, as darkness fell across the field, a number of flickering lights appeared, and these reflected off people's faces and lit up the field into a huge and peculiar landscape the like of which can hardly be imagined.

Although desperately weary, we could hardly close our eyes because of the very strangeness of it all: the sounds of shouting, wailing, children crying, dogs barking – and every so often from the other side of the wall, the far-off rumble of a damaged house falling, mingled with screams, or the shooting of sparks into the sky where a thatch had suddenly caught fire.

As it grew darker it grew colder, so that although Anne and I curled up as close as a pair of spoons, we became chilled as the damp rose from the earth. There were other dangers apart from cold, too, for the enormity of what had happened to the City had not changed the essential part of some people's wicked characters, and loose fellows prowled around looking for unguarded objects to steal; indeed I fell asleep once, only to wake at feeling a fellow's hand under my skirts and upon my pocket. I sat up immediately and shouted abuse and he ran off into the darkness.

Thus, managing to sleep only now and again, we passed the night, not knowing what would become of us.

The following morning there was some excitement and lightening of mood when the king himself came to speak to us. A fanfare of trumpets sounded his arrival, then the crowds parted and he, attended by a few gentlemen, wearing an elegant riding jacket and sitting atop his fine black horse, spoke about the dilemma that the City found itself in.

'The judgement which has fallen upon London is immediately from the hand of God, for be assured that no Frenchmen, Dutchmen or Catholics had any part in bringing you so much misery,' he said in a clear and decisive tone. 'I assure you that I find no reason to suspect anyone's involvement in burning the City, and desire you to take no more alarm. I, your king, will, by the Grace of God, live and die with you, and take a particular care of you all.'

We were all much moved by this and, as he went off to speak to another group, many of us shed tears at his kind words and chivalrous intentions (and I am sure did not give one thought to his indiscretions or bastard children). Anne was particularly overcome by him and spoke admiringly of his princely manner, looks and virility, saying she thought him the most noble man alive.

That afternoon we heard that, to prevent the remaining small fires gaining more of a foothold, a detachment of two hundred soldiers was coming from Hertfordshire with carts laden with spades and buckets. Everyone at Moore Fields was very glad to hear this, for we were all exhausted and a great lassitude had crept over us. I dreamed of nothing more than being back in my bed-chamber in Chertsey, in clean clothes, with Mother bathing my grazes and making me soothing camomile drinks. This lovely vision, however, seemed as far off and impossible as the one promised by Count de'Ath on entering his cabinet.

Chapter Thirteen

The Devastated City

*'By water to St Paul's wharf. Walked thence and saw
all the town burned, and a miserable sight of Paul's
church, with all the roofs fallen and the body of the
quire fallen . . .'*

On Friday and Saturday the move back into the City
began, for the lethargy that had fallen on everyone
had somewhat passed, and by then most of us were
anxious to see what remained of London now that the
fire was halted, and whether or not anything survived
of our homes. Those re-entering the City were asked
to be vigilant, to watch for anything suspicious and to
stamp out any glowing embers they might see so that
they wouldn't catch flame.

Faced with having to move on, some now chose not
to go back into the City at all, saying they could not
bear seeing the calamity which had befallen their
homes and possessions. These folk started journeying
on foot to wherever they could, to places where they
had family or friends and could mayhap start again,
for it had been decreed that cities and towns

everywhere must receive and welcome distressed refugees from London and permit them to trade.

I could not decide what to do. Although I longed for home, I didn't want to leave London without getting word to Tom and telling him where I'd gone. Also, knowing there was little chance of obtaining a lift on a carriage or a cart, we could not yet face making the arduous trek to Chertsey on foot. We were very weary, for we'd slept little on the Fields because of the continuous noise and movement from those around us, and also the alarms sounding whenever wind-blown firebrands came over the walls. Besides, when I'd slept, I'd had terrible nightmares that I was once again in the doorway of St Paul's with the ring of flames all around me and about to burn to death. Each time, I woke to Anne shaking me and telling me I was crying out in my sleep, and was glad she did so, for I had this childish superstition that if I actually fell asleep and dreamed I was dead, then I would not ever wake.

Eventually (Anne being very anxious to do so) I decided we would go back to Crown and King Place and see if anything remained of our shop. Once we had seen it, we could then decide if we should stay put and start again – for we'd heard that several people had already put up rough stands or tents upon the rubble and ashes of their former homes, and some few were already trading by obtaining provisions from outside London to sell.

Accordingly, with Kitty safely inside her basket, we set off, going through Moorgate, where two burly guards had been posted to stop thieves coming out with stolen goods. We knew that there was much looting and pillaging taking place in the City, for treasures that had been sealed up in cellars, buried in gardens or left in the few houses which had survived the fire were now ripe for the taking. Guards were also on duty about the City ready to quell any disturbances between the citizens and foreigners for, in spite of what the king had said, people were still not certain of how the fire had started, but were mighty anxious to place the blame somewhere.

We'd already glimpsed the devastation through Moorgate, but this did not prepare us for the spectacle we saw when we were past the walls and into the open space beyond them.

For this is what it was: an open space. As far as the eye could see, from the City walls right down to the Thames, all was laid to waste, with little to be seen but random heaps of rubble and stones under a sifting, shifting layer of ash. There were no grassy squares or winding cobbled lanes or dim passageways . . . the beautiful city with its pretty houses, grand buildings and ancient churches stood no more.

Anne and I surveyed it all, and I felt too heavy to speak, for I had never seen such desolation and could hardly comprehend how it was possible for such a thing to have happened and for such a mighty city to have fallen.

'Where do we go from here?' Anne spoke at last, but I just shook my head wordlessly, for all landmarks had gone and without those it seemed impossible to trace where our shop had been.

We walked on a little further, to where the remains of a church stood. This, being of heavy stone, had somewhat survived, for although the roof and windows had disappeared (there just being some traces of red- and blue-stained glass melted and fused into the ground nearby), remains of the spire still stood, and at least a part of each wall.

'What church is this?' Anne asked.

I stood looking at it doubtfully. 'St Alphage, I think,' I said. 'Although I don't know this parish well.'

We walked on. 'And if so . . .' I pointed to two great heaps of smoking rubble, 'here was Clothworkers' Hall . . . and over there, Brewers' Hall.'

We stood silent once more, lost in thought. Around us from several places rose thin spires of smoke. Further off, a grey and steamy fogginess seemed to hang over all, and through this could be seen dismal figures such as ourselves, picking their way over the ashes like so many grey ghosts. As soft ash floated up with each movement, making us cough, piles of dirt and dust eddied about any remaining stumps of walls. There was black soot-dirt from burned wood, grey dirt from the reduced stones and red and yellow dirt from the bricks that had caught aflame. In places where it had been blown by circles of wind this detritus was inches thick, and looking at it I could not think how it would ever be possible to make London clean again.

Anne came and put her hand through mine. 'I don't like it,' she said tremulously. 'Shall we go home to Mother?'

I squeezed her hand. 'If we can,' I said. 'But let's try and find Crown and King Place. Just in case . . .'

Just in case . . . I knew not what. Just in case there had been a lull in the fire and it had jumped right over our row of shops and left them intact. Just in case a trained band had obtained fire squirts and directed them on to our shop so that it had escaped. Miracles *did* sometimes happen, I already knew that.

Working from St Alphage, we made our way through the wreckage towards where we thought our shop had been. On the way we saw some small signs of revival: a man who had made a table from two planks of wood and was selling beer from it, and another who had fashioned a rough tent from some canvas and had set up home on what remained of his dwelling. One family also seemed to be living in the cellar of what had been their house, for the trap door to this was open, voices came from below, and a child was seated atop, playing forlornly amid a pile of cinders.

A man stopped us to say that owing to an order of the king, all churches, chapels and other public places in the east of the City that had survived were open freely to receive goods that might be brought to them for safekeeping.

I thanked him as he passed on. 'But we have nothing to leave in them,' I said to Anne.

'Just Kitty,' she said.

People had reached what had been their houses and were standing inside, looking lost and bewildered. I saw very few tears, however, for people seemed too shocked for that. Some, finding their own places, had pinned a paper to a blackened stave of wood, or left word on a pile of stones to say what shop it was, or had hung a piece of material or some object (I saw a quill, and later a pewter mug) to denote what had once stood there.

We moved on and, by careful register of what

remained of churches and some Halls of the Guilds, found our way through the remains of the City to what was left of Crown and King Place. Here we surveyed where our little row of shops and houses had stood, and I knew then that a miracle had *not* happened, and that our shop had been laid to waste and destroyed utterly, along with all the others, and I felt very sad and low.

Here, too, we found Mr Newbery sitting on a stump of wood inside what had been his premises, a tankard in his hand. He had no wig, nor even proper dress, but was wearing an old, loose Indian robe such as those worn by gentlemen of leisure at home. This gown was torn and dishevelled, however, and was spotted all over with small burn marks, as if he had walked through a shower of sparks whilst wearing it.

He rose and gave us a slight bow, swaying on his feet. 'Ah! You found your way back, then,' he said, with as much ease as if he had been receiving us in his parlour. I nodded, staring at him (as I knew Anne was), for his bald pate had big smuts of soot all over it and his cheeks seemed to be liberally powdered with grey ash. 'It took me a good long time to get myself here, for all the taverns are down and I couldn't work out where I was.'

'Did our neighbours all survive? Have you seen anyone?' I asked him.

'Oh, several,' he said. 'Few have died.' He then added in his usual manner, 'Although I heard that at Bridewell the flames raged with such intolerable heat that the very dead in their graves were burnt!' and I could not help smiling to myself at this.

'Are you going to stay here?' Anne asked him.

He nodded. 'I managed to preserve my clothes and some of my goods by taking them to a friend in Bishopsgate. He boxed them and buried them in his garden for safekeeping, and luckily the fire did not get that far.'

'But where will you live?' I asked.

'Soldiers are erecting makeshift tents for people, so I shall retrieve my goods and begin trading again as soon as I can. I want to be here to give directions for the rebuilding of my shop.'

'I see,' I said, and then asked to be excused, adding that we were mighty anxious to go inside our own place.

'Oh, not a thing remains of it!' he called after us.

Our shop had been separated from his by two small and mean dwellings. These were now no more, and a half-stump of oak was all that was left of our doorjamb. This was charcoaled and reduced, but meant we could see where our premises began. Shuffling around the debris on the ground with our feet (which we had to do with care, some of the ashes still being hot), the outline of the floor could be seen, and the division into the back room; also, oddly, a burnt stub of the sturdy bush of rosemary which had stood in our yard.

I cannot explain how strange it felt to be standing in our shop – and yet not our shop, for it was filled with debris from the roof and upper floor, and open to the skies. To the right we could look along to where Mr Newbery could be seen drinking from his tankard, and to the left could be glimpsed, through the devastated houses, the broken spire and ruins of our parish church.

Kitty, who usually remained quiet whenever she was in her basket, suddenly started to meow, as if knowing she was home, but of course we did not dare let her out.

'There's a note here, pinned to a strut of wood!' Anne said suddenly.

'Really?' I moved to her quickly, my long skirts making the dust lift and swirl. 'Let me see.'

This small piece of parchment was nailed to a charred brace, and I removed it carefully, my heart pounding, for I could already see that it was in Sarah's careful script.

I read it out:

'Having heard of the dreadful fire, we are come to London and I wait with Giles Copperly to bring you and Anne back to Chertsey. As we may not bring the carriage into the City, the ways all being blocked with rubble, we stay on the Southwarke side and will remain here until you come to us. Please God that you are both safe. Your sister Sarah.'

Thinking of my elder sister waiting on the other side of the river for us, anxious for news, made my eyes brim with tears, and I turned away to dab at them with a piece of my skirt.

Anne uttered a long sigh and then pulled at my sleeve. 'Oh, can we go now?' she implored me, and a moment later added, 'A carriage belonging to Giles Copperly! Do you think he and Sarah are betrothed?'

I shook my head unknowingly.

'There's no reason at all to stay here now!' Anne went on. ''Tis awful and I hate it and we can't possibly make sweetmeats *here*!'

'I know,' I said, biting my lip. I was anxious to get away too, but reluctant to go without telling Tom. Looking down at Sarah's note, however, I thought immediately of what I could do – employ the same method as she had and leave a few lines in case he should come by.

I had no quill, of course, and sought to borrow one from Mr Newbery, but he told me that all his presently lay buried in the strongbox in his friend's garden.

'I shall pin Sarah's own note back to the wall, then,' I said to him, 'so it should be clear enough that we've gone to Chertsey. If anyone comes for me then please direct them to it.'

'Indeed I shall!' Mr Newbery said rather grandly, and with a slur to his voice, making me wonder how much ale he had already drunk that day.

'We hope to see you again soon, Mr Newbery,' I said. 'Although I don't know when.'

He waved the tankard. 'Be assured that if any other young man asks after you, I shall tell him where you've gone.'

I'd already turned away when what he'd said registered with my fuddled brain: if any *other* young man . . . 'Has someone asked for me already, then?'

'A lad came a while back. In quite a mess, he was!' He glugged his ale. 'Been in a fight, I should imagine.'

'What did he want?' My heart was fluttering but I fought to stay calm. Had it been Tom – or only Bill? Had I told him where the shop was that night at St Paul's?

Mr Newbery shrugged. 'He just asked for you and I

told him I hadn't seen you, neither dead nor alive.'

'And where did he go? In which direction?' I asked urgently.

Mr Newbery waved his tankard and ale slopped from it. 'Who knows. In the direction of wreckage and rubble.' He smiled, pleased with himself. 'For in every direction is wreckage and rubble!'

I left him then and, calling to Anne that I would be just a moment, hurried up the lane (as best I could because of the devastating ruins) towards the corner where Doctor da Silva's shop had stood. If it had indeed been Tom who'd asked for me I thought that, finding himself with nowhere else to go, he might make for the apothecary's shop where he'd once lived.

This was not too difficult to find, for it had stood at the convergence of several lanes, and the outlines of these could still be traced. Reaching what I thought was the remains of it, I had further confirmation that I was in the right place by seeing what was left of several heavy iron chains and padlocks from when the shop had been enclosed in the plague time. This ironwork was in a heap on the ground, fused together by the heat which had passed over it.

Scrambling over stones I found Tom lying within the rubble, propped against some brickwork. His knees were drawn up, his head down on them, and he gave no indication of having heard my arrival.

I gasped with shock at the sight of him for, as well as being covered in dirt and ash, through his torn and bloodied shirt I could see dark bruises across his shoulders and large abrasions on his back.

'Tom!' I called.

He lifted his head and gave me a weak smile, then

closed his eyes. 'Excuse me not rising, Hannah.'

'What happened to you?' I put out my hand to touch his shoulder, causing him to wince. 'Did you fall from a carriage or – or get in a fight?'

He shook his head and sighed wearily. 'It isn't a pretty tale.' There was a pause. 'I was stoned by a mob.' I gasped. 'Along with Count de'Ath – although I should not call him that because that isn't his real name – and it was that which led to the trouble.'

I looked at him and longed to put my arms around him, for he looked so broken, but I was scared of hurting him. '*Stoned?*'

He nodded and explained in a croak. 'We – some of the folk of Bartholomew Fair – had moved on to the common land in Islington. Local men got to hear that Count de'Ath was there, and, thinking him a Frenchman, sought him out and were about to take him and hang him, saying it was he and his compatriots who had caused the fire.'

He paused to take several slow breaths, then went on, 'A soldier intervened and stopped them, saying it could not be proved that anyone started it, and for his pains was stoned out of the village with us.' He paused again here and I stroked his face tenderly, for there was a small space on his cheek which wasn't bruised.

'The Count jumped on a horse and galloped off, and most of the mob ran after him, leaving me to evade the rest and walk back here. I didn't know where else to go.'

'You must come back with us!' I said immediately. 'Sarah is waiting at Southwarke with a carriage, and we are going home to Chertsey.'

'I cannot . . .' he protested weakly.

'You must!' I said. 'Tom, I insist.' My mind raced ahead. 'You will be able to obtain lodgings in our village. And work, too, later, if you wish.'

He did not say anything, but he looked at me with such great relief that my eyes filled with tears again for pity of him.

'Come now,' I said, and I put my hand under his arm to help him to his feet. 'We shall have a grand ride home in a carriage and—'

He let out a cry and clutched his elbow. 'I fear I shall not be good for work with a broken arm.'

'You will mend!' I said with false cheer, but seeing him standing, I hid my dismay at the pitiful, wretched sight he made. His arm hung useless, fine ash had stuck to his open wounds, and his skin, where visible, was blue with bruising. 'You shall have the root and leaves of comfrey to mend your broken bone, and alkanet and pennyroyal to heal the bruises and cuts. You know the herbs as well as I do!'

He tried to smile at me and just about succeeded. Slowly then, with his good arm about my shoulders, we made our way down towards Crown and King Place. We passed other citizens who were either shocked, burnt, dirty, troubled, dazed – or all of those things – but none spoke, nor hardly looked at us with any interest, for everyone was deep in their own troubles and woes, and much brought down with them.

At Crown and King Place Mr Newbery was not now to be seen, but Anne was standing by, looking anxious. On seeing Tom's condition, her eyes widened and she gasped. 'Did you get caught in the fire?' she asked. 'What happened?'

'We'll tell you on the journey,' I said. 'We're taking Tom back home with us. He has nowhere to go. And no work,' I added.

'Perhaps he can work with Father,' she said. 'He's always complaining he has too much to do.'

'Perhaps,' I nodded.

Anne went to take Tom's other, broken, arm but I shook my head at her. 'You manage Kitty, I'll manage Tom.'

Leaving what remained of our shop then, we began to walk very slowly, passing others trudging at a snail's pace and looking around them in bewildered fashion. In the ash-fogged light we were all grey wraiths, moving through a wasteland of rubble and stones. Twice we came across still-glowing coals and directed passing soldiers to stamp them out, and going by what remained of St Dominic's we found that the tower was down, its great lead bells melted completely and fused into the stones in a strange, mountainous lump.

Once or twice on our journey Tom swayed and almost fainted and we had to sit on the ground for a while until he recovered, but pretty soon we came in sight of London Bridge and I knew there would soon be an end to his ordeal.

It was while we were waiting our turn to get on to the bridge through the narrow passage that had been forged between the heaps of wreckage, that Anne slid her hand into Kitty's basket and drew something out. 'While I was waiting for you, I looked around in our shop and found this,' she said.

I took what she offered and gasped with surprise,

for I saw that it was part of the metal sign which had hung above our shop. It was much reduced and had melted and buckled through the great heat, but a part of the painted image could still be seen. Gazing at it, I was torn between smiling and weeping. 'The sugared plum,' I whispered. 'To think that this is all that remains of our shop.'

Anne shrugged, murmuring that she'd thought I'd like to keep it, and Tom looked at me with sympathy. 'London will be rebuilt, and your shop along with it,' he reassured me gently. 'And when it is, I'll make you another sign.'

I smiled at him – indeed I would have kissed him had I been able to find space on his poor face – for I knew what he said about London was true. I felt that my fate was with Tom, but it was also with London, and one day we would return and there would be another shop, trading anew under the sign of the Sugared Plum.

But for now we would cross London Bridge, find Sarah and go home . . .

Notes on London's Plague, 1665

All the quotations at the chapter headings are from Pepys's *Diary*, which I used for background information. I also used a book published in 1926 called *The Great Plague of London* by W. G. Bell, where I found most of the stories of ordinary people. *Restoration London* by Liza Picard was also invaluable. The idea for Sarah's sweetmeat shop came to me when I read in seventeenth-century Court Records a young girl's answer to the question of what she did for a living: 'I make sweetmeats and chocolett cakes for persons of quality and gentlemen's houses . . .'

During September, after Hannah and Sarah had left London, the numbers of people dying of plague continued to rise. Over 8,000 people died every week in September. Following this, as the weather became colder, the numbers on the Bills of Mortality slowly began to fall. The end of the Great Plague was at last in sight. By the following February, the city was deemed to be free enough of plague for the king and his court to return.

Although London was far and away the largest city in Britain, it was small compared to the size it is now. It is thought that about 300,000 people lived in it – and that one third of those (that is, more than 100,000) perished during the Great Plague. Most of these were the poor, who could not get away from the city.

Accounts have been found for the killing of as many

as 4,380 dogs in the city alone and probably three times as many cats. This was, of course, misguided, because the animals may have been controlling the very vermin that are thought to have spread the plague.

Nell Gwyn, the orange seller who rose to become a mistress to King Charles II, was fifteen in 1665. She is depicted in records as merry, witty and lovable as well as strikingly attractive. Pepys was an admirer, referring to her as 'pretty, witty Nelly'.

The plague was a terrifying and mystifying disease and people were prepared to try anything to avoid catching it. Everyone was very superstitious – even Pepys carried a 'lucky rabbit's foot' in his pocket. People saw what they thought were portents of death in the form the clouds took, or in natural but inexplicable phenomena like comets. They sometimes carried a piece of paper with the word ABRACADABRA written in a triangle, thus:

A
AB
ABR
ABRA
ABRAC
ABRACA
ABRACAD
ABRACADA
ABRACADAB
ABRACADABR
ABRACADABRA

They took all the conconctions mentioned in this book and many more. One of these recipes begins: 'Take black snails and cut and gash them with your knife, then take the liquor which comes from them and add it to a goodly quantity of wine . . .' It was also thought to be beneficial to drink your medicine from a hanged man's skull.

It is now known that the plague was spread by rat fleas carrying the plague bacilli and jumping from their hosts, the rats, to humans. The bacilli attacked the body's lymphatic system, causing inflamed and painful swellings in the lymph glands, called 'buboes'. No one knows exactly why or how it died out, but bubonic plague never again hit this country quite as badly as it did in 1665. It was feared that it would return as the weather grew warmer in 1666, but it did not, and although the rest of the country was hit, London remained relatively free of the plague. On 2 September, 1666, however, another terrible disaster occurred: The Great Fire.

Notes on the Great Fire of London

The Great Fire of London began on Sunday 2nd September 1666 in Pudding Lane and was finally halted (some say at Pie Corner) by nightfall on Wednesday 5th September.

Year of the Beast In the Bible, 666 is the number of the beast, who has the ability to bring down fire from heaven. 1666 had long been heralded by hellfire preachers and puritans as the year when God's punishment would fall on sinful London.

Samuel Pepys All the quotations at the chapter headings, and some of the stories of the characters, are from Pepys's *Diary*. Pepys was perhaps the most famous observer of the fire and wrote movingly of it (he was also the man who buried a whole Parmesan cheese in his garden). Two other books I used were *The Great Fire of London* by W. G. Bell, first published in 1923, for its accurate detail, and *Restoration London* by Liza Picard, an amusing and invaluable source of background material.

Nell Gwyn was sixteen in 1666 and had been acting with the King's Company for a year. By 1668 she had become the king's mistress and two years after this she had a child by him. Strikingly attractive and a practical joker, Nelly never hid her humble beginnings and the people loved her for this.

Bartholomew Fair All the sideshows and stalls mentioned (and more) were at the real fair, which was held for two weeks at the end of August. I have taken liberties with history only in that Bartholomew Fair was not held in 1666, for fear there would be a reoccurrence of plague.

Numbers of deaths Early counts had it that only a handful of people perished in the fire, but now it is believed that many more may have died, for such was the disruption to ordinary life that there were no Bills of Mortality published for three weeks after the fire and so no way of telling just how many perished in that fierce, all-consuming heat.

Numbers of houses burnt It is thought that about 15,000 houses and Guild Halls were burnt, including some of the most palatial and beautiful buildings in the city, and about eighty churches, including St Paul's, of course. There was no such thing as fire insurance and no way of obtaining recompense for what had been lost.

Rebuilding It took many years to get back to some normality (St Paul's Cathedral was not completed until 1711) and for some years the rubble was occupied by shacks and alehouses built to entertain all the workmen employed on the rebuilding of London. Jetties (the fronts that jutted out from houses) were now banned, as were all-wood structures. The streets were also made wider to help prevent fires catching from one side to the other.

Plague One of the most commonly-held beliefs was that the fire 'finished off' the plague of the previous year. The truth is that plague had more or less ceased in London by September 1666, but what the fire did was to burn out the worst of the filthy, unsanitary and horrendously overcrowded buildings in which people lived (sometimes ten to a room), thus ensuring plague would find it difficult ever to get a foothold again.

Who started the fire? In October 1666 a Frenchman named Robert Hubert, who had confessed to starting the fire, was hung, but there were doubts at the time as to whether he was sane, or had even been in the country at the time. Many thought that Thomas Farriner, the baker in Pudding Lane, was responsible, because he had not guarded his fire well enough. Others thought Dutch, Spanish – or a group of Catholics – were to blame. The people of London were desperate enough to blame anyone, and religious and racial intolerance are not new.

Recipes from
the Seventeenth Century

Sugared plums

Sugared orange peel

Candied angelica

Marchpane fruits

Frosted rose petals

Sugared plums

Place about twelve firm, pitted plums in sufficient water to cover and cook gently until just tender. Strain the liquid, keep back about half a pint in a jug and add 6 oz sugar. Boil this up and pour over fruit.

Leave for two days, then drain off water into a saucepan and add another two ounces of sugar. Boil up and pour over fruit.

Repeat this process every day for eight to twelve days, until the liquid is as thick as honey. Leave the plums soaking in this for a further three to ten days, according to how sweet you want them to be.

Remove and place the plums in a very low oven or airing cupboard until thoroughly dry, then dip each fruit quickly into boiling water, drain off excess moisture and roll in caster sugar. Pack in greaseproof paper until needed.

Sugared orange peel

Wash two large unwaxed oranges, and use a small sharp knife to cut off the tops and bottoms. Slice off the peel very thinly, from top to bottom, taking care to get only the zest. Cut the zest into long neat strips, then cut it in half, so that each strip is about 4 x 1 cm. Boil a saucepan of water, add the orange peel and boil for three minutes. Drain and plunge the peel into cold water. Repeat this blanching process twice more, using fresh boiling water each time.

Put 500ml of cold water and 500g caster sugar into a saucepan and boil until the sugar is dissolved. Add the drained peel and simmer for one hour. Drain and dry on a rack for three hours.

Candied angelica

Cut several tender angelica stems into equal lengths, cover with water and boil for five minutes. Peel off the outer skin and simmer until the stems turn light green. Drain and dry on a cooling rack. Cover with plenty of sugar and leave for three days. Then place in water and simmer gently until they turn green again. Drain, roll in caster sugar and dry on a rack.

Marchpane (Marzipan) fruits
(A modern-day version)

450g ground almonds
225g icing sugar
225g caster sugar
2 eggs
1 tbs. lemon juice

Whisk the eggs and lemon juice. Stir in the sugars and ground almonds, and use your hands to form the mixture into a ball.

Divide this ball up according to how many different fruits you intend to make, and knead a few drops of colouring agent into each new ball.

Make up your fruits by shaping as necessary, and refrigerate until needed.

Frosted rose petals

Break apart full pink or red roses and remove the white bottom edge of each petal. Sprinkle the petals with rose water (or dip them in a bowl of it) then lay them to dry on kitchen paper in the sunshine. Sift icing sugar over them. Every two hours or so, repeat the process, turning them over each time, until the petals have dried to a crisp. Lay in boxes between white paper.

Recipes from the Still Room

Most grand houses had a still room (the word 'still'
comes from 'distilling'). Here the women of the
household would prepare pot pourri, balms and scented
waters, and distil flowers in order to obtain precious
drops of their essential oils.

Rose water

Pot pourri

Herbal hair rinses

Scented water to bathe in

Pomander balls

Rose water

Gather petals from three or four full roses that have not been treated with pesticides. Place in a saucepan with a pint of water. Heat gently until the petals become transparent, but do not allow them to boil. Let the mixture cool, then strain through a sieve into a jug, pushing the petals with your fingers to extract all the liquid. Keep mixture in the fridge (it will keep for a week or so) and use as a cooling spray on face or body.

Pot pourri

Pick apart several full roses and dry out on a paper towel in a warm spot, turning them occasionally. Add dried marjoram, thyme, rosemary and lavender flowers or any other strongly scented herbs, plus the dried, chopped rind of an orange and a lemon. Add some dried bay leaves, cloves and a teaspoon of cinnamon. Mix well together and stir occasionally.

Herbal hair rinses

Using a herbal infusion to rinse your hair after washing will condition your hair and leave it shiny and sweet-smelling. Use a tablespoonful of dried herbs to two pints of boiling water, leave covered until cool, then strain and bottle. After washing and rinsing your hair, use a cupful or two of the infusion in a jug, pouring through your hair several times.

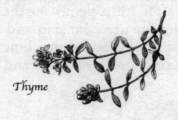
Thyme

Herbs to use

Camomile and dried marigold flowers will add highlights to light hair; sage works well on darker hair. Adding nettles and dried elderflowers will help combat dandruff. Lad's love (sometimes called southernwood), still to be found in cottage gardens and from herbalists, was a seventeenth-century remedy to make hair grow thicker and faster.

Marjoram

Sage

Scented water to bathe in

To one pint of water add eight tablespoons of dried herbs, or double this of fresh ones, mixing them according to whatever you have in abundance. Put into a pan and simmer gently for ten minutes, then cool completely and strain, pressing down the herbs to extract as much liquid as possible. Use a quarter of this mixture to scent your bath, and for an extra-special touch, scatter fresh petals on the water. As a guide, rose and lovage are cleansing and deodorising; rosemary and hyssop are refreshing; lime flowers and lavender are relaxing; and camomile and lemon balm are soothing.

Rosemary

Pomander balls

Can be made with any citrus fruit. Divide into sections and pin ribbon or lace around to mark the quarter-sections. Stud all over in straight lines with cloves (using a knitting needle first to make the holes), then place the fruit in a paper bag containing cinnamon and shake to cover. Take out and dry completely in an airing cupboard, then add extra trimmings and a hanging loop. The fruit will shrink as it dries so you may need to adjust the ribbon-markers.

Orange

Glossary

atonement being in harmony with God, from the 16th-century phrase *at onement*.

cabalistic sign a sign used in a secret or occult doctrine or science.

cambric a fine white linen or cotton fabric.

charnel deathlike.

charnel house a building or vault in which bones or corpses are kept.

cony rabbit.

cutpurse a thief or pickpocket who stole by cutting the drawstrings of money purses.

electuary a purgative medicine mixed with honey or sugar syrup in some sweet confection.

fustian a hard-wearing fabric with short velvety nap (pile); made of twilled cotton, or cotton mixed with linen or wool.

groundlings those who stood on the ground, the cheapest part of a playhouse, to watch a theatrical performance.

haberdashery small items for the dressmaker, such as ribbons, laces and silks, as well as hats and caps, and fabric articles for the household.

halberd a weapon which combined a spear and battleaxe on a pole of up to about two metres in length.

marchpane an archaic word for marzipan, the main ingredients of which are ground almonds and sugar.

meet an archaic word meaning proper, fitting, or correct.

milch-ass an ass, or donkey, whose milk was sold by its owner.

patch Through the 17th and 18th centuries fashionable men and women wore patches, like beauty spots, on their face and/or visible parts of the upper body to make them look more attractive and often to cover blemishes.

patten a wooden-soled over-shoe raised up on a circular metal frame and worn to keep one's shoes and long skirts above the muck on the ground.

periwig In the 1660s, a periwig of false hair hanging in curls from a central parting was an essential part of a fashionable man's attire and often disguised a lack of his own hair.

pesthouse a hospital that cared for people with an infectious disease.

poultice a moist and often heated mixture of substances applied to sore or inflamed parts of the body to improve blood circulation and reduce inflammation.

Puritan In the 16th and 17th centuries the more extreme English Protestants aimed to purify the Church of England of most of its ceremony and other aspects they deemed to be Catholic. Adhering to strict moral and religious principles, the Puritans were opposed to luxury and sensual enjoyment.

quarantine enforced isolation, usually of people and animals who have an infectious disease or who may be carriers of it.

swaddle In the 16th century it was thought beneficial to swaddle a new-born baby by wrapping it tightly in linen or other cloth.

worsted a fabric with a hard, smooth, close-textured surface, made from a closely twisted woollen yarn.

ALSO AVAILABLE NOW

The Remarkable Life and Times of Eliza Rose

ROMANCE, TREASON, MURDER AND ROYAL INTRIGUE

A new gripping and vivid adventure
by Mary Hooper

Turn the page for a tantalising extract . . .

Prologue

Somersetshire, 1655

The castle bedroom is large and richly furnished. Paintings and costly tapestries line the panelled walls and in the centre is a vast four-poster bed hung about with heavy drapes. Childbirth being a close and private matter, no outside light is allowed to penetrate the room, so the window shutters are secured tightly and heavy damask curtains hang across them. Light is provided by the fire burning in the grate and several silver candlesticks holding tall wax candles. A large white china bowl of lavender and rose petal pot-pourri standing on a table diffuses a faint fragrance.

There is a tap on the door and a woman within opens it. Notwithstanding her years, she is both handsome and elegant. A maid carrying a copper scuttle, full of coal, makes as if to enter. She is stopped by the woman, who takes the scuttle from her.

'Please, madam, it's very heavy,' the maid says. 'And you'll get all covered in smuts.'

'That's of no account,' the woman says. 'I don't want my daughter disturbed.'

The maid glances at a younger woman lying on the

bed. 'How does she?'

'She progresses well.' The older woman goes to shut the door.

'Are you sure that I can't get the midwife for you? Or the housekeeper or the doctor?'

'No one, thank you,' the woman says firmly, and, the maid not going away, has to shut the door in her face.

'Who was that?' the younger woman calls.

'Hush! No one – just the maid with some coals.'

'Did she –'

'Hush!' the older woman says again. 'She didn't see or say anything.' She puts some coal on to the fire and then wipes her hands and goes over to the bed where the woman lying on the linen oversheet is in the final stages of labour. She waits while another pain ebbs and flows through the woman's body and then, when there comes a moment of calm, helps her sit up on the bed and places pillows behind her. Then she holds a cup to her lips.

'What is it?'

'A herbal drink: tansy and juniper. I had it prepared by my own apothecary. 'Twill help and give you strength for the final ordeal.'

The other groans. She looks towards one of the tapestries on the far wall. 'Is the babe still there?' she whispers.

'You know he is. He's arrived and is quite safe.'

'Suppose he cries?'

'Then there's only you and I to hear him.' She dabs a cloth to the other woman's temple.

'Are Kathryn and Maria well?'

'Kathryn and Maria are very well and happy. They

are with their nurses. Now, concentrate on this coming child and –'

A mighty pain seizes the other woman and she throws herself back on to the pillows, turning to bury her face among them to stop herself from screaming.

'Soon, now. Soon,' murmurs the older woman when the pain passes. 'It can't be much longer.'

'You've been saying that for hours!'

There are heavy footsteps outside, then the door opens and a man calls from the doorway. 'Is he here, then? Is my son in the world?'

'Not yet,' the older woman says, and she and the woman in bed exchange anxious glances.

The man strides into the room. He has a large nose, puffy eyes and is weak of forehead and chin. He's been hunting and his hands are stained with the blood of small creatures.

'What, still not arrived?'

'Soon,' the woman on the bed says weakly. 'Very soon.'

'But where's the midwife? Where are the goodwives and neighbours to attend the birth?'

'My daughter wants complete quiet this time,' came the reply. 'She has asked – nay, insisted – that I should be the only one attending the birth.' She tries to smile at the man. ''Tis all feasting and gossip when the neighbours come in and 'tis difficult to get any rest.'

'That is the custom, though,' the man says, but then he shrugs. He puffs out his chest. 'My son!' he says. 'I've long waited for this.' He looks from one woman to the other carefully. 'And you're quite sure that it will be a boy this time?'

'Very sure, my lord,' the older woman says with

confidence. 'The hour the child was conceived and the potions my daughter was taking have ensured that your next child will be male. Besides, we have consulted various wise women throughout her time.'

'Quite so,' said the man. 'Because if –'

'Please!' The older woman holds up her hand. 'Please don't alarm my daughter at this time with your threats and intimidation. I can assure you, sire, that the coming child will be a boy. I'm perfectly sure of it. There will be no need for my daughter to be turned out of doors.' She looks at the man coldly as she speaks, for there's no love lost between the two of them, and then the woman on the bed lets out a sudden, piercing scream. The man hastily leaves the room, asking to be informed the moment the birth has taken place.

As his footsteps retreat the younger woman says, 'I screamed so that he'd go!'

Her mother nods, smiling. 'It was well-timed.'

'I was scared that there would be some noise from the passageway.'

'Hush!' the reply comes. 'Just forget the babe's there. All will be well.'

An hour goes by and the pains begin to come one after the other without a gap between. The older woman, knowing it is almost time, goes to the bedroom door and bolts it. Then she climbs on the bed to help her daughter, rubbing her back and murmuring endearments and encouraging words.

At last, with one final push, one tremendous effort, the child is born. Even before the cord has been cut the younger woman is struggling to sit up and look down at the baby.

'What is it?' she asks frantically. 'Is it a boy?'

Her mother shakes her head and sighs. 'No. Another girl.'

'Let me see ...'

''Tis better if you don't.'

'Is there anything wrong with her?'

'Not a thing. She's a healthy size and all complete.'

The older woman swiftly cuts the cord, then wraps the child in a linen cloth, swaddling her round and round.

'Let me ...' the new mother says, and the other relents and holds the tiny bundle towards her. 'So much like Maria!' she murmurs, taking the child.

'Quickly!' the other says.

'Poor little child,' says the young woman. 'Will your new mamma love you as I do? Will she tell you fairy tales?' She looks down at her daughter for the first and last time. 'Once upon a time,' she whispers, 'there was a beautiful child born in a castle ...'